A Single Woman

Maggie Christensen

Cover and interior design: J D Smith Design

Editing: John Hudspith Editing Services

Dedication

To my lovely niece, Carole, who introduced
me to the beauties of Orkney

Also by Maggie Christensen

Oregon Coast Series
The Sand Dollar
The Dreamcatcher
Madeline House

Sunshine Coast books
A Brahminy Sunrise
Champagne for Breakfast

Sydney books
Band of Gold
Broken Threads
Isobel's Promise
A Model Wife

Scottish books
The Good Sister
Isobel's Promise

Check out the last page of this book to see how to join my mailing list and get a free download of one of my books.

One

Isla

Isla Cameron stood in the doorway observing the room filled with people she barely remembered, and wished she'd given in to her initial inclination to refuse the invitation to her school reunion. What did she have in common with these people? People she hadn't seen for twenty-five years and hadn't had much in common with most of them even then. So why was she here? Curiosity, she supposed, was what had brought her out on this cold December evening, when she'd have been much more profitably occupied finishing off her report for the Board of Governors meeting in two days' time.

Taking a deep breath and smoothing down her already immaculate black pantsuit, a red frilled blouse modestly filling the neckline, she walked into the room noisy with the chatter of the crowd of men and women in their early forties who'd elected to relive their youth. She accepted a glass of champagne from a passing waiter and looked around the room, trying to recognise what time had done to her old classmates.

'Isla! It *is* Isla Cameron, isn't it?'

Isla turned to be confronted by the lively face of someone she *did* remember well. She and Kirsty McLennan had been best friends all through high school, only losing touch when Kirsty had gone to Aberdeen to study Law and Isla had taken time out.

Back then, it had been a desire to get away when her mother had

1

died unexpectedly a week after she sat her Highers. Isla had wandered across Europe and Asia, finally coming to rest in Australia, where she'd worked for a time in a series of cafes before returning home to take up her place at Glasgow University.

By that time, all her peers had moved on with their lives and she'd had no interest in trying to reconnect with them. This night might be a mistake. But it was good to see Kirsty again.

'Kirsty McLennan!'

'Kirsty Reid, now. Has been for years. You never married?'

Isla thought back to her few disastrous affairs before she made the decision to focus on her career.

'No.' She smiled – a tight, polite smile. 'But tell me about you. Are you a solicitor or a barrister maybe? I didn't know you were back in Glasgow.'

Kirsty laughed. 'Neither, I'm afraid. I met Duncan at Aberdeen University and married right after we graduated. We came back to Glasgow so he could join his dad in the family firm, and I started a family. I help him out a bit in the office, but no glittering law career. Not like you. You've become quite famous as the headmistress at Glenferrie Girls Academy.'

'Oh!' Isla was surprised Kirsty knew what she was doing. 'Hardly famous. How do you…?'

'My niece,' Kirsty interrupted. 'Fiona MacLeod. I helped Alasdair settle on a good high school for her – though the wee girl had her own ideas. But I remembered you from our own high school days and I knew she'd be safe with you.'

Isla knew the girl Kirsty was talking about. Fiona MacLeod was someone who'd make her mark wherever she went. Confined to a wheelchair, the teenager was not one to let her disability stand in her way. She was popular with her peers, bright academically, and took a lead in many of the school's activities. There was something about the wee girl that tugged at her heartstrings. It reminded Isla of… no, she wouldn't go there. It only ever led to heartbreak.

'Fiona's your niece?' she smiled. 'She's a lovely girl. She doesn't let anything stand in her way.'

'You're right there. She's had a lot to cope with in the last little while.'

Isla racked her brains. She did try to keep up with all of her students, but with over five hundred girls, it was impossible to be on top of everyone. 'Her mother…' she said at last, '…didn't she…?'

'Elspeth passed away. It's been two years now, and the family have coped well, but it leaves a huge gap. I'm not sure they'll ever get over it completely.'

Isla remembered. Young Fiona had come to Glenferrie part-way through the school year, just after the tragedy that had taken her mother so suddenly. She had quickly fitted in, was well-liked, mature beyond her years, perhaps as a result of her tragic loss. 'Isn't there another child? A boy?'

'That's right. Robbie's a year older than Fi – older than our wee Jamie, too. It's difficult to know what he's thinking. He's a boy, and a teenager to boot.'

'And the father?' Isla didn't know why, but she was curious.

'Alasdair?' Kirsty sighed. 'I think he's just been going through the motions, getting through every day as best he can. He seems to be spending more time with the kids than he did before – he always left that to Elspeth.' She grimaced. 'It took her death to bring him to his senses. They have a good *au pair*, but it's not the same.'

Isla was beginning to lose interest. She always tried to stay out of her students' family lives. Fiona MacLeod's family was no concern of hers. She looked over Kirsty's head to see that the others were making their way to the dining room and, at that very moment, a loud voice announced dinner was about to be served. Isla had hoped to slip away before the meal, but now found herself part of the crowd moving toward the double doors on the far side of the room.

Placed at a round table with a group of people she knew she should recognise, Isla tried to make polite conversation. But she'd never felt comfortable with this group at school, so why would things be any different twenty-five years later? She should never have come.

She thought longingly of her comfortable flat, her warm fire, her cosy armchair set exactly where she liked it, and Sooty, the black cat who'd arrived on her doorstep one wet night almost a year ago and was now part of her life.

'Sorry?' Isla realised her neighbour had asked a question.

'I was asking if you'd attended any of the earlier reunions.'

'No.' Isla almost shuddered at the thought of having done this once and been willing to repeat the process. 'But… twenty-five years…' she said, as if to explain her presence tonight.

'Aye, it's a long time since we set off to change the world. And did you?'

'Pardon?'

'Change the world?'

'Oh, I don't think so. Did any of us?' Isla tried to recall the name of the man she was speaking with. She peered down at the table in an attempt to read his name card, but it had tipped over.

Seeing the direction of her glance, he grinned. 'Colin Walker. We were never in the same class. You were too bright for me, I'm afraid, but…'

'Colin.' Isla had the vague recollection of a school dance, an over-attentive boy from one of the lower classes who she'd spent the evening trying to avoid. Was this him?

'Look a bit different these days.' He gestured to his thinning hair, and to the incipient paunch. 'I've never forgotten you.'

Isla shifted awkwardly in her seat. This was the last thing she needed. A ghost from the past, one she'd managed to avoid back then, sitting right next to her and… 'I'm sorry,' she said, pushing her chair back, 'I need to…'

Isla made her stumbling way to the toilet and, holding onto the edge of the basin, stared at herself in the mirror. The face that gazed back at her was youthful for her forty-three years. She'd aged well, but she wasn't interested in any male attention. She shivered at the expression she'd seen in Colin's eyes. It was one she'd seen all too often.

There was something about her appearance, the soft dark hair, the clear Scottish skin that seemed to attract the unsought and unwanted attention of men like him. Or maybe it was her slim figure that led some men to believe she was looking for a knight in shining armour to take care of her and whisk her off into the sunset. She almost snorted at the idea of the man she'd left at the table being anyone's idea of a knight, in shining armour or not.

'Are you okay? I saw you leave the table. Just tell me where to get off, if you'd rather be alone.'

Turning, Isla saw Kirsty standing just inside the door, a concerned expression on her face.

'I'm fine. It's okay. You can come in. I won't bite your head off.' She turned and leant her back against the basin. 'It just all got too much. I don't know why I came. I have nothing in common with all those people and,' she shuddered, 'I've been seated next to a guy I spent one whole evening avoiding at a school dance.'

Suddenly she realised how ridiculous she must sound, and the two began to laugh.

'I know,' Kirsty said. 'Some of them are pretty awful. But I've stayed in touch with a few of the women. They're not so bad. Why don't you join *us*?'

'Thanks, but I don't think so. Not tonight.' She patted her hair and took one more look in the mirror. 'I'll just fetch my bag and coat and be off. But it's been good to meet *you* again.'

'Before you go…'

Isla looked up.

'Maybe we can catch up again – away from all this?'

'Sure. Give me a call at school.'

Brushing past her former classmate, Isla slipped out of the door, and picked up the bag from where she'd left it on the floor by her chair. She murmured her apologies to the other occupants of the table, and made her way to the cloakroom and out of the hotel, oblivious to the whispered comments which followed her disappearance.

Once outside, Isla breathed a sigh of relief. She drew the collar of her camel hair coat up around her face. It was a frosty night and she could smell snow in the air. Maybe they were going to have a white Christmas after all.

Two

Bel

'Nana Bel…'

Bel Reid smiled inwardly, just as she always did each time Fiona called her that. When she returned to Scotland, almost two years earlier, to reunite with Matt Reid, the family had been reeling from the loss of Elspeth, Fiona's mother and Matt's daughter. The distraught twelve-year-old, in need of someone to take the place of the mother she'd lost, had asked permission to use that name, and Bel had been thrilled.

'What is it, Fi?'

Fiona manoeuvred her wheel-chair closer to where Bel was sitting in a sunny spot overlooking the courtyard, two West Highland Terriers at her feet.

'I'm worried about Dad.'

The girl frowned, and Bel thought, not for the first time, how mature Fiona was for a fourteen-year-old. True, she'd had to grow up quickly when her mother died, but Bel suspected she'd always been what Bel's aunt and namesake would have called *an old soul*.

'I think he's lonely.'

Lonely? Bel considered Fiona's words. Alasdair had been a widower now for two years – two years in which he'd made every effort to become both a mother and father to his two teenagers.

'What makes you think that?'

'Well…' Fiona gave a sigh, '…he's home more than he used to be, but he stays locked away in his study. He didn't… When Mum…' she stumbled on the word. 'He was always at work, but now, it's as if he doesn't want to leave us, as if he's afraid we'll disappear. But he's still not really with us most of the time. I've tried to talk to Robbie about it, but he just shrugs and goes back to his computer games.'

Bel smiled. Fiona's brother was a typical fifteen-year-old – totally absorbed in himself, his football and his computer. What his dad did or felt would be of no interest to him.

'What about Sofi?' Bel asked, knowing the *au pair* had become part of the family over the past two years.

'Oh, she's great. And her English is improving no end.' Fiona beamed. It had been *her* idea to employ an *au pair*, one her father had initially rejected. 'But Dad doesn't have much to do with her, and Robbie doesn't always treat her well.' She pursed her lips, her annoyance with her older brother apparent.

'So, your dad. What would you like me to do?' Bel knew Fiona had something in mind. The girl was too astute to have brought the subject up without a plan.

'Can you ask Grandpa to have a word with him?'

Bel bit her lips to hide a smile. *So, Matt was to take Alasdair to task?* He wouldn't thank her interference, but she'd come to love Fiona as if she were her own granddaughter and found it hard to refuse this heartfelt plea.

'Okay, sweetheart. Your dad loves you both very much, you know. He may just be finding it hard to show it at the moment. He's missing your mum, too. But I will ask Grandpa to talk to him.' She squeezed the girl's hand. 'Now, you were going to show me your latest photos.'

Having finally got Bel's agreement, Fiona allowed herself to be distracted. The pair then spent the next hour going through the latest shots Fiona had taken with her new camera, a birthday gift from Bel and Matt which had opened up a whole new world for her.

*

It wasn't till evening, that Bel had an opportunity to make good her promise.

'I had an interesting chat with Fi today,' she said, when she was brushing her hair.

Matt was already in bed and impatient for her to join him. 'Come here,' he said, throwing back the duvet on her side of the bed.

She leapt in to find herself enfolded in his arms, and gave thanks, as she did every night, that she'd found this wonderful man and he loved her.

'Now what's this about Fi?' he asked, burying his face in her neck. 'What's she been up to now? Can't it wait till morning?'

Bel extricated herself and propped herself up against the pillows, ruffling Matt's hair with one hand. 'She thinks Alasdair is lonely.'

'Okay... And?'

'She wants you to have a word with him.' Bel smiled at Matt's stunned expression.

'Me? Why me?'

'Well,' Bel stroked his forehead gently, 'I guess she thinks you might know what to say since you lost a wife too.'

They were both silent for a moment. It wasn't something they talked about. Matt's wife, Ailsa, had died in the accident that had injured Fiona. He'd been a widower for five years when Bel and he met. He must know what loneliness was like.

'Hmm,' Matt said at last. 'But he has the weans, and that *au pair*. It's not as if he's all alone in that big house. Not like...' His face took on a closed expression. It was one Bel had come to recognise, one he adopted when there was a topic he didn't want to discuss. It was as if he retreated into the past, a past where she couldn't join him.

Alasdair's not like you, Bel thought. And it had been his daughter... it had been Elspeth who had persuaded him to sell the big house and build this lovely modern edifice of wood and glass on the lochside – a house which rose up from the heather and gorse-covered terrain and appeared to be part of the landscape, with Ben Lomond looming high behind it.

'I'm sure you're the best person to do it, Matt.'

Matt rubbed his chin, and Bel knew he was picturing Alasdair's own parents – his bluff father, more at home on the golf course than anywhere else, and his mother, a sweet lady, but totally under her husband's thumb. They meant well but, as Fiona clearly knew, weren't the ones to turn to with her problem.

'I suppose I could,' he said at last, 'though God knows what I'll say – or how he'll take it. You're much better at that sort of thing than I am. Or maybe Kirsty?'

But they both laughed at the thought of Matt's daughter-in-law attempting to break through Alasdair's reserve. Kirsty was charming, but not known for her sensitivity. She was a wonderful wife and mother, a brilliant organiser, but had a tendency to put her foot in it, to say it like it was, rather than take a more tactful approach.

'No, maybe not,' Matt said. 'Well, I don't have to do it right now. I have better things to think about.' And with that, he drew Bel to him and all thought of Alasdair was forgotten.

But at breakfast next morning, Bel brought the subject up again.

'About Alasdair…'

'Och, don't you think Fi's got it wrong. The man's most likely depressed rather than lonely. I don't see how he can be lonely with two teenagers rampaging about the house all the time. And I'm no psychologist if that's what he's needing.'

'You managed to put him right about Elspeth,' Bel reminded him. She recalled how he'd told her about taking his son-in-law to task when his daughter had been feeling down, how Alasdair had taken Matt's advice back then. 'He listens to you.' She smiled across the table as she spread marmalade on her toast.

Matt covered her hand with his, causing her to stop what she was doing. 'Thanks for your vote of confidence, sweetheart, but I'm not sure what I can do.' He released her hand and rubbed his chin. 'I know where he is right now. It's not a good place. I guess I thought – we all thought – the children would help him pull out of his grief, just as Elspeth helped me. But I guess Robbie's too caught up in himself. The lad's always been a bit full of himself and tended to ignore the needs of others. And Fi…' His lips curled up into a fond smile. 'Fi's always trying to put the world to rights.'

'So, will you?'

'Talk to him? I'll try to have a word on Sunday when they come to lunch. But I'm not promising anything. These things take time. Can't be rushed.'

'Hmm.' Bel wasn't satisfied, but knew better than to push Matt any farther.

Three

Alasdair

Alasdair closed down his computer and sighed. He picked up the photo of Elspeth sitting on his desk. It was one taken when they were engaged and a favourite of his. It had sat on his desk ever since and… His eyes began to mist, and he angrily knuckled the tears away.

God, how he missed her! The two years without her had been an eternity, and yet it still seemed like yesterday he'd stood in the hospital corridor with her father and brother and wept for a life ended too soon. How was he going to get through the rest of his life without her reassuring presence, her smiling face, the memories they'd shared?

'Da…ad.' The insistent voice of his daughter insinuated itself into his thoughts. Fiona was amazing in how she'd managed to adapt, first to her own disability then to her mother's death. She had none of the guilt he felt when he remembered how he'd become so wrapped up in his work he'd failed to recognise Elspeth was ill. It had taken his father-in-law to bring him to his senses but, by then, it had been too late. The monster inside his wife had ensured her early death – an early menopause, a hysterectomy, an infection. The doctors could explain it away, but Alasdair knew he was partly to blame. He must be. How else could an otherwise healthy woman in the prime of her life suddenly succumb to an infection?

'Da…ad,' Fiona called again. 'Dinner's ready. Shall I come and fetch you?'

'I'm coming,' he replied, and rose to make good his words.

Once seated at the kitchen table, Fiona on one side, Robbie on the other, and Sofi, the *au pair*, sitting next to Fi, they began to eat. As always, the empty chair at the other end of the table seemed to be accusing him. It was where Elspeth always sat, and he couldn't bear for anyone to take her place.

He knew that, when she'd been alive, he spent too much time at the office. He'd told himself it was his desire to provide well for his family, but had it been? Or had he chosen to leave it to his capable wife to bring up their children, forgetting that in doing so she'd abandoned her own career? That, too, fuelled his guilt and was what made him begin to delegate more, to bring work home instead of spending so much time in the office.

But had anything really changed? Without Elspeth, the house was an empty shell, despite the presence of Fiona, Robbie and Sofi. Sofi! How would they manage without *her*? And to think it had taken Fiona's pleading for him to approach the organisation through which she was employed. That had been… almost two years ago, he realised with a shock. He had a vague recollection the arrangement had only been for two years. Did that mean she'd be leaving? That some other girl would have to take her place?

It was too much to even think about right now.

'How was school?' he asked, passing the dish of vegetables to his son.

'All right,' Robbie all but grunted.

'It was good,' Fiona said with a wide grin. 'We had photography for Art class and Ms Smythe was impressed by the ones I took out at Grandpa's. Can we go again soon?'

'We'll be there on Sunday,' Robbie piped up. 'Uncle Duncan's promised to take Jamie and me out in the boat.'

'On the loch? It might not be the weather for it. Looks like snow.'

Robbie muttered under his breath, and Fiona rounded on her brother. 'It's rude to mutter at the table, Mum always said…' her voice petered away as she saw her father's face close up.

He couldn't help it, but any mention of Elspeth tore him apart. He knew it was unfair to the children, especially Fiona, who wanted to talk about her mother a lot. 'We'll see,' he finally said.

'It'll soon be Christmas,' Fiona tried again, with a sideways glance at her dad. 'Will we be going to Nana Bel and Grandpa's again this year?'

'It should be our turn,' Robbie said, as if suddenly becoming aware of the conversation. 'We were there last year, and at Aunt Kirsty and Uncle Duncan's the year before...' His voice died away as they all remembered that Christmas, the one just after Elspeth died.

There had been no real festivity. None of them had felt like celebrating, but Kirsty had insisted Elspeth would want them to carry on for the children's sake. So there had been the usual Christmas dinner, but it had been a very subdued affair and none of them had enjoyed it. Alasdair could barely remember the day, and last year hadn't been much better, though Bel had tried her best, regaling them with tales of Christmas down under in Australia.

But Fiona was right. It would soon be here again; one more Christmas without Elspeth. He missed her every day and, as she became older, wee Fiona looked more and more like her mother – so much so it sometimes hurt to look at her.

Lost in thought, he suddenly became aware Robbie was waiting for an answer. 'I don't think we could manage it, Robbie. We'll talk about it on Sunday. Maybe your Aunt Kirsty will want to do the honours again.' But that would bring back more memories. Perhaps they should forget about the whole thing. Pretend it was just another day. But, seeing the eager faces of his two children, he knew that wasn't possible. No, for their sake, he needed to leave this well of despondency into which he'd sunk at Elspeth's death, and which he seemed to be incapable of climbing out of.

'You went back home for Christmas last year,' Fiona said to Sofi. 'Will you be doing the same this year?'

'No. My friends and I, we are planning a ski-ing trip. Your slopes here are not what we are used to, but it will be my last chance. I will be leaving you soon after.' She threw what looked like an apologetic glance toward Alasdair. 'You did remember Mr MacLeod. Our arrangement. It is only for twenty-four months and it will end. I will be sorry to go.' She smiled at Fiona and Robbie. 'Maybe you will like to have a nice new girl to help you?'

Damn! He'd been right. And he'd done nothing about her replacement. Alasdair roused himself sufficiently to reply. 'We'll be sorry to lose you, Sofi. It's been good to have you. We'll miss you, especially Fi.'

'Can't you stay?' Fiona asked.

'No, *Liebchen*. My two years. It is ending. I must go back to the university in my home town. My parents are missing me too. But think of the fun you will have teaching a new girl all about yourselves and about Scotland and Glasgow.'

'I wish...' Fiona began. But no one discovered what she wished because at that moment the phone rang, and Alasdair excused himself, glad to have a reason to leave the conversation.

Entering the study, he picked up the phone, irritated to hear his sister-in-law's voice. *What did she want now?* He liked Kirsty, and she'd been a good friend to Elspeth, especially during her illness, but she was a bit too feisty for his liking, always coming up with some plan or other which entailed action from the rest of the family.

'Good evening, Kirsty.'

'My, my. Very formal tonight, Alasdair.'

'We're having dinner.' He knew he sounded testy, and the call *had* been a release from Fiona's conversation, but he didn't intend to let Kirsty know that.

'I'll be quick then. Duncan and I were having a chat about Christmas...'

Alasdair sighed. He couldn't escape it, and soon all the shops would be decorated with Santas, Christmas trees and holly – if they weren't already. He'd been managing to avoid the centre of town quite successfully, even though he knew both Robbie and Fi would expect presents under the tree.

'... and we thought we could all discuss it at Dad's on Sunday, see if he and Bel are willing to do it again this year. It should really be your turn, but I know...' She cleared her throat. 'Anyway, Duncan and I thought we'd do something on Christmas Eve. We owe a few dinners and such, and a Christmas Eve do might work for friends and family. So I thought I'd sound you out first – just to make sure you'd nothing else planned.'

Planned? Alasdair hadn't planned anything for the past two years. He felt as if time had stopped with Elspeth's death. He got through each day, went to the office, came home, ate dinner, tried to have a conversation with the children, to spend time with them on weekends. But he knew he was going through the motions. It was as if he was at the bottom of a deep hole. Sometimes he wished he was the one who'd died.

From somewhere deep in his memory he could hear Elspeth saying the same thing about her mother – wishing she'd been driving that day, the day Ailsa had been killed and Fiona so terribly injured. He'd dismissed it at the time, considered it ridiculous. Now it didn't seem such a bad idea – not about Ailsa's death – about Elspeth's. If the children were to lose one parent, why not him? They'd be much happier with Elspeth than with him. Children – even teenagers – needed their mother. He was a poor substitute. Was that why he habitually hid himself away in his study? He was well aware it was a tactic to avoid the reality of his situation. In there with the door closed, a glass of whisky at his elbow, he could pretend everything was the way it used to be – that Elspeth was in the kitchen cooking up something for the family or sitting embroidering in the living room in front of a favourite television programme.

'Alasdair, are you still there?' Kirsty's voice brought him back to the present.

'What? Yes. Christmas? I hadn't...'

'So you're free? Good. We'll go ahead. I'll need to get the invitations out soon. People get booked up. You know what it's like. See you at Dad's on Sunday.'

She hung up, and Alasdair was left looking at the silent receiver. He replaced it slowly. Yes, he knew what it was like. Everyone full of Christmas cheer, getting drunk, exchanging gifts, kissing under the mistletoe. *How was he going to bear it?* He dropped his head on his arms and broke into wracking sobs.

Four

Isla

'And how do you propose to fund this… venture?' Rachel Callaghan removed her glasses and narrowed her already small eyes, her lips curling up in disdain.

Isla flushed, but was determined not to let this woman – who'd been her nemesis ever since her appointment to the board eighteen months earlier – fluster her. She smiled across the table. 'It'll fund itself, Rachel.' She let her gaze encompass the other board members who were no doubt expecting her to give in to the older woman. But, this time, Isla wasn't about to back down. 'It'll be good for the girls to experience another country, and France isn't so very far away. I'm sure they'll…'

'Maybe we can invite Ms Cameron to provide us with a more detailed plan at our next meeting? We have quite a full agenda to get through and…' Bernie Houston, Chairman of the Board, looked pointedly at his watch.

Isla saw her opponent visibly wilt, but knew from the gleam in her eyes as she replaced her spectacles, that the battle wasn't over yet. She determined to enlist the support of some stalwart parents before the next meeting, and forced her mind back to the remaining items on the agenda.

'How did it go?' Isla's deputy, Maree Stoddart, was waiting at the door to the office. 'Did they agree?'

'Not yet. Bloody Rachel Callaghan put her oar in as usual. They've asked for more information. But at least it gives us time to drum up some support.'

'I've had wee Fiona MacLeod on at me wanting to know if she'll be able to go. I don't know...' Isla saw Maree bite her lip. 'She's up for anything that one, but overseas?'

'We'll see.' Isla went into her office and dropped the bundle of papers she was carrying onto the desk before pouring herself a glass of water.

Mention of Fiona MacLeod reminded Isla of the email she'd received that morning. Kirsty had wasted no time in contacting her. After twenty-five years without communication of any sort, it had only taken her old friend two days to reach out again. But Christmas Eve? Isla hated this time of year. It brought back too many memories. She'd planned to spend it holed up in her flat with a good supply of wine and the latest books from her favourite authors. Hadn't her foray into the past with the reunion been enough?

But Isla had a sneaking curiosity to find out more about the family Kirsty had married into. She'd googled Reid solicitors Glasgow and had come up with a family firm – Matthew and Duncan Reid with an office in Anniesland – but not much more. She was surprised her old schoolfriend had become a glorified office clerk and homemaker instead of the legal eagle she'd aspired to for most of her high school years.

But who was Isla to condemn the choices others made with their lives? When she was backpacking around Europe, she'd never have imagined she'd end up as the – let's face it – tight-arsed principal of an elite girls' school in her native city. She closed her eyes as her mind travelled back through the years and over the path which had led her to this point.

We were all so idealistic, then, she thought, *with no real clue of what life had to offer us. We thought the world was our oyster and, yes* – she remembered the question asked of her at the reunion – *we did imagine we were going to change the world. Instead the world changed us, shaped us into what we are today.*

She opened her eyes again to see it was dark outside and there were a few flakes of snow whirling around. If she didn't leave now, she'd be caught up in the predicted snow storm. She packed up quickly and, as she locked the office door behind her, heard her steps echo in the now empty building. There was a ghostly feel to it when all the girls had gone, as if the once stately home was waiting for someone or something.

Isla gave herself a shake to dismiss such creepy thoughts. It was just an empty school building – nothing more – and tomorrow it would once again be full of the bustle and noise of five hundred girls and their teachers, all excited about the coming Christmas celebrations.

She pulled open her car door, brushing off the snowflakes which had landed on her shoulders and slid into the driving seat with a sigh. Tuning the radio to Smooth FM, she attempted to be soothed by the relaxing sounds of her favourite station, only to find that the events of the meeting combined with Kirsty's email were going round and round in her head, drowning out the haunting voice of Whitney Houston.

Glad to reach home, Isla frowned as her front door got stuck on the pile of Christmas cards on the mat. Another reminder of the annual festivities she preferred to ignore. Yes, she'd sent out the usual batch herself, but if she had her way, she'd have chosen to ignore the entire celebration, go to sleep in the middle of December and wake up again in the New Year.

She remembered Kirsty's invitation again. Could she bear to be part of a Christmas Eve event – a family celebration with all its reminders of what she'd lost? Heading to the bedroom to shed her coat and outdoor shoes, she caught sight of the photo on the wall beside the bed. The dark-haired young girl with the wild curls and winning smile would have been fourteen by now, too – the same age as Fiona MacLeod.

Sighing, she made for the shower, tossing her garments into the laundry basket. It would be good to see Kirsty again, she decided as the hot water cascaded over her, but it would be breaking all her rules about not socialising with parents, and Fiona's dad was certain to be there.

Still undecided, she drew on a robe and made her way to the kitchen where, after eyeing an unopened bottle of Malbec, decided a glass of Makar gin would take the edge off the chill she was still feeling. Isla had just poured herself a small measure, topped it up with tonic, and was trying to decide what to eat when her phone rang. She smiled at the familiar number.

'Shona! I've been meaning to ring you.'

'Me too. How are you? I know this time of year is difficult for you.'

Bless her. Isla had met Shona MacMillan at Glasgow University, both of them having taken time out before starting their degrees. With this in common, being older than most of their cohort, they'd drifted together and become firm friends over the three years of their undergraduate program, moving on together to Jordanhill for the Dip Ed that would enable them to teach.

Isla took her phone and glass into the living room and curled up in an armchair, glad the central heating had turned on at its appointed time and the room was now at a comfortable temperature. She could hear a gale blowing outside and, as if to welcome her home, Sooty leapt up to settle down on her lap.

'So, how're you coping?'

Trust Shona to get straight to the point. She'd been there for Isla during what had been the most difficult period of her life, had supported her and helped her see she did have a future, though maybe not the one she'd planned. It had been Shona who'd encouraged her to apply for the position of Headmistress at Glenferrie Academy, something she'd always be grateful for. It suited Isla down to the ground, despite her initial concern about being in an all-female environment surrounded by girls all day and every day. She couldn't have gone on to complete more and more degrees as her friend had done, to end up as a lecturer at the same college where they'd both received their teaching diplomas.

'Okay, I suppose,' she replied. 'Survived the board meeting today, and term will soon be over.'

'That's why I'm calling. Christmas...'

There was a pause, and Isla knew what was coming. Every year, Shona took off to Europe and spent the festive season on the ski slopes – a different location each time – and every year she begged Isla to join her.

'Where is it this year?'

'Val d'Isère-Tignes. It's in the French Alps, near the Italian border.'

'I know where it is.'

'It's one of the largest resorts in France – three hundred kilometres of slopes, eighty-two lifts and...'

'And I suppose one of your party has just dropped out?' Isla asked with a chuckle.

'Am I that transparent?' There was an answering gurgle from the other end of the phone. 'Well, what about it? You know it doesn't help to hole up in that flat of yours for the holiday. It doesn't...' Shona paused, '...it doesn't bring her back.'

'No.' Isla sighed. But being part of a crowd of raucous ski-buffs intent on making the most of the few days or weeks in the snow wasn't her idea of fun.

'I hate to think of you on your own.'

'I won't be.' Isla made a sudden decision. 'An old school friend has invited me for Christmas Eve. So, you see, I won't be spending the entire holiday on my own.'

Five

Bel

Sunday promised to be a beautiful day. There was still snow lying on the ground, but it was only a surface covering and an overnight frost was making it glisten like diamonds. Bel loved the Sunday ritual which Matt had reinstated after his daughter's death, and when Bel joined him in Scotland. It had helped her immediately feel part of this extended family, though she was sorry not to have been able to become friends with Elspeth, too. The few times the pair had met, the other woman had been antagonistic toward her, fearing she was trying to take her mother's place. Both Matt and Alasdair had assured Bel that, before she died, Elspeth had changed, had come to accept Matt loved her, but Bel still harboured regrets she'd not been able to make her own peace with Matt's daughter.

Bel hummed under her breath as she mixed the marinade of garlic, rosemary, lemon zest and oil, and rubbed it into the lamb she was preparing to roast. They'd all be here in a couple of hours and she wanted to ensure everything was prepared.

Gazing out at the still waters of the loch and Ben Lomond looming up in the distance, seeing her little Toby rollicking with Matt's Hamish in the courtyard, and hearing Matt's singing in the shower, she found it hard to believe that, only two years earlier, she'd thought she'd lost him for good. It was partly thanks to wee Fiona that he'd contacted Bel again and she'd taken the huge step of joining him here, in the country she'd vowed never to live in again.

Now Fiona was trying to fix her *dad's* life. But that might prove to be a more difficult proposition. If, as Matt suggested, the man was suffering from depression, there wasn't much any of them could do. They could listen – if Alasdair wanted to talk – but, so far, he'd bottled up his feelings, pretending everything was fine, he was coping and, when pressed, that he just needed time.

'Something smells good.' Matt's arms reached around Bel's waist and she found herself being pulled into his embrace. 'Mmm. You smell good, too.' He buried his nose in her hair, before releasing her gently. 'I guess I'd better get out of the cook's way and see what wine we have. Red, do you think?'

'Probably. Though the menfolk might appreciate something a tad stronger on a cold day like this.'

'Missing Sydney's sunshine?'

'No.' Bel realised she wasn't. Though sometimes the wrench of leaving her adopted home did sometimes give her cause for nostalgia, she never regretted her decision. 'But that reminds me. The letter from Pete's solicitor. I suppose I should do something about it.'

Bel would like to ignore the legal document which had arrived a few days earlier. It brought back memories she'd been at pains to suppress, memories of the ex-husband who'd arrived on her doorstep claiming refuge in his dying days. She'd agreed for a time, then managed to find him a place in a nursing home, the home in which he'd died several months earlier.

'It's a lot of money.'

'Yes.' Bel frowned. 'He told me he'd left everything to me, but I never imagined… I don't want it, I don't deserve his money. I never wanted…' Her eyes misted over, and Matt took her in his arms again, his chin on her head, his hands patting her back.

'Dinna fret. But it's yours now. I don't see how you can do other than accept it. But what you do with it is your choice. Maybe a charity if you don't want to be burdened with it yourself?'

'Burdened. It's a strange way to put it. But you understand me so well. That's exactly what I feel it is – a burden. It's as if Pete has reached out from the grave to ensnare me again. But I won't let him.' Bel felt a surge of energy as Matt's words sparked an idea. 'I know what I'm going to do with it.'

Matt raised one eyebrow. 'That was quick.'

'It was your reference to a charity that made me think of it. Aunt Isobel… *Isobel's Place*… Maybe…' She stopped speaking, her thoughts not having gone any further.

'You're thinking you could expand the old girl's legacy? Build on the respite care home she had us set up?' Matt pulled on his ear. 'It's a thought.' He paused for a moment. 'Would you like me to put out some feelers; see what could be done?'

'Would you?' Bel smiled with relief. She'd be glad to get rid of the entire inheritance. She hadn't asked for it. Pete had said there was no one else, that she'd been his one and only love. That, in itself, made her feel bad. Somehow it felt disloyal to Matt to accept money – and such a lot of money – from her ex-husband. But if it could be put to good use, if it could help more children with a disability and their carers, she would feel much better.

Matt grinned. 'You have a lot of the old woman in you, you know.'

'Well, I couldn't be like a better person.' But Bel felt a twinge of guilt at the way she'd treated her aunt when she was a young girl. It hadn't been till Isobel was dying, and Bel travelled across the world to be at her side, that the two had become close.

'You did the right thing in the end.' Matt drew Bel to him again. 'No more guilt, now. Promise?'

'I promise. Now, let me get on with this leg of lamb or there'll be no lunch and a houseful of hungry people.'

'I'm going.' Matt held up his hands in mock surrender, turning in the doorway to add, 'Might check your idea out with young Fi. She has a good head for what's needed in that regard.'

'Good plan. Now, go!'

All too soon the family arrived, and Bel marvelled yet again the amount of noise five adults and three teenagers could make, not to mention the two dogs, who ran around getting underfoot as they begged for attention.

'Need some help?' Kirsty appeared in the kitchen. 'Dad's disappeared into the study with Duncan and Alasdair, the boys are lost in their iPads, and Fi is keeping the dogs occupied.'

'Thanks.' Bel straightened up from the oven where she'd been checking on the roast. 'Almost done. If you could set the table? I didn't manage to get to it earlier.' She blushed, remembering why her usual organisation had fallen apart. Once the meat was in the oven and the potatoes and vegetables ready to go in too, she'd ducked into the bedroom intending to make a quick change from her trackpants and old sweater into something smarter. But the best-laid plans... Matt had followed her in, and what ensued had done little to help the lunch preparations. Afterwards she'd had to shower before changing into the tailored black wool pants and lilac tunic she'd donned minutes before Alasdair and his two arrived, quickly followed by Duncan, Kirsty and Jamie.

Lunch was barely over when Robbie, who had maintained his usual silence throughout the meal spoke up. 'Uncle Duncan...'

'Don't bother your uncle, Robbie. Let him finish his coffee,' Alasdair said.

Robbie looked mulish, but Duncan grinned at his nephew. 'It'll be the boat you're going to ask about. What do you think, Dad? Is the weather going to hold? I promised these two we'd take a wee trip across the loch, weather permitting.'

'Oh, Duncan, I don't think...' Kirsty began, but Matt nodded.

'As long as you're back before it begins to get dark. I wouldn't like you to get caught out there.'

'We'll be back, Grandpa. Come on, Jamie.' Robbie pushed his chair back, followed by his young cousin, leaving Fiona looking bereft.

'I think Nana Bel wants to ask your advice, Fi,' Matt said, 'And maybe you would have an opinion to offer too, Kirsty. Alasdair...' he turned to his son-in-law, '*I'd* like *your* opinion on a new blend of scotch I recently purchased. Come back to the study with me. We can leave the women to their own devices.'

Duncan soon left with the boys – after many adjurations to wrap up well, take care and be sure to put on their lifejackets – and Matt and Alasdair disappeared into Matt's study.

'Well, what's this about? Women's business?' Kirsty asked as the three began to clean up.

'Not exactly.' Bel finished loading the dishwasher. 'Let me make a cup of tea and we can sit down. We'll think better that way. Tea for you, too. Fi?'

'Can I have some of your special tea? The one with the fancy name?'

'Red Zinger? Of course you can. I have to buy it on the internet,' Bel explained to a puzzled Kirsty. 'It's a herbal tea I like – a mix of hibiscus, peppermint, orange, lemongrass and something else, cherry I think. Fi's developed a taste for it. I might have a cup too. Would you like to try it?'

'Why not? I'm always up for something new.'

The three carried their mugs of the red tea into the living room and, while the two women settled themselves on the sofa, Fiona manoeuvred her chair alongside, Toby jumping up on her lap while Hamish, the older of the two dogs, lay at her feet.

'Now!' Kirsty said, clearly unwilling to wait any longer.

Cradling her mug in both hands, Bel stared down at her feet. 'I've had a letter from a solicitor in Australia. He's representing my former husband's estate – Pete died recently and I'm his beneficiary.'

'That means he's left you some money, doesn't it? Will you have to go back to Australia?' Fiona wanted to know.

'No. It's not like that, Fi. And, yes, quite a lot of money, actually.' Bel could see Kirsty's eyes widen, not surprisingly. Bel had never mentioned her first husband. She'd never had reason to till now.

'So, where do we come in?'

'I've decided I don't want to keep it. It wouldn't feel right, not now I'm married to your grandpa, Fi. So I'm going to give it away – put it to a good cause. You were so helpful when we were setting up Aunt Isobel's house. Andrew – the architect,' she said to Kirsty who was looking mystified, 'wanted Fi's advice on bench heights and things like that. Well, I thought, we thought – your grandpa and I – you might have some ideas as to how we could improve what we started there.'

'Wow!' The young girl's eyes gleamed. 'You want me to be involved again?'

'We need some ideas. *Isobel's Place* is up and running, so we need to know how we can improve on what we offer there, or extend it in some way. I don't need your ideas straight away, but if you could think about it?'

'How much money are we talking about, Bel?'

Trust Kirsty to go straight to the bottom line.

'I'd rather not say, Kirsty. It hasn't cleared probate as yet and there are probably going to be fees etcetera before we know the final amount.

Matt and I just thought we should be prepared with a plan for when it does come through.'

'I can do that,' Fiona said eagerly. 'And can I go visit with you next time? I haven't really been there since it started to operate. Going might give me some ideas, and I can talk with the children there. You can talk to the staff – they most likely won't want to listen to me.'

'Good idea. I'll have your grandpa talk to your dad about it.' Bel saw Fiona's face light up at the mention of her grandpa and dad together and hoped Matt was using his time in the study to make inroads into finding out what Alasdair was thinking – to listen, if his son-in-law was prepared to open up.

Talk of the devil. At that very moment, the two men walked in to join them, Alasdair's jaw clenched tightly and a pinched expression on his face.

Six

Alasdair

Alasdair drove the two children home in silence, reliving the conversation in Matt's study. At first Matt had been very jovial, pouring them both generous measures of a very palatable malt and going into great detail about the distillery he and Bel had visited the previous week.

Then, in Alasdair's opinion, things had become ugly. His father-in-law, not one to beat about the bush, had come straight out and intimated that Alasdair wasn't being fair to Robbie and Fiona, wasn't spending enough time with them, leaving their upbringing to the *au pair*. And, as if that wasn't enough, Matt had suggested he see his GP, tried to recommend a grief counsellor, going as far as to give him a number to call.

Alasdair sighed, his lips tightening as he steered his way carefully down the A82 through Balloch and Dumbarton and headed towards home. Then there was his blasted sister-in-law and her damn foolish plan for Christmas Eve. As if it wasn't enough that they'd all be getting together on the day itself, she wanted to start the celebrations the evening before with a "grown-ups-only gathering".

Kirsty had sprung that on them just as they were leaving, in the process of putting on their coats, giving him no time to respond, but saying, 'I mentioned it on the phone, Alasdair, and if Bel and Dad are going to do Christmas, Duncan and I thought it a good chance to return some hospitality. He'd seen the glance Bel shot towards Matt but had no recollection of a discussion about Christmas Day. It must have been one of the times he'd tuned out. He found himself doing that more and more these days. He sighed. Maybe Matt was right; maybe he did need help. But not some shrink who had no idea what it was like to lose the most important person in your life. It was like losing an arm or a leg, though even that would be preferable. That wouldn't keep him awake at night, wouldn't fill him with guilt, wouldn't…

'Dad – guess what?' Fiona's voice piped up from behind him, interrupting his thoughts.

'What, darling?'

'Nana Bel told us she's a beneficiary to someone and she wants my input on how we can improve *Isobel's Place*.'

Robbie roused himself from his phone at her words. '*Your* input?'

'Yes, *my* input, smarty-pants. She said she and Grandpa had talked about it and I'd been so helpful before – Andrew said so!'

Alasdair could hear the smugness in her voice, reminding him how like Elspeth she was becoming. She had her mother's gift for organisation and her caring nature, but also a touch of her self-righteousness which was not such an attractive feature. What he would give to have her back again self-righteous or not. 'That's enough, you two. If you can't be nice to each other best say nothing.' A glance in the rear-view mirror showed Fiona sticking her tongue out, and Robbie return to gazing at his iPhone.

Maybe Matt was right, maybe he wasn't being fair to them. They'd be out of their teens before he knew it and off to God knows where. Is that what he wanted – to be left alone?

'Hey you two,' he said, before he could change his mind. 'What about we go into town to see the Christmas lights, then have fish and chips – if you've any room left after that big lunch.'

'Really, Dad?' The surprise in Fiona's voice startled him, and he was conscious of even Robbie looking up from his phone. Had he been such a grouch about Christmas? Yes. He answered himself. He'd ignored the natural desire of his children to participate in the Christmas festivities, even going to the extent of refusing to make any plans.

That's why Kirsty's assumption he'd go to her Christmas Eve bash had irritated him so much. He just wanted the whole thing to be over.

He'd forgotten Robbie and Fiona had lost Elspeth too. He wasn't the only one grieving. But they were younger, more resilient, and they deserved some fun.

'Really,' he replied, carrying on past the turnoff on Great Western Road.

Once in the centre of town, Alasdair parked the car and unloaded Fiona's wheelchair, surprised to discover even Robbie, usually blasé about such things, appeared excited to see the display of lights. The three made their way to George Square, stopping to admire the large illuminated Christmas trees, with strands of lighted snowflakes strung between them, and the strings of tiny lights among the branches of the live trees, plus the huge decorated Christmas tree in the middle of the square.

'Look!' Fiona pointed to the crowds of people. 'It's the Christmas markets.' She turned her face up towards Alasdair. 'Dad, can we…?'

Alasdair shrugged. They were here now and could probably get something to eat right here at one of the stalls.

'Can we have a real Christmas tree this year?' Fiona asked as they saw a line of them leaning against one of the stalls. 'We always… when Mum…' She bit her lip as Alasdair felt himself tense. This is what he'd been afraid of – all the reminders of how it used to be.

'Oh, look,' she said again, before he could reply. 'A big wheel. I wish…'

'Can I come back with my pals, Dad?' Robbie, too, seemed mesmerised by the display.

'We'll see.' Alasdair was beginning to wish they'd gone straight home. This carnival atmosphere was what he'd been at pains to avoid. Now, surrounded by crowds of happy people all intent on having fun, there was no way of evading the fact that it would be Christmas in a couple of weeks – another Christmas without the woman he loved, another celebration to get through, only a few weeks after the anniversary of her death.

As if sensing his emotional turmoil, Fiona reached out a hand to clasp Alasdair's. 'Can we visit Mum's grave tomorrow, Dad? I want to wish her a Happy Christmas.'

Alasdair nodded, unable to speak, his eyes too full of tears.

Seven

Bel

'How did it go with Alasdair? You did have a word, didn't you?'

Bel and Matt were relaxing on the sofa, the two dogs asleep at their feet making occasional grunting noises as they chased imaginary rabbits in their dreams. Although enjoying the family lunch and loving her recently acquired grandchildren, it was nice to be alone with Matt again. This was the time she enjoyed most – the time when there was just the two of them.

When Matt didn't immediately reply, she twisted around to see his face. 'Well, did you?'

Matt sighed and tightened his arm around Bel's shoulders, drawing her towards him, his mouth on her hair, before replying.

'A word. Yes. I guess that's what it was.'

'And?'

'He didn't take it well.' Matt sighed again.

Bel straightened up, forcing Matt to meet her eyes. 'What do you mean "didn't take it well"? What exactly did you say?'

Matt drew a hand through his hair. 'I can't remember my exact words. I think I may have suggested his GP could help and... I gave him the name of the therapist I used when Ailsa...'

'You did what? Good God! No wonder he looked as if he'd been struck by lightning when the two of you joined us.'

'I could have handled it better,' Matt acknowledged, 'but I didn't see any point in beating around the bush. Alasdair's depressed. A blind fool can see that. He needs help.'

'He's still grieving. You all are, but *he* feels Elspeth's loss most. And then Kirsty started blabbing on about her Christmas Eve bash as if that was going to help engender the Christmas spirit and take away the pain.'

'That's her way. She wouldn't be Kirsty if she didn't try to cheer us all up. And she's right when she says Elspeth wouldn't want her death to spoil Christmas for us every year.'

Bel had no reply to that. She'd never got to know Elspeth well enough to know what she'd want or not want. But Matt and his daughter had been close.

'Mmm'

'And what about you? Did Fi agree to look at possibilities for helping you spend your inheritance?'

'That was easy. She's thrilled at the idea of being involved again and wants to visit *Isobel's Place* to see how it's going now and talk to the residents. I told her we could arrange it – maybe after Christmas?'

'Yes. Let's get all that out of the way first. Thanks for managing to get us out of Kirsty's do, by the way. I tend to share many of Alasdair's feelings about her Christmas Eve bash.'

'That was easy, too. I just had to say I had too much to do with preparing for the next day. It was almost the truth, if not entirely.' Bel relaxed into Matt's arms again and picked up the glass which had been resting on the low table in front of the sofa. She took a sip, the creamy liquid sliding smoothly down her throat and leaving behind a nutty aftertaste. 'Nice. Is this the one we bought at that new place – the one you used to inveigle Alasdair into the study?'

'Not so much of the inveigle. We both had a good dram before I approached the subject. Maybe I should have poured a bigger measure.' He chuckled.

'No. He had to drive home.'

Matt frowned. 'Aye. One car accident in this family was enough.'

Bel immediately regretted her words.

'On a cheerier note. I checked my emails after everyone left – while you were walking the dogs – and there was one from Celia. Remember her? She was my house guest for a bit and bought me out at Isabella,'

Bel said, referring to the up-market boutique she'd owned in Sydney's Mosman before returning to Scotland and becoming Matt's wife.

'You mean the ex-model you thought I was interested in?' Matt joked, running his fingers along Bel's neck and making her shiver with pleasure.

'That's the one.' Now secure in Matt's love, Bel had all but forgotten her initial jealousy at her former housemate's always immaculate and elegant appearance.

'What's she up to now? Didn't you say something about a divorce?'

'Yes.' Bel's expression became grave. 'But it seems her husband died before it could be finalised and she's his sole beneficiary. It means she'll be able to pay off my share of the shop. So, more money...' She shook her head.

'I don't know – you wealthy widows.'

'Matt!' Bel pretended to be shocked, though she did feel somewhat surprised at his flippant remark.

'Sorry. I don't know where that came from. But she had a few problems with her husband, didn't she? Wasn't she afraid of him?'

'Something like that.' Bel didn't want to discuss what was really none of their business. 'The main thing is that Isabella will be all hers.'

'And are you sorry? Do I detect a hint of regret?'

'No...oo.' But, in truth, Bel did feel something akin to regret. With the finalising of the ownership of the boutique she'd spent so many years establishing, her last links with Sydney and Australia would finally be severed. Then she looked at the face gazing down at her with concern. This was the man she'd left everything for, the soulmate she'd finally found at the ripe old age of sixty-five, at a time of her life when she'd never thought to find love again – the man she'd travelled half-way across the world to be with. 'No,' she said more definitely. 'I made the right decision.'

Matt's lips joined hers in a kiss so intense it took her breath away. *What had she done to deserve such happiness?*

Eight

Isla

Christmas Eve dawned as a bright frosty day. The snow of the previous few weeks, and the slush that followed it, had disappeared leaving the roads and pavements slick with ice, making every foray outside risky.

Isla grimaced at Sooty as she prepared for Kirsty's pre-Christmas celebration, trying to decide on an outfit that would be warm and smart without being too dressy. After discarding several perfectly good ensembles, she finally settled on a dress in what the fashion magazines called winter white with splashes of black, paired with a pair of black high heels. She deliberated on the heels, then decided she'd only have to walk between the car and the house. Surely she could manage that without slipping and falling?

Grabbing the requisite bottle of champagne and the large box of Ferrero Rocher, both picked up on a hurried trip to Sainsbury's earlier in the day, she was ready.

Peering out the window to check she had the correct address, Isla was surprised to see Kirsty's home was an older style house. The large two-story semi-detached sandstone building stood in a beautifully landscaped garden, two stone pillars guarding the entrance to the driveway, and stained-glass windows beside the front door. For some reason, she'd expected her old school friend to have chosen a more modern home.

She manoeuvred the car into a parking spot nearby and, checking the icy pathway, she grabbed the bottle and the chocolates, slid her bag up her shoulder and got carefully out of the car. She pressed the remote control to lock the car. Isla took a deep breath. She could do this.

She could hear the loud voices even before she pressed the doorbell, to be greeted by a rosy-faced Kirsty wearing a red glitter wrap dress with a cross over neckline – very Christmassy – and a big grin.

'Isla! I'm so glad you could make it.' Kirsty gave Isla a hug with one arm, the other hand holding a half-full glass. 'Come in. Let me take your coat and get you a drink. Oh, thanks,' she added, seeing the bottle and box Isla was carrying. 'Just put those down here.' She pointed to the hall table which already held a number of bottles and packages, before leading Isla into a bedroom and adding her coat to the pile already on the bed. 'Now, what'll it be? Champagne?' Without waiting for a reply, Kirsty headed off through the house, leaving Isla to follow her into a room at the back, from which all the noise was emanating.

Mesmerised, Isla stood just inside the doorway. It was like the school reunion all over again, only this time she knew no one.

'Here we are.' Kirsty had returned with a glass of champagne. 'Now, let me see,' she said, her eyes darting around the room before settling on a balding man by the window. 'Alex, come and meet my old school friend. This is Isla Cameron. Isla, Alex Jackson. He's a teacher too, so you should have a lot in common.' She floated off as the doorbell rang again, and Isla was left feeling awkward.

Isla smiled weakly and took a sip of champagne. The man looked as embarrassed as she felt. 'Where do you teach?' she asked, after a pause during which the tips of the man's ears turned red, making her feel sorry for him.

'I teach PE at the local high school. You?'

'Glenferrie Academy.' Isla thought it best not to reveal she was the headmistress there, knowing some men found that intimidating.

'Posh, huh?'

There was no reply to that, so Isla took another sip of champagne, wondering if coming here tonight had been another mistake. Seeing a buffet table at the other end of the room, she used that as an excuse. 'I think I'll grab something to eat,' she said, before moving away and castigating herself for her rudeness. But she didn't want to spend the next half hour or so debating private versus public education.

Isla picked up a plate and was filling it with a vol au vent and a miniature quiche when Kirsty appeared again at her side, drawing her into a group and introducing her to a tall dark man who she linked arms with. 'This is Duncan – my better half,' she said with a smile which told Isla Kirsty's marriage was a happy one, 'and these are out neighbours – John and Judy Torrance.'

The conversation was easy as they discussed the latest films and the recent Citizen Theatre's production of *The Macbeths* which all had seen. Then, as happens at such events, the group melted away, and Isla was left standing by the doorway into the hall, feeling isolated. Gazing around, she noted that, despite the age of the home with its moulded cornices and ceilings and old-fashioned fireplaces, Kirsty and her husband had injected a modern atmosphere with white walls and modular furniture.

This section of the house seemed to be the only part retaining its original décor with three floor-length stained-glass windows. Now on what must be her third glass of champagne, Isla moved closer to the large Christmas tree standing in front of the middle window, her eyes filling at the obvious signs of Christmas.

'It can be a sad time.'

Having imagined herself alone, Isla turned quickly to see a tall, wide-shouldered, fair-haired man standing almost hidden by the branches filled with Christmas ornaments and tinsel.

'You escaped, too?' he asked, with a conspiratorial grimace.

Isla nodded, hoping he didn't see her tears.

'Look,' he stammered, 'I need a breather. Why don't you join me – get away from all that…' He gestured in the direction of the room they'd both left where the sound of carols was beginning to drown out the chatter.

Isla hesitated. What she really wanted was to go home, but she needed to sober up a bit before she could consider driving on the icy roads. Fresh air would clear her head.

Seeing her waver, the man spoke again. 'Get your coat and we can sneak away.'

About to do as he said, Isla looked down at her heels. They were not made for walking on icy roads.

'You'll be fine. The pathway around the garden has been cleared.

'Okay.'

By the time she'd put on her coat, her companion was opening the door, and the pair slipped out, closing it silently behind them.

After the centrally-heated house, the frosty air hit them like sharp needles, their breath forming clouds in the cold air.

'By the way, I'm Alasdair,' Isla's companion said.

'Isla.' She shook his outstretched hand before returning hers to her pocket, while wondering what on earth she was doing out here with a strange man on Christmas Eve.

'How do you know Kirsty?' he asked, as they walked.

'We're old school friends, though until a school reunion a few weeks ago, we hadn't seen each other since. You?' Isla didn't really want to know, but felt obliged to ask.

'Sister-in-law, for my sins.'

Isla almost stumbled in surprise. If Alasdair was Kirsty's brother-in-law, then it followed he was also Fiona MacLeod's father and, if she remembered correctly, it was around this time of year his wife had died.

'Are you okay?' he asked.

'Yes, thanks.' Should she tell him? Tell him what? That she was his daughter's headmistress? What would be the point of that? They were two strangers, grabbing some fresh air, escaping from a party it seemed neither of them wanted to be part of. That was all.

At the corner they turned, and without any further conversation, they walked back and stepped into the Reid home just as silently as they'd left.

In their absence, the gathering seemed to have become even more raucous, the loud beat of music and chorusing of old hit songs emanating from the living room. It was like being at one of the parties Isla remembered from her schooldays. She'd never been a social animal. She grimaced.

'Not your scene either?'

'No. I think I'll make my thanks to Kirsty and leave.'

Still in her coat, Isla peeked into the room catching sight of Kirsty in the centre of a jolly group of choristers. She hesitated, unsure how to interrupt.

'You'll never manage it. Call her in the morning,' Alasdair advised. 'I'm going, too. Tomorrow…'

'Is Christmas Day. Yes.'

Isla supposed he'd be involved in some sort of family celebration. She shivered. She would be alone. For her, it would be just another day, nothing special, no celebration. Another day when she'd try to keep the memories at bay.

Nine

Alasdair

Alasdair awoke to the sound of happy voices and Christmas carols coming from downstairs. He turned over and closed his eyes, but there was no hope of his going back to sleep. A shower helped bring him fully awake and, dressed in a pair of jeans, checked shirt and an Aran sweater which Elspeth had knitted, he made his way downstairs.

The kitchen was empty, reminding him Sofi had departed for her ski trip a few days earlier. He filled the kettle and pulled out the griddle. Robbie and Fiona would expect their traditional Christmas breakfast of pancakes with fruit and maple syrup, and, regardless of how he felt, he wouldn't disappoint them.

'Thanks, Dad.' Robbie sauntered in holding the new iPhone Alasdair had given him for Christmas. 'Fi's setting hers up now.'

Alasdair felt guilty he'd not given more thought to the children's gifts. He'd left it to the last minute when, running out of ideas and time, he'd rushed into the Apple store in Buchanan Street on Friday to purchase two of the latest iPhones.

It wasn't what Elspeth would have done. The family would have made lists well ahead of time and they – usually Elspeth – would have made the purchases before Christmas to leave a bundle of wrapped parcels under the tree. Instead, he'd merely written Fiona and Robbie's names on gift tags which he'd attached to the packages from the store.

'Breakfast will be ready soon, son.' Alasdair busied himself, taking eggs and milk out of the fridge and beating them in a bowl along with vanilla essence. 'Can you set the table?'

But Robbie had disappeared again, no doubt having stuck those earpod things back in his ears to block out anything Alasdair might say. He sighed. Being a parent of teenagers wasn't easy. He was dropping the first batch of batter onto the stove, when he heard the familiar swish of wheels and Fiona's lively voice at his elbow.

'Thanks, Dad.' His daughter's face was beaming. She held up her new phone. 'This is really cool.'

So, maybe his hurried purchase hadn't been so bad after all. But in his heart, Alasdair knew that very little thought had gone into it. 'Glad you like it, Fi.'

'And I got a book voucher from Gran and Pop.' She grinned, 'So did Robbie, but I don't think he's impressed.'

Alasdair smiled. Trust his parents to take the easy way out, too. Maybe he'd inherited it from them. They'd elected to spend Christmas on a cruise. 'You won't miss us, son,' his mother said, when they broke the news. 'We know it's not a good time for you. You won't want to be celebrating.' While he appreciated the sentiment, he had a strong sense of abandonment. Was this what his children felt when he refused to participate in their school events?

Alasdair made a vow. In the coming year things would be different. He'd change. Attend all of Robbie's football games and all of Fiona's school events. He'd be there for his kids. And he'd better start organising a replacement for Sofi. He could manage over the Christmas period when the office was closed but, come the New Year, Sofi would be gone, and they needed help in the house.

'We can make a trip into town next week if you want to redeem them. I don't go back to work till after New Year.'

'That'd be great.' Fiona was setting the table as she spoke, manoeuvring her chair around the kitchen as adroitly as always. *She was amazing.* With every reason to be moody and depressed, his daughter was always cheerful, always making the best of things and trying to help others to do the same.

It was sobering for Alasdair to realise he could learn a lot from his daughter. His son was a different matter. Even when Elspeth was alive, Robbie had tended to disappear into himself with his phone, and now he was even more insular. He'd hide himself away in his room or on his blasted devices – and now, thanks to Alasdair, he had a new one to lose himself in! The boy had taken to ignoring everyone around him and only appearing for meals or a favourite television program. That needed to change, too. Alasdair was beginning to feel that, by shutting himself off from his children he was letting Elspeth down, letting himself down.

Yes, he realised, as Matt had suggested, he was suffering from depression. But he wasn't going to take his father-in-law's no doubt well-meaning advice. He wasn't going to visit his GP to be prescribed little blue happy pills, nor was he going to visit any shrink. He was going to take himself in hand. His thoughts went briefly to the woman he'd met at Kirsty's the previous evening. He wasn't the only person in Glasgow who found this time of year difficult. It was a matter of willpower, and he had that.

Feeling more optimistic than he had in ages, he dished up another batch of pancakes. 'Tell your brother breakfast is ready, Fi, and if he doesn't come right away there'll be none left for him.'

Gleefully, Fiona wheeled herself away, yelling, 'Robbie, breakfast!'

*

Despite his good resolutions, the day had been trying.

Bel and Matt had done their best, and Kirsty and Duncan had too, but they were all conscious of the ghost of Elspeth casting a damper on the proceedings. In an attempt to break with tradition, Bel had produced a seafood feast, telling everyone it reminded her of an Australian Christmas, and recounting tales of queuing up at the fish markets on Christmas Eve to be sure of having the fish fresh for Christmas Day.

They'd all tried to keep cheerful for the sake of the children – as they'd done the past two years, but it had been difficult, and Alasdair was glad when the sky began to darken and he was able to use the excuse of an oncoming storm to leave.

'Drive carefully.' Matt and Bel stood arm-in-arm in the open doorway, the two dogs at their feet, as Alasdair drove off. He followed

Duncan's car along the road till they hit traffic at the approach to Dumbarton. Fiona had fallen asleep in the back of the car and, as usual, Robbie was totally engrossed in his new phone.

The house was cold and empty when they arrived back, and Alasdair turned up the heating before pouring himself a glass of the scotch Matt and Bel had given him for Christmas. It was the same malt Matt had plied him with the previous Sunday – a nice drop. He'd been careful with his drinking over lunch, conscious of the drive home and the possibility of striking bad weather. But now he was home, he felt able to drink more freely.

The two teenagers disappeared into their rooms immediately they returned – Fiona to immerse herself in the bundle of books she'd received from both her grandparents and her aunt and uncle, and Robbie to no doubt listen to music or text his friends. Alasdair had read about all the damage too much screen time could do, but wasn't really sure what he could do about it without alienating his son.

Taking his drink into the study, he fired up his computer, remembering his vow to take control of his life. First, he checked out the website of the organisation which had found Sofi for them and emailed his request for a replacement detailing the duties required. Then he opened a series of emails from Fiona's school. They'd been building up for a few weeks and he'd managed to ignore them. Now, given his recent resolve, he knew he needed to become more involved.

Flicking through them quickly, he found he was able to delete most of them, referring as they did to events already having occurred – ones he perhaps should have attended. No should about it. He knew his daughter would have loved him to have been at the Carol Service and the end-of-year prize-giving. Fiona had even won a prize for her photography. He was proud of her. So why hadn't he attended? Had he even known the date?

He took another sip of his scotch and opened yet another email. Glenferrie Academy certainly liked to keep in touch with its parent body. But it was a good school. Fiona was happy there. It had been a good decision to move her there after Elspeth died – to a school where no one knew of her loss.

He read the subject line – Proposed trip to Colmar. Had Fiona mention this to him? He had a vague idea she had said something about it, wondering if she'd be eligible to go. Since the girl's accident, neither he nor Elspeth had ever let her disability stand in the way of Fiona doing anything she set her mind to. But a school trip to Europe? That would entail more support than the school would have bargained for. Still, he was curious as to how it might be managed and, the more he thought about it, the more he knew Fiona wasn't going to be easily dissuaded from going.

Alasdair scrolled down the email. There was to be a meeting of interested parents held in the first week of term – on Friday January 12th at four p.m. in the school assembly hall. He entered the time and date into his phone. He'd be there.

Ten

Bel

'Happy New Year, darling. May we have many more of these together.' Matt's words were almost drowned out by the screeches and bangs from the television as the screen showed the celebrations in Edinburgh with a gigantic fireworks display.

'I'll drink to that.' Bel raised the glass of champagne she'd been holding in anticipation of this exact moment. It was strange, she thought, how quickly she'd fallen back into the old Scottish custom of waiting for *the bells* before toasting the New Year. Back in Australia, the party would have started much earlier with most people well into their cups by now.

She was snuggled up to Matt on the sofa and their two West Highland Terriers lay asleep in front of the log fire that cast a warm glow into the room while a storm raged outside, the rowan trees by the fence swaying in the wind. At first, she'd thought it odd that Matt had chosen to shun window coverings for the floor-length windows. It had been okay to live with bare glass in Sydney, but with the Scottish weather...

However, she'd soon come to realise there was method in his madness. The triple glazing provided protection from the elements, while offering fantastic views over the surrounding countryside.

'One more glass, then I think it's bed for us.' Matt refilled their glasses and lifted his again. 'To a year of renewal. To helping Alasdair come to terms with his grief, and to you finding a way to use your swag of money for good.'

Bel clinked her glass with his, her mind turning from the celebration of the New Year to their concerns about Alasdair. 'I thought he looked a little better at Christmas, didn't you? Maybe that talk you had has borne fruit.'

'Maybe. But did you see what he gave the kids for Christmas? Those phones must have cost a packet – but didn't require a great deal of thought. Elspeth would never have...'

'Shh.' Bel put a finger on Matt's lips. 'They're his kids – a different generation. Maybe...' She bit her lip. How could she know what Elspeth would have done? It was a tricky subject and one Bel tried to keep clear of. 'Robbie and Fi seem thrilled with them,' she said after a long pause.

'Mmm.'

'Now, you mentioned something about bed.' Bel began to rise, only to find herself pulled back down.

'Let's wait till the fire dies down a bit,' Matt turned off the television and the side lamp, leaving the room bathed in firelight, 'and enjoy each other's company. I'm so glad I found you.'

'We found each other,' Bel said, as she felt Matt's lips on her forehead. Thinking how they'd almost lost each other completely, she shivered involuntarily.

'Cold?'

'No. Someone just walked over my grave.' She laughed. What a ridiculous thing to say. She'd have to watch those old Scottish sayings that seemed to bubble from her lips now she was back in Scotland. There had been too many deaths to make a joke of it. 'Sorry. Don't know where that came from.'

Matt pulled her closer. 'Let me warm you up.'

*

Bel awoke to a calm winter's morning. The storm had passed leaving behind a scattering of leaves and branches, and a weak sun was breaking through the clouds of the night before. She turned into Matt's arms. 'It looks like a lovely day. We should...'

She was silenced by his lips meeting hers in a long kiss. 'Yes, we should…'

When they surfaced some time later, Bel had a satisfied smile on her face. What a start to the New Year! 'Now we must get up,' she said. 'I can hear the dogs. We need to let them out and maybe take them for a walk.'

'You mean we can't stay here all day?' Matt said lazily, his lips turning up in the way she found irresistible.

'No, we can't. How about a special breakfast? Maybe poached eggs with mushrooms and tomato on…'

'Your special bread? Sounds delicious.' But, instead of allowing Bel to rise, he held her legs in a scissor hold.

'There won't be any breakfast if you don't let me get up.' But she allowed him to hold her for a few more moments before managing to disentangle herself from his grasp.

Bel glowed with pleasure as she stood in the shower letting the warm water flow over her. She was so happy even, if she had to come half-way across the world to do so! Bel shuddered to think what her life might have been like if Aunt Isobel hadn't insisted she make the trip to visit her in her final weeks. Meeting Matt Reid, her aunt's solicitor, was the best thing that had happened to her. And now, here she was, back in Scotland, living on the side of Loch Lomond with this lovely man.

She stepped out of the shower to find him waiting to wrap her in a towel and smother her with kisses.

'Your turn in the shower now,' she said, evading his arms. 'I need to start breakfast.'

Bel dressed quickly, then went through the house to open the back door for the dogs who could barely hide their delight at her arrival. She laughed at their excitement as they raced around the yard. They looked like twins, despite the fact Matt's Hamish was a much older dog than Bel's little Toby. The dogs had taken to each other right away when the pair had met, and now it was rare to see one without the other tagging along.

Breakfast over, the pair decided on a walk, the dogs cavorting around their ankles as Bel and Matt pulled on their matching sheepskin coats and Bel slipped her feet into a pair of sheepskin boots, her toes curling up in their warmth. There had been no need for such warm clothes during the forty-odd years she spent in Australia, but it hadn't taken her long to get properly kitted out for the Scottish winter.

Striding along, the dogs running at their feet, her hand grasped tightly in Matt's, Bel brought up the subject that wasn't far from the forefront of her mind. 'Pete's money. I can't stop thinking about it. How do you think we can use it? *Isobel's Place* is up and running. Aunt Isobel left enough for the ongoing upkeep.'

'You talked to Fi, didn't you?'

'Yes. She suggested she visit, talk to the residents and carers, but…'

'Then let's arrange that before school starts and see what she comes up with. She'll have much more of an idea what's needed than we do.'

'But it's such a lot of money. Fancy old Pete having all that stashed away.'

'He had enough to pay for a carer of his own, and yet he chose to latch onto you.' There was a bitter note in Matt's voice forcing Bel to remember how the two men had vied for supremacy when they'd met in Sydney – almost like two dogs fighting over a bone.

'Well that's all over now. And the better man won.' She squeezed the hand holding hers. 'We'll need to organise it this week, then. School starts next Monday.'

'I'll talk with Annie,' he said, referring to Annie Baird, the motherly woman they'd appointed to run the home.

'Good idea.'

For the remainder of their walk, they forgot about their worries as they devoted their energies to keeping up with their small white companions.

Eleven

Isla

The tall sandstone house stood at the far end of the circuit from Queen Margaret Drive. Isla enjoyed the sense of privacy she felt here, as if she was on top of the world. What had once been a large family dwelling had been divided into flats after the war, and she'd been lucky enough to snap up the top one. With three bedrooms plus a large living area, kitchen and the usual facilities, it was a rare find in this part of Glasgow.

Isla stood in the bay window gazing out towards the Botanic Gardens, wondering if she'd brave the weather. The day had been fine so far, but the clouds were building up and it was tempting to stay inside, spend the day by the fireside with a mug of hot chocolate, one of the books she'd bought herself for Christmas, and Sooty in her lap.

She stretched her arms and yawned. She really should take some exercise. Shona would be back and would no doubt want to get together to share her Christmas stories and berate Isla for refusing to join her once again. She was a good friend, but her continued attempts to persuade Isla to *get a life* were irritating. Isla was very happy with the life she'd made for herself, solitary though it was.

Making a sudden decision, she reached for her quilted down coat, slipped her feet into the pink suede boots which had been an impulsive purchase at the beginning of winter, and locked the door behind her.

Once outside, Isla pulled up her collar, glad she'd thought to pull on the pink wool beanie which matched her boots. She smiled to herself, imagining what her students would think to see their elegant headmistress in such unusual garb. But none were likely to do so. Walking quickly and swerving to avoid the puddles left by overnight rain, she stuffed her hands in her pockets, glancing up at the other houses as she went along.

Most of them had now been renovated in the same way as Isla's, or turned into hotels or offices. These days, people were no longer able to maintain such large residences as family homes. Take this one, she thought, seeing the sign *Isobel's Place*. It had been one of the last to go, only a few years earlier. She seemed to recall reading about it. The old woman who'd owned the house had managed to keep it right up till her death when, at her expressed wish, it had become a respite home for children with a disability and their carers.

Isla approved of that, and it made her think of young Fiona MacLeod and the man she'd taken the walk with on Christmas Eve. She sensed a lot of grief in him, grief that met her own. It had been good to get out of the cheer at Kirsty's and, she admitted, he had been pleasant company as they'd strolled around the garden– no more interested in conversation than she was.

She was close to *Isobel's Place* when she saw a large For Sale notice in front of the neighbouring house. She wondered what it would become next, recalling that it had held the offices of a firm of accountants for many years, before becoming a sort of hostel for students. Change happened. It would be of passing interest to see who the new owners would be in the prized location.

Isla had barely reached the end of the road when the heavens opened. So much for beating the rain! Turning, she made her way back, barely noticing a large car stop outside *Isobel's Place* as she hurried past, head down.

Isla was just shaking the rain off her coat, when she received the anticipated call from Shona suggesting they meet for dinner, and refusing to take no for an answer. After agreeing to meet that evening, Isla settled herself by the fire with the chocolate drink she'd envisioned earlier. She sighed with pleasure. There should be time to finish the Lin Anderson book lying beside her chair. She curled up to lose herself in the exploits of forensic scientist Rhona MacLeod.

*

It was still raining heavily when Isla headed out that evening so, instead of walking down to Byres Road, she hopped into her car, deciding to limit her alcohol consumption to one glass of wine with dinner. It would probably be wise anyway, as she intended to spend the next couple of days preparing for the term ahead and would need a clear head.

Driving slowly and peering through a steamed-up windscreen, Isla couldn't find any parking on Byers Road so turned up Great George Street and along to park in Lilybank Gardens Car Park.

Once inside the restaurant, Isla shook her umbrella and looked around seeing Shona already established at a corner table. She was pleased to see it was well away from the large Christmas tree that still graced the room despite it being close to twelfth night, when all good folk should have dismantled their decorations. She took a seat with her back to it.

'Happy New Year!' Shona rose to greet her with a hug.

'Same to you. What a night!'

'You drove down?'

'I certainly did. You?'

'I walked.' Shona's top-floor flat on Highburgh Road was almost as far away as Isla's, but her friend never seemed to worry about the weather. 'Now what'll you have? I got us a bottle of red for starters.'

'One glass for me.' Isla sat down, noting her friend had already made inroads on the wine.

'Spoilsport. You really missed out this year. The ski-ing was superb and the company…'

Isla saw a familiar gleam in Shona's eyes.

'You met someone?'

'Hugh Crawford. He's an accountant, divorced, lives on the South side and…'

A waitress appeared with menus, interrupting Shona's flow of words.

'Sounds right up your ally.' Isla grinned at the other's enthusiasm. She'd become used to Shona's relationships over the years. They always started out well, her friend full of optimism that this time, this one, would be it, only to have it fall into disappointment after a few weeks or months when the new fellow didn't come up to scratch.

'But what about you?' Shona asked, after the two women had ordered, and Isla was taking her first sip of wine. 'You were going to that Christmas Eve thing your old schoolfriend was having. You *did* go, didn't you? You didn't chicken out again?' Shona glared at her.

Isla sighed. Her friend knew her only too well. 'I went.'

'And?'

'It was just what I expected. Christmas tree, carols, lots of people intent on getting drunk…' Her voice died away as she remembered the one person who hadn't been focussed on how much alcohol he could consume.

'What?'

'Sorry?' Isla felt she'd lost track of the conversation.

'You disappeared on me. Where did you go? Did *you* meet someone?'

'No!' Isla took a gulp of wine, almost choking. 'You must be joking. You know very well I swore off men years ago.'

'But that was when… You had another reason back then. It's different now.'

'I'm still the same person, Shona. No matchmaking required. I'm…'

'I know, I know. Happy as you are. Fulfilled by your job. You keep telling me that. But, don't you sometimes wonder?'

'No.' Isla dropped her eyes to avoid her friend's gaze, her fingers drawing imaginary lines on the wooden table.

But Shona was just getting into her stride. 'It would do you good. There's no sense in continually brooding over what might have been. It's a new year – time for some new resolutions.'

The arrival of their meals prevented Isla from having to reply, and by the time Isla had finished her smoked haddock, cod and prawn fish pie, and Shona her red pepper and quinoa burger with fries, the place had become more crowded and a group at the other end of the room had begun to sing.

'Time to go, I think.'

'My treat.' Shona rose.

Once outside the pub, the two women stood for a moment. The rain had cleared, and the air was chilling.

'Thanks, Shona. My turn next.'

They hugged, and Isla watched her friend cross the road, before turning to walk to her car with relief. *She knew her friend cared about her and was only trying to help, but she wished Shona would leave it alone.* Isla had made her decision fourteen years ago. She saw no reason to change it now.

Twelve

Alasdair

It was a clear evening, the streets glistening with ice, the white coating of frost on the trees in the driveway looking like necklaces of diamonds. Alasdair locked the car and joined the figures already making their way towards the well-lit school building. Like many other similar establishments, Glenferrie Academy had originally been the home of a wealthy Glasgow merchant, back in the days of the tobacco lords.

This wasn't Alasdair's first visit to the school. He'd come with Fiona on her first day. But at that time, he hadn't taken much in, leaving the talking to Kirsty who'd made most of the arrangements and accompanied him and Fiona. So, it was as if he was seeing it for the first time and he was impressed how the school had managed to transform the old building into a welcoming place for its young students.

Fiona seemed happy enough here. She'd been delighted to see him leave, waving him off before returning to help the new *au pair* with an assignment for her English lessons. Anaïs was French and had only arrived the previous weekend. She'd been with them for two days before Sofi left, and now Fiona was enjoying practicing her French with the new addition to their family. That was something he'd managed to do right, Alasdair thought, as he shrugged off his coat and found a seat in the hall which was quickly filling up with other parents. Most were couples, though several were women on their own, and he saw a few glancing his way with curious expressions.

Alasdair managed to avoid their eyes, focussing on a lectern at the front of the room where, presumably, the headmistress would soon appear to provide information on the proposed trip to Europe. Fiona had been full of praise for Ms Cameron ever since she became a student here, and Alasdair had formed a mental picture of the woman.

She'd be in her fifties, grey hair, androgynous – a typical academic, somewhat severe. A woman who devoted herself to teaching – to becoming headmistress – in a girls' school, had to be a bit of an oddball.

Suddenly he sensed a restiveness in the room. A tall elegant dark-haired woman wearing something blue and floating approached the lectern, looked out at her audience, and smiled.

'Good evening, everyone. Thanks so much for coming out on such a cold evening…'

Alasdair heard no more for several minutes as he tried to adjust to the woman who stood in front of him – the woman he'd last seen at his sister-in-law's Christmas Eve bash, the woman who'd joined him in escaping from the throng of party-goers, the woman who appeared to hate Christmas just as much as he did.

Isla Cameron defied all his preconceived notions of what the headmistress of a girls' school should be like. If asked, when walking with her on Christmas Eve, he would have picked her as belonging to one of the more caring professions – a nurse, or perhaps a physio. But here she was – Fiona's headmistress.

Then it struck him. She'd said she was an old school friend of Kirsty's. So, while he was ignorant of her identity – to him she'd been merely a sympathetic stranger with whom he'd been able to find solace from Christmas festivities – she must have been fully aware who *he* was. Why did that make him feel uncomfortable – as if, somehow, he'd been deceived?

Alasdair forced his attention back to the purpose of the evening. He was here to learn more about this proposed trip, to determine if and how Fiona might be able to participate, not to speculate on the motives of her headmistress.

'I can assure you this will be no holiday,' Isla said with a smile, her glance taking in the entire room and faltering when her eyes met Alasdair's. She seemed to waver for a moment before continuing, 'We will have a full itinerary planned to include visits to places of interest,

French conversation, and sessions on the history and geography of the region. I will be accompanying the group myself, along with two of my most senior staff – Maree Stoddart and Jenny Hamilton. Like me, both teachers have been on staff at Glenferrie for over ten years, and we all speak French fluently, she said with a chuckle. 'We plan to take a smallish group of around twelve girls, so there will be limited places available. And, as I said in the email you will all have received,' she smiled again, 'only girls in fourth and fifth years as we believe they have the potential to benefit most from the trip.'

There was some muttering among the audience and, as if recognising their restlessness, Isla paused. 'Now, I'm sure many of you have questions.' She looked around expectantly.

As she answered questions relating to costs, accommodation, timing, etcetera, Alasdair studied the woman his daughter admired so much. Here, in what was her more natural surroundings, she exuded a confidence which had been missing on Christmas Eve when all he saw was a vulnerable woman as anxious as he was to leave the party.

'Isn't Colmar located in the wine country?' Alasdair heard one woman ask in a slightly disapproving tone.

He saw a faint shadow cross Isla's face. It was fleeting, and he doubted anyone else had noticed it, but he'd been observing her closely at the time and caught a glimpse of it before she made a swift recovery to reply, 'You are quite correct. Colmar is on the Alsace wine route and the local vineyards specialise in Riesling and Gewürztraminer wines. We will make every effort to include a visit but, rest assured, there will be no wine-tasting.' This brought a ripple of laughter and signalled an end to the evening.

On his way out, Alasdair collected one of the information folders being handed out, wondering how he was going to explain to Fiona that it would be too difficult for her to make the trip. He'd almost refused to accept it from the smiling woman at the door – no doubt one of the two teachers who'd be accompanying the girls. He dropped it on the passenger seat when he got into the car, planning to throw it away later. There was no sense in Fiona getting her hopes up. They could maybe make a family trip to France at some future stage to satisfy her desire to travel. It was a pity Robbie's school wasn't organising something like this. It would do the boy good to get away from his blasted devices for a bit. But the only thing that would get him interested in going to Europe would be if there was a World Cup game to be held there.

Next morning, an excited Fiona arrived at the breakfast table. 'Well, Dad, did you get all the information? Doesn't it sound great?'

'Don't know what you're so excited about,' Robbie muttered. 'It's just more school stuff.'

'It's a trip to France, stupid. We can speak French to real French people. Sorry, Anaïs.' She threw a glance at the *au pair*. 'I know you're French, but it'd be different to be surrounded by your countrymen – or is it people?' She screwed up her face as if trying to work out the correct term. 'Well, anyway, it's different. And, smarty pants,' she turned back to her brother, 'it's not like school at all. We'll get to visit all sorts of cool places. It'll be amazing.'

Alasdair didn't want to burst her balloon of enthusiasm, but he needed to let her down lightly. 'I'm not sure, Fi. It might not be possible. Ms Cameron said the places were limited.'

'But she'd want me to go! I came top in French last year and with my photography Ms Smythe said I could be the recorder for the trip – take photos and even some videos.' She was beaming at the idea of her work finding a larger audience, and Alasdair hated to disappoint her.

'We'll see,' he said after a pause.

'You know what that means, Fi.' Robbie grinned as he poured cornflakes into a bowl and splashed milk over them, leaving drops on the table.

Fiona made a face at her brother before helping herself to cereal. 'I know it may be more awkward for me, Dad, but I really want to go. Maybe you could speak to Ms Cameron about me – see what you can work out?'

Alasdair sighed. Fiona had never allowed her disability to define her, and both he and Elspeth had always treated their daughter as they would if the accident had never happened. But the fact remained that the school could well see her presence on the trip as a liability – one which they'd prefer not to have to cope with.

'You will, Dad, won't you?' Fiona gazed at him with such a pleading look in her eyes that Alasdair found it hard to refuse. She looked so like her mother, he had trouble refusing her anything – but this?

'I said I'd think about it,' he repeated, and downed the last of his tea before rising to leave.

'You're driving Fi to school today, Anaïs?'

'Certainly, Mr MacLeod.'

'Alasdair,' he repeated for what must have been the twentieth time since the girl had arrived. She clearly came from a respectful family, but *Mr MacLeod* made him feel ancient.

Driving towards his office in the centre of Glasgow, Alasdair couldn't dismiss the disappointment in Fiona's eyes. He knew exactly to what Robbie was referring. He – and Elspeth – had habitually used the term *We'll see* when faced with difficult decisions. Decisions which they'd already made and knew would disappoint the children.

This time, maybe he should do as Fiona asked and at least discuss possibilities. That meant meeting with Isla Cameron, and he was surprised how pleased he was at the prospect of seeing her again.

Thirteen

Bel

'Are you ready?' Matt called through to the bedroom where Bel was adding a touch of lipstick.

'Be with you in a moment.' Bel put the final touches to her makeup, patted her hair and slipped on the new camel-coloured cashmere coat she'd bought on a recent trip into town – one of several coats she now owned, much to her amazement. But, even after two years, she still felt chilled in the Scottish winter, and her wardrobe now consisted of a variety of wool and tweed garments she'd never have worn in Sydney. Looking down at her present outfit – a lilac crew-necked chenille jumper teamed with a pair of black cord pants, she reflected that her former customers at Isabella would scarcely recognise her.

Bel felt her excitement build as they drove towards Glasgow. When, on their visit to *Isobel's Place* two weeks earlier, they saw the For Sale sign on the neighbouring property, Fiona had clapped her hands and grinned. 'There's your answer, Nana Bel. Buy that house and you can double the size of *Isobel's Place*. Easy peasy.'

But it wasn't that simple. It had taken several days to establish the sale price, then to have the dwelling valued. Their initial inspection revealed that the previous owners had divided it up into tiny rooms – almost cubicles – which they'd rented out to students, not all of whom had treated it well. Before Bel was willing to make an offer, she and Matt had decided to enlist the opinion of Andrew Forrest, the young architect who Bel's Aunt Isobel had commissioned and who'd worked with them on the original renovation of *Isobel's Place*.

Now they were on their way to meet Andrew at the property to determine if it was a viable proposition. How Bel hoped it was! To be able to increase the service they were already offering – right next door. She was sure her aunt would have been thrilled.

'Hi folks!' Andrew was waiting for them and turned from his study of the building as Bel and Matt got out of the car.

'What do you think?' Matt shook the younger man's hand, and Andrew gave Bel a peck on the cheek.

'Difficult to say from the outside, but my first impressions are good. These places were built to last, but there's no telling what the years – and the occupants – have done to the inside.'

'Mmm.' Bel recalled the dry rot they'd found in her aunt's house. That hadn't been cheap to fix. Then there had been her own termite infestation in Sydney. She knew all about the perils of old houses.

'Let's go in. I managed to get a key.' Andrew pulled a keyring from his pocket and the three made their way up the steps to the front door. It opened with a creak and they walked into a hallway smelling of something Bel couldn't quite recognise. She wrinkled her nose and sniffed.

'Damp,' Andrew said, 'and mice. It's to be expected if the place has been lying empty for a while?' He glanced at Matt.

'The realtor said it has. The owner is overseas and the last tenants – students, he tells me – left sometime last year. It's lain empty since then, waiting for the owner to make a decision about it. Seems there was some thought he might take up residence himself, but he visited at Christmas and when he saw the state of the place...'

'Right. At least it isn't rats.'

Bel shivered and drew the collar of her coat up around her chin. Mice she could cope with, but rats? That was something else. It brought back memories. She remembered seeing rats running along the top of the back wall of the next-door house in her childhood. That was where the rubbish bins had been kept, and she suspected the creatures had been foraging in them. As a child, she'd been scared to go near that part of the yard, and she still didn't much like the thought of them close to the house.

Bel and Matt followed Andrew through the house, the architect poking and prodding at the walls, before ending up in the large kitchen which was almost a replica of the one Bel had found in her Aunt Isobel's house when she arrived in Scotland to visit her.

The sudden reminder brought tears to Bel's eyes but, before she could say anything, Matt said, 'Takes me back. Just like next door.' He put an arm around Bel's shoulders as he spoke and gave her a squeeze. 'So, Andrew, what's the verdict? Can we do the same sort of renovation without it costing Bel an arm and a leg? And is there any way of combining the two? That is what you'd like, isn't it?' he asked Bel.

She nodded, unable to speak – the picture of her Aunt Isobel sitting in just such a kitchen at the forefront of her mind.

Andrew tapped his lips with a finger. 'Hmm. Need to get a building report. I'd recommend one anyway.' He turned to face Bel. 'Your aunt looked after her home. Apart from the dry rot, it was in excellent condition. This place is another matter. It's been left to get into disrepair. I'm not sure it's a good buy.'

'Oh!' The excitement Bel felt on their way into town had been slowly draining away and now it disappeared completely. 'Can you arrange the inspections for us? That would be best, wouldn't it, Matt?' she asked, looking up at her husband.

'I think so. It looks as if we're done here.' He went over to the window which was covered with cobwebs, and sat over a cracked white sink. 'Regardless of what they say, Bel, it looks like it'll need a complete gutting and refitting. Are you up for that?'

Bel's stomach clenched, and she chewed her lip. It was going to be a much bigger job than she'd envisaged. But Pete's legacy would cover it, and she couldn't think of a better use for his money. 'Let's see what the reports say.'

As the door closed behind them, she turned and looked up at the outside of the old sandstone building, trying to remember who'd lived there when she was growing up next door. Closing her eyes, she pictured the street as it had been back then – few cars, carefully tended hedges and pots of colourful blooms, white-edged steps, net curtains and… Yes, she could see it as if it was yesterday, the net curtain of this house being cautiously drawn back, a bespectacled face peering out at

Bel and her friends. The owners all these years ago had been a pair of spinster sisters – that's what Bel's mum and aunt had called them – the Miss Hoggs. They'd been nice enough to the young girl next door – chocolates at Christmas, an egg at Easter – but very inquisitive. Bel had always felt she was being spied upon.

In retrospect, the poor women probably had little else to interest them, and the goings-on of their neighbours provided the entertainment for which people now turned to television programs. Bel wondered idly if the present owner was some relative of those women who'd died many years ago, when she was in Australia.

'Ready to go?' Matt was pressing the remote control to open the car, and Andrew was leaning in to farewell her.

It was chilly standing there on the pavement. 'Yes. Thanks, Andrew. It was good of you to come this morning.'

He gave her another peck on the cheek and shook Matt's hand again. 'I'll be in touch when I have the reports for you. It may take a couple of weeks.'

'I don't think the buyers will be lining up for this place, so there's no rush.'

Bel slid into the car and they set off.

'How about a bite of lunch?' Matt asked. 'We could drive into town, now we're here. Take a trip down memory lane. Remember…?'

Bel did remember. When they'd first met, Matt had taken her to lunch after her first meeting with Andrew. That had been the start of something she hadn't thought she wanted. But Aunt Isobel had known better.

Fourteen

Isla

Isla was about to pack up for the day when Jean, her Personal Assistant, popped her head round the door.

'Yes?' Isla looked up from her computer which she was in the process of closing down.

'You haven't forgotten, have you? You have a parent interview in ten.'

Blast! She *had* forgotten. Isla ran her eye down her diary and there, sure enough, at five fifteen, was the entry she'd been trying to avoid. Alasdair MacLeod – Fiona MacLeod's father. A note jotted beside his name said *Colmar trip*.

'He wants to...' Jean began.

'I know what he wants,' Isla said tiredly. She'd been inundated with parents wanting to discuss the proposed trip ever since the meeting and now almost all the positions were filled. Almost. And she knew Fiona was keen to claim one of the remaining spots. She had no problem with that, though heaven knows how they were going to accommodate her. But the girl would be an asset to the group with her permanently positive attitude and her photographic skills. In fact, Moira Smythe, the Art teacher, had already offered to accompany them at her own expense if Fiona was permitted to go.

'You'd better get me some coffee, Jean. Make it two cups.'

Isla hadn't spoken to Alasdair MacLeod since Christmas Eve, but she'd noticed his surprise when he caught her eye at the meeting and had felt guilty. Why, she wasn't sure. It wasn't as if she'd lied to him or hidden who she was. They'd been two lonely people escaping from a party neither of them wanted to be at. Two strangers passing in the night. *Why did that sound like the theme of a movie or the lyrics of a popular song?* She'd gone home that night with the melody of *Some Enchanted Evening* playing in her head, only to curse the silly romantic fantasy that had come out of nowhere. She was past all that, and the man had recently lost his wife.

Ten minutes. Just time to check her hair in the mirror she kept on top of the filing cabinet and renew the lipstick that had worn off during the day, before Jean returned with the two coffees and announced his arrival.

'Good afternoon, Mr MacLeod. Won't you take a seat? Coffee?' Isla wasn't sure how to play it. They'd met – yes. But under very different circumstances.

'Alasdair. We met…' He appeared puzzled.

'Yes. I remember.' Isla opened the folder on her desk to hide her embarrassment. This had never happened to her before. Until now, despite Glasgow's limited social scene, she'd always managed to avoid encounters with the parents of her students outside the confines of the school.

She knew she should have refused Kirsty's invitation.

'So, Isla – I can call you Isla? Ms Cameron sounds very formal.'

'Yes, of course.' Isla bit her lip, not sure why she felt so flustered. She was used to dealing with parents – did it all the time. *Why did this man make her feel nervous?* She took a sip of coffee and swallowed. 'You wanted to discuss the Colmar trip?'

Alasdair drew a hand through his hair. 'Yes. It's Fi – Fiona. She's set on going, and I'm not sure it's practical for her. Elspeth – her mother – and I always encouraged her to believe she can do anything other children can do, but this may be a bridge too far, even for her.' He looked imploringly at Isla as if hoping she might have an answer, either as to how his daughter could participate or how he could break the news to her she couldn't go.

'There are still a few places available,' Isla said, reading from the list in her folder. 'Two to be exact.' She looked up again to meet his eyes, noting for the first time how they were a deep brown, unusual with the blond of his hair. She'd known one other man whose brown eyes had… She quickly suppressed the memory that had arisen unbidden.

'Hmm. But…'

'What exactly is your concern, Mr… Alasdair?' Isla picked up a pencil and tapped the desk, knowing exactly what his concern was, but wanting him to be specific. She saw him take a deep breath.

Alasdair cleared his throat before replying. 'It's not that I doubt the school's level of care. I know Fi is extremely happy here and all her needs are catered for. She's never been made to feel different. That's important. But, on a trip like this… What if something happened? What if…? I can't bear the thought of losing her, too.'

Isla's throat ached as she recognised the dilemma Alasdair was facing. She could understand that, while he hated refusing his daughter anything, he was terrified she might meet with an accident, or become ill, while far from home. She gave what she hoped was an understanding nod. 'Of course not,' she said quietly, thinking quickly how to deflect his emotion. 'How do you manage at home?' she asked. 'It must be difficult as a single parent.'

She saw Alasdair's eyes widen as if he'd never thought of himself that way.

'We have help,' he said, after a pause. 'An *au pair*. Anaïs is our second girl. She's French. Fi's been madly practicing her French on her in anticipation of…' His voice died away. 'Hell, I don't know how I'm going to tell her. It was Fi's idea I meet you like this. She refused to accept my telling her it might be too difficult. She's so determined.' He covered his face with his hands. 'Sorry, I…' He cleared his throat again. 'Sorry,' he repeated.

The mention of a French *au pair* caught Isla's attention.

'How reliable is this *au pair*?'

Alasdair appeared to recover from his distress. 'Anaïs? Well, she's only been with us for a few weeks but, so far, she seems fine. Fi likes her. She's fitting in well.'

'I wonder…' Isla tapped with her pencil again, conjecturing if what she was about to suggest would seem invasive of his privacy. 'What are her duties?'

Alasdair seemed surprised, but replied, 'She helps Fi dress, shower, etcetera, though Fi's pretty independent these days and can manage a lot by herself. Anaïs is just there for support when required. She also drives Fi to and from school, looks after the house, some cooking, cleaning, shopping and so forth. Why?'

It was Isla's turn to take a deep breath. 'How would you feel about this Anaïs accompanying Fiona on the trip – to support her if necessary?' When Alasdair didn't immediately reply, she continued. 'Her being French would be a significant bonus for us, but I'm afraid you'd have to pay her way, along with your daughter's.'

Alasdair picked up his cup, and Isla waited patiently, allowing him to consider her proposal. It was an ideal solution. If he accepted, it would mean not one but two additional adults on the trip. At least, she assumed the *au pair* could be regarded as an adult. She had no idea how old the girl was, but old enough to have left home and taken a position in a foreign country.

Alasdair placed his cup carefully on the table before replying. 'I suppose it's a possibility,' he said at last. 'But... I'd need to think about it, sound out Anaïs, and...' He looked across the desk to meet Isla's eyes. 'It's certainly food for thought. Can I get back to you? How soon do you require an answer?'

Suppressing the unexpected quiver she experienced when their eyes met, Isla checked her folder before replying, 'I can keep a place open for one more week. We would like to have Fiona with us,' she smiled, 'but you do understand there will be a number of other girls who'd also like to come?'

'Thanks.' For the first time since he'd entered the office, Alasdair smiled, his face crinkling up and making him appear attractive. Isla had the distinct impression it wasn't something he did often. She idly wondered what it would take to make this buttoned-up man open up. He was clearly still grieving for Fiona's mother.

'So, I'll be back in touch.' Alasdair rose and reached out to shake Isla's hand before leaving.

Isla exhaled loudly as the door closed behind him. There was something about Alasdair MacLeod that made her want to reach out to him. She'd experienced it faintly on Christmas Eve, then again when their eyes met at the meeting. She shook her head in annoyance. She was imagining things. She was tired. It had been a long day. She had no need to reach out to Alasdair MacLeod or any other man.

Fifteen

Alasdair

Alasdair sat in his car recalling the meeting he'd just had with Isla Cameron. She was a cool customer – not at all what he'd expected. Though what had he expected? Some recognition they were like-minded – on the basis of their walk on Christmas Eve? Then, she'd seemed vulnerable, he'd felt a connection, though not one he wanted to pursue. Today she'd been all business. Well, he couldn't fault her for that. *He* operated that way all the time, had done for years. It was one of the things that had irritated Elspeth.

Elspeth! Thinking of his deceased wife brought his mind back to Fiona and her desire to be part of this damned trip to France. If it hadn't been for that, he wouldn't be here in the first place. He'd never have needed to see Isla Cameron again. But he had and, for some unknown reason, the woman had managed to get under his skin.

But she had come up with a possible solution. He turned it over in his mind. To have Anaïs accompany Fiona on the trip would set his mind at rest to some extent, but… In Alasdair's mind, there was always a *but*. He needed to give it more thought, maybe run it past the family on Sunday. He knew Fiona would be all in favour – anything that would get her to France – and most likely it would appeal to Anaïs, too.

He started the engine and drove home.

*

'Well, Dad?' Fiona greeted him as soon as he entered the house, 'What did she say? Can I go?'

'Steady on, Fi. Let me get my coat off first.' Alasdair shrugged off his overcoat and hung it up in the hall closet, while Fiona sat impatiently in the hallway. 'Can it wait till after dinner?'

'Ohhh!' Fiona's disappointed voice was almost more than he could bear, but he needed to think this through a bit before he revealed her headmistress's proposal.

Walking through to the study, Alasdair poured himself a measure of scotch from the bottle Matt had given him for Christmas. He began to relax as the warm liquid coursed through his body. It was a good drop. His father-in-law certainly knew his malts.

'Dinner, Mr MacLeod.' Anaïs' gentle accented voice interrupted him. 'Alasdair,' he corrected automatically, knowing it would most likely take another few weeks for the girl to feel comfortable using his first name.

Fiona managed to maintain her patience throughout the meal but, as soon as the family retreated to the living room, and before Robbie switched on the television for their favourite quiz show, Fiona turned on her father again.

'Now, Dad!'

'It's not simple, Fi. Ms Cameron would like to include you...'

Fiona beamed.

'But there are some considerations.'

Her face fell again.

'We still haven't made a decision. There are a few matters I need to think about. I've promised to decide within a week. She's going to keep a place open till then.' As soon as he'd uttered the words, Alasdair regretted them seeing how Fiona's face lit up again. He didn't want her to get her hopes up, then be disappointed. She'd suffered enough disappointments in her life. But he had to decide what would be best for her, not what she wanted. He hoped Matt and Bel would have good advice to offer – maybe even Kirsty. She knew Isla Cameron after all.

It crossed his mind he could ask Kirsty about her – find out what her history was – before suppressing it. He could just imagine how Kirsty's mind would work overtime if he even mentioned Isla's name.

'Don't know why you want to go, anyway. They all speak foreign there. If it was me…' Robbie began superciliously.

'It's not you. It's me we're talking about. *I* can speak French, not like…'

'That's enough!' Alasdair interrupted, just as the introductory music to their program came on, Robbie having managed to find the control and turn on the set. 'Now, let's all settle down and have a pleasant evening. It's the beginning of the weekend. Maybe we can all do something nice together tomorrow.'

*

A drive down to the coast on Saturday, followed by the movie *Maze Runner* and an unprecedented dinner at McDonald's, had seemed to satisfy both teenagers, and they were all in a good mood as they drove out to Loch Lomond on Sunday morning. Robbie's football games had yet to start and Alasdair was conscious of his vow to attend all of them, while aware he'd need to find something else to occupy Fiona – and a suitable treat for her in return. This wasn't going to be easy, but it was still January and he was determined to try harder this year.

In the bustle of their arrival at the lochside home, Alasdair forgot all the things he'd been worrying about on the way and was soon helping Duncan and Matt prepare the barbecue, while Bel and Kirsty relaxed indoors with a glass of wine. The children had all disappeared as soon as they arrived, Alasdair assuming Fiona had gone to raid her grandfather's library or take more photos, and the boys to disappear into cyberspace on their iPads or phones.

'It's a bit on the cool side to eat out here,' Matt said, handing Alasdair a beer, 'but it gives the women a rest from cooking.'

'Good beer, Dad,' Duncan said.

Matt grinned. 'A new pub's opened in the village. They're doing all right. So, what have you guys been up to since last weekend?' he asked.

Duncan began to regale the pair with a challenge he was experiencing with a difficult client, while Alasdair remained silent.

'You, Alasdair?'

'Took the kids to the coast and a movie yesterday,' he said, then hesitated.

'And?' Matt must have realised there was something bothering him.

'Nothing. Not now, anyway. But I'd like your and Bel's opinion on something later. It's about Fi. Oh, nothing serious,' he added, seeing Matt frown. 'It's to do with school.'

*

Lunch over, Duncan offered to join the three children and the dogs in a ramble over the hills, leaving Alasdair free to have his desired talk with Bel and Matt. He'd tried to persuade Kirsty to join them, but sensing something was afoot, and with Alasdair's agreement, she stayed behind.

'Now, what's this all about?' Bel asked, when they were all seated with coffee. 'Matt said it was about Fi?' A frown appeared between her eyes.

Alasdair gazed out the window to where the others were making their way across the muir, Fiona encouraging Duncan to keep her up with the boys, and the two dogs gambolling at their feet. She was so adventurous, so independent. He sighed.

'There's this school trip – to France.'

'And Fi wants to go?' Kirsty guessed.

'Oh, surely…' Bel began, only to be interrupted by Matt.

'She's always been a wee terrier when she wants something. I bet she's been harping on about it.'

'You're right. It's at times like this, I wish Elspeth was here. She'd know what to do. But her headmistress…'

'Isla. Isla Cameron,' Kirsty said.

'You know her?' Bel seemed surprised.

'We were at school together. Only met up again recently at a school reunion. But I knew who she was before that.'

'Let Alasdair finish,' Matt broke in.

'Aye.' Alasdair took a gulp of coffee before continuing. 'I went to a school meeting about it, and it seemed to me it was going to be way too difficult for Fi to go. Maybe when she's older...' He paused. 'Anyway, Fi wouldn't listen to reason and kept on at me to meet with her Ms Cameron, so I did.' He felt himself redden. 'Seems the school would like her to go – maybe it fulfils their diversity policy or something. She started asking me all sorts of questions – about our *au pair* – and ended up suggesting she go too – to accompany Fi.'

'And how do you feel about that?' Bel's voice was gentle.

Alasdair dragged a hand through his hair. 'I don't know. That's why I wanted to ask your opinions. On the face of it, it sounds practical, but what if... What do you think Elspeth would say?'

He looked pleadingly at Matt, but it was Kirsty who replied, 'I think she'd go along with what Isla is suggesting. You've never wrapped Fi in cotton wool, though,' she thought for a moment, 'Elspeth did try to cosset her a bit when she was smaller. But she's fourteen now and more sensible than most of her peers. She's had to grow up quickly...' Her voice faded.

'Rubbish,' Matt said. 'She's always had an old head on young shoulders. I'm not sure what her mother would say. I tend to disagree with Kirsty. I think Elspeth would be more cautious. But,' he sighed heavily, 'she's no longer with us, and we can't spend the rest of Fi's life wondering what her mother would think or do. What's your take on it, Bel?'

Matt turned to his wife who'd been silent during the latter part of the conversation.

'How does Fi's headmistress – this Ms Cameron – think Anaïs would help?' Bel asked.

'Much the way she does at home. She's started off well and by July she'll be well and truly one of the family. Fi loves her already and the pair chat away in French. Ms Cameron sees that as a plus too, and it'll be another adult in the party – if you can call a nineteen-year-old an adult. I'd pay for her, of course.'

'I can see how that would appeal,' Bel replied.

'Isla wouldn't be swayed by any monetary concerns. She always stunned the rest of us by her strong ethical standards, and I can't imagine she's changed any over the years,' Kirsty put in. 'I don't want you to think I'm batting for her, but I do think it would be good for Fi to get away for a bit. You've all been stuck there in that house since Elspeth passed away. Would probably do you *all* good to get away.'

There was a stunned silence.

Kirsty was well known in the family for being outspoken, but this was going too far.

'I think I know what's best for my family,' Alasdair said stiffly, wondering if it had been such a good idea to ask for advice. *Why hadn't he just refused Fi permission to go? Why did he feel the need to bring it to a family discussion? And why this family? Why Elspeth's family?*

He knew why. If he'd asked his own parents, they'd have told him it was none of their business, or his mother would have gone on and on about the *puir wee soul who'd lost her mother.* Her ongoing sympathy and platitudes made him cringe. He'd been grateful for her help in the immediate aftermath of Elspeth's death, but, even then, Fiona hadn't found her to be much help.

They were interrupted by the return of the others and, in the ensuing chaos, with dogs and children everywhere, nothing more was said about Fiona, her headmistress, or the proposed trip.

It was only as they were driving home, Fiona chatting ten to the dozen and Robbie lost in his phone as usual, that Alasdair realised nothing had been decided. He was still no closer to reaching a decision. And Isla Cameron would be wanting a decision.

Sixteen

Isla

Isla stood gazing out the window, watching the sky darken, then turned to survey the light-filled room. She loved this place with its peaceful views over the Botanic Gardens. She'd bought it when she'd accepted the position at Glenferrie; when she decided she was going to spend the rest of her life as a single woman. She had no need for a garden or access to a park or playground. It was low maintenance and that suited her fine.

Sooty leapt down from the white canvas-covered sofa and wound himself around her ankles, purring loudly. Isla picked him up, burying her face in the creature's fur until her pet decided he'd had enough and jumped down again, prowling around the room before finally settling in his favourite spot at the foot of the bookcase.

Sunday! It was supposed to be a day of rest, but Isla had been up since dawn working on the report she was preparing for the next board meeting. It was the one on the proposed trip to Colmar; the issue that caused Rachel Callaghan such angst at the last meeting. This time, Isla was determined to be well-prepared. She already had the support of the parent body – even those parents whose girls weren't going to be part of the excursion assuring her of their backing. And the group was almost complete. She was just waiting to hear from Fiona MacLeod's father to finalise the names.

Fiona was such a lovely girl – bright and cheerful and not afraid to speak her mind. Isla's own mind went to Fiona's father. Alasdair MacLeod had made an impression on her on the two occasions they'd met. There was something about him that spoke to her. It wasn't that he was attractive – though he certainly was. It was as if, in him, she'd met a kindred spirit.

Isla shook her head. Now she sounded foolish – even to herself. But, picturing his face, the way his lips became taut as if with pain, the deeply-etched lines around his eyes and mouth, she knew she was looking at someone who'd suffered, who was still suffering – just as she had, as she was – and she ached to help him make the pain go away. *Where had that come from?* Alasdair MacLeod was the parent of one of her students. Yes, he'd lost his life partner. So had many men she met, women too. She didn't feel the urge to comfort them. What was it about this man?

Shona's arrival put an end to Isla's self-recriminations. In an effort to return Shona's hospitality of three weeks earlier, Isla had invited her friend to dinner. But faced with the daunting task of deciding what to cook, she'd resorted to Marks and Spencer's ready-cooked meals. The lamb shanks with honey roast vegetables were already in the oven, the mango and mangetout waiting in the refrigerator, and the Brussels pâté sitting on the coffee table along with a plate of crackers, an opened bottle of Margaret River Cabernet Sauvignon and two glasses. She'd developed a taste for Australian wines during her sojourn in that country and preferred them to the thinner French ones, even though she had more first-hand experience of the varieties grown there.

'Hey!' Shona burst through the open door like a whirlwind. 'You'll never guess.'

Isla grinned. Ever since they met, Shona had been like this – full of the joys of life. Regardless of what life threw at her – and she'd had her fair share of disappointments – she quickly bounced back, ready for more.

'Probably not,' she replied, 'but take your coat off first and let me pour you a glass of wine before you launch into whatever you have to tell me.'

They were barely seated when, taking a gulp from her glass, Shona began to speak. 'Gee, this is a nice drop.' She picked up the bottle to examine the label. 'Another of your Australian wines. But I digress.'

Isla smiled and took a sip from her own glass, knowing Shona would eventually get to what had excited her.

'Hugh has a friend.' She stared at Isla intently. 'Now, don't go all coy on me. I know what you said about men, but hear me out.'

Isla sighed. She thought Shona had given up trying to matchmake. After what happened – almost ten years ago now – her friend had tried to take her out of herself, as she put it, by trying to set her up with a variety of men, many of whom had been very nice, but not for her. For the past few years, it seemed Shona had given up, accepted that Isla was not in the market, was not looking for a relationship, was perfectly happy being single. Now this! She cradled her glass in both hands and prepared to listen.

'I know what you keep telling me, Isla, but, my God, it's been nearly ten years. Surely...'

She glanced sideways at Isla who sat as if frozen. *Could she bear to hear this?*

'Anyway,' Shona continued, undaunted by Isla's icy posture. 'Daniel Henderson is his name. I met him at a dinner party with Hugh last weekend. He's around our age, tall, good-looking, and...' she paused as if this was the detail that would seal Isla's agreement, 'he's recently arrived from Oxford to take up a lectureship in Education here in Glasgow.'

'I didn't think you were going to set me up with someone who was living somewhere else,' Isla said drily. 'I don't care if he's the best thing since sliced bread. I'm not interested. Not now, not ever. Now, drink up and try this pâté I bought specially for you. Dinner will be ready soon.'

'But...' Shona began, as she picked up her glass, '... you can't live like this forever. You must...'

'Stop it! You're my dearest friend, Shona. But you have to realise, I'm not like you. I can't turn my emotions on and off when someone new comes along. I learnt that the hard way and I think I'm completely insulated from all those feelings you seem able to call up at the drop of a hat.'

'But won't you even...?'

'No! It wouldn't be fair on the poor guy. I did try, several times – remember? And it never worked. You just have to accept that I've used up all the love I was gifted with and I channel my finer feelings into my work.'

'Mmm. Speaking of your work. You mentioned something about a trip to France – back to Colmar. Is it wise? Won't that bring back memories?'

Isla spread pâté on a cracker, popped it into her mouth, and took a gulp of wine while deciding how to reply. Finally, she raised her eyes to meet Shona's.

'I think it's time. I was happy there. I can't avoid the past forever. I feel…' Isla wondered how to explain to her friend. 'I feel I need to go back to where it all began. Maybe…' she sighed. 'Maybe that'll help.'

'And how are your plans going? Is the dreadful Rachel still opposing it?'

'I'll find out next week – at the Board meeting. But I now have the support of the parents and the group is almost finalised. I'm just waiting for one confirmation.' She pictured Fiona MacLeod and her father.

Shona must have seen something in Isla's eyes, or maybe she'd given an involuntary smile. She raised an eyebrow.

'There's one girl… she's in a wheelchair… her father's going to confirm with me this week.'

'That's a big undertaking. What's the father like?'

Isla wished she hadn't mentioned Fiona and her father.

'Oh, you know. Typical buttoned up businessman. Widower, so overly concerned about his daughter.' Isla tried to sound nonchalant. 'He's going to decide if their *au pair* can accompany her.'

'And what do *you* think?'

'I'd like her to come. She reminds me…' No, Isla couldn't say it. 'She's a bright kid and would benefit a lot from the chance to widen her horizons. She's a very gifted photographer too, and would produce an amazing record of the trip,' she said instead, hoping her friend hadn't noticed her slip up.

'Right. Well, I hope it works out for you,' was all Shona said, helping herself to crackers and pâté. 'Mmm. This is delicious. Have you been working away in the kitchen?'

'Afraid not. You'll be eating Marks' best tonight.'

The pair laughed at a memory from their uni days. Over lunch in the Student Union one day, Isla had admired the jumper a mutual friend was wearing – a navy heavy-knit. When she replied 'It's Mark's,' and Isla had mentioned they had nice knitwear there, the other had looked shocked and responded, 'Mark's my brother.' Neither Isla or Shona had ever forgotten the incident which was now burned into their memory.

To Isla's relief, Shona didn't return to any discussion of the man she'd earmarked for her friend, instead she spent most of the meal alternately singing the praises of the new man in *her* life who, it seemed, *was* the best thing since sliced bread, and condemning the increased bureaucracy in her workplace.

By the time Shona left, all Isla's earlier feelings of annoyance had disappeared, and she hugged Shona warmly as the pair agreed to meet again soon.

Once she was alone, however, Isla's mind went back to the earlier conversation. *Why couldn't people leave her alone? Why did they assume she must be lonely, that a woman needed a man in her life for it to be fulfilling?*

She idly wondered whether Alasdair MacLeod had the same problem. If, now he was a widower, friends and family were rushing to matchmake, urging him to remarry, to provide a mother for his children. She thought not. *It was different for men. But was it? And why did the idea rankle?*

Seventeen

Alasdair

'What have you decided?' Fiona spooned up her porridge, then lifted the bowl to drink the remaining milk, leaving a white rim around her lips.

'About what?'

'Dad! About France, of course. I can go, can't I?' Fiona met his gaze, her pleading expression so like one he'd often seen on her mother's face, he had to look away.

'It's not…'

'That easy. I know. So you keep saying. But surely?'

'You are going to France?' Anaïs joined them at the table, placing a mug of coffee at Alasdair's elbow. '*C'est vraiment bon. Quand va-tu? Pour les vacances?*'

Fiona didn't reply, instead looking across at Alasdair. Anaïs followed her gaze. With both their eyes on him, Alasdair shrugged. He knew when he was beaten. 'It depends on you, Anaïs. Ms Cameron – Fi's headmistress – suggested you accompany the group – to help Fi.'

'I don't need,' Fiona began, stopping when she saw her father's grim expression.

'*Moi? Mais…*' Anaïs' eyes widened in surprise.

Alasdair gulped down his hot coffee before replying. 'It would help to have another adult – and your being French would be an advantage too. They're planning to go to Colmar in July – in the school holidays.

I'd pay for both of you, of course, and you'd still receive your salary from me, Anaïs. So...' He dragged a hand through his hair. 'What do you think?' he asked.

'What a wonderful idea!' Fiona seemed to have changed her mind about requiring help, or maybe she'd come to the conclusion this was the only way she'd be allowed to go. 'You will agree, Anaïs?'

'If your father thinks...' She turned to Alasdair with a frown. 'I do not know Colmar. It is far from my home town. In Alsace. Close to the German border. They speak German there too. Why do they choose such a place to visit? There are many other pretty spots, I think.'

'I don't know.' Alasdair dragged a hand through his hair again.

Fiona chuckled. 'Grandpa would say you look as if you've been dragged through a hedge backwards, Dad. You'll need to fix up your hair again before you leave for the office.'

Until now, it hadn't occurred to Alasdair to wonder why this particular location had been chosen for the trip. Maybe Isla Cameron, or one of the other teachers, had contacts there.

'So, you'll let Ms Cameron know?' Fiona wasn't going to let up.

'I will.' Alasdair sighed, knowing he'd promised to give Isla Cameron his reply this week. He could phone her, he supposed, but something – he wasn't sure what – made him want to see her again. Taking out his phone he made a note to set up another appointment at the school. He expected he'd have to complete some paperwork, he told himself, and it would be simpler to do it there.

*

It was mid-week before he managed to find time to arrange the meeting at Glenferrie – two days during which Fiona continually badgered him, asking if he'd done it yet. He'd be glad to get it over with and was beginning to wish he'd put paid to the whole idea. But now, not only Fiona, but Anaïs, too, was making plans for the trip.

The sun was already beginning to set when Alasdair drove into the school grounds at five o'clock. The large building loomed up before him out of the darkness like a ghost ship. The grounds were deserted apart from a red Peugeot which he presumed belonged to the headmistress.

Alasdair parked his own black BMW SUV next to it, wondering what prompted the woman to choose a red car – a colour he'd always associated with brash young men and speed. He'd always preferred to choose the more conservative black for his own vehicles.

He walked into the building, his feet echoing in the empty corridors, and made his way to the office where he'd met Isla on his previous visit. He knocked on the partially closed door, before pushing it completely open.

Isla Cameron was seated behind the large wooden desk, head down, fingers busily typing on a keyboard. The window behind her looked out onto the school's extensive playing fields, empty at this time of night and, inside, a tired-looking plant stood forlornly on top of a gray filing cabinet along with a small round mirror.

He cleared his throat.

Isla looked up, and he caught sight of the Isla Cameron he remembered from Christmas Eve, before her professional persona took over.

'Mr MacLeod.'

'Alasdair,' he automatically corrected her.

She appeared not to hear him.

'You've reached a decision?'

'Yes, Fi – Fiona – has my permission to go, and Anaïs – our *au pair* – she's agreed to go, too.'

'Good.' Isla exhaled. 'I'm glad you've agreed to my suggestion. I'm sure Fiona will prove to be an asset to the group – Anaïs, too.'

Alasdair was surprised to hear Anaïs' name pronounced correctly and with a distinct French accent. It had taken him some time to get it correct himself. He wondered about Isla Cameron's background. Had she lived in France – have French connections? Cameron was a Scottish name, as was Isla, but that wasn't to say she'd lived here all her life. He found he was curious about her. For the first time since Elspeth's death, a woman piqued his curiosity.

'What happens now?' he asked, feeling lightheaded at this unexpected insight.

He watched, mesmerised, as Isla Cameron drew a sheet of paper from the folder on her desk. 'I need to ask you to fill in a form giving your formal approval. There are some things we still need to have in hard copy,' she smiled – a smile that lit up her otherwise solemn face. 'And we'll need details for Anaïs, too. We can arrange for payment later, once it has all been approved by the board. That's one part of it that *can* be done online.'

'Wait a moment.' It just occurred to Alasdair what she had said. 'You mean the school board still has to approve this? It hasn't been finalised?'

'It's a mere detail. The board meets next Tuesday.'

But Alasdair noted the fleeting frown that had appeared between her eyes.

'I can complete that form now.' He drew out a pen. 'Unless you need to get away?'

'No.'

Alasdair had the impression she had little to go home to, that the school was her life. He wasn't sure why that occurred to him, as he quickly filled out the requisite information, signed the form, and handed it back.

'Well, if that's all.' He rose, for some reason reluctant to go, but unable to find a reason to prolong the meeting. He stood, fastened his coat, and retied his scarf. 'I'll say goodbye then.'

'Goodbye, Mr MacLeod.' Isla barely glanced up from her perusal of the form which she was placing back into the folder.

What a cold fish, Alasdair thought, as he got back into his car and set off for home. But her students seemed to like her. Maybe they saw a different side of her, the side he'd seen, albeit briefly, at Kirsty's do, a side of her he'd dearly like to explore.

Eighteen

Isla

'Do say you'll come!' Shona was at her most persuasive. 'It's the last night and there were rave reviews. Listen…'

Isla could do nothing but listen as, on the other end of the phone, her friend began to read from a review, 'Rona Munro's *Bold Girls*, first staged in 1991, is one of those disquieting works that lures its audience in gently before gradually exposing them to the sadness and desperation at its core.'

'Oh, I don't know, Shona. It doesn't really sound like my thing.'

'What else are you going to do?'

'Well…' Isla cast around for a reason, an excuse, anything that would get her out of going to the Citizens Theatre with Shona, but couldn't come up with anything on the spur of the moment.

Latching on to Isla's hesitation, Shona continued, 'It starts at seven-thirty. Shall I pick you up, or meet you there?'

'I'll meet you in the foyer,' Isla said, realising she'd been trapped into going. When was she going to learn? *Hadn't Kirsty Reid's evening been enough?* But this was the theatre. There was no likelihood of being bored by overly enthusiastic revellers or reminded of a celebration she was at pains to ignore.

To her surprise, Isla enjoyed the evening so much that, when Shona invited her to a charity dinner arranged by a colleague the following weekend, she agreed. It wasn't until she was back home drinking a warm mug of hot chocolate, Sooty purring loudly in her lap, that she took time to consider what she might have let herself in for.

By her own admission Shona was still heavily involved with the man she'd met ski-ing over Christmas. He'd been in London this weekend, hence the spare theatre ticket, but surely he'd be partnering Shona to the dinner? Well, Isla reasoned, she'd been the spare wheel often enough in her life. One more time wouldn't hurt. It was for a good cause, and at least the company should be intelligent.

It would be interesting to meet this paragon of Shona's. Usually her friend's male companions disappeared long before she got to be introduced.

And, as Shona kept pointing out, she needed to get out more. Isla sighed. Maybe Shona was right. Maybe it was time to become more sociable. A New Year's resolution, perhaps? Having made the decision to return to Colmar, she hoped she could finally find closure – put the past behind her and look to the future.

Isla cupped her mug in both hands. If she closed her eyes, she could see herself back there.

Just turned thirty, with no prospect of a permanent relationship, and surrounded by other people's children every day, Isla was desperate to have one of her own.

When the summer holidays came around, she headed off to Europe with no clear plan, no idea of where she might end up. After two weeks of meandering through Holland and Belgium and several days in Paris, she headed east, finally reaching the wine-growing Alsace region in the north-easterly part of the country.

Driving into the city of Colmar, Isla was struck by the cobblestone streets lined with half-timbered buildings which appeared medieval or early renaissance. She later learned this was the old part of the town but, by then, she was caught up in the enchantment of the place and its people.

And she'd met Olivier – Ollie. Despite his French name, Ollie was all American. He'd come to the region to spend his university break with his uncle – interning for his Viticulture course back home in California. Phillipe Carlier owned one of the largest vineyards in the neighbouring countryside, and his nephew was helping with the harvest.

Isla and Ollie met when she was on a wine-tasting trip and the young American student started up a conversation with her, claiming to be starved of English-speaking female company. While Isla knew this couldn't possibly be true, she was flattered by the attentions of the tall, tanned American with thick blond hair and deep brown eyes who must be eight to ten years her junior. He confided he had a girl 'back home' who wore his class ring – soon to be exchanged for an engagement ring – but that didn't seem to prevent him paying attention to Isla.

For the affection-starved school teacher, it was balm to the soul and, even though she knew there was no future in it, she fell into the relationship with all the fervour of an unsophisticated young girl.

In retrospect, her desire for a child may have fuelled her passion, but for Isla, it was a summer of love – one which she knew she'd look back on with nostalgia.

And that's where it had all begun.

Colmar!

Isla's thoughts went back to the board meeting held the previous Tuesday, and she smiled remembering how impressed they'd been at her thorough report. Even Rachel Callaghan had been cowed into supporting it when Isla had produced evidence of the backing of the parent body and the list of attendees which included the daughters of several prominent business men and one member of the Scottish parliament.

Alasdair MacLeod was one of the prominent businessmen. Isla had been surprised at the response to Fiona MacLeod's name being on the list. She had been unaware of Alasdair's reputation in the city, only knowing he was something in insurance, and not even sure how she came to know that.

Now she was informed he was Regional Director for one of Glasgow's largest insurance companies, and well known to all the board members. That he was willing to entrust his daughter to her care for the overseas excursion practically sealed the deal.

It figured, she thought, that the buttoned-up man she was beginning to get to know, was a respected businessman. It was as if there were two versions of him – the vulnerable one she'd met on Christmas Eve and the more formal one of their two more recent encounters. What would it take, she mused, to find out who the real one was?

*

'Here she is!' Shona's voice reached Isla across the crowded room and, as she made her way to join her friend, Isla was glad she'd agreed to come. The room, filled with round tables all covered with white tablecloths and sporting the insignia of the charity were surrounded by a melee of well-dressed chattering strangers.

As she reached her friend, Isla was enveloped in a warm hug, then, 'This is Hugh.' Shona smiled and drew forward a tall man who could have been any one of the men Shona had been with over the years. He took Isla's hand and gave her a peck on the cheek. 'And this,' Shona said, as if revealing a secret surprise, 'is Daniel – Daniel Henderson.' She beamed at Isla as the man Isla hadn't noticed till now, moved towards her, hand outstretched, a wide grin on his face.

'So, you're the famed Isla, Headmistress at Glenferrie Academy?' he said, his accent sounding more English than Scots. Isla stared incredulously at the tall blond man, then turned to glare at Shona.

She'd been set up. The evening was going to be a disaster.

Somehow, Isla managed to remain polite throughout what was, for her, a long and boring dinner. The food was good, as was to be expected, but placed as she was between Shona's Hugh and his friend, Daniel, the conversation was even more difficult than she anticipated. The men appeared to be intent on attempting to prove to each other how well they could handle their drink – the numerous bottles of wine ordered and consumed bearing testimony to their prowess.

On Hugh's other side, Shona seemed to be enjoying their rivalry, but Isla, who was restricting herself to a maximum of two glasses, found it all very childish and wished herself anywhere else. She was wondering how soon she could leave without appearing rude, when the speeches began, only for her to find Daniel's hand on her thigh. She moved away.

The speeches over, the waiters began to serve dessert. Isla rose and, pointing in the direction of the doorway to the ladies, walked across the room and out into the hallway. For a moment she enjoyed the reprieve from the noisy dining room, before entering the toilets.

Once there, she stared at herself in the mirror. How had she allowed herself to be talked into this again? Her New Year's resolution to get out more hadn't included meeting men, especially not ones like this Daniel Henderson. Then she reconsidered. He was probably quite a nice guy – when he wasn't trying to prove something to his friend.

As she entered the hallway again, she almost walked into a man standing close to the doorway of the function room.

'Sorry,' she muttered, her eyes downcast.

'Isla!'

She looked up to see Alasdair MacLeod grinning down at her. *He looks much more attractive when he smiles,* she thought, as she had before, then flushed with embarrassment.

'Escaping again?'

'No... yes,' she admitted. 'I seem to have been shanghaied into something I didn't expect.'

'Yes. I saw you fending off Henderson's attentions during dinner. Doesn't hold his drink well. Never did.'

'You know him?'

'From school. Have you known him long?'

'Too long!' Isla said bitterly. 'I met him for the first time tonight. My friend,' she pointed towards the table she'd been seated at, where Shona was holding forth, waving her glass around, 'didn't tell me she'd organised a dinner partner for me.'

'I was about to leave. Do you want to join me? Maybe we could find our own spot for a coffee and dessert?'

'I couldn't.' But could she? Isla peeked into the function room once again to see the group she'd been dining with were now engaged in some weird game. She shuddered.

'You have your bag. Coat?'

'In the cloakroom.' Isla threw one more glance back at her dining companions. They were laughing and carousing. They'd barely miss her.

Isla was torn. She was Shona's guest. Her friend would expect her to stay. But she couldn't imagine going back in there to become part of whatever drunken game they were playing. On the other hand, she didn't want to give Alasdair the wrong idea.

She glanced into the room again, then met Alasdair's eyes. 'Alright,' she said, 'let's get out of here.'

Nineteen

Alasdair

It was a clear night, the stars sparkling in the sky above them as they walked.

'Where are we going?' Isla asked after a few minutes.

'The Rogano.' Alasdair wasn't familiar with many city eateries, but the Art Deco styled restaurant was one he frequented for lunch at least once a week. 'They know me there. We can get coffee and the dessert you missed out on.'

'Oh!'

Alasdair glanced sideways at his companion. *What was she thinking?* He knew the restaurant was one more usually patronised by Glasgow's powerbrokers and fashionista. It might not be Isla's normal venue for eating out, but it was only a five-minute walk, and a place he knew well.

'Here we are,' he said, as they turned into Royal Exchange Square.

It was a relief to get out of the cold and, once seated with coffee and servings of crème brûlé with Highlander shortbread, they both began to relax.

'You seem to be making a habit of rescuing me.' Isla said, her face softening into a smile.

He'd been right. The smile made her look completely different. It wasn't the professional smile she'd used at the parent meeting. This one seemed more genuine – as if she was really pleased to be here.

'Glad to be of service. Though you don't give the impression of someone who often needs rescuing. What was tonight all about?'

Isla exhaled loudly and, picking up her spoon, stirred her coffee. 'Shona – my friend – she's always trying to *help* me – to force me to get out more. The charity event seemed to be innocuous. It's for a good cause.'

Alasdair nodded. That's what had enticed him along. The group was doing good things for kids like Fiona and deserved all the support they could get.

'She did tell me her new partner would be there – it was to be an opportunity for me to meet him. But…' she paused, '…what she didn't tell me was that he'd be bringing along a friend. I should have realised. I've known Shona for years – since uni. And she's always trying to matchmake. She can't keep a man herself, so God knows how she thinks she can find one for me.' She said the last sentence under her breath, and Alasdair could barely catch the words.

'And that was bad – why?'

'I'm perfectly happy being single,' she said without hesitation.

Alasdair wasn't sure why, but he felt a chill run through him.

'The school keeps me busy, and I enjoy my independence,' Isla continued, before Alasdair could respond.

Neither spoke as they spooned up their desserts.

Despite the comfort of the restaurant, Alasdair felt awkward. Isla was his daughter's headmistress. He was still grieving for Elspeth. What was he doing sitting here with this elegant self-contained woman? What did they have to talk about? He was completely out of practice with women. Other than his mother, Bel and Kirsty, he didn't think he'd spent time alone with any woman since Elspeth died.

The waiter came to remove their empty dishes. Alasdair ordered more coffee.

'Have you…?'

'I…'

They both began to speak at once then laughed.

'You go first,' Isla said.

'I was going to ask what made you choose Colmar. It's an unusual choice.'

He saw Isla's lips tighten, then relax. 'I spent time there when I was younger. It's a lovely medieval city – should be a very different experience for the girls.'

'Fi's certainly looking forward to it. You mentioned something about her Art teacher going, too?'

'Yes. Lee's very impressed with Fiona's photographic skills and means to encourage her to branch out on the trip – videos, podcasts and such.'

'Mmm.' Alasdair didn't have much experience with such things, but no doubt Fiona would be able to explain them to him.

Isla picked up her coffee and drained the cup. 'I should go now. Thanks for rescuing me – and for the coffee and dessert. It was kind of you.' She smiled again.

'Must you?'

Alasdair rose with her, reluctant to see her go. 'I can walk...'

'No. No need. Stay where you are.'

And she was gone in a flurry of blue, her coat whirling behind her as she swept through the door.

Alasdair resumed his seat, ordering a Taylor's ten-year-old tawny port. He sipped his drink slowly, trying to make sense of what had just happened. He'd just spent an hour or so with a woman – a woman who intrigued him, a woman who was his daughter's headmistress.

But she was an independent woman. By her own admission, Isla had no need for anyone more in her life, she was content to remain single – an admirable, if unusual occurrence in one so elegant, so...

Stop right there, he told himself. What was he thinking? Elspeth was barely cold in her grave and here he was considering... what?

But despite living with two children and an *au pair*, despite going to the office every day and seeing family on weekends, Alasdair knew it wasn't enough.

He was lonely.

Twenty

Bel

'Look at this, Matt!' Bel's voice drew her husband to look over her shoulder at the computer screen.

'What?'

'It's the new website. Celia has taken Isabella online. Doesn't it look wonderful? I never imagined...' She gazed mesmerised at the stylish heading and title page featuring the boutique she'd owned back in Australia. It belonged to Celia now and, after much procrastinating, the new owner had finally taken the plunge and joined the internet revolution. 'Her son-in-law has been badgering her for ages to let him set it up, and now it's done.'

'Still no regrets?'

'None.' Bel turned her head to smile at the man standing behind her. 'Now what I actually wanted to check was the email from Andrew, but I opened one from Celia first.'

'What does Andrew have to say?' Matt leaned closer, and Bel inhaled his familiar aroma – a mixture of soap and the tang of the outdoors.

'Let me see.' Bel scrolled down to open Andrew's email.

They read it together.

'So, that's that. What do you think?' Bel said when they'd finished.

'It'll be a lot of work, but not impossible. And he does say...'

'Yes!' Bel said jubilantly. 'We'll be able to knock through to Aunt

Isobel's.' Although the old woman had been gone for nearly three years now, she still thought of what was now *Isobel's Place* as her aunt's house – and the house she'd grown up in.

'You'll go ahead?'

'I think so. If we put in an offer now, it'll be at least April before it's all finalised and the better weather should be here by then. We can plan a July opening, before the fair holidays.'

Matt laughed. 'No doubt about you, darling. You're already planning the opening and you haven't bought the house yet.'

'But we will, won't we?'

'It's your money, Bel. Not my decision to make.'

'But you know how I value your advice.'

'Then I say go ahead. Andrew's reports say the building is sound and it's certainly a big plus to be right next door. I love to see you excited like this.' He dropped a kiss on the top of Bel's head. 'Now, remember it's our day with Fi. Wasn't it today we promised her a special treat and we're to hear more about her French jaunt?'

'You're right. How could I forget? We can tell her this news, too. She'll be thrilled. I should get dressed. Are you going like that?' She raked her eyes down Matt's early morning deshabille.

'Probably not,' he chuckled. 'Beat you to the shower.'

*

'Where are we going today?' Fiona's excited voice reached them from the back seat of the car as they left the Anniesland house behind.

Bel looked back. 'How does the GOMA sound? The Margaret Tait exhibition is still on and, since you're into film and videos, Grandpa and I thought...'

'Oh! *Stalking the Image*. We heard about that at school. It's her centenary year. How splendid!'

Bel hid a smile at this old-fashioned word. She was really enjoying their Saturdays with Fiona – originally designed to provide her with company while Alasdair took himself off to watch Robbie play football, they had evolved into a special time with her and Matt. Fiona was delightful company, continually surprising them with her grown-up take on things.

As they wandered around, Bel and Matt were kept informed and amused by Fiona's pithy comments. But after an hour they had all had enough.

'Lunch?' Matt suggested. 'McDonald's?' He looked at Fiona for her agreement.

'Can we eat here?' Fiona said to their surprise. 'My friend Cassie came here in the holidays and she said the food was really good. Anyway, McDonald's isn't such a treat any more, now that even Dad takes us there.'

Bel and Matt exchanged a smile over Fiona's head. How times had changed. Bel recalled Matt telling her how both Fiona and Robbie had been delighted to be taken to the restaurant frowned on by their parents.

'I think Dad's trying to please us – now that there are just the three of us,' Fiona continued. 'But it doesn't bring Mum back.'

All three were silent as they entered the lift and descended to the café.

'Now,' Bel said, when they'd been served with soup and chicken sandwiches accompanied by hot chocolate for Fiona, and coffee for Bel and Matt, 'tell us about your trip.'

'Well,' said Fiona, between bites. 'You know Dad finally agreed, and that Anaïs is coming too?'

Bel smiled.

'I think Ms Cameron talked him into it. She's so cool. Ms Smythe was going to come too – she's my Art teacher, the one who told us about this exhibition. But she's not coming after all. However...' Fiona took a deep breath, a wide grin on her face. '...she wants me to be the official photographer for the group – take all the photos and make videos of where we go and what we do. It'll be special – she wants to set up a display when we get back; invite the parents and everything.'

'Wow! That sounds wonderful.' Matt couldn't keep the pride out of his voice. 'And will we get to see them too?'

'Of course! I'll set up a YouTube account so you can see them while we're there.' She munched on her sandwich. 'But you don't need to wait till then.' She gave a secret smile. 'School is having an Easter exhibition of our work and Ms Smythe wants to include some of the shots I took at the loch. You *will* both come to that, won't you?'

Fiona looked from one to the other.

'We certainly will. Are they ones we've seen before?' Bel asked.

'Yes, but they're to be blown up and framed and everything. Most of those on display will be from the more senior students, but Ms Smythe said mine were as good, if not better.' Fiona wriggled in her chair, too excited to sit still.

'Well done! I think that deserves an ice cream,' Matt exclaimed.

'Can we stop at Desserts on the way home?'

'Sure can.'

Fiona smiled smugly. 'Wait till I tell Robbie.'

'Nana Bel has some news for you, too,' Matt said with a smile.

Fiona turned to face Bel. 'You bought the other house!'

'Not news, then.' Bel laughed.

'I knew it! Oh, that's so good. When…?'

'Steady on,' Matt said. 'These things take time. Bel has to put in an offer. If it's accepted, then the entire process will take around six to eight weeks to finalise.'

'Then there will need to be a lot of work done,' Bel continued. 'But it should all be up and running by the middle of the year – and we'll be able to go through the wall to my aunt's old house – to *Isobel's Place*.'

'So *Isobel's Place* will be twice as big?'

'It will.' As she spoke, Bel felt her Aunt Isobel's presence as surely as if she was standing at her shoulder. She shivered. But it was a welcoming presence. She knew the old woman approved of what she was doing, and she hoped Pete would have approved of her use of his legacy, too.

Twenty-one

Alasdair

Alasdair looked out of his office window and wondered why his work, once the centre of his existence, now failed to hold his interest. He rose and walked to the window, seeing the familiar tall buildings of his home city spread out before him, but today the red and blonde sandstone didn't provide the pleasure he was accustomed to feel.

He sighed. Whereas he'd always had Elspeth at home, known she was there – an anchor keeping him steady, someone to return to at the end of a busy day, now, it was different. He still had the children. The house echoed with their voices and laughter, but he couldn't summon up any enthusiasm for them, for his life.

Maybe his father-in-law was right. He was depressed. But he wasn't going to seek help from a quack. He was quite able to find his own way back from the blackness that, some days, threatened to engulf him.

Unexpectedly, a face appeared in his mind's eye – a calm face, one which he knew would understand. Isla Cameron. She wasn't Elspeth. She was completely unlike Elspeth. And yet…

His hand went to the pocket where he kept his mobile phone, then hesitated. Should he call? What would he say?

'Mr MacLeod?'

He turned from the window to see his secretary standing hesitantly at the door. Grace Allen had been with him for years, was extremely efficient, managed his diary and kept him safe from people she regarded as timewasters. For the first time, he wondered what she thought of him. She was such a harridan, he'd never dare ask, but he recalled several business associates commenting on her protectiveness.

Elspeth had once accused him of encouraging her, suggested the woman was in love with him. He'd rubbished the idea, of course. Grace was almost old enough to be his mother. *Her* face had never disturbed his dreams.

'Your appointment's here.' Grace was giving him a puzzled look. 'Mr Grierson – Strathclyde office.'

'Of course.' Alasdair came back to the present and the matter in hand. 'Give me five minutes, then show him in.' He needed a few minutes to refocus his thoughts on this meeting.

But, the meeting over, Alasdair was still haunted by thoughts of Isla Cameron, by the memory of her sad eyes, of her reluctance to be part of a couple.

That decided him.

He wasn't looking for a relationship either. But it would be pleasant to have a companion with whom he could exchange views, another adult with whom he could make intelligent conversation, perhaps even share the odd visit to the theatre or cinema, or even dinner. If he made it clear at the outset that he wasn't looking for anything more than that?

Before he could overthink his next move, he took out his phone and pressed the speed dial for Glenferrie Academy.

A very cheerful voice answered. 'Good afternoon. Glenferrie Academy. This is Jean Beattie speaking. How may I help you?'

Damn! It hadn't occurred to Alasdair his call wouldn't go straight through to Isla. Though why should it? He had his own efficient gatekeeper in Grace. Thrown for a moment, he hesitated, cleared his throat, then, 'It's Alasdair MacLeod here, Fiona MacLeod's father. I'd like to speak with the headmistress, with Ms Cameron.'

'Good afternoon, Mr MacLeod. I'll see if Ms Cameron is available.'

Alasdair was put on hold, the rendition of some neutral music tempting him to end the call before it had begun. But he'd given his name. He waited.

'Good afternoon, Alasdair MacLeod. Is there something about Fiona you want to discuss with me?' Isla's softly accented voice reached his ears. It had such a restful effect. He could see her there in her office, tapping on her desk with her pen, an open folder in front of her – or maybe a laptop?

He cleared his throat. 'No, not Fi. It's... I... I wondered if you'd have dinner with me some time. I'm not... I'm quite aware of your view about men following you. I can assure you I have no such intentions. But... you need to eat, and I would enjoy some adult company – your company,' he quickly added, lest he sound too needy.

There was silence at the other end of the phone. Alasdair wished he knew what she was thinking. He may have made a dreadful mistake in imagining she'd agree to a dinner engagement with him. He wasn't accustomed to this. He hadn't invited a woman to dinner since he was nineteen. He'd forgotten how.

The silence went on for so long, he began to wonder if Isla had hung up. Then he heard a muffled sound he couldn't identify, followed by, 'Thank you. That's kind of you. I appreciate your consideration of my concerns regarding the male of the species. On that basis I'd be delighted to join you for dinner. Did you have a particular day in mind?'

Somewhat stunned by the formality of her reply, Alasdair thought quickly. He'd extended the invitation without any real idea of the outcome; with no real expectation of success. 'Friday,' he said, remembering the children would both be busy – Fiona was having a friend for a sleepover, and Robbie was going to a birthday party. He wouldn't be missed. He could claim to be working late, though why he felt he needed this subterfuge, he wasn't sure.

'Friday,' Isla agreed, with a smile in her voice.

'Seven? Can I pick you up?'

'No,' she answered swiftly. 'I can meet you at the restaurant. Where did you have in mind?'

Alasdair hadn't thought that far ahead and, while one part of him was curious about where she lived, another was glad to keep their evening on a more formal footing. 'Can I let you know – text you?'

Isla gave him her mobile number, and Alasdair finished the call. He drew a hand round the inside of his shirt collar, relieved it was over. He'd much rather take on a business opponent than make another call like that one.

Twenty-two

Isla

Isla stared at her phone in surprise. *What had she just agreed to?* The call from Alasdair MacLeod had been unexpected, and she'd barely been able to suppress her amusement at his invitation and his strange choice of words. Her first instinct was to refuse – to claim work, too many other engagements. But there was something about the man, and his tentative approach, that tugged at her heartstrings – much the way his daughter did.

So now she, who had always vowed never to mix her work and social life, was committed to dinner with the father of one of her students. She leant back, picturing the man she'd agreed to dine with. He was a bit of an enigma. She knew he was widowed, was something important in the insurance industry, had two children, hated Christmas as much as she did, but not much else.

Her musings were interrupted by a gentle knock at the door. It opened, and Maree popped her head around. 'Staff meeting in ten minutes. I have the coffee machine on.'

'Thanks, Maree. I'll be right there.' As she gathered the papers she needed for the meeting, Isla recalled how delighted the staff had been when she agreed to use some of the proceeds from the last fundraiser to purchase a state-of-the-art coffee maker for the staffroom. Most of the staff had been with the school since before she took over as headmistress, and she was well aware of the importance of maintaining a stable cohort of staff and ensuring their continued motivation and support. It was amazing how a seemingly small item like a coffee-maker in the staff-room could add to their sense of loyalty and commitment.

As expected, the staff meeting went without a hitch. Everything was now in place for the Colmar trip, so the main focus of discussion was the Easter Art Show which Lee Smythe was organising. It was to take place on the Thursday evening before the Easter break, only three weeks away. Lee was intent on getting help in both setting up for the event and in attending on the evening itself.

'The girls will help, of course, and they're mainly seniors and very capable. But, as you're all aware, I'll need some of you to supervise them and ensure it all goes to plan. There will be a host of parents and, hopefully, board members present, and we've invited a wheen of local dignitaries.'

'Well done, Lee. I think we should all congratulate our Art Mistress on managing to put all of this together. I understand we have some impressive talent on display this year.'

'Yes, indeed. Sandra Ellis has a couple of excellent figure drawings, Gail Thomas is displaying her usual prowess in water colour cityscapes, and we have a new entrant in Fiona MacLeod. Fiona is a younger contender, but has made great strides in photography in the past year, and we're displaying several shots she took out by Loch Lomond.'

Fiona MacLeod! The MacLeods seemed to be following Isla around.

A muttering among the group, accompanied by the sound of cups and saucers rattling, signified to Isla that it was time to draw the meeting to a close.

'I think that's all for today.,' she said. 'Please let Lee know if you're able to help on the thirtieth. I'll be there, of course.' Along with Alasdair MacLeod's family she thought, as she rose to leave. *Why was she permitting her life to become entangled with his?*

No sooner was Isla back in her office, than her phone rang.

She could hear Jean on another call, so she answered it herself, expecting it to be a parent with some request or query. But, with Fiona MacLeod and her family still on her mind, Isla wasn't overly surprised to hear Kirsty Reid's voice.

'Sorry I haven't been in touch before now,' Kirsty said in a breathless voice. 'Life's been hectic.' \

Isla could picture Kirsty, red-faced with enthusiasm, dashing from one place to another, full of energy, and taking on more than she could cope with. She'd been like that as a schoolgirl – head of the debating team, a leading light in the drama group and the choir, and a valued member of the hockey first eleven. Isla had never known where she found the energy. She didn't imagine she'd changed much over the years.

'We must catch up. There was no time to talk on Christmas Eve, and you disappeared really early. I looked around and you'd gone.'

Isla blanched, hoping she wasn't going to have to explain her early departure. But Kirsty continued without drawing breath, 'I have to be out your way on Thursday and wondered if they let you out for lunch.'

Isla thought quickly. She wasn't in the habit of leaving the building during the school day unless she had an unavoidable appointment. Would lunch with Kirsty fit into that category? Probably not, but it was an attractive prospect. Alasdair MacLeod *was* Kirsty's brother-in-law, and her old school friend wasn't noted for her tact – or her ability to keep her mouth shut. It would be an opportunity to find out more about the man who was beginning to intrigue her before they met for dinner.

'I think I can manage that,' she said with a laugh. 'Where did you have in mind?'

'There's that little Italian on the main road. How about we meet there? Around twelve or twelve-thirty?'

'Twelve-thirty. And I can only stay an hour. I have meetings in the afternoon.' Isla wasn't sure whether or not she did, but an inner caution led her to set a time limit on their lunch.

'Great! See you then, and we can have a proper catch-up.'

Isla put down the phone, a thoughtful expression on her face. *A proper catch-up* – what did Kirsty mean by that? They'd chatted at the reunion, filled each other in on what they were doing and such like. A shiver ran up Isla's back. *Kirsty couldn't know about her and Alasdair, could she? But what was there to know?* Isla itemised the times the two had met: Christmas Eve, at the school – twice, three times if you counted the Colmar information evening – at the charity dinner. That was it. Really not much. And now there was to be dinner.

No, she decided, Kirsty couldn't possibly have any idea they were even acquainted. She wasn't intending to say anything and she couldn't imagine Alasdair would have mentioned her to his sister-in-law. Isla might not know much about the man, but she was sure he was one to keep his personal life under wraps – especially from a gossip like Kirsty.

Having satisfied herself she had nothing to fear, Isla walked out to where her PA was busy on her computer in the outer office. 'Can you block out my diary for a couple of hours on Thursday, Jean? Twelve till two.' At Jean's raised eyebrows, she added, 'I'm having lunch with an old school friend.'

She was surprised to see her secretary's face relax into a smile. 'It's about time you took some time for yourself. You work too hard – here at the crack of dawn and till all hours of the night. Don't think I don't know.' She tapped her nose. 'The place won't collapse if you go out to lunch once and a while.'

'I'll have my mobile, and you can ring me if anything crops up.'

'And you have a good deputy in Maree Stoddart. She can cope if we have an emergency, though I can't imagine what might happen over lunchtime.'

Isla could imagine all sorts of emergencies arising while she was gone, but decided not to dwell on them.

*

By the time twelve o'clock on Thursday arrived, Isla was looking forward to seeing Kirsty Reid again. Kirsty had always been more outgoing to Isla's serious and considered approach to life – apart from that one time. But Kirsty knew nothing about that period of Isla's life. It had all happened long after the pair lost touch.

Not only was she happy to renew their old friendship – a surprising one, considering how different the two were – Isla was also curious about the family Kirsty had married into – the Reid and MacLeod family. To her shame, she'd googled Alasdair MacLeod the previous evening after two glasses of red wine. What she'd discovered had surprised her. An ex-student of Hutchesons' Grammar, he'd graduated from Glasgow University with first class honours in 1998 which made him around forty-two to Isla's forty-four. That surprised her. She'd assumed he was older from his serious demeanour and formal way of speaking, but perhaps that was just his way. It appeared he and his wife had met at university and married soon after they graduated. Their children had come along some years later.

Joining an insurance company on graduation, he'd moved around before attaining his present position of Regional Director in one of Scotland's largest firms and had been touted as the next CEO until taking a lower profile on the death of his wife.

Isla closed the computer at that point, having had a surfeit of photos of Alasdair both with and without his family at various gatherings over the years. *What was she doing? Why was she so obsessed with knowing more about him?* She tried to justify her interest by the fact she was having dinner with him, but knew that wasn't the reason. However, it did give her some background before she spoke with Kirsty.

Kirsty was already seated at a window table and reading the menu when Isla arrived.

'Sorry if I kept you waiting,' she said, taking a seat opposite.

'Not at all. I've only just arrived. Good to see you again.'

The pair ordered, then sat back to take stock of each other. Today, Kirsty appeared more relaxed than Isla remembered, while Isla felt slightly nervous.

'So!' Kirsty began. 'I understand you're taking my niece to France. I'm really pleased for her. There was a family conference about it, you know.'

Isla didn't, and said so.

'Oh, yes. Sunday lunch – always at my father-in-law's place on Loch Lomond. At least, since he re-married a couple of years ago. Lovely lady – Bel – lived in Australia but grew up here in Glasgow. Alasdair – Fi's dad – wanted our opinion. Well,' she admitted, 'probably not mine. I tend to take the extreme view that the girl's mother over-protected her. But Alasdair seemed unsure which way to go. He came to see you, didn't he?' She gave Isla a speculative look, and Isla could feel herself redden.

'Yes. Thanks,' she said to the waitress who chose that moment to serve their meals, giving her much needed breathing space. 'We had a parent meeting and Fiona's dad subsequently made an appointment to discuss the possibility of her joining the group.' She said nothing about their further meetings or the proposed dinner engagement.

'Mmm. Well, it seems to have worked. She's really excited about it. And I hear the *au pair*'s going, too. That was Fi's idea – the whole *au pair* thing. The puir man couldn't cope when Elspeth died, and his mother was worse than useless. I did what I could, but…' She spread her hands as if to demonstrate her helplessness.

Isla couldn't imagine Kirsty ever feeling helpless. She was a woman who'd dash in where angels feared to tread, as the saying went.

'Anyway, it seems to have worked out. Alasdair says he's reduced his workload, but I think,' she pointed at Isla with her fork, 'he's still hiding from reality.'

'What was Fiona's mother like?' Isla asked.

'Elspeth? She was lovely, if a bit set in her ways. She missed her own mother. Ailsa was killed in the accident that left Fi in a wheelchair. I always felt Elspeth blamed herself for that.' She took a mouthful of pasta and chewed reflectively. 'She felt it should have been her in the car that day. Matt never blamed her though.'

'Matt?'

'Elspeth's father. Of course, you don't know the family. They weren't there on Christmas Eve.'

Isla had been content to let Kirsty babble on, grateful not to have to contribute, but now it was her turn to be the focus of Kirsty's attention.

'So, why Colmar? I'd have thought Paris, or somewhere closer to the coast. Colmar is on the other side of the country, isn't it? I googled it. Looks like a nice place, but…' She raised an eyebrow.

Without hesitation, Isla gave her standard reply about spending time there when she was younger, forgetting Kirsty would want to delve further. 'When you were younger? When? Before or after uni? I seem to remember you headed off overseas after school. I heard about your mum. That must have been hard.' She put a hand on Isla's for a moment before continuing, 'Is that where you ended up?'

'No, Colmar was later. It was when I was teaching. I'd just turned thirty. I went to France for the entire summer holiday, visited the castles, worked in a winery. I needed a break from teaching and that was it. I loved it there.' She could feel her face soften as she remembered.

To Isla, her thirtieth birthday had been a milestone, a sign that the marriage and children thing had passed her by. If she wanted a child of her own, it was up to her to find a way. Ollie had presented her with the perfect solution.

After long days picking grapes, it had been a relief to lose herself in the comfort Ollie's arms offered. She hadn't been in love with him. But with him, she'd been able to forget the failed relationships, the quarrelling children she taught, the staffroom fault-finding, the friends who were married with children, and feel young and desirable again.

When, returning home, she discovered she was pregnant, she hugged the secret to herself, confiding only in her best friend Shona. And, when little Morag was born, her heart had overflowed with joy and hope for the future.

'And what about you?' Kirsty spoke again. 'At the reunion you said you'd never married. Anyone special on the scene?'

God, Kirsty didn't mince words. She hadn't changed from the meddlesome schoolgirl who wanted to know everyone's business – and settle it for them.

'No one. Glenferrie keeps me pretty busy.' *And I have a date with your brother-in-law.* But Isla didn't say that aloud.

'I wonder...' Kirsty gazed across the table, a glint in her eye – the sort of one Isla recalled from their schooldays. Kirsty was hatching a plan.

'Coffee?' It was the waitress again, come to remove their empty plates.

Isla ostentatiously checked her watch. 'No thank you. I really must get back,' she said to Kirsty.

But Kirsty had one more salvo to fire before they parted. 'All those girls,' she said. 'But you can close the door on them at the end of the day. Isn't it a bit of a cop out? Don't you ever long for children of your own – regret you missed out?'

Isla froze.

Then, from somewhere she didn't recognise, the words fell from her lips. 'I had a child. A little girl. She died.'

Twenty-three

Isla

'I'm sorry.'

'I don't want your sympathy. I'm not sure why I told you. I prefer to keep it to myself. I'd be grateful if you didn't tell anyone.'

'But...'

What had she done?

Isla hurried away from the restaurant, barely remembering taking leave of Kirsty, recalling her shocked expression, the questions in her eyes; the questions Isla knew she couldn't bear to answer.

Morag's death had remained a secret between her and Shona for ten years. Ten years during which she'd thrown herself into her career to assuage her grief, caring for other women's daughters instead of her own. She knew what grief was. She lived with it every moment, every day. That might be why she recognised the expression in Alasdair MacLeod's eyes. He was living with grief, too.

And now, Kirsty McLennan knew her secret. It was easier to think of her by her maiden name, the one she'd known her as all those years ago. Kirsty Reid was a stranger, but Kirsty McLennan was the friend who'd have risked her life for her back when they were in their teens.

Could Isla trust her not to spread it around? And did it really matter after all this time? But, strangely, she wanted to be the one who told Alasdair about Morag. She didn't want him to hear it as a piece of gossip from his garrulous sister-in-law.

*

Isla felt nervous as she prepared to meet Alasdair the next evening. He'd texted to first ask if she liked Italian, then again to say he'd booked a table at Sorrento on Byres Road and hoped that met with her approval. She smiled when she read the formal words. He was certainly different from the men Shona had produced for her over the years; different from the Daniel Henderson she'd been partnered with at the charity dinner. Shona had graciously accepted her apology for leaving the dinner early, having pleaded a headache. Thankfully her friend had said no more about Daniel.

She dressed carefully, choosing a soft blue woollen dress and black shoes with slightly higher heels than she was used to wearing. As she slipped on her coat, tied the belt and hitched her leather bag over her shoulder, she reflected that she had taken a lot more care than usual in her preparations for the evening. Was she making too much of Alasdair's invitation?

It was a cool, but clear night, so Isla decided to walk down across the bridge and along Byres Road to the restaurant. It was one she enjoyed and had patronised often with Shona, and Italian food was her favourite.

As she walked in the door, the familiar atmosphere engulfed her like a warm hug. And there, sitting at a corner table, was her dinner companion.

Alasdair rose to greet her, seemed about to give her a peck on the cheek, then recoiled and stretched out a hand. Smiling inwardly, Isla placed her own hand into his firm grip. They sat down and smiled awkwardly at each other.

'Do you?'

'Thanks.'

They both spoke at once, then laughed.

'I love this place,' Isla said, her eyes roaming around the room, seeing the familiar red and white checked tablecloths which reminded her of Italy, the exposed brick walls, the large potted orange tree which she could see through the archway.

'Good choice, then. It's my first time.'

'What made you choose it?'

'I asked my sister-in-law. You know her – Christmas Eve – Kirsty Reid.'

Isla's stomach lurched. He told Kirsty they were dining together? What had Kirsty said?

'I told her I was entertaining a colleague from Edinburgh,' he said, allaying her fears. 'I'm afraid she can be a bit of a gossip. Not that I'm ashamed of taking you to dinner. Far from it, but... the family... they're still grieving Elspeth's death. I don't know...'

'I understand. I think you're still grieving too.' Isla was tempted to cover his hand with hers, but resisted.

Alasdair sighed heavily. 'Not everyone understands. It's been two years now, and I miss her every day. But, meeting you... I hope I don't speak out of turn. You seem like a breath of fresh air.'

Isla had been called many things in her life, but a breath of fresh air?

'I'm sorry. I'm babbling. What must you think of me?'

It was clear to Isla that Alasdair was feeling uncomfortable. This was probably the first time he'd dined with a female since his wife died. She couldn't relate to that sort of grief, but she remembered her own grief after Morag's death – how she'd burst into tears every time she tried to speak. She couldn't remember how long her paroxysm of grief had lasted, but it had taken all Shona's support and, finally, her new responsibilities at Glenferrie Academy to give her life a fresh focus.

'I understand grief,' she said.

They were interrupted by a waiter and, after a brief examination of the menu both ordered lasagne with Alasdair, after consulting Isla, also ordering a bottle of Chianti to accompany it.

'Tell me about your wife,' Isla said, when the wine had arrived and been poured.

Alasdair began to speak. He told of how he and Elspeth had met as students, married, had two children, how he had become more and more engrossed in his job, his guilt at spending too much time at the office, her illness and finally her death. 'Maybe...' he said, '...if I'd been home more, I'd have realised how sick she was. I could have...' He thrust a hand through his hair.

This time Isla really had to restrain herself from reaching out to him. 'I'm sure you did all you could – that she understood. You were building a future for your family.'

'That's what I told myself. But what if it wasn't enough? Since...' He cleared his throat. 'I've delegated more, stayed home, but... I now tend to shut myself up in the study leaving the children to the *au pair*. I'm letting *them* down too. Hell, sorry. I don't know why I'm telling you all this. You're a stranger. You must think I'm mad.'

'Not mad. No. Sometimes it's easier to talk to a stranger. Have you spoken about this to anyone else?'

'No. My father-in-law suggested I talk to my GP or to a counsellor. But I couldn't bear it. My only fear is what it's doing to my children. Are they suffering because of my actions?'

'Well, if Fiona is anything to go by, I'd say not. She has every sign of being a happy well-adjusted young girl – more mature than most, but I suspect she's always been that way.'

Alasdair smiled. 'You're right. Fi's always had an old head on young shoulders. But how come you're so easy to talk to? So understanding?'

Isla paused as their meals were served, then decided it was her turn to disclose her own past. She drew a deep breath before beginning. This was a story she hadn't revealed to anyone. Shona was the only one who knew the whole story and, until her disclosure to Kirsty the day before, she hadn't mentioned Morag's death in the past ten years. *What made her want to tell Alasdair her story?*

'I was thirty,' she began, 'teaching in a school in Maryhill. I enjoyed teaching, but being with children every day – other people's children – made me long for one of my own.' She sighed and ran a hand through her hair, then took a gulp of wine before continuing. 'I'd had a few relationships that hadn't gone anywhere. I'd given up hope of finding *The One*. It was summer, school holidays. I took off for Europe to get away from everything, and there I...'

'Fell in love?' Alasdair guessed.

'Not exactly. But I did have a passionate affair and came home pregnant.' Isla decided to gloss over the facts about Ollie.

'So what happened?'

'I took maternity leave, had the child – a lovely little girl with dark curls and a winning smile.' Isla felt her eyes moisten, remembering her beautiful daughter. She brushed away the tears. 'Sorry,' she sniffed.

'Take your time.' Alasdair leant forward, his eyes filled with concern.

'She'd just turned four. It was the year of that terrible flu. She…' Isla couldn't stem the tears.

'I'm so sorry.' Alasdair's hand covered hers.

They sat in silence as she attempted to regain control.

'I'm sorry. I shouldn't have…'

'No. *I'm* sorry. I shouldn't have asked.'

'Is everything all right?' A waiter appeared seemingly from nowhere and nodded at the still untouched dishes of lasagne.

'Fine,' Alasdair said, then turned his attention back to Isla. 'Do you want to leave?'

'No. I'll be fine in a minute. Maybe… I'll be back.' Isla rose and made her way to the loo where she sluiced her face with cold water, grimaced at her reflection, and re-applied some lipstick.

By the time she returned, Alasdair had eaten his lasagne and there were two cups of coffee on the table.

'Thought you could probably do with this,' he said. 'I had them leave your lasagne.'

'Thanks.' But Isla looked at the now congealing pasta and pushed it away in favour of the coffee.

'Not quite the evening you anticipated,' she said, after taking a sip. But, now they'd both shared such intimate information, she felt more comfortable with him. It was true what they said about a problem shared, though it wasn't exactly a problem. She'd kept Morag's death and the circumstances surrounding both that and her birth as a closely guarded secret. But there was really no reason why it should remain so.

'Hardly strangers now,' Alasdair said, as if reading her mind.

It was true. He was no longer just the parent of one of her students. He'd become her confidant, a sympathetic ear, a friend, even, or a potential one. And the buttoned-up insurance executive had again shown her his more human, more vulnerable, side.

'I guess we should leave.'

'Yes.' Isla drained her coffee, while Alasdair arranged to pay the bill.

'Where did you park?' he asked, as they were both donning their coats.

'I walked,' Isla replied, as they reached the door to discover a fine drizzle had begun.

'Let me drive you.' Alasdair took her firmly by the elbow and, giving her no opportunity to refuse, steered her to where a large black BMW SUV was parked by the kerb.

'Where to?' he asked, when they were both seated, seatbelts fastened.

'Kelvin Drive.'

Alasdair gave her a curious glance. 'Kelvin Drive? That's where *Isobel's Place* is. Isobel MacDonald was Bel's old aunt. Bel's my father-in-law's new wife,' he explained. 'A coincidence.'

Isla was familiar with the building – passed it every day – and had often wondered about its name.

'This is me,' she said, as the car approached her building.

They stopped. Isla felt Alasdair's eyes on her, the dim light of the street lamp casting shadows on his face. He leant towards Isla and touched her cheek with one finger. She shuddered as if burned.

'I hope you'd be willing to try again. Now that we're privy to each other's secrets – grief and guilt – maybe we can start again?'

'I'd like that.' Isla opened the door and stepped out, standing on the pavement heedless of the light rain, as she watched the big car turn and speed down the road.

How did he know? She wasn't only tormented by grief, but by guilt that she hadn't been able to save her beloved daughter.

Twenty-four

Bel

'Alasdair seemed a bit brighter yesterday,' Bel said. They were on their second cup of tea and Matt was engrossed in the papers which lay open on the table.

'What did you say?' He looked up, his face vacant. 'Sorry, Bel. I was caught up in the news. I didn't have time to read the papers yesterday.'

'I was speaking about Alasdair, saying he seemed to have perked up a little. He wasn't as down as he's been. Maybe he decided to get help – or maybe he's met someone.'

Matt folded the paper. 'Met someone? It's not something to joke about. How could he have met someone – and I presume you're talking about someone of the female gender. Elspeth's barely been gone...'

'He's a man, Matt. And that family needs...'

'I'm not going to sit here and listen to you talking about a replacement for my daughter.' He downed the last of his tea. 'I promised to drop in on old Archie Taylor in the village today.' He pushed back his chair and made for the hallway.

'Will you be back for lunch?' Bel called after him, but there was no reply.

Now I've done it, thought Bel. She'd been careful to avoid mentioning anything about Elspeth ever since she came back to Scotland. Matt's daughter had been a thorn in her flesh when they'd first met, but it had been Elspeth who had disapproved of Bel, not the other way round.

She'd resented Bel taking what she saw as her mother's place in Matt's life – been jealous of their relationship.

Now the boot was on the other foot and, it seemed, Matt couldn't bear the thought of his son-in-law finding someone else. It had been two years. In Bel's mind, that might be quite long enough for Alasdair to meet and befriend a possible successor to Elspeth, or even just to make friends with another woman.

She'd made the comment without thinking, as a way of trying to explain the change she'd noticed in Alasdair at lunch the previous day. It was subtle, a lightening of his demeanour, a slight change in his attitude to the children – less judgemental, more flexible. Maybe she was imagining it.

She sighed as she loaded the dishwasher. Whatever she'd noticed, she should have kept it to herself – or left it as a change in his manner. It was the suggestion of another woman in his life that had angered Matt so much. Bel stopped what she was doing and gazed out the window at the scene she'd come to love – the blue water of the loch, the yellow and purple of the gorse and heather on the muir, and Ben Lomond rising up behind them in all its majesty.

She should have known better, but it was done now. She bit her lip in annoyance at her own stupidity. This was the first time she and Matt had disagreed over anything major. They'd often laughed about the fact that they had such similar views and values. Other couples might argue, but not them. Well, that was over now – and it was all her fault.

Since it appeared she was going to be on her own for the best part of the morning, Bel decided to take the dogs for a walk and had just called them when her phone beeped. Checking the screen, she saw Kirsty's number. *What did she want?*

'Hi Kirsty. How are you?'

'Fine. It's a glorious morning for a drive, and I thought I'd just check you were going to be in. I have a copy of that book we spoke about yesterday and I can pop over and drop it off.'

There was a pause, while Bel decided how to respond. Anniesland to Inveruglas was hardly in the *pop over* category. It was close to an hour's drive.

She remembered the book to which Kirsty was referring. It was the latest Caro Ramsay – *Suffering of Strangers*. Bel had mentioned she was keen to read it, and Kirsty had promised to lend it to her. She did want to read the book, but did she want to see Kirsty? The two dogs, frolicking at her feet decided for her.

'Matt's not home, and I was about to take the dogs for a walk.'

'Great. So you'll be back by the time I get there?'

Seeing there was no way of avoiding a visit from her effusive daughter-in-law, Bel weakly agreed.

Kirsty's car was already in the driveway when Bel returned. The long walk across the muir had calmed her, made her realise she and Matt had not really quarrelled; it had forced her to conclude that any mention of a future relationship for Alasdair was out of bounds if she wanted to retain a harmonious relationship with her husband.

'Let me see to the dogs and I'll put the kettle on,' she greeted Kirsty, who stepped out of her car on Bel's arrival.

When the dogs were fed and watered, they settled by the fire and, the tea made, the two women joined them.

'The book – in case I forget.' Kirsty set it down on the coffee table. 'You'll enjoy it. I did.'

'I'm sure I will. I've read her other ones. So what have you been up to?'

Although they'd only seen each other the day before, it had been a family occasion and there had been little time for the two women to talk together.

'Oh. Much the same as usual. Keeping Duncan's books, ferrying Jamie around.' She picked up her cup, then put it down again. 'And I caught up with an old friend – Isla Cameron – Fi's headmistress.'

'Yes, you said you knew her.' Bel absentmindedly stroked Toby's ears as the dog moved closer to her feet.

'We met for lunch last week. I think she's a lonely woman. She runs that big school almost single-handed. And you'll never guess what she told me?'

Bel shook her head, knowing that, whatever secret the woman had revealed, was now going to be repeated. Kirsty just couldn't help herself. She didn't mean to gossip – at least Bel didn't think she did – but she appeared incapable of keeping anything to herself.

'She may be single, but she had a child who died.' Kirsty paused as if for effect. 'I think she needs a man in her life.'

'Maybe so. More tea?' Bel lifted the teapot to refill their cups.

'Thanks. But don't you think so? She's surrounded by girls all day, every day – other women's daughters. Don't you think that's odd? She's not too old to have one of her own, if…'

'Is she looking for a relationship?'

'She says not, but…' Kirsty took another sip of tea. 'I mean, what woman isn't?'

'*I* wasn't, Kirsty,' Bel said, as gently as she could. 'And I was a lot older than this woman you're talking about. I was quite happy being single. Not all women need a man to lead a fulfilled life.'

'But you'd been married. You…'

'Well, if your friend had a child, then she's been in a relationship too. Maybe he was the love of her life and she lost him. He may have died. Anything might have happened. Did she say anything about that?' Knowing Kirsty, Bel was sure she'd have asked.

'No. She closed right up after she mentioned the child. Didn't want to say any more. In fact, I think she regretted telling me.'

'Hmmm.' Bel had heard enough. She felt sorry for the poor woman who'd revealed her innermost secret to Kirsty, but if they were old friends she must have realised the nature of the woman she was telling it to. 'You'll stay for lunch?'

'That would be lovely.'

'It'll be leftovers from yesterday's roast. I was planning to make sandwiches and I can open a tin of soup.'

'Sounds fine – more than I'd have made myself at home.'

Bel would dearly love to have shared her conversation with Matt, but knew that to do so might open up a can of worms. Kirsty had the reputation of being blunt, and Bel dreaded to think what she might say, not only to her, but to Matt at lunch – if he did return for it.

'Now, tell me about how Jamie's doing with his football,' Bel said, knowing the change in subject would have Kirsty talking for hours.

Matt walked in as Bel was opening a tin of vegetable soup.

'You're back!' Bel barely raised her eyes from her task, unsure how Matt might be feeling and embarrassed at Kirsty's presence. 'Kirsty's here,' she warned, as he came to enfold her in a hug and whispered, 'Sorry.'

'Hello, Dad. My, you two are such lovebirds, you put Duncan and me to shame.' She walked over to join them in the kitchen area.

'Not in the office today?' Matt asked.

'I came to drop a book in for Bel. It's such a lovely day – and I do get time off for good behaviour now and then,' she laughed. 'Though I did promise to deliver some documents in Dumbarton for Duncan on the way back.'

They had finished their soup and were starting on the sandwiches when Kirsty dropped her clanger.

'I was telling Bel about seeing Isla Cameron. You know – Fi's headmistress,' she explained at Matt's obvious puzzlement. 'I think she's a lonely woman, and it occurred to me...' she picked up a sandwich, '...that Alasdair must be lonely, too.'

Sensing what was coming Bel gave a slight shake of her head, but Kirsty, either not seeing it, or determined to ignore it, ploughed on regardless.

'Maybe we should get them together.'

Bel could see the storm clouds in Matt's expression, but Kirsty appeared ignorant of the tempest she'd stirred.

'I don't think so,' Matt said, his mouth taut, his body tensing. He rose and left the table. The study door slammed.

'Oh, dear!' Bel said.

'What did I say?' Ignorant of the furore she'd caused, Kirsty widened her eyes. 'I only said what anyone's going to think. Alasdair's been on his own for two years. He's a young man. He has two children. He's not going to stay on his own forever.'

'Elspeth was Matt's daughter.'

'And my friend. And she'd not have wanted him to spend the rest of his life grieving for her, or for her children to be without a mother figure.'

'Maybe not. But it's too soon for Matt.'

There was little conversation during the remainder of their lunch. Each woman was very aware of the angry man in the neighbouring room, and Bel was wondering how she was going to handle Kirsty's *faux pas*, especially after her own earlier comments.

When Kirsty finally left, the sound of her car driving off brought Matt back into the kitchen.

'Would you like something more to eat?' Bel asked, in an attempt to pacify him, recognising he was still tense with anger.

He ignored her question. 'She's gone, then. What on earth was she thinking? Did you put her up to it?' he accused.

'Of course not. She's just being Kirsty. It's what she does. You should know that by now. But I feel sorry for her if she's trying to matchmake her friend. From what I've heard, Isla Cameron is fiercely independent and doesn't suffer fools gladly. I'm sure she won't take kindly to being the object of Kirsty's machinations.'

Twenty-five

Isla

'This takes me back,' Isla said to Shona. They were walking up Bath Street towards the Mitchell Library after parking at Charing Cross City Parking.

'Poring over books and hoping the hot guy from the table across the room would ask you out for coffee? And it did happen.'

Isla smiled at the memory of stolen moments while supposedly studying for her university exams. They'd always preferred the city reference library to the University Library or Reading Room. Those places were fine during the day, when they needed to be on campus for classes. But in the evenings, it was more exciting to frequent the Mitchell where the clientele was mixed and there was the possibility of meeting men from other colleges. She'd loved the atmosphere there, too – the deep silence that pervaded it, the sense of it being a place of learning.

'No chance of that tonight. I'm really looking forward to the programme. What a great event *Aye Scotland* is. And this is its eleventh year. I love Clare Mackintosh's books. Have you read her latest?'

'It's on my bedside table – under a few others, I'm afraid. I'm not as big a fan as you are. But I am looking forward to hearing Sarah Vaughan. I loved *Anatomy of a Scandal*.'

'I haven't read it.'

By this time, they'd reached the entrance and followed others up the steps and into the building.

The event lived up to their expectations, and Isla sighed with regret when it came to an end.

'I could have listened to them all night,' she said as they rose to leave. 'And to be chaired by Michael Malone!'

'Michael J Malone,' Shona corrected her. 'There's another Michael Malone as I discovered when I was searching for him on Amazon.'

'Really?'

'How about we have coffee before we go home? There's something I need to tell you.'

'Sure.' Isla was puzzled. They'd been together all evening. What did Shona have to say she couldn't have said earlier? The tickets to the *Aye Write Festival* were part of her attempt to persuade Isla to get out more. After the debacle of the charity dinner, she'd given up trying to matchmake, and the round of events featuring Scottish writers was her way of attempting to whet Isla's taste buds for some sort of social life. So far, it had been a success.

Since both were avid readers of crime novels, the previous week they'd enjoyed a session with Alex Gray and Leigh Russell, held in the university chapel, and a fascinating session with Simon Cox and Ragnar Jonasson on exploring Icelandic crime from two different perspectives. There was one more to go, on Saturday afternoon, when Isla was looking forward to seeing and hearing another of her favourite authors, Lin Anderson. It suddenly occurred to her that her favourite Anderson character, Rhona Macleod, shared a surname with the man who was occupying more of her thoughts than she liked.

But Shona had changed her mind. 'I know. There's a tapas bar in Elderslie Street. I've heard it's really good. Why not try there?'

'Shona! It's Wednesday night. We both have to work tomorrow. I agreed to coffee, but...'

'Come on, Isla. Live dangerously. It's not late. One glass of wine?'

Reluctantly Isla agreed, and found herself being led in the opposite direction of their parked cars and towards the tapas bar.

Once there, served with glasses of sangria and sharing a plate of chorizo and mushroom croquettes, Isla was forced to admit it was a good idea. After they'd rehashed the event, with Isla now determined to read the Sarah Vaughan book, Isla asked, 'What did you want to tell me?'

'Oh.' Shona put down her glass, 'About Saturday. I'm not going to be able to make it.'

'What?' Isla couldn't believe her ears. This had been all Shona's idea in the first place, and the Saturday event was one she didn't want to miss. 'Why not?'

Shona looked down at her drink before replying, then she raised her eyes to meet Isla's. 'Hugh's booked us into Crieff Hydro for the weekend.'

'Very posh! Well, I can see how you couldn't refuse.' Isla tried, unsuccessfully, to keep the sarcasm out of her voice. 'So, he's still on the scene?'

'Very much so.' Shona buried herself in her wineglass, then added, 'I think he's the one, Isla. I've never felt like this before.'

Stunned by the serious note in her friend's voice, it took Isla a moment or two before she said, 'I'm glad for you. I hope it does work out. You've certainly kissed enough frogs.'

Shona laughed. 'I wouldn't exactly call them that. But there have been a few who...' She laughed again. 'Anyway, what about you? I don't know why you didn't like Daniel. He's a good friend of Hugh's, and we could have made an awesome foursome. If you'd played your cards right, you might have been going to Crieff with us.'

Isla shuddered, remembering the clammy hand on her leg, the raucous laughter and the drunken antics of Shona's companions that evening. Then she recalled the man who'd rescued her – his kindness, his understanding of her plight, his ineffable correctness. There weren't many like him these days – or if there were, she hadn't met them.

'What are you thinking?'

Shona's voice brought her down to earth.

'You had a faraway look in your eyes. You haven't met someone, have you? You'd have told me if you had – right?'

'Of course not.' Isla took a hasty gulp of wine, almost choking as it went down too quickly. 'Where would I meet anyone?'

'True. Pity. There's a spare ticket for Saturday now. Take it anyway. Maybe that old schoolfriend you mentioned would like it – or one of your staff.'

'Thanks.' Isla couldn't think of anyone she'd like to take to the author event, but it was one she didn't want to miss. There was no need to refuse the ticket. It would only make Shona more determined to manufacture a social life for her and that was the last thing she needed.

But, driving home, Isla's mind went into overdrive. She recalled how, in one of the conversations she'd had with Alasdair, they'd discovered a shared enjoyment of tartan noir. In fact, she was almost sure *Bloody Scotland* had been mentioned.

Could she offer him the spare ticket?

Should she?

Dare she?

Twenty-six

Alasdair

Alasdair picked up the phone without checking the number. It was Anaïs' night off and he was cooking dinner – not one of his best skills. Since Elspeth's death, he'd tried to familiarise himself with many of the tasks he'd always left to her – cooking was the one that defeated him more often than he liked, but he was determined to master it. Tonight, despite Fiona's offers to help, or even take over, he'd planned to try his hand at a roast dinner. It couldn't be too hard, could it?

He'd put the meat in the oven and was preparing the potatoes and pumpkin when the phone rang.

'MacLeod.'

There was silence at the other end, making him wonder if he'd been too abrupt. He answered his calls this way at work, but, at home he was more accustomed to giving his first name. 'Alasdair MacLeod,' he corrected himself.

'It's Isla Cameron.'

He felt a thrill run through him at the sound of the soft voice, more hesitant than it had been in her office.

'Isla! How lovely to hear from you.'

'I hope you don't think me too forward, but I have a spare ticket for an *Aye Write* event on Saturday at three. It's the *Bloody Scotland* panel and I thought… I wondered…' Her voice trailed off.

Saturday afternoon. He'd been going to Robbie's games on

Saturdays, part of the vow he'd made to spend more time with his children. But he knew he'd enjoy the panel. He'd loved the book – the collection of stories from many of his favourite Scottish crime novelists. 'It sounds attractive. Can I let you know?'

'I'm sorry. It's short notice, I should have realised.'

'No, it's not that. My son, Robbie, plays football. I need to check with him. I can let you know tomorrow – unless you want to offer it to someone else?'

'No, that's fine. So, tomorrow?'

'I'll call or text you.'

Hell! What was he to do? How could he choose between Robbie's football game and a literary event with Isla? He returned to the vegetable preparation, the two alternatives playing out in his mind. But he really had no choice. Robbie had to come first. He should have refused straight away.

Alasdair poured himself a beer while dinner cooked, drinking it in the kitchen and cleaning up as he did so. By the time everything was ready, he'd become reconciled to missing the opportunity to meet the *Bloody Scotland* authors, deciding instead to pull the book from the shelf and re-read his favourite stories.

'Dinner!' he called into the living room where Fiona was watching one of her favourite programs, and Robbie was on his iPhone as usual. The boy would feel his hand had been cut off if he was to do without it for an entire day.

'Not bad, Dad,' was Fiona's assessment, after a few mouthfuls, 'We'll make a cook out of you yet. What d'you think, Robbie?' She gave her brother an elbow in the ribs.

'Steady on! What are you talking about?'

'Dinner. What planet are you on? Why so grumpy?'

'I've been benched for Saturday's game,' Robbie mumbled.

Surprised, Alasdair looked up. 'Why?'

He saw Robbie shift uncomfortably in his seat. 'Mr McCallum says I wasn't playing my best, and I told him…'

'You argued back?'

Robbie looked down.

'It doesn't work, son. He's your coach and what he says goes.'

'I know,' he muttered, 'but…'

'No buts. Is it just for this game?'

'Yeah,' Robbie kicked the leg of the table, and speared a roast potato with his fork. 'There's this new kid. He's going to give him a try.'

'Well, mind your P's and Q's and you'll be back on the team before you know it.'

'So you don't need to come to see me sitting on the sidelines,' Robbie said bitterly.

'We'll talk about that later.'

Of course he'd go. Wasn't that what a good dad did? But to watch Robbie sitting there, disconsolate, while this new kid took his place. Did he really want to do that? Did Robbie want him to watch his humiliation?

Robbie gave him his answer. 'No, Dad. I don't want you there. It won't be the same.'

Alasdair sighed. He was trying to do his best. He could stay home with Fiona. But, as if reading his mind, she said, 'Remember I'm spending the weekend with Grandpa Matt and Nana Bel. We're going to finish my project on Australia. She's promised to look out her old photos and check my research.'

Alasdair had forgotten. That meant he'd be free to accept Isla's invitation. But, instead of relief at the prospect of seeing the authors he admired, all he felt was guilt. As the two teenagers chatted, Alasdair reflected that his guilt stemmed from the fact that, regardless of what he'd told Isla, of what he'd told himself, he wasn't immune to her attraction. And this made him feel he was being unfaithful to Elspeth's memory.

'Dad!'

Fiona was speaking to him.

'Sorry. Did you say something?'

'See,' she said to her brother, 'I told you he wasn't listening. I was asking what you'll do on Saturday when you're left alone – work, I suppose.' Her face took on a disapproving expression which reminded him of her mother.

'Actually, no.' Alasdair made up his mind. 'There's an author event on at the Mitchell Library. The authors of a book I enjoyed are speaking. I was offered a ticket and thought I'd have to refuse but since Robbie doesn't want me and you'll be at Inveruglas, I might just go.' *There was no need to mention Isla Cameron.*

*

The book lay on the coffee table where he'd dropped it the previous evening. It comprised short stories inspired by some of Scotland's iconic buildings and, written by twelve of Scotland's best crime writers, had been a birthday gift from his father-in-law. The previous evening, after the children had gone to bed, and in anticipation of today's event, he'd poured himself a measure of whisky and settled down to re-read them.

He'd read those by Lin Anderson and Val McDermid and was half-way through Elaine Thomson's *Stanley Mills* when sleep got the better of him.

Now, with Fiona out at Loch Lomond, Robbie at his game, and Anaïs off for the weekend, Alasdair was alone in the house. He gave one last glance around to ensure everything was tidy – something Elspeth had been strict about, saying you never knew what might happen. He patted his pockets to make sure he had his wallet and his car keys, picked up his phone and closed the door behind him.

Turning on the radio on the drive into the city, Alasdair caught up with the sports action on BBC radio FM which almost made up for missing Robbie's game. He wondered how Robbie was faring. Although he knew his son had brought it on himself and didn't blame the coach for his decision, he felt for the boy. It would be hard for him to have to sit and watch his team play without him, and Robbie was proud. He'd take this demotion badly. It was probably as well Alasdair wasn't there to see it.

He thought about the woman he was driving to meet. She was a strange one. Though it might be that Alasdair was out of practice in making friends with women, in talking with women other than family or work colleagues. And he felt a little uncomfortable about the personal details they'd shared over dinner last time they met. Still… He was comforted by the fact that there would be little time for conversation today – they'd be listening to other people talk.

Alasdair parked his car and headed towards the Mitchell Library. He'd arranged to meet Isla at the entrance and, as he approached, he could see her slim figure, wearing her blue sheepskin coat, standing by the door. He hurried towards her.

'I hope I haven't kept you waiting.'

'Not at all, I only just arrived. Thanks for coming.'

'My pleasure.'

'I thought it would appeal to you. My friend – the one I've been coming to these events with – she made other plans.'

'You've been to some of the earlier sessions?'

'Yes.' Isla seemed to relax. 'This is the last one. They were all excellent and have added to my pile of books to read.' She grimaced. 'Shall we go in?'

The session was as good as Alasdair had expected and, as it drew to an end, he decided he'd invite Isla for coffee so they could discuss it. She had admitted she'd not read the book yet and purchased a copy at the end of the session.

It was in this amiable mood that they walked out of the library, and Alasdair turned his phone back on to see a flurry of missed calls, several from a number he didn't recognise and one from Bel. His immediate thought was that something had happened to Fiona.

'I need to get this,' he said, pressing *return call* and putting the phone to his ear, his throat constricting.

'Alasdair. Thank goodness!'

'Bel. What's the matter? Fi – has something happened?'

'Fi's fine. She's right with me. It's Robbie.'

'Robbie?' What could have happened to Robbie? He was to have spent the afternoon sitting on the sidelines while his team played.

'The school called Matt when they couldn't reach you. There was an accident. He's…'

'But he wasn't playing. That's why I wasn't there!' Alasdair knew his voice had come out as a wail.

Out of the corner of his eye he saw Isla mouth, 'Is everything okay?' He shook his head. *What on earth had happened?*

As if reading his mind, Bel continued, 'I don't know exactly what happened, but Matt's driven into Glasgow. Robbie's been taken to the Queen Elizabeth. Matt left over an hour ago, so should be there by now. I think he said something about Robbie's leg. They were taking him to Emergency.'

'Thanks.' He closed the phone and stood, frozen for a second, before replacing it in his pocket and dragging a hand through his hair. Hell!

He should have been there. He shouldn't have listened to Robbie. *He* was the grown-up. He should have made his own decision.

'What's the matter?' He felt a gentle pressure on his arm and turned to see Isla gazing at him with an expression of concern. He'd completely forgotten about her.

'Sorry. It's Robbie – my son. He's been hurt. I have to go.'

Twenty-seven

Alasdair

Alasdair drove into the hospital car park. Despite the late Saturday afternoon traffic, he'd made the trip in around fifteen minutes. He was a mass of nerves and questions as he rushed across the road to Emergency. Once inside, his eyes searched around before seeing Matt sitting in a row of chairs, head bowed.

'Matt!'

Matt's head jerked up. He rose to grasp Alasdair by the shoulder.

Alasdair flinched. It brought back memories of when Elspeth... He shook away the memory. It hadn't been this hospital. It hadn't been the Emergency Department. Robbie was a fit young boy.

'Glad you're here, son.'

'What the hell happened?'

Matt pulled Alasdair down into a seat beside him. 'He broke his leg. They're fixing him up now. One of the teachers brought him in. He's gone now.'

'But...' Alasdair dragged a hand through his hair which was now almost standing on end. 'He wasn't even playing today.'

'From what I understand, the boy who was taking his place turned an ankle early in the game, and the coach relented and brought Robbie back into his old position. He was playing well till this happened.'

'Have you seen him?'

'Briefly. Before they took him off to be x-rayed. He was pretty out of it but wanted me to know he scored a goal and may have won the game for them.'

Alasdair gave a bitter laugh. 'That's my Robbie.' Then he became serious. 'What happens next?'

'I guess we wait here to find out.' Matt pulled on his ear. 'Happened to Duncan once. He was younger than Robbie at the time. Fell off his bike if I remember correctly. If it *is* broken, he'll probably be out of commission for six to eight weeks. No more games for him this season.'

Just then a nurse appeared and, looking from one man to the other, asked, 'Mr MacLeod?'

'That's me.' Alasdair stood up, his heart in his mouth, expecting the worst. He hated hospitals. Had done ever since Elspeth's death. 'Is Robbie…?'

'Not to worry, Mr MacLeod. Your son has a clean break in the tibia. He's a healthy young lad. He'll do well. We'll put a cast on it, and you'll be able to take him home. Let him rest up for a bit before he tries to put any weight on it, and he may need to use crutches for a while. It'll slow him down, but he'll soon be fit and kicking a ball around again, though probably not this season.'

She disappeared again.

'Not much we can do here for now. How about we find a cup of tea, or maybe even something to eat?' Matt checked his watch. 'It's nearly six. There must be somewhere open here.'

Alasdair allowed himself to be led to where two food outlets were still serving customers. He watched while Matt ordered soup, coffee, and chicken sandwiches, then joined him at a table.

'I should have been there. It was my responsibility.' Alasdair clenched his jaw. He ignored the food and drink sitting in front of him.

'Dinna fash yourself, son. There was nothing you could have done. It would have happened whether you were there or not. Though I'll not deny Robbie would have liked you to see him score the winning goal.'

Alasdair groaned.

Why had he listened to his son?

'It should have been *me* driving him to hospital. I should…'

'Don't blame yourself. Why don't you have something to eat? You'll be no good to Robbie if *you* collapse on us.'

Alasdair picked up a sandwich and took a bite. It tasted like cardboard. He sipped his coffee, surprised to feel a rush of energy as the caffeine entered his system.

'Where were you anyway?' Matt asked.

'An author event. They were discussing that book you gave me for my birthday.'

'Any good?'

'Yeah. The book was great, and it was interesting to hear the authors talk about it.' Alasdair suddenly remembered how he'd left Isla outside the library with little explanation. *What must she be thinking?* He should get in touch with her. But not from here. Not when he was with Matt.

He was trying to think what to do, when Matt drew out his phone.

'I need to call Bel,' he said, putting it to his ear.

Alasdair managed to finish his coffee and take a few more bites of the sandwich while listening to Matt's side of the conversation.

'Fi wants to talk to you,' he said, handing over the phone.

'How's Robbie?' Fi's voice was filled with concern. 'Should I get Nana Bel to drive me to the hospital?'

The pair might argue a lot, but they were close, and Alasdair knew how worried she must be. Fiona was no stranger to hospitals. She would be picturing her brother there and knew he could be feeling lost and afraid.

'No need for that. I haven't seen him yet, but the doctors say he'll be fine and can go home once they put a cast on his leg. He'll need to rest for a while, then he'll be able to get around on crutches.'

'Or he can have a chariot like me.' Fiona sounded almost gleeful, her worry vanishing at the news. 'Can you get him to ring me when he gets home?'

'Will do. I have to go now. Grandpa and I have to get back to the Emergency Department. We need to be there when Robbie's ready to leave.'

'Give him a hug from me,' she said, her earlier gleefulness forgotten. 'He's going to find it difficult not being able to get around.'

'I will.'

Alasdair closed off the call and handed the phone back to Matt. 'Fi's right. It's going to be hard for Robbie. He's such a livewire. Apart from the time he spends on his iPhone and iPad, he's always on the go. I'm not sure how he'll cope.'

'He'll manage.'

'You're optimistic.'

'Have to be when you've lived as long as I have and seen as much.' Matt pulled on his ear. 'It may be the making of him. Help him understand how his sister has to cope with her disability every day. He'll only be *hors de combat* for a few weeks. She has a lifetime to live with it.'

By the time the two men returned to the waiting room, it was close to seven o'clock.

'You don't need to stay,' Alasdair was saying to Matt, when an orderly brought Robbie out in a wheelchair. Maybe Fiona hadn't been too far wrong in her comments.

'Here's the boy, now. I wish Fi was here,' Matt chuckled, his thoughts seemingly going in the same direction as Alasdair's.

'Dad!' There was relief in Robbie's voice. 'You're here.'

'Where else would I be?' Alasdair tried to hide his emotion at the sight of his son. There was a burning sensation behind his eyes.

'Fi can't crow about her chariot, now.' Robbie said, but there was a suggestion of fear in his eyes.

'You're his dad?' the orderly asked, pushing Robbie up to them. 'You can take the wheelchair for a couple of days, but we'll need it back. And you can take these with you too.' He indicated the crutches lying on Robbie's lap which Alasdair hadn't noticed, being more concerned with the expression on his son's face. 'Take him in to your GP. He'll have the results of the x-ray and will keep an eye on Robbie for you.' The man produced a sheaf of papers. 'Here are some instructions for the cast. It's fiberglass and this young man needs to take care of it. Will you be okay?' he asked Robbie, who nodded.

'Can we go home now, Dad?' His eyes were tired, his face paler than usual, and there were white lines around his mouth. He was still dressed in his football kit which was looking decidedly muddy.

'Sure thing. Fi sends you a hug.'

'Bet she'll laugh if she sees me in this thing.' He grimaced. 'Do I have to go home in it?'

'Best to do what the doctor suggested, at least for now. After a few days, you should be able to get around on the crutches.'

Robbie scowled. 'It wasn't my fault. Frank Reilly got in the way and knocked me down, just when I…'

'That's enough. It happened. It was an accident. Now, say goodbye and thanks to your grandpa and let him get off. He has to drive back home to Nana Bel and Fi. She wanted to come here, but I told her you'd be home soon anyway. And she'll be back tomorrow. Anaïs will be back then, too, so we'll have to muddle through till then.'

'Can we have pizza tonight? I'm hungry.'

Alasdair smiled with relief. This was more like Robbie. 'I think we can manage that. But an early night for you, young man. And no computer games.'

'Oh, Dad!'

But Alasdair could tell his son was beginning to fade. It had been an eventful day for him, and for Alasdair, too. He'd be glad to get home.

Twenty-eight

Isla

Isla watched Alasdair's departing back, wishing she could do something. She had an empty feeling inside. It had been so good to share the author event with him – to share his enjoyment as the writers discussed the intimate and sometimes deadly connection between people and places in their stories. She'd been hoping she and Alasdair might continue the conversation they'd started on the way out. In fact, she was sure he'd been about to suggest coffee to do just that.

Then he'd heard the news about his son, and headed off to the hospital. She couldn't blame him for that. She'd have done exactly the same – if Morag had lived, if Morag had been in an accident. But here she was, alone on yet another Saturday evening.

Isla wasn't sure why that bothered her. It never had before. But, suddenly, the prospect of eating alone, sitting at home with only her cat for company, wasn't an attractive prospect. She reminded herself of all the times she'd left social gatherings early, preferring to go home to a good book rather than listen to one more empty conversation, fend off one more drunk, or pretend to be interested in some inane discussion.

She gave herself a mental shake, checked the copy of *Bloody Scotland* in her bag, and decided to buy a bottle of wine and an Indian takeaway on the way home. She was no young girl mooning over what might have been. She was a grown woman who was on her own by choice and quite content to remain that way.

After enjoying the takeaway – a treat she didn't often allow herself – and one glass of a sparkling Shiraz, Isla was settling down to read in front of the fire, Sooty curled up in her lap, when her phone buzzed.

Putting down her book with a sigh – and a coil of anticipation in her gut – Isla pressed to accept the call.

'Hello? Isla Cameron here.'

'Isla. It's Alasdair. Alasdair MacLeod.'

Isla smiled. How many Alasdairs did he think she knew who would be calling her at this time on a Saturday night?

'How's your son?'

'Well, he's home – and in bed now.' He sighed.

Isla could picture Alasdair running a hand through his hair – something she noticed he did when he was worried or annoyed. He sounded exhausted.

'The leg's broken, but should heal well. But it's going to slow him down quite a bit for the foreseeable future. I brought him home in a wheelchair, but he's eager to try the crutches the hospital gave us. I don't know…'

'And Fiona? How's she taking it?'

'She's still with her grandparents. Back tomorrow – and the *au pair* will be back then too.'

'It won't be easy for you with two…' Isla bit her lip. Maybe she was speaking out of turn. *What did she know about his family?*

But he seemed not to hear. 'I'm sorry I rushed off like that – I couldn't contact you sooner. What must you think of me? Will you forgive me?'

'Of course. I understood. He's your son. You had to go. I'm glad it's nothing more serious.'

'Yes.' There was a pause before he continued, 'Thanks again for inviting me. I now owe you a return jaunt.'

Isla felt herself bristle. She thought they were becoming friends. Friends didn't talk about owing. It wasn't a game where each took turns. Or was it? Was she so far out of the loop these days that she had trouble operating in normal society? How many friends did she have, besides Shona? There were her staff, but they hardly fitted into the category of friends.

In the past ten years – since Morag died – she'd managed to avoid her former friends and colleagues, alienating them to such an extent they'd gradually all disappeared from her life. It hadn't worried her. She'd been glad. It allowed her to grieve in peace, and she was spared their cloying sympathy. Now she wondered if it had been a mistake.

'I hope your son makes a speedy recovery,' she said stiffly, not sure why she felt rejected. 'We'll see you next Thursday.'

'Thursday?' Alasdair sounded bewildered.

'The Easter Art Show at Glenferrie. Fiona has several of her landscape photographs on display. She's very excited about it.'

Had he forgotten?

'The Art Show. Yes. She is. I was planning to attend – and her grandparents too. I don't know about Robbie…' He paused, seeming to drift off into another place. 'He'll likely see his broken leg as a good excuse to give it a miss. Fi will be infuriated if he doesn't go.' He chuckled, clearly envisaging some lively altercations between the two. 'But that'll be nothing new. I'm sorry. I should let you go. You must have other things to do. I apologise for interrupting your evening. And sorry again for earlier.'

Isla stared at the now silent phone, then rose to pour herself another glass of wine, before settling to read again. She'd almost finished the first story in the book – the one by Lin Anderson – before Alasdair's call and was intrigued by the time slip taking the reader back to Viking times, while enjoying revisiting the character of Magnus from Anderson's novels. She'd finish it, then make some hot chocolate before going to bed, she decided.

But, once she reached the end of the tale, she sat gazing into the fake coals of her gas fire. Sooty, who had left her lap when the phone buzzed, was now lying stretched out in front of the flames and seemed fast asleep.

Isla thought about what she had read. The connection of people and places Anderson had talked about and the place itself. Maeshowe. She remembered it, too. She'd been there – to Orkney. Her mind went back to a long-ago summer before her mother died. She must have been around twelve or thirteen at the time, captivated by tales of ancient Vikings, the strange stone circle, and the Neolithic chamber, imagining all sorts of weird things happening there.

It had been a happy time. She couldn't recall what had drawn them to visit the northern islands, but did remember it as a time when her life had been much simpler, one of the last holidays she'd taken with her parents. At the time, she vowed to study History and to return. She'd kept the vow to study History, majoring in History and English, but had never returned to Orkney. How wonderful it would be to take a break away and go back to that place of peace and wonder.

She stood up and stretched, her sudden movement startling Sooty whose back paw had been resting on her foot. The cat looked around, mewed in annoyance then curled up to go back to sleep.

It would be the easiest thing; book a flight, find a place to stay.

And the Easter holidays were coming up.

Isla made a snap decision.

She'd go to Orkney.

Twenty-nine

Isla

There had been no word from Alasdair all week, and Isla determined to forget any ideas she might have had about him.

Her focus was on the Art Show that night and her trip north next day. Despite her last-minute decision, she'd managed to book a flight to Kirkwall leaving in the early afternoon. She'd been dubious about finding a flight on Good Friday but the gods must have been with her, although she'd had to pay a premium price. She also managed to find a one-bedroom cottage on Airbnb, preferring her own company to a busy hotel or a room in someone's home.

'Are you planning to go home first?' Maree's curly red head peered in through the office door.

'I was.' Isla checked her watch. Last day of term was always a busy one and today had been no exception. But there was nothing that couldn't wait and, after a week relaxing in Orkney, she'd be in a better frame of mind to tackle the outstanding matters on her desk – with no staff or children to interrupt her. She closed down her computer. 'I'm going now. I'll see you back here.'

'Six-thirty? It kicks off at seven with an introduction from you and a formal opening by Guy Nicholson.'

'Sounds good. Lee was lucky to get him,' she said, referring to the up-and-coming Glasgow artist.

'Not luck.' Maree tapped her nose.

'Oh! I didn't realise.' So, Lee Smythe and the artist were a couple? 'I'll walk out with you.' Isla took her coat from its hook and put it on, picked up her bag and took one last look around the room before switching off the light and closing the door.

She needed the break.

As she drove home through the busy traffic, her thoughts went to the evening ahead. It was an annual event, but this year was the first time one of the junior students had work on display. Fiona MacLeod was an exceptional girl. And her father was different too – very restrained and formal. He'd be there tonight. She sighed, remembering how he'd left her standing outside the Mitchell Library.

Sooty greeted Isla by threading himself through her ankles and purring loudly. 'I know, puss. You're hungry, and I have to go out again. And I'm going to be away for a whole week. But you won't be abandoned.' She filled her pet's bowl, glad her neighbour had agreed to drop in each day to make sure he was fed and watered and to provide the required TLC.

Isla had a quick shower and changed into the black and white dress she'd worn on Christmas Eve. It was a bit dressy, but the parents would expect that, she decided, as she slipped her feet into her black high heels. Grabbing a glass of apple juice, she consumed a slice of quiche without taking time to sit down, and was ready for the road again.

It began to rain as she entered Great Western Road and joined the line of traffic heading west. Not the best sort of night, but Isla knew the parents would be out in full force. Nothing would deter them from attending the event many considered to be the highlight of this term. Even parents of those students whose work wasn't on display always seemed to enjoy the evening, oohing and aahing as they moved around the exhibits. Tonight would be no different.

Holding her umbrella carefully and stepping over the puddles which were already forming in the almost empty car park, Isla made her way towards the well-lit building. Stopping just shy of the steps, she reflected how much she'd achieved since taking over as headmistress ten years ago. Back then, the school had declining enrolments, and the grounds had been in a state of disrepair. Now it was a showpiece, an establishment of learning to rival any in the city. She'd thrown herself into the job, making it her priority, and this was the result.

But, as Shona was wont to point out, it had been at the expense of a personal life. Maybe her friend was right. Maybe it was time to draw back a little, to make more time for herself. Was that what she'd been thinking when she invited Alasdair MacLeod to the author event?

Pushing all thoughts of the man to the back of her mind, Isla mounted the steps to be greeted by a group of prefects.

'Oh, Ms Cameron. The display is wonderful. You should see how fantastic Sandra and Gail's pieces look now they're all framed and hung.'

Gail Thomas preened, while Sandra Ellis, a pale, slight girl, blushed shyly.

'Well, let me get in, girls, and I'll take a quick look around before everyone arrives.'

Two of the girls took Isla's coat and umbrella and carried them away to the staffroom, while the others led her into the hall which had been transformed into a gallery. The walls were covered in a variety of art-works – paintings, photos and prints, while a number of ceramic and metal sculptures were displayed in the middle of the room. To one side a long table held the drinks and nibbles and, on the stage at the far end, were four chairs and the podium from which she gave her weekly homily to the students.

'Isla!' Lee Smythe, looking stunning in a royal blue and purple print caftan appeared with a dishevelled bearded and bespectacled man in tow. 'This is Guy – Guy Nicholson.'

'Mr Nicholson. How lovely to meet you. We're delighted you agreed to open our show this year.'

'Guy, please. Mr Nicholson makes me want to look around to see my dad. I'm pleased to be here. Lee dragooned me into it.' But the fond look he gave Lee belied his words.

'Miss!' Isla turned to see her two guides looking frustrated.

'Sorry. If you'll excuse me? I promised these girls I'd have a look around before everyone arrives.'

Moving around the displays, Isla was again impressed with what had been achieved in the past year. She took a particular interest in the photographic section, noting the three items bearing Fiona MacLeod's name. The girl was so talented. She'd managed to capture the essence of the place with one image showing the loch in the early morning, the rising sun casting its light across the water, another taken midday focussed on two fishing boats sitting on the smooth surface of the loch, while the third cleverly captured a mirror image in the loch of the peak of Ben Lomond rising above it.

As the room began to fill with people and the buzz of chatter reached a crescendo, Isla slipped away from her chaperons and made her way to the stage. Lee and Guy were already there, along with Bernie Houston, Chairman of the Board.

'Another successful evening by the look of it.' Bernie rubbed his hands together in the manner that usually made her cringe. But tonight, she was determined not to let anything upset her.

'The girls have worked really hard, and Ms Smythe has encouraged them to produce good results.'

Bernie made his usual little speech complete with wisecracks, then Isla thanked everyone for coming, praised the girls and Lee, and introduced the guest speaker.

There was a hush as the dishevelled man stepped forward to the podium, then moved aside from it saying, 'I'm not used to such formality, so I hope you'll excuse me if I make this brief and talk to you like I would to a group of friends – of other artists. I'm talking to those of you who have their works displayed here tonight.' He waved his arm to encompass the school hall. 'And to those who have aspirations for the future.'

To Isla's dismay, he then sat down on the edge of the stage, his legs dangling, while he continued to speak, holding the microphone in one hand, and gesticulating with the other.

What had they let themselves in for?

Isla cast a sideways glance at Bernie, whose face was turning red, and Lee, who was grinning. She turned her attention back to the speaker, who now held the audience in the palm of his hand. He spoke of his own challenges as a struggling artist, of the stroke of luck that led to his present fame, and finished with words of encouragement which led to tumultuous applause.

With a sigh of relief, Isla thanked him, then began to move among the parents, who were collecting glasses of wine before moving around the room, many escorted by their excited daughters.

With a glass of wine in her own hand, Isla was chatting to one set of parents, graciously accepting their congratulations on yet another successful Art Show, when a small whirlwind appeared at her elbow. She turned to see Fiona MacLeod sitting there, an enormous grin on her face.

'Did you see my photographs, Ms Cameron? They're on the far wall. Dad says…'

At that moment, Isla noticed Alasdair MacLeod standing behind Fiona.

'I said she had the makings of a photographer,' he said.

Fiona grimaced. 'I *am* a photographer, Dad. Ms Smythe says so.'

'You are indeed, Fiona.' Isla met Alasdair's eyes and it was as if a secret message passed between them, as if time stood still.

'You know my brother-in-law.' Kirsty Reid's voice broke into the moment.

'Yes.' Isla felt herself redden.

'And these are Fi's grandparents – Duncan's dad and stepmother.' Kirsty brought forward an older couple – the man's hair streaked with grey and the woman's a silver helmet. Both were tall, and the woman was wearing a smart tunic and wide-legged pants in an unusual shade of lilac. A pashmina in a deeper purple was thrown seemingly carelessly over her shoulders.

'Lovely to meet you, Mr and Mrs Reid. You must be very proud of Fiona's efforts.'

'They look wonderful hanging there. We'd seen them before, of course. Fi took the shots close to our home,' Kirsty's father-in-law said.

'You live by Loch Lomond? How lovely! Now, I must move on. Enjoy the rest of the evening.' Isla left the group and took a mouthful of her wine. She was conscious she'd been babbling. *Had they noticed whatever it was between her and Alasdair – or had she been imagining it?* She took three deep breaths, put a smile on her face, and joined another group of parents admiring their offspring's artwork.

The evening was almost over when Isla found herself being cornered by an embarrassed Alasdair MacLeod.

'I want to apologise again.' He bent towards her so that his words were only for her. Isla glanced around, but the rest of his family, including Fiona, appeared to be intently studying a collection of wire sculptures at the other end of the hall. 'You were kind enough to invite me to the *Aye Write* event and I rudely dashed off. I'm sorry.'

'You said.' Isla wished the floor would open up and swallow her. She did not want to have this conversation – not here.

'You've done well, tonight.' He gestured to the now emptying room.

'Not me. It was mostly the girls who set this up, along with my Art mistress.'

'Yes, Ms Smythe. Fi speaks highly of her.'

There was a pause. Isla, disturbed by his nearness, wondered if she could slip away without appearing rude. 'Was there anything else?'

'Yes.' He pulled on his ear. 'You'll be on holiday now… I wondered… Could we meet again? I promise not to run away next time.'

'I'm off to Orkney tomorrow. The story of Maeshowe reminded me of a family holiday when I was much younger. It intrigued me, and I decided it was time for a return trip.'

'Oh.' He seemed surprised. 'Well, maybe when you get back? If you'd be willing to spend more time with me.' His lips turned down as if he expected Isla to refuse.

She took pity on him. 'I'll be back on the seventh. What did you have in mind?'

He looked flustered, and Isla smiled. Alasdair was as out of practice at this as she was.

Whatever this *was!*

'Dad and Bel are taking the kids for a few days. Robbie's able to move around on crutches now, but he's getting a bit stir crazy, and Fi loves it out there. They thought the change would do them both good.' He rubbed his chin. 'So, I'm a free man for the second week of the holidays. I had planned to work at home. How about a leisurely lunch – maybe drive out into the country?'

'I'd like that.' Isla meant it. The thought of a nice quiet lunch somewhere, an opportunity to get to know him better was attractive. After her week's holiday she'd be rested, more prepared to embark on this new friendship – or whatever it turned out to be.

'Good.' Alasdair exhaled. 'I'll make a booking and text you. Tuesday okay?'

'Tuesday.' she agreed.

Thirty

Isla

Isla stepped from the plane into a cold windy day. She picked up the hire car she'd booked, along with a map of the islands, and was soon heading into the town itself.

She was just drawing up to the cottage which was to be her home for the next seven days when her phone buzzed. She checked the number. Shona! Perfect timing.

'I suppose you're there already,' her friend said in an accusing tone. 'I don't know why you've chosen to bury yourself away in that godforsaken place over Easter when you could have been enjoying a week in Arran with us.'

Isla held the phone away from her ear, Shona's voice still audible. A week in Arran with Shona and her cronies was the last thing she wanted. She knew her friend had only her good at heart, but the very thought of a drunken trip with Shona and her crew of friends – one of whom would no doubt be the one she'd been matched up with at the charity dinner – made her shudder.

This place was steeped in history and she had only herself to please. She could stay home or wander around the island to her heart's content without any interference from friends – well-meaning or otherwise.

When she was able to get a word in, Isla replied, 'You know I'm always grateful for your willingness to include me, Shona. But I'm not the social animal you seem to imagine I am – or should be. Orkney will suit me fine. I love what I've seen so far – on my way from the airport. I'm sitting outside the place I've rented, and it looks exactly like I expected. There's a real sense of history here, plus a distinct Nordic influence. I'm looking forward to visiting some of the historical sites, and there are several silver stores and galleries I plan to check out. There's even a craft trail and a jewellery trail, and I may take in one of the distilleries. I'll have no time to get bored.'

She heard Shona sigh.

'Well, maybe you'll meet someone there and come back in love with a…what do they call them? An Orcadian?'

'Fat chance! But let's catch up when I do get back. I'll tell you about my week, and you can fill me in on what I missed.'

Shona agreed and, encouraging Isla to keep an open mind and an eye out for local talent, hung up.

Isla laughed. Shona would never change. But she was a good friend, had seen Isla through the most difficult time in her life. She hoped Hugh would prove to be the right one for Shona who seemed to spend her life moving from one man to the next hoping each would be the one to rescue her from her single state – from the single future she regarded as a fate worse than death.

*

Four days later, Isla was glad she'd come. Already, she'd stood in the Ring of Brodgar, full of wonder at the people who'd raised those ginormous stones; walked, stooped, along the stone passage into Maeshowe and vowed to watch the live webcam footage come December when the sun would be shining straight into it. She'd stepped back five thousand years at Skara Brae, admired the replica of the interior of a prehistoric house at the visitor centre, and been amazed at the sophistication of their way of life.

She'd also spent an enjoyable afternoon wandering around a silver gallery and was now the proud owner of a beautiful necklet with blue markings signifying the ceaseless movement of the waves, and a pair of matching earrings. And she'd purchased a bracelet for Shona who had a birthday coming up.

Today she planned to visit Saint Magnus Cathedral. She'd already read up on the history of the Romano-Gothic building and was keen to see the structure at first-hand. Built from red and yellow sandstone, it was one of the few which had survived relatively unscathed from the ravages of the Reformation. She'd learned it was named after the martyr Magnus Erlendsson, Earl of Orkney, who'd been killed on the orders of his cousin, and whose relics still rested in a pillar in the cathedral, having been taken there from the St Magnus church in Birsay. It appeared the route they'd taken to reach the cathedral had now been made into a pilgrimage of fifty-five miles. Weather permitting, Isla intended to walk at least one section of it.

As Isla hurried along to join the group which was already entering the cathedral, she almost tripped, glad she'd chosen to wear flat shoes. There were six others, and she barely noticed them as their guide showed them around and explained the architecture and history of the building. Although she'd already studied the guidebook, nothing had prepared her for its magnificence, for the overwhelming sense of peace and majesty.

She was standing in the nave, her head back, admiring the intersecting arches, when she heard someone say, 'Isla Cameron. It *is* you, isn't it?'

Turning quickly, Isla was astonished to see a man she'd hoped never to meet again. Standing behind her, a sheepish expression on his face, was Daniel Henderson. What on earth was he doing here? Why wasn't he in Arran with Shona and the rest of her crowd?

'Oh!'

'I'm afraid I owe you an apology,' he said with a deprecating smile. 'Last time we met... my behaviour was abysmal. I have no excuse. We'd all been drinking before we arrived and...' He spread his hands. 'What can I say? I don't normally behave like that. I don't blame you for leaving.'

Isla was lost for words. 'What are you doing here?' she asked frostily, her body tensing up to repel any unwelcome advances.

'The same as you, I expect. I'm on holiday. I'm not familiar with this part of Scotland. I'd heard a lot about its history and decided to come to see for myself.'

Isla suddenly realised that, while they'd been talking, the others in the group had moved on. 'We should join them,' she said, pointing to their backs, before leaving Daniel to catch up.

It wasn't till the tour was over and they left the cathedral, that she found herself standing next to Daniel again.

'This is crazy,' he said. 'I can't let you go on thinking of me as the fool you met at the dinner. Let me at least buy you lunch to make up for my rudeness.'

Isla glanced around. The others had all left. She tried to think of an excuse, but couldn't come up with one. He knew she was on holiday, had no deadlines to meet, nowhere to be at a specified time. 'That would be kind of you,' she said.

*

Fifteen minutes later, Isla was sitting opposite Daniel – my friends call me Dan – Henderson in the Café Lolz, with a bowl of Cullen skink, a thick soup made of smoked haddock, potatoes and onions, and a delicious-looking bere bannock.

'This looks lovely,' she said, unfolding a napkin and wondering how she was going to make it through a meal with him. But to her surprise, the conversation flowed smoothly as they compared notes on their respective sight seeing. Isla was able to recommend a visit to Scapa Flow which Daniel had yet to see, and he went into raptures over the Italian Chapel.

'I'm going back this afternoon to take more photos,' he said. 'Why don't you join me?'

Unable to come up with an excuse, and with the distinct feeling she was being coerced into accompanying him, Isla reluctantly agreed.

As they drove south, along the eastern shore of Scapa Flow, she glanced out of the corner of her eye at this man who seemed to be taking over her day, surprised to discover he was more agreeable than she remembered. Dressed in the inimitable Barbour and with a Burberry scarf tied casually around his neck, he was quite attractive with his thick blond hair and pale blue eyes. And today his behaviour was impeccable. Maybe he was being truthful when he said he'd behaved out-of-character on their first meeting. Maybe she should give him another chance.

Daniel was right. The chapel was amazing. 'And, when you think this was all done by prisoners-of-war – from two Nissen huts,' Daniel said. 'It beggars belief. I read about it in the guide book. They were sent here to build barriers to protect the British fleet in Scapa Flow – they were called the Churchill Barriers, after Winston Churchill.' He coughed. 'My interest is in that particular period of history.'

Isla was fascinated. He really was very knowledgeable. She'd learnt over lunch that Daniel – she couldn't bring herself to call him Dan – lectured in History at Glasgow University, returning to his native city after spending the previous ten years in England. That explained how he'd been at school with Alasdair MacLeod, she supposed, thinking of him for the first time that day. Was she being disloyal to him by spending time with Daniel Henderson? No, why should she even imagine that? Alasdair was only a friend, and Daniel was...' Well, he was becoming a friend, too, but this wasn't a friendship she envisaged continuing beyond today.

How Shona would laugh, Isla reflected, if she could see her now.

'We should team up,' Daniel said casually on the drive back. 'We're both on holiday on our own and it's more fun to have someone to share things with – to discuss. Don't you agree?'

Isla forbore replying that she enjoyed being alone – that was one of the reasons she was here. But to her surprise she'd enjoyed his company, his knowledgeable remarks, his witty asides. Maybe he wasn't so bad after all? She recalled Alasdair saying how Daniel could never hold his drink. Had it been the drink that made him such obnoxious company on their first meeting? If so, there was little likelihood of a recurrence of it here on Orkney. She decided to take a chance.

'Sounds like a good plan.'

Thirty-one

Bel

'Here they are,' Bel called to Matt who was attempting to brush Toby's coat. Her little dog was perched up on a high stool and Hamish, worried about missing out on his master's attention, was weaving in and out between Matt's ankles.

'Be with you in a sec,' Matt replied. 'Be still, Hamish. You've had your turn. I've left this too long, but I wanted them to look their best, and it's Easter Sunday.'

Not sure what difference that made, but glad Matt had become as fond of her little Toby as she was, Bel hurried to the door to greet Duncan and Kirsty, closely followed by their son, Jamie, his head down, his thumbs busy on his iPhone.

'I thought I told you to leave that at home?' Kirsty said. She gave Bel a wry glance. 'Teenagers! We passed Alasdair on the way. They'll be here soon. How's Robbie doing?'

Bel smiled. Kirsty didn't change. She wasn't inside the house yet and hadn't stopped to draw breath.

'We'll soon see,' Bel said as another car drew up and Alasdair got out, followed by Robbie awkwardly manoeuvring on a pair of crutches.

By the time Fiona and her wheelchair had been unloaded, Matt had appeared, the two dogs behind him. They immediately made for Robbie, no doubt curious about his strange new metal legs.

Once inside, Robbie collapsed onto the sofa, his crutches falling to the floor. He screwed up his face. 'I'll never get used to these things.' He gave the crutches a kick with his good foot.

'You should have kept the wheelchair.' Fiona deftly placed herself by the arm of the sofa. 'Then we'd have been twins.'

Robbie scowled. 'Two days were long enough. I don't know how you do it. How can you be so upbeat all the time when...'

'You do what you have to,' his sister said seriously. 'There would be no sense in my getting down and making everyone around me miserable. Remember that when you start grumbling about being out of the team for the rest of the season, for not being able to get around, for...'

'Okay, okay, bossy boots.'

Bel listened to this exchange with a slight pang. She was so impressed by Fiona's attitude. Matt had hoped Robbie's accident might have made him more understanding of his sister's disability, but so far there was no sign of it. She sighed. There were several more weeks to go. Things could change.

The conversation at lunch revolved around the Art Show, and Fiona beamed with pride at the praise of her photographs, while Robbie continued to sulk.

'What's happening with *Isobel's Place*, Nana Bel?' Fiona asked during a lull in the conversation. 'Has the renovation started yet? When will it be done?'

'Not as soon as we hoped, honey,' was Bel's reply. 'Andrew's being very careful to make sure there are no problems before he lets the workmen start. But the building's ours now.'

'Good!'

'Why are you so interested?' Robbie grunted.

'Because it's an interesting project for me – that's why. If I didn't have family and Anaïs to help me, or if they needed a break, it would be good to know I had somewhere like that to go to for a holiday.'

'Some holiday!' Robbie almost sneered.

'Can I try your crutches after lunch?' Jamie asked Robbie, effectively changing the subject. 'I've always wondered how it feels.'

'You're welcome to them.' Robbie pushed the food around his plate.

'Is it not to your liking?' Bel asked. 'I thought baked ham was a favourite of yours.'

'It's okay,' he muttered.

'Robbie! Mind your manners. That's no way to speak to your grandma.'

'Oh, leave him alone, Alasdair. He's finding it hard to adjust to being off his feet. He'll soon get used to it and be moving along as if he hasn't a care in the world,' Bel said, though she doubted it. The boy seemed seriously depressed. Couldn't Alasdair see that?

She reflected that he probably could. But Alasdair clearly didn't know how to handle his son in this mood – and no doubt he felt he should have been at the game, instead of...

'You went to one of the *Aye Write* events, Alasdair, didn't you? How was it?' she asked, in an attempt to change the subject and take the heat off Robbie.

'Good. The *Bloody Scotland* event. It's the name of a book,' he said, as both Jamie and Robbie sniggered.

'Oh!' Kirsty said. 'I think Isla Cameron was going to that one. She told me she had tickets for several of the events, and I'm pretty sure that was one of them. Did you see her?'

Alasdair didn't reply immediately.

Bel glanced in his direction to see a flush creeping across his cheeks. He coughed.

Could Alasdair have something to hide?

Seeing his embarrassment, Bel quickly said, 'You were lucky to get a ticket. Matt and I tried ages ago, but were too late.'

'A friend had a spare one.'

Kirsty appeared to have forgotten her question, focussing instead on the book. 'We should choose that one for next month's book club, Bel. What do you think?'

Since moving back to Scotland, one of the many social groups Bel had been invited to join was a book club set up by Kirsty and composed of several of her friends. Most were younger than Bel, but all shared a liking for reading about crime and although it was the group's stated policy for each member to take turns in selecting the book of the month, in practice, Kirsty usually took control.

'You'll enjoy it, Bel,' Alasdair said, clearly glad to be let off the hook and making Bel even more curious as to why Kirsty's question had embarrassed him. He knew Isla Cameron, of course. She was Fiona's headmistress, and Bel had seen them talking together at the Art Show the previous evening. *Isla Cameron. Kirsty was right. She would be a good match for Alasdair.*

Then she remembered Matt's anger at the very suggestion his son-in-law might find another partner. She decided to keep her suspicions to herself. It would never do for Kirsty to get even an inkling of them. And she may be completely wrong. But she decided to keep her eye on him and perhaps...

'Did you ever find anyone to replace Catherine?' she asked Kirsty, referring to the book club member who had deserted them just after Christmas to visit her daughter in Canada.

'No, but...' Kirsty seemed to wrack her brains before adding, 'Isla Cameron would be perfect. I'll contact her after the holidays. And she'll no doubt have read the book by then, too.' She sounded pleased with herself, with no thought her old friend might refuse. Bel pondered if, by bringing up Catherine when she had, she'd inadvertently suggested Isla as her replacement. But it didn't matter. Bel hoped Isla would agree. She'd like to find out a bit more about this woman who'd been a school friend of Kirsty's and who, if her suspicions were correct, was more to Alasdair than his daughter's headmistress.

*

When lunch was over, Matt suggested they go for a walk. 'It's a great afternoon and the dogs have been in all morning,' he said, when the dishwasher had been loaded and Jamie and Robbie were looking longingly at their iPhone and iPad respectively.

'Good idea,' Fiona said, reaching for her jacket.

Robbie only grunted, 'I'll have to stay here.' He lifted one crutch from the floor. 'These won't be much use up on the muir.'

'Do you have a wheelbarrow, Dad?' Duncan asked with a grin. 'I'm game to push him in it while you take Fi. Will you join us, Bel? Kirsty?'

The two women agreed and, with a lot of cajoling and laughter, Robbie was soon ensconced in Matt's shiny new wheelbarrow with a red handle.

'I feel a fool,' Robbie complained, lying back on a hastily collected cushion, his plastered leg sticking out in front of him and the other hanging over the side.

'Don't be such a wimp,' Fiona adjured him when they were all ready to go. 'Who's going to see you other than us?'

'Let's have a race,' Fiona said to Matt as they all trundled across the heather, the dogs running back and forth between them.

'Oh, I don't think…' Alasdair began. But it was too late. Matt and Duncan were off, leaving Bel and Kirsty laughing at their antics and Alasdair looking concerned.

'It's all right for you two to laugh, but these are my kids that are rattling around. What if they tip them out?'

'They won't,' Bel said, sobering up. 'They love them just as much as you do. Besides, Fi's used to travelling this way, even if it's a new experience for Robbie.'

By the time they'd caught up, the two teenagers were arguing as to which of them had won the race, while their drivers were sitting on the ground, and the dogs were off in a dip in the hillside, noses down.

'Here – Toby, Hamish!' Bel called to the dogs, who came running back at the sound of her voice.

The trip back to the house was a slower affair. Matt continued to push Fiona, while Alasdair took charge of Robbie, leaving Duncan to walk with the two women, while Jamie ran ahead with the dogs.

'You shouldn't encourage him, Duncan,' Bel said as they strolled across the rough grass where the blooming gorse stretched out into the distance like a yellow carpet.

'He's my dad.'

Bel wasn't sure whether he meant this as an explanation of Matt's behaviour or his own, so decided not to reply. By the time they reached the house they were all in need of more sustenance.

'Tea, I think,' Bel said. 'I made a batch of hot cross buns yesterday, and I believe there are some Easter eggs lurking in the kitchen. This elicited a yell of 'Yeah' from the three children, proving that regardless of their seemingly cool teenage demeanour, they could still be swayed by the thought of chocolate eggs.

Tea served, the adults formed one group and the children another. Bel, sitting on the edge of the adult group, was able to overhear much of the teenagers' conversation.

'How did you do your leg in?' Jamie asked Robbie.

'I was pushed. Wait till I see Reilly again. I'll give him what for. I'm out for the rest of the season because of him. Stuck with these.' He kicked at his crutches. 'I don't know how Fi does it.'

'Does what?' Fiona asked.

'Copes with being stuck in that chair of yours all day, every day. It would drive me mad. Before… I never realised how hard it must be for you. And, this afternoon – it's usually me wheeling you around. But, when Uncle Duncan started to push me in that wheelbarrow, I thought I was going to fall out. Don't you ever wish…?'

'What's the point? I hated it at first. I wanted to run and jump like I used to. But then, I started to understand that this was what life had in store for me and I decided to accept it, to make the most of what I had, to…'

'Count your blessings,' Robbie said sarcastically.

'If you like. There's no sense in moaning about what you can't change. So it's best just to get on with it. You're lucky. Your leg will heal in a few weeks and you'll be back on your feet again. It would take a miracle for that to happen to me.'

Fiona sounded so matter-of-fact that Bel felt her eyes moisten. The girl had such an old head on young shoulders. She'd had to suffer so much in her short life, but harboured no sense of regret, no feelings that life had been unkind to her.

'I'd never realised,' Robbie said slowly, as if suddenly coming to the recognition of what his sister had gone through, of what her life was like.

Bel smiled to herself. Some good would come out of this. Of that, she was sure.

Thirty-two

Isla

Isla smiled as she read Alasdair's text. Like the man himself, the text was formal and to the point. He hoped she'd had a good trip, was feeling relaxed and remembered their arrangement for lunch. If she was agreeable, he'd pick her up next day at eleven o'clock.

She'd spent the past two days at school catching up on paperwork and preparing for the term ahead. A relaxing day away from all that was exactly what she craved. She wondered what Alasdair had in mind. It was difficult to predict. He was such a mystery to her. Despite having shared a few outings with him and revealing details of a past she was accustomed to keep private, she didn't feel any closer to understanding what made him tick.

She texted her acceptance and headed to the kitchen to prepare a hot chocolate. She'd promised herself a quiet evening with a good book and no worries about school or anything else.

As she settled down by the fire, her phone buzzed again. Another text. This time from Shona to thank her for the bracelet. They'd only managed to meet briefly the previous Sunday after Isla's return. On her way home from Arran and with Hugh waiting in the car, Shona had only made a fleeting visit to check she was back, and hadn't taken time to open the birthday gift.

Shona had looked blooming. Hugh seemed to be good for her. Isla hoped Shona wouldn't be disappointed again, or decide it was all too hard. She knew that feeling only too well and didn't intend to let her own guard down readily. But... She read Alasdair's text again. Was this a friendship she really wanted to pursue? There were so many potential obstacles – not least of which was his ongoing grief for his wife. Then there were his children. Fiona, she knew, but being her headmistress was a world away from being a friend of her father's. And the son, Robbie, was an unknown quantity – a teenage boy with, no doubt, all the usual hang-ups, at what Shona called the hairy and smelly stage.

But, Isla reminded herself, it most likely wouldn't come to that. They were merely meeting for lunch. She tried to dismiss the small voice that was telling her she was already finding him an attractive companion, enjoyed his company and was looking forward to getting to know him better.

*

Alasdair didn't speak much as they drove out of Glasgow. Isla wondered where they were heading, but didn't want to ask, assuming Alasdair would tell her when he was ready. She was right.

As they reached the outskirts of the city, Alasdair turned to her. 'I thought we might drive out towards Ayr. I've heard there's a passable restaurant there in an old country house. It's good to get out of the city, and we might be able to catch a sea breeze. He glanced at Isla and she saw an unexpected twinkle in his eye as his face crinkled up into the smile she remembered. Today he was dressed casually in a pair of chinos, and an Aran sweater over a pale blue shirt. His *Barbour* had been thrown into the back seat.

Isla relaxed. The tension she'd felt earlier disappeared. She was going to enjoy this trip, glad she'd taken care with her appearance and had chosen to wear a pair of tailored black slacks topped with a royal blue polo-neck jumper.

By the time the car turned into a long driveway bordered by poplars, Isla knew she'd made the right decision agreeing to come. Once out of Glasgow, Alasdair had relaxed, become a different person from the uptight businessman who'd arrived to pick her up. It was as if, leaving the city behind, he'd also sloughed off his everyday persona and become once again the man she remembered from Christmas Eve and the author event, albeit less vulnerable. Which was the real Alasdair? Isla hoped it was this man, the one who could laugh at himself, recount amusing anecdotes of his children, and who was interested in her.

'Impressive,' she said, her eyes meeting his as he helped her out of the car.

'I haven't been here before. A colleague mentioned having spent a weekend here, and it sounded good.'

'Well, it certainly looks well-appointed.' Isla gazed up at the large white stucco building with its red brick trim. It had obviously started life as a country house – a very large country house with a turret on one end and an imposing arched entrance topped by a crenelated parapet. 'I wonder who lived here?'

'Some wealthy laird. no doubt.'

'Mmm.' Isla could imagine horse-drawn carriages pulling up on the gravelled forecourt, lords and ladies in elegant gowns alighting to be shown in by liveried servants. 'It's a bit like a Scottish Downton Abbey.'

'You like that sort of thing?'

Isla thought she could detect a note of condemnation in his voice. 'I enjoy the historical aspect,' she said defensively.

'Elspeth liked it. I could never see the attraction I'm afraid.' His face seemed to close up at the memory of his dead wife.

Isla bit her lip. Why had she said something to remind him of his wife? They'd been getting on so well.

His face cleared. 'There are a lot of these scattered around the countryside. Mostly renovated like this one and turned into hotels and restaurants. Shall we go in or do you want to stay here admiring it?'

'Sorry. Of course.'

Once inside, Alasdair mentioned their reservation and they entered what appeared to be a sitting room furnished with comfortable armchairs and low tables. Isla had no sooner sunk into a chair than a waitress appeared.

'What would you like to drink?'

About to ask for a glass of wine, Isla changed her mind. 'I think I'd like a gin,' she said. 'It seems more in keeping with this place.' Her eyes flickered across the walls on which watercolours of the surrounding countryside were cleverly displayed.

'One gin – Makar?' Alasdair raised an eyebrow to which Isla nodded, '…and a light beer.' He leant back in his chair, relaxed once more. 'This is nice. I've been looking forward to getting you to myself again. Now, tell me more about the wonders of Orkney. Is the stone circle as spectacular as they say?'

'Even better.' Isla enjoyed describing the beauties of Orkney to Alasdair, all the more so as he was clearly absorbed in what she had to say. As she spoke, his eyes rarely left her face, moving only when their drinks arrived. But, to her surprise, instead of being embarrassed by his attention, Isla found herself glowing at his obvious interest.

When the waitress reappeared to let them know their table was ready, Isla had almost forgotten they were here to have lunch, so engrossed had she been in describing her impressions of the previous week.

'And you didn't mind being alone up there?' Alasdair asked, when they were seated at the white linen-covered table close to a window which looked out onto manicured lawns and beautifully landscaped gardens.

'I loved it,' Isla replied as she unfolded her napkin, keeping her eyes downcast to hide the slight untruth. What did it matter if she failed to tell Alasdair she had had company, the company of his old school mate – the one from whom he'd rescued her only a couple of months earlier?

As they ate – a salmon dish for her, and steak for him – Isla couldn't help but compare the two men. While Daniel had proved to be amusing company, Alasdair, although a more relaxed Alasdair than she'd been privy to before today, was the more serious of the two. She had the distinct impression he'd never let her down, would be able to handle any crisis. Daniel, on the other hand, would be more of a fair-weather friend – someone who might be fun for a time, but would run a mile when things got tough.

What was she thinking?

'Penny for them?'

Isla blushed. 'They're not worth it.' She took a sip of the wine Alasdair had ordered to accompany their meal – a Sauvignon Blanc from New Zealand – and decided to change the subject. 'How's your son?'

'Robbie? Coming along. He's beginning to get around more easily on his crutches, and I do believe he's developing a better understanding of what it's like for Fi. I think I told you the pair are out at my father-in-law's place this week. They love it there – the muir, the dogs. Elspeth and I never saw fit to get a pet for them.' He paused as if hesitant to say anything untoward about his wife. 'She was pretty houseproud and I...' he rubbed his chin, '...I went with the flow. Do you have any animals?'

'A cat.'

At that point, the waitress arrived to remove their plates.

'Dessert or...?'

'Coffee would be lovely.'

'You don't strike me as a cat person,' Alasdair said, after some deliberation, 'although,' he cocked his head to one side, 'you do share some of their characteristics.'

'I do?' Isla wasn't sure whether to be flattered or insulted.

'I have the impression you prefer to walk alone, are innately curious, don't suffer fools gladly, and I can imagine you metaphorically flexing your claws.' He chuckled.

Their coffee arrived, and they sat drinking silently, lost in their thoughts.

Finally, they rose to go.

While they'd been in the restaurant, a light breeze had blown up, but the sky was till clear, despite the slight chill in the air.

'Are you game for a stroll along the front?' Alasdair asked, walking to the car. 'We used to come to Ayr on holiday when I was a kid; I have fond memories of the beach here although it's changed a lot since then.'

Isla looked at Alasdair, his hair tousled by the wind, and could imagine him as a little boy, probably not unlike his own son. She wondered if he'd brought Robbie and Fiona here.

As if reading her mind, he said, 'Elspeth and I used to come here, too. When the kids were younger, of course. Fi loved building sandcastles and paddling in the sea before...'

'How old was she when she had the accident?' Isla asked gently.

'She was seven,' he sighed, and muttered, 'and Elspeth never forgave herself.'

Isla glanced up at his face to see a frown etched on his forehead. She longed to reach up to smooth it away but managed to restrain herself. That would be an intrusion on his grief.

'I'm sorry,' he sighed again. 'I didn't intend to inflict my pain on you. Let's go to the beach.'

'Let's.'

Maybe the sea air would succeed in blowing away the worry from his face – a face she was coming to like more than was good for her.

Alasdair seemed to recover his equilibrium on the way over to the beach, and the stiff breeze that greeted them when they stepped out of the car again almost took their breath away.

'I'd better make sure you don't blow away,' Alasdair said with a smile, his earlier sadness seemingly forgotten as he grasped her hand.

As their fingers entwined, Isla had a sense of coming home. Despite the cold of the day, his hand was warm in hers, his fingers firm. She felt as if she was tethered to a strong tree, one which might bend in the wind but would stand strong against all adversity.

'I said I wanted to get to know you better,' Alasdair said as they struggled against the breeze. 'Glenferrie Academy. What led you there? It seems a strange position for a young, vibrant woman like yourself.'

Isla glowed with pleasure at the compliment but was a little surprised by his dismissal of the role of headmistress at the prestigious girl's school. She bridled. 'What's wrong with Glenferrie?'

'Nothing. Nothing at all. But...' He stopped and turned his head to meet her eyes. '...it must be a lonely position to be in. I know how much you're loved by your students – Fi talks about you a lot – and I'm sure you're respected by your staff, but what about friends, family?'

'No family. As for friends.' Isla paused. She really didn't have any, besides Shona. 'I have one good friend. We met at uni and have always kept in touch. She supported me when my daughter died.' Isla kept her eyes down, watching her feet in the shoes she'd chosen to wear which were quite unsuitable for walking along the promenade. 'When that happened, I couldn't bear everyone's sympathy, so I ignored them, shut myself off, and one by one they disappeared.' She looked up again. 'But my New Year's resolution – egged on by Shona – is to get out more. And now I've reconnected with your sister-in-law.'

'Watch out or she'll make you one of her projects.' Alasdair gave a grim laugh. 'I'm not sure I've escaped.'

'She was like that at school, too. Always wanting to set the world – and everyone around her – to rights.'

'Her heart's in the right place.' Alasdair paused. 'But I know what you mean about avoiding sympathy. I felt like that when Elspeth died. I just wanted to shut myself away. But there were the kids. I may not have been completely fair to them either. I reduced my hours in the office but brought work home. And it was easier for me to closet myself in my study than to face them, to face the emptiness in the house.'

Isla squeezed his hand to find an answering pressure.

'We're a right pair.'

Isla wasn't sure why, but she found his comment comforting.

Thirty-three

Isla

Isla was filled with doubts as she drove along Great Western Road. She was reminded of the last time she'd made this trip. She'd been full of misgivings then, too – and look what had happened.

When Kirsty called to invite her to join her book club, her initial reaction had been to refuse. She recalled Alasdair's comment about her becoming one of Kirsty's *projects*. Then she remembered her promise to Shona, her resolution to get out more. She'd never belonged to a book club, preferring to choose her own reading matter and to read alone. The thought of having to read a book chosen by someone else, a book she might never have chosen herself, might not even want to read, had filled her with trepidation. And the risk of having to lay bare her thoughts on the said book in front of a room full of strangers... She almost turned the car around.

But Kirsty had assured her they all enjoyed the same sort of crime novels she did. And they were to discuss a book she'd already been reading – she'd finished the stories in *Bloody Scotland* the night before and part of her was interested to hear what others thought of it. Well, she decided, if she felt uncomfortable, she didn't need to go back.

With this in mind, Isla felt more confident as she turned off the main road. It was a plus that this meeting was to be held at Kirsty's home, a house with which she might not be familiar, but at least had visited once already.

Kirsty had told her they were 'All women like us'. Isla wasn't sure what she meant. She and Kirsty had had a lot in common at one time. But, since leaving school, their lives had gone in very different directions. She supposed Kirsty meant they were all of a similar age and university educated. But Isla suspected that, like Kirsty, the others were all married, no doubt with children. This was borne out by the fact that the group met on a Saturday afternoon when 'the men are at the football'.

When Isla reached her destination, there were already several cars parked in the driveway. She parked her Peugeot at the kerb, picked up her book from the passenger seat, hooked her bag over her shoulder and, taking a deep breath, made her way to the front door.

'Glad you could make it,' Kirsty greeted her, answering the door before Isla could have second thoughts. 'Come on in and meet the girls.'

Isla cringed. This was why she always avoided such gatherings. Girls! She and Kirsty would never see forty again and she suspected that would be true of the others, too.

She went in to be introduced.

As she'd expected, the other group members were facsimiles of Kirsty – well-heeled, well-dressed west-end matrons. But they seemed a nice bunch. They were friendly and welcomed her into the group as she was introduced as 'My old school friend Isla Cameron who's now headmistress at Glenferrie Academy'. There were a few gasps, but, to Isla's relief, no one announced their daughter or daughters were among her students.

Kirsty served tea and the conversation became general. Kirsty looked at her watch. 'We're just waiting for... ah, here she is,' she said as the doorbell sounded.

She left the room, returning accompanied by the tall elegant woman, older than the others, to whom Isla had been introduced at the Art Show. 'You remember Isla,' Kirsty said. 'Fi's headmistress. You met at the Art Show. Isla, this is Bel Reid. She's married to my father-in-law.'

Isla thought this was a strange way for Kirsty to introduce her mother-in-law, while the thought that this was Alasdair's mother-in-law too went through her head. She remembered the meeting at the Art Show – and how eager she'd been to get away from Bel and her husband. She glared at Kirsty. Had she done this on purpose? No. How could Kirsty know?

'Isla, how lovely to meet you again. Fi talks about you a lot.'

Did Isla imagine it, or did the woman's eyes examine her with a greater intensity than was warranted?

'Now we can start,' announced Kirsty.

Isla found the afternoon passed quickly at first. Each of the group shared their impressions of the book and identified their favourite stories, then they had a free and more wide-ranging discussion. When the others discovered Isla had recently visited Maeshowe, they pressed her for details and ended up sharing reminiscences of Hebridean trips taken or planned.

As the discussion waned, Kirsty disappeared, only to return wheeling in a small tea-trolley on which were glasses, several bottles of wine, and a platter of cheese and biscuits.

'We always finish this way,' she explained, clearly seeing Isla's surprise. We're not about trying to outdo each other – only biscuits and cheese are permitted – but it's nice to have a glass of something to sustain us for the evening ahead.

Amused, Isla shook her head at the offer of cheese, but accepted a glass of wine, and, in the ensuing medley, found herself seated next to Bel.

'I was interested to hear about your trip to Orkney,' Bel said. 'I've never visited the northernmost islands, but your description has whetted my appetite. I love the sound of the Viking museum and the cathedral.'

'You sound as if you're from away,' Isla said, detecting a not unfamiliar accent. 'Australian?'

'Oh dear! I thought I'd managed to lose it. I grew up here in Glasgow, but I went to Australia in my early twenties and only returned a couple of years ago. I thought I'd lost any accent I might have had.'

'It's only a hint. I recognised it because I spent time in Australia myself – on a gap year before the reality of university study took over. My mother died when I was in my last year at school and I needed to get away.'

Isla wasn't sure why she was telling Bel all this. She was usually a very private person, but there was something about this older woman that prompted confidences.

'I'm sorry. That must have been difficult for you. Your father?'

'Long gone.' At least Isla would keep that to herself. The man who'd been her father had left her mother with a young child, never to be seen or heard of again.

'Where did you stay in Australia and how long did you spend there?'

Isla enjoyed reminiscing about her days on the continent on the other side of the world, discovering Bel had lived not far from where Isla shared a flat and worked as a waitress. It would all have changed now, of course, but it was nice to recall those years when she'd been a free spirit.

It was with surprise she realised the room was beginning to empty. 'I should go,' she said, 'I've loved talking with you.'

'I've enjoyed it too,' Bel said. 'It's not that I miss the old place, but it's nice to talk about it with someone who's lived there. I hope this means we'll be seeing you again. Next month's meeting is at our place. We live out in Inveruglas, if you're not adverse to a drive out to Loch Lomond. We'll be reading Anne Cleeves' new book. I assume you read her?'

'Yes. And I've already read *Wild Fire*. I'd love to come.' Isla meant it. Despite her misgivings, the afternoon had been pleasant, and the women friendly. She'd enjoyed talking with Bel, although the fact she was Alasdair MacLeod's mother-in-law might prove to be a sticking point; she was also Fiona MacLeod's grandmother. It seemed all of Isla's rules were being broken.

Thirty-four

Bel

'That went well,' Bel said, as she helped Kirsty load the tea- trolley with the dirty glasses and empty platter. 'Your friend Isla should be a good addition to the group, if she decides to continue with us.'

'What makes you think she won't?'

'Nothing, really. But I got the impression she wasn't quite sure it was for her – that she was weighing us up.'

'And finding us wanting?' Kirsty laughed.

'No. But she does hold an important position in the community, and I guess she may feel she needs to keep herself isolated from the rabble. Not that you and your friends are the rabble,' she chuckled. 'Anyway, we had a lovely chat about Sydney. Did you know she spent some time there between school and uni?'

'I knew she travelled when we left school. That's when we lost touch. Before that, we did everything together. Then I went on to uni, met Duncan, and the rest is history.'

The pair went into the kitchen. Kirsty started loading the dishwasher, then turned abruptly to face Bel. 'I was thinking...'

Bel sighed inwardly. When Kirsty started thinking, she always had some plan in mind. What was it this time?

'Mmm?'

'Isla. I know I've said it before, but she's perfect. She's single, intelligent, the right age. She lost a child, you know.'

'You said.' Bel wondered what else the woman had told Kirsty – no doubt in confidence.

'She didn't say much about it, other than it was a little girl. But, as far as I know, she never married. And she's been at Glenferrie for around ten years. I think she's still grieving for her daughter. Though you'd think she'd find it hard spending all her time with other people's daughters. It's a bit odd don't you think?'

'That may be her way of handling it,' Bel said gently, feeling sympathy for the young woman who, she suspected, was now going to become one of Kirsty's *projects*.

'I was thinking,' Kirsty repeated, 'what she needs is a man in her life, and what Alasdair needs…'

Oh, dear, thought Bel, *here it comes. Once again Kirsty is going to leap in where angels fear to tread.* She hadn't known Kirsty long enough herself to have experienced much of her tactlessness, her complete lack of understanding that there were some matters – and some people – you didn't meddle with. But Matt had forewarned her about his daughter-in-law's impetuous behaviour – how her impulsiveness and loose tongue often got her into trouble. And if Bel was right, she was heading for trouble right now.

'… is a woman in his life,' Kirsty continued. 'Elspeth was a good friend, as well as my sister-in-law, but it's been two years now, and anyone can see he's lonely and depressed. Isla would…'

'Don't you think that's up to Alasdair?'

'Och, you know what men are like. He probably just needs a bit of a shove in the right direction.'

And you're dying to give him that shove.

'And you think Isla Cameron is the right direction for him?'

'Don't you? And she's Fi's headmistress, too. Perfect!'

'Don't you think that could present problems – for her and for Fi?' Bel knew she was playing the Devil's advocate. She was conscious she'd had the same idea herself and speaking with Isla had reinforced it. They *would* make a good match. But she knew Matt wouldn't see it that way.

'And there's Matt to consider,' she added.

'Matt?' It was clear Kristy hadn't considered Matt's views. 'What's it got to do with him?'

'He *was* Elspeth's father.'

'And?'

Bel sighed. Sometimes Kirsty could be so obtuse.

'I don't think he's quite ready for someone to replace Elspeth in Alasdair's life just yet.'

'But he must see...' Kirsty's voice trailed off, no doubt seeing the wary expression in Bel's eyes. '*He* married *you*.'

'Yes.' Bel picked up the tea-towel and replaced it on its rail to give her time to consider an appropriate response. 'But he'd been widowed longer than Alasdair has. And I guess he sees things differently when it's his daughter's widower. It's not such a surprise, surely? Elspeth had trouble accepting Matt's relationship with me.'

'All the more reason for him to see sense where Alasdair's concerned.' Kirsty's lips formed a determined line.

Bel sighed again. In her heart, she agreed with Kirsty, but her loyalty lay with her husband, and she knew his views on the matter.

'Let it go, Kirsty. If Alasdair and Isla are meant for each other, they'll make their own way, without any outside interference. You said they've met?'

'But...' Then Kirsty seemed to think better of whatever she'd been going to say. 'I do know he met with her at the school – about Fi's Colmar trip – and I saw them talking together at the Art Show.'

'Well, then. Why not just let fate take its course? What will be, will be. But Matt would never forgive you if he knew you'd been instigating some sort of relationship between them.'

Or me, she thought, regretfully. *But Kirsty is right, Isla Cameron might just be what Alasdair needs.*

Thirty-five

Isla

The book club had turned out well, Isla reflected over breakfast next morning. And she had promised Bel she'd go next month. Since meeting Kirsty again – and Alasdair, she had to admit – she'd developed a curiosity about the family. This was so unlike her, it gave her pause for thought. What was it about them that had her accepting invitations she'd have had no trouble declining only a few months ago?

If she was honest with herself, it was the enigmatic Alasdair MacLeod whose image kept popping into her subconscious when she least expected it. She gave herself a shake. The Easter break was over, and everything would be back to normal tomorrow. Back to *auld claes and parritch* as her grandmother used to say. Funny how those old sayings stuck in her mind. Sometimes she wished her grandmother was still alive – or her mother. For a moment she felt saddened, missing her lovely and devoted mother who'd died too soon. How she'd love to be able to have her here; to be able to unload all her troubles and worries onto her older and wiser shoulders. Maybe she'd have been able to help her sort out her life.

She sighed.

Placing her cup and cereal bowl into the dishwasher and ensuring Sooty still had some food in his bowl, she peeked out the window. The sky which had been overcast earlier, had cleared to a fine day – perfect for a walk, as long as she rugged up well.

Once outside, she lifted her head to the sky and took a deep breath, the chilly air almost closing her throat. The road was deserted as she walked briskly along, the church bells chiming in the distance reminding her of her recent trip to Orkney, and Kirkwall's magnificent cathedral.

Her thoughts then turned to the man she'd met there. Daniel Henderson. Unlike Alasdair MacLeod, Daniel seemed straightforward. There was no deceased wife. According to Shona, he'd married in his twenties and divorced not long after. Since then, he'd flitted from one woman to another, rarely staying long enough to become involved. Glad she'd shunned any romantic involvement with him, while enjoying his company in Orkney, Isla nevertheless was somewhat surprised he hadn't attempted to contact her since their return.

Turning into Kelvingrove Park, Isla smiled at the antics of a group of teenagers, the boys wheeling around on their skateboards, while the girls huddled together giggling. Some things didn't change.

Isla walked on, mentally planning the agenda for the next day's staff meeting. She often found she could think more clearly away from her office and home. She'd just determined to give Maree greater responsibility, when she caught sight of a familiar figure walking towards her.

'We meet again,' Daniel said. 'I thought I'd bump into you somewhere. Shona said you live around here. I've been intending to ask her for your number, so this is serendipitous.'

Isla gulped. *What was he doing here? Didn't he live on the other side of the city?*

As if to answer her unspoken question, he added, 'I had to come into the university library to pick up a book I need,' he held up a thick tome Isla hadn't noticed, 'and I decided it was a lovely morning for a walk.'

She glanced at him suspiciously, but he seemed genuine – and he couldn't have known she'd be in the park this morning.

'Shall we walk together?'

Without waiting for her reply, he turned on his heel to face the same direction as Isla and took her by the elbow.

'I was impressed by the Italian chapel we saw,' he said. 'It's led me to review a set of lectures I'd planned on the effects of war in Scotland. I decided to include one on prisoners of war in the two world wars. Did you know there were quite a number of camps for both Italian and German prisoners, and I believe some liked Scotland so much they stayed on afterwards.'

'Hence all the ice-cream and chip shops,' Isla laughed.

'Maybe,' he said, with a smile. 'But what brings you out here on a Sunday morning?'

Isla slowed to match his more leisurely pace as the pair chatted on, till the large shape of the Art Gallery loomed up in front of them.

Daniel took out his phone and checked it. 'It's gone eleven. The gallery has a pretty decent café. Can I persuade you to join me for a cup of tea?'

Isla hesitated.

'Or coffee, if you prefer.'

By this time, they were standing still, and a cool wind was blowing up, rustling the leaves and ruffling Daniel's hair. It would be churlish to refuse, and the thought of a cup of warming tea did have some appeal. 'Tea would be good,' she said.

'So, back to work tomorrow?'

They were on their second pot of tea, and Daniel had ordered a plate of chicken sandwiches, which arrived on delicious small crusty rolls, when his voice became more serious. 'I don't know what Shona has told you about me.' He tapped the table with the fingers of his right hand, then ran them through his hair. 'I've done a few things I'm not proud of over the years – got into a few scrapes, and Hugh has bailed me out on more than one occasion.' He grinned sheepishly – exactly like one of her students caught out smoking in the toilets, Isla thought, smiling to herself. But whereas with her students it never failed to annoy her, in Daniel, it was almost endearing.

'But,' he continued, 'I've turned over a new leaf. When I accepted the position up here, I made a vow to myself I'd act my age, instead of pretending I was still in my twenties or thirties. The first time you saw me was a regression, I'm afraid – as I already explained. But that's in the past. I want to see you again, and I need to assure you that's not who I am – not anymore.'

Isla wished herself somewhere else. She'd set out for a solitary walk and, by now, should be back home with her cat, eating her lunch, not sitting here listening to his ramblings.

Was he for real?

She glanced at her companion who seemed perfectly serious. He leant towards her and she caught a whiff of a mixture of soap and spicy aftershave.

'You never married?' he asked unexpectedly.

'No.' Isla spoke sharply. It was none of his business. It had been her choice to remain single. She'd had offers. But no relationship had measured up to the passion that had created her Morag. And she'd never met anyone she wanted to share her life with, not even Ollie.

She sometimes wondered about him, wondered if she'd have contacted him, had Morag lived. By now, her daughter would have been coming up for fifteen, would be full of curiosity, asking about her birth father. Would Isla have been able to resist her questions? Would it have been fair to deny her that knowledge? Had it been fair to leave Ollie in ignorance of the fact he'd fathered a daughter?

At the time, she'd had no doubts. She'd returned to Scotland, ignorant of the fact she was pregnant, but with the hope that maybe she was already carrying the child she yearned for. In the following weeks, Ollie was due to return home too – back to the fiancée who awaited him, to a life very different from Isla's, in a country across the ocean.

In her view, it would have been foolish to have contacted him about a child whose very existence could upset his entire life. And, if she was honest with herself, she had no intention of sharing what she saw as her own little miracle with anyone, not even her father. Then, when Morag died, there had been no point. Ollie had probably fathered several children by now, was a pillar of the community, a Californian vigneron with a bevy of blooming and tanned offspring ready to take over the family business when he grew too old to manage it.

'You were wise,' Daniel said.

It took a moment or two for Isla to understand what he meant, then he continued, 'No ex. No children. A wise lady.'

At that moment, Isla didn't feel very wise. What was she doing here? 'I should go.' She started to rise, only to have him put a hand on her arm.

Tempted to shake it off, she paused.

'Can I invite you to a movie?'

Isla wasn't sure what she'd expected, but this wasn't it. 'A movie?'

'They're showing a digitally enhanced version of the old movie *Grease* at the Glasgow Film Theatre next Sunday. I was planning to go myself, but it would be much more enjoyable with company.' He raised an eyebrow.

How did he know? She'd never seen the movie but loved the music. She'd heard it was coming to the theatre but had been too busy with other matters to check the dates.

Daniel must have noticed her hesitation, the interest in her eyes. He was quick to capitalise on what must have appeared as tacit agreement. 'It's an afternoon show. We could have an early dinner afterwards.'

She capitulated. What harm could it do, after all? 'All right, but...'

'Great. Shall we meet there at one?'

Feeling as if she'd been cleverly manipulated, Isla agreed with a smile. He was a nice man. He was a friend of Shona's. And there was no sense in mooning over Alasdair MacLeod. Their day out had been good, she'd felt... She wasn't sure exactly what she'd felt. But the man was still grieving. He had a family, a life. And he hadn't been in touch since. What had she expected? Isla pulled herself together as she left the café and began to walk home, determined to forget the entire Reid and MacLeod family and get on with her life.

She was almost home when the phone in her pocket vibrated and, looking at the screen, she saw Shona's number.

'Hi Shona,' Isla quickened her pace as a few drops of rain began to fall. The earlier clear sky had darkened, and it looked as if it was going to pour down.

'Fancy a movie tonight?'

Isla almost laughed. She hadn't been to the movies in months, and now two invitations in the same afternoon.

'I don't think so. School starts tomorrow, and I...'

'All the more reason to get out of the house. I know you. I bet you spent most of last week holed up in that office of yours at Glenferrie, and you have the rest of the school year all planned out.'

'Well...' Shona knew her too well.

'I knew it.'

'What's the movie?' Isla felt herself weakening. While one part of her longed to be alone in her flat with only her cat for company, another part thought it would be nice not to spend the evening completely by herself.

'*The Guernsey Literary and Potato Peel Society.*'

'Oh!' Isla couldn't keep the eagerness out of her voice. It was one movie she *did* want to see.

'Is that a "yes"?'

'I guess. I'll meet you there.'

*

'Well? Glad you came?'

The pair were leaving the cinema, stopping only to put up their umbrellas. The rain which had threatened earlier had really set in.

'You know I am. It was wonderful. I *am* glad I came. Thanks.'

'How about a glass of wine before heading back? It's a dirty night.'

Isla looked up at the black clouds, at the rain pelting down. She thought of her warm, cosy room, the fire flickering in the light of her reading lamp, her cat lying at her feet, then she looked at Shona's eager face. 'Okay. Just a quick one.'

Once they were seated with glasses of an indeterminate red wine, Shona began to dissect the movie.

Isla listened for a bit without comment then said, 'I've joined a book club – at least, I think I have.'

Her words stopped Shona in her tracks. 'You have? Where? Who?'

Wishing she'd kept it to herself, Isla said, 'Kirsty Reid – remember the old school friend I told you about? The one I met at the school reunion? I went yesterday, and it was okay. I may go again.'

'That's wonderful!' But Isla had the impression Shona wished it had been she who had introduced Isla to a book club, not some old school friend. 'What are they reading?'

'All crime, mostly Scottish. Yesterday it was *Bloody Sunday* which I already had.'

'Mmm. Sorry I missed that *Aye Scotland* session, but Crieff was fantastic.'

'You and Hugh – it's serious?'

Shona blushed. 'I hope so. Oh, Isla, I've never felt like this. He's…'

She waved her hands in the air as if unable to find words sufficiently superlative to describe her new companion. 'And what about you?'

It was Isla's turn to blush. She shook her head. 'You know me. I prefer being on my own, present company excepted.'

'Well, let's do this again. Did you know there's going to be a showing of *Grease* at the GFT next Sunday? Why don't we meet up for that too?'

Isla dropped her gaze and stroked the stem of her glass. 'I'm sorry, Shona. I can't. I'm already going to it.'

Shona's eyes widened. 'You are? Who with?'

While she'd dearly love to keep that information to herself, Isla knew her friend would soon find out. Daniel and Hugh were friends, and he'd have no reason to keep their meeting secret. 'Daniel Henderson,' she muttered.

'But... you only met him at that charity do when we were all drunk – and you left before you could get to know him.'

Isla exhaled. So, Daniel hadn't mentioned their meeting on Orkney to his friend? But it was probably only a matter of time. Perhaps they hadn't met since Easter, or perhaps men didn't share these things the way women did. Well, she'd done it now.

Shona's eyes were standing out on stalks, ready to hear how Isla and Daniel had managed to meet – without her help.

Isla took a deep breath, knowing Shona was about to put two and two together and make at least five. 'I don't want you to get the wrong idea,' she began. 'There's nothing going on between me and Daniel Henderson. I don't even like him very much.' *But was that true?* 'Easter weekend – when you all went to Arran – I went to Orkney. You knew that. It's where your birthday present came from. And when I was there, I bumped into Daniel. He was on holiday too, and we did a few things together – two city slickers in the wilds of the north, you know?' She laughed self-consciously.

Shona fingered the birthday bracelet on her wrist. She was hanging on Isla's every word.

Isla took a sip of wine, then continued, 'We didn't have any intention of seeing each other again. Then, this morning, I bumped into him – in Kelvingrove Park.' As she said it, the coincidence hit her again. There was something odd about it, but how could he have manufactured that meeting? No, she was being daft. 'We ended up having tea, and he invited me to *Grease* next Sunday That's all.'

'That's *all*? You spent time with Daniel Henderson in Orkney and you didn't tell me?'

'There was nothing to tell.'

'Hmph. Will you see him again? After next week, I mean. We could make up a foursome. I'd love it if...' Shona's eyes gleamed in anticipation.

'I doubt it. Don't get your hopes up. I've no intention of us becoming *an item*. It's a one-off.'

'Pity.'

But Isla could see her friend didn't believe her and was working out how she could get her and Daniel together again. She knew from what Daniel had said, that he'd like to strengthen their friendship. But she wasn't sure she could cope with the complications such a relationship would bring. And there was Alasdair MacLeod to consider. How had Isla managed to get herself into this situation? For someone who proclaimed to be satisfied with her single life, she now had two men eager to invite her out. Or was that putting it too strong?

The two women hugged and parted. When Isla returned to her car, she automatically turned her phone back on, only to see she had a message.

It was from Alasdair MacLeod.

Thirty-six

Alasdair

'Come on, you two. Anaïs is ready to drive you to school.' Alasdair drained his cup and rose from the table. The *au pair* was standing by the door, car keys in her hand.

'I'm ready, Dad. I just have to collect my bag,' Fiona called from the living room, making good her claim by wheeling herself to the door with a smile.

'Do I have to go?' Robbie grumbled from where he was still sitting at the breakfast table. He was wearing his school uniform but was otherwise not ready for the day ahead.

'It's the beginning of term,' Fiona reminded him. 'I can't wait. Just think – it's only nine weeks till we're off to France.' She beamed at Anaïs, who gave a shy smile.

'It's all right for you, Little Miss Sunshine,' Robbie muttered.

Alasdair sighed. Nothing changed. At Easter, he thought he'd detected a more empathetic side to Robbie – an understanding of what life might be like for his sister. He should have known it couldn't last.

Robbie pushed his cereal bowl away from him. 'But can't I stay home, Dad?'

'No, son. It's a school day and there's nothing wrong with you apart from a broken leg – a leg which will heal. You'll most likely find you're the hero of the hour. You scored the winning goal, didn't you? Now get your bag and your coat. Anaïs is waiting.'

Still grumbling, Robbie pushed himself up, balanced on his good leg, and steadied himself on his crutches. 'Hey, I'm getting good at this,' he said in a surprised voice, making his way across the room to where Anaïs was waiting with his coat and bag. He gave Alasdair a grin. 'Maybe you're right, Dad, and it won't be so bad. I'll tell them all how I saved the day and put myself in mortal danger.'

Alasdair laughed. The boy was incorrigible.

After the trio had left, Alasdair poured himself one more cup of coffee and picked up the paper. He didn't have to be in the office till later, so he had time to catch up on the news. But the newsprint blurred as he remembered the text he'd sent the previous evening. He'd waited over a week to contact Isla sensing she could be scared off if he tried to push their friendship, but anxious to consolidate the closeness he felt they were beginning to establish.

He took out his phone. Still no reply. He frowned. What did it mean? Did it mean anything? It had taken him ages to compose a text he thought conveyed his intention – one that was friendly without being too intimate. Had he made a mistake? Should he have called? He was so out of practice with all this business, he had no idea. He scratched his head. She'd be back at school today and no doubt busy.

Maybe he should have got in touch on the weekend. But he, along with Matt and Duncan, had taken the boys to the football on Saturday. Then there had been the family lunch on Sunday with Kirsty doing her usual thing of looking as if butter wouldn't melt in her mouth, while no doubt planning something that would put the cat among the pigeons. Come to think of it, Bel had been giving him some strange looks, too. They couldn't know about his outing with Isla, could they?

He sighed, closed the paper and downed the last of his coffee. He had more to think about than his unsatisfactory love life. There was a management meeting to prepare for, an interview with the finance editor of the Herald this afternoon, and the new security manager would be awaiting his arrival at the office.

*

Alasdair thanked the journalist for what had been a reasonably pleasant interview. Edwin Gallagher was new to the paper and determined to make his mark. The feature on Alasdair was to be the first in what he styled as a *Focus on the Giants of Glasgow's Business Industry* and, as such, he'd been fairly gentle with him, focussing on Alasdair's career from university to the present time and ignoring any personal details.

Alasdair had been glad about that. He had no desire to have his personal life bandied about by all and sundry. As soon as Gallagher walked out, Grace walked in with a couple of post-it notes.

'You had several calls while he was here,' she said, 'I was able to deal with most of them, but you may want to handle these two yourself. The manager at the Renfrew branch seems to need your advice about one of his staff, and… there's one from your daughter's headmistress. I thought it might be important.'

'Thanks.'

Isla had responded – and with a call, not a text. Alasdair tried to subdue an unexpected jolt of pleasure at the sight of her name on the yellow square of paper. Maybe the call wasn't in response to his text. Maybe it was something to do with Fiona. But the number written there wasn't for the school – it was Isla's mobile number. He sat for a moment before picking up the phone and dialling.

His call was answered immediately.

'Alasdair. Thanks for calling back. I'm sorry if I interrupted you in the office.'

'Not at all.' He leant back and smiled at her diffident tone.

'I wanted to thank you for the drive and lunch last week. I've been remiss, I should have called sooner.'

There was a pause.

'No. My fault. I should have been in touch before now. I let things pile up – family matters. But it's good to talk with you now. This was the first day of term. How was it for you?'

He listened while Isla gave him a humorous and, no doubt, edited version of her day.

She paused again.

'You mentioned getting together again – for another meal. I wondered…' Alasdair heard her take a deep breath as if steeling herself for her next words, '… would you like to come to my place for dinner – on Saturday?'

Alasdair's head jerked up. She was inviting him into the place he was sure was her sanctuary. From what he'd gleaned from their brief acquaintance, Isla Cameron didn't allow many people to broach the walls she had erected between her and the outside world. This invitation was a sign – a sign she wanted to pursue a relationship with him.

Trying not to sound too eager, Alasdair said, 'Thank you. I'd like that.' He thought for a moment then added, 'Saturday would be good.' He was sure he could negotiate with Anaïs, and surely Robbie and Fiona wouldn't mind, if he spent the day with them. How did other single parents manage to carry on a relationship, he wondered, and at what stage did the children become involved? Well, any prospect of that was a long way off.

'Lovely. I'll see you at around seven then?'

Alasdair's next call wasn't such an easy one. It was some time before he was able to reassure the branch manager that the recalcitrant employee could and should be dismissed, and to provide advice on how he could prevent the situation from happening again.

But, as he packed up to leave for the day, it was Isla's call in the forefront of his mind, and he was humming as he threw his briefcase onto the back seat of the car and drove home.

*

Carrying a bottle of wine and with an empty feeling in the pit of his stomach, Alasdair anxiously pushed back a stray lock of hair and pressed the bell to Isla's flat. He'd debated buying flowers or chocolates but decided against them, fearing she'd get the wrong idea. Now he wondered if he should have, but it was too late for doubts.

'Welcome!' Isla was smiling at him and wearing something soft and blue. He'd noticed she often wore blue – it matched her eyes.

Unsure if he was being too forward, he leant forward to give her a peck on the cheek, as he did so, inhaling a sharp scent quite different to the floral notes of Elspeth's he was accustomed to. He was glad Isla didn't immediately draw away, but neither did she attempt to prolong the contact, giving a nervous laugh as she accepted the proffered wine.

'Perfect,' she said, checking the label of the Spanish Rioja. 'I've made a lasagne. I hope it's as good as the one we had at that restaurant you took me to.'

'I'm sure anything you cook will taste delicious.'

Who is this awkward guy? Alasdair thought, trying to bring his brain into gear. Good job he had decided against the flowers and chocolate. He'd have been even more tongue-tied.

But, just as he was wondering if this whole evening was going to be a disaster, a ball of fur flung itself at his feet and began to wind around his ankles, purring loudly.

'Sooty!' Isla remonstrated. 'I'm sorry,' she said to Alasdair. 'I don't understand. He's not used to strangers and doesn't normally welcome them like this.' She bent to pick the cat up, but Alasdair beat her to it.

'He's a lovely little fellow,' he said, fondling the ears of the little creature who began to purr even more loudly at his ministrations.

This broke the ice as the pair shared anecdotes about pets in general and cats in particular.

I really should get a pet for the kids, Alasdair thought, despite part of him feeling it would be disloyal to Elspeth's memory.

By the time they sat down to eat, they had made a dent in the tray of nibbles Isla provided – a collection of raw vegetables and dips – and were part-way through their first glass of wine. Before serving the meal, Isla turned on some music, the low tones of a blues singer Alasdair knew he should recognise wafting across the room.

'You have a nice place here,' he said, helping himself to the lasagne and a serving from a large bowl of green salad, 'and this looks and smells delicious.'

'Thanks.' Ignoring the compliment about the food, Isla continued, 'I bought this place around the same time as I took up the post at Glenferrie.'

'And, prior to that?' Alasdair was interested in knowing a bit more about the background Isla seemed determined to keep secret.

'A house in Bishopbriggs. When Morag was born, I decided to do the whole suburban thing – semi-detached, back garden, neighbours.' She grimaced. 'Afterwards, everything about it reminded me of what I'd lost. I couldn't stay there.'

'I can understand that. Sometimes I'd like to move myself – the house has so many memories. But it's the children's home, and they've had enough to cope with – losing their mother.'

He could see the empathy in Isla's eyes.

Robbie and Fiona had lost a mother, and Isla had lost a child.

'And…' Alasdair hesitated, unsure how to proceed, but he had to know, '…her father?'

'Knew nothing about her.' Isla took a swig of wine. 'It was better that way. There was never anything serious between us, and he had a fiancée back in California. No doubt he'll be the head of a thriving family now.'

Alasdair didn't understand how she could have kept something like that to herself – to have given birth to a child then lost her, and to suffer all alone.

'I had friends,' she said. 'Shona has always been there for me. She may be a little flaky at times, but she's loyal.'

But Alasdair knew it wasn't the same. His heart went out to her. He wanted to say something to comfort her. But there were no words. He looked down at his half-eaten portion of lasagne.

As if she knew what he was thinking, Isla spoke again. 'I didn't want everyone's commiserations. I hate that sort of thing. I just wanted to get on with my life, to put my memories in a box – a box I only open when I'm alone.' She sat silent, as if frozen, then gave a nervous laugh. 'I don't know why I'm telling you all this. I haven't spoken about Morag – about how I felt – to anyone since.'

They finished their meal without referring to the matter again. But the thought of the bereaved mother leaving the home she'd shared with her beloved daughter, and all her friends and neighbours to take on a new role, to live in this flat away from all the reminders of her past life, struck a chord.

When they finally retired to the living room with coffee, it seemed natural to join Isla on the sofa, to put his arm around her shoulders and pull her to him in a long kiss – a kiss which she reciprocated.

Thirty-seven

Isla

Isla stood with her back to the door, and touched a finger to her lip where Alasdair had kissed her again before leaving. She felt like singing, like dancing around the room. There was a glow inside that she'd never felt before – not even with Ollie.

But how did *he* feel?

It had seemed so natural when Alasdair's arms went around her, their lips met and, for a few seconds, her world stood still. Isla wrapped her arms around herself and floated through the house, oblivious of the demands of her pet who, now that the visitor had left, wanted her attention. Her mood remained upbeat as she cleared the table and stacked the dishwasher. Deciding to pour herself the remainder of the wine, she took a fresh glass from the cupboard, then stopped midstream, one hand in the air.

What was she doing?

What was she thinking?

This was Alasdair MacLeod, a school parent, a grieving husband, a man she'd decided could be nothing more than a friend. Did she really want to complicate her life? At this moment, she decided there was nothing she wanted more. She emptied the few remaining drops of wine into the glass and tossed them down, before picking up Sooty, giving him a hug and depositing him in his cat bed for the night.

*

After a surprisingly sound night's sleep, Isla awoke and stretched lazily, remembering the thrill of being in Alasdair's arms. Despite all the obstacles, she knew she wanted him in the way she'd wanted Ollie. But, this time, it was different. She was older; her feelings were more mature. Alasdair was no twenty-year-old looking for a bit of holiday fun. She thought back to their conversation and shivered, the fluttering in her stomach reminding her of his lips on hers, his hand on her cheek, the promise of more.

'You've captivated me,' Alasdair said, brushing the hair back from her forehead. 'I never expected to feel this way again. Meeting you, spending time with you… it's brought me back to life. I was wandering around in a dream, on autopilot, dreading each day, trying to keep going for the sake of the children. Then… when we met… when I walked into your office… there you were, calm, elegant, very much in control, but with an inner sadness that met mine. Och, you must think I'm daft, talking like this, when we barely know each other. But I feel I've known you all my life, as if, for the past two years, I've just been marking time till we met. And to think you were there all the time – part of Fi's life.'

At that point, Isla had daringly reached up to stroke his face, her forefinger smoothing the lines on his forehead, tracing his eyebrows, nose, and ending at his mouth which opened to allow his tongue to delicately touch it. The resultant jolt of desire had forced her to move away, to mutter something about more coffee, and Alasdair had decided it was time to leave.

But before he did, he'd extracted a promise from her to join him again for dinner the following Saturday evening at his home. 'I can farm out the children to their grandparents,' he said. 'They often go there for the weekend. It'll give us time alone, time to…' Although Alasdair hadn't specified exactly what he meant by that, Isla had a fair idea. Next Saturday couldn't come quickly enough.

But that was a whole week away, and today she was going to see *Grease* with Daniel. Now it appeared her relationship with Alasdair was on a firmer footing, she regretted agreeing to the movie. After Alasdair, Daniel came a poor second. *Whatever had possessed her?*

Fortunately, they'd arranged to meet at the cinema. Isla planned her arrival so they'd have little time for conversation prior to the showing and intended to leave immediately afterwards. Daniel could think what he liked. She had no desire to see him again, but she'd let him down lightly.

Driving into town, she couldn't help being amused at the situation she was in. For someone who was determinedly single, who proclaimed to anyone who would listen that she had no need of a man in her life, she now had two.

'Here you are. I thought you'd had second thoughts.' Daniel greeted her with a peck on the cheek.

Isla flinched. 'Sorry. Running late. Shall we go in?'

Despite her regrets about her companion, Isla enjoyed the movie. She'd been a small child when it was released and had never managed to see it till now. The music was amazing, and she found herself lost in the story of the young lovers, even though she could never identify with the role Olivia Newton John played. Isla could never have transformed herself like that for a man. Was that what attracted her so much to Alasdair, she wondered? The fact they were so similar in their outlook on life.

They were making their way out of the cinema, Isla preparing to refuse the invitation to drinks and dinner she was sure Daniel was about to extend, when she heard a voice call out, 'Ms Cameron!'

Turning to see which of her students had spoken, and thinking not for the first time how difficult it was to get away from school and everything related to it, she saw Fiona MacLeod with a boy on crutches who must be her brother – and Alasdair. For a moment, she was unable to speak. What must he think of her? Only last night they'd been… and today, here she was being squired around by a man she'd evinced no interest in, a man she'd been at pains to avoid. She felt herself redden.

'It's Ms Cameron, Dad,' she heard Fiona say as she wheeled herself toward Isla, Alasdair and her brother following. 'Did you enjoy the movie, Miss? Wasn't the music wonderful? And the dancing? I wish I could dance like that.' But there was no sense of wistfulness in the girl's voice. It was a simple statement of fact.

'Henderson,' Alasdair said stiffly with a nod of acknowledgement to Isla.

'MacLeod.'

Isla saw Daniel's eyes move from her to Alasdair and back again. She took a deep pained breath and closed her eyes. When she opened them again, Daniel was staring at her with a strange look on his face.

'Do you two know each other?' he asked.

'Ms Cameron's my headmistress at Glenferrie,' Fiona bubbled, not giving her father time to reply.

'Isla,' Alasdair said at last.

Isla saw Fiona's eyes widen at her father's use of her first name.

'You came to see *Grease*, too,' she said weakly, then regained her composure sufficiently to reply to Fiona. 'Yes, Fiona, I loved the movie. Did you know the music before today?'

'We played a few tracks in the car on the way in,' Alasdair replied for her. 'You?'

'Yes.'

Why did Isla have the impression their conversation wasn't about the movie; that there was another agenda playing itself out between them?

Alasdair jerked as if suddenly remembering something. 'We should go. I promised the kids we'd go to McDonald's. Well…' He seemed reluctant to leave.

'Let's go, too. 'Bye, MacLeod.' Daniel took Isla by the elbow and led her away.

She didn't look back but could feel Alasdair's eyes on her as if they were boring holes in her back. As they walked off, she heard Fiona ask, 'How do you know Ms Cameron's name, Dad?'

She didn't hear his reply.

When they were completely out of earshot of the trio, Isla wrenched free of Daniel's grasp. 'Yes,' he said. 'How does MacLeod know your name? What have you been hiding from me?' His words were jocular. His tone was anything but.

Suddenly afraid without knowing why – this was the man she'd spent a few pleasant hours with in Orkney, had shared tea and scones with only a week earlier – Isla wrapped her arms around her body as if to protect herself.

Thinking quickly, Isla said in as calm a voice as she could muster, 'We've met a few times to discuss Fiona's participation in a trip to

France. He must have seen my signature on the paperwork.' She held her breath while Daniel seemed to consider how plausible that was, only letting it out when he nodded.

'Now,' he said, rubbing his hands together, 'I think drinks and dinner are called for. I've booked a table...'

'Oh!' Isla put a hand to her forehead. 'I'm sorry, Daniel. My head. I have a migraine coming on. I think it must have been the volume of the music. I won't be much company tonight. Thanks so much for the movie. I did enjoy it. But I need to go home now and lie down.'

She saw the light go out of his eyes, then it reignited. 'How about I...' he began.

'No.' Isla held up a hand. 'I need to be alone in a dark room. I'm sorry,' she repeated.

'Well, if you're sure.' Daniel seemed reluctant to let her go, but after a weird tussle in which he tried to kiss her on the cheek and she tried to shake his hand instead, they parted.

Once in her car, Isla closed her eyes and leant back. Her head was now throbbing with a real headache as she contemplated what had just happened. How could she have been so stupid as to think she could juggle two men – two men she'd regarded as friends, two men who seemed to harbour a dislike of each other that went back to their schooldays? And the confrontation with Alasdair had shown her a different side of Daniel, one of which she'd prefer to remain in ignorance. So much for his claim of being a changed man.

She shivered and determined to avoid him in future.

Thirty-eight

Alasdair

What had happened?

Alasdair gazed into space, his chicken wrap and coffee forgotten, while Robbie and Fiona tucked into their burgers and fries and sipped their milkshakes. Isla and Henderson! He'd hardly been able to believe his eyes. That slimy bastard was the last person he'd expected to see her with. He couldn't imagine how they came to be together after she'd fled from him at the charity dinner. The Isla he was coming to know was independent, a private person, very correct and sensitive. Whereas, Daniel Henderson…

Alasdair remembered numerous occasions at school when the guy had managed to implicate others in mischief of his own making, while getting off scot-free himself. At university things had become worse, with Henderson's drunken exploits serving as a cautionary tale to every fresher. Then, there was his bullying behaviour, his misogyny, his jealousy – the list went on. Surely Isla could see him for what he was? Although, he was able to turn on the charm when it suited him. Alasdair remembered Elspeth recounting how one of her friends had been fooled into dating him for a while – until he showed his true colours.

But Isla! He'd thought she was more discerning. And, after last night… He rubbed his chin.

'Something wrong, Dad? You're not eating.' Fiona's concerned voice broke into his thoughts.

'No, I'm fine.' He took a bite of his wrap to prove the point, but it tasted like sawdust. 'How are the burgers?' he asked. It wasn't fair to inflict his mood on these two.

'Great!' Robbie replied. 'Can I have another milkshake, Dad?' He slurped up the remainder of the thick liquid with a gurgle.

'I think not.'

'Aw!'

'We should get back as soon as we're finished here.' He took another bite from the wrap, before deciding he'd lost his appetite.

'I'm finished,' Fiona said, carefully folding the wrapping from her burger. 'Thanks, Dad.' She turned to her brother. 'You should thank Dad, too, Robbie. He only brought us here because *we* like it. See, he didn't even eat what he ordered for himself.'

Alasdair smiled at his daughter's flawed logic.

'Thanks, Dad,' Robbie said, grudgingly. 'Where would you have preferred to eat?'

'Probably somewhere boring like Romano's,' Fiona replied for him, demonstrating how well the girl knew him. 'Mum always said…' She hesitated.

'It's okay to speak about your mum.' Alasdair realised how rarely they did. Immediately after Elspeth's death, the pain had been too great, but now, it didn't hurt so much to hear her referred to. 'Go on, Fi. What did your mum always say?'

'She said if she had half the money you spent in Romano's, we could all go to the French Riviera.' She buttoned her lip as if revealing a secret.

'Did she indeed?' Alasdair laughed. 'I think what she meant was that I often lunched there with business associates – I even met your grandpa there for lunch once.' Alasdair remembered that meeting so well. His father-in-law had requested they meet so he could set him straight about his apparent neglect of his wife. At first, Alasdair had been annoyed at the old man's interference, but it had turned out for the best; the subsequent trip to Gleneagles had cemented their ailing marriage – too late, as he now knew to his cost.

'Ready Robbie?' Alasdair asked, seeing his son lean over to pick up his crutches. 'You're halfway there, son,' he said, referring to the eight weeks the doctors had told Robbie he'd need for his leg to heal.

Robbie's face brightened. 'I'll be right for the summer holidays,' he said, 'and Sports Day. Just wait till I get my own back on Reilly. I plan to beat him to a pulp – on the sports field, I mean, Dad,' he added, clearly seeing Alasdair's glare. 'I'm a much faster runner than he is.'

They packed up and left.

On the trip home, the conversation was all about the movie. At Fiona's urging, Robbie admitted he'd enjoyed it too, but added, 'Next time, I want to choose the movie, and it won't be anything soppy. The new Star Wars one is out next month. Can we go to that, Dad? You'll probably like it too, Fi,' he said condescendingly to his sister.

'We'll see.'

'You know what that means,' Fiona said.

'It doesn't anymore, does it, Dad?'

With a jolt, Alasdair realised how he'd changed in the past two years. When Elspeth was alive, he'd used that phrase a lot with the kids as a way of avoiding making any promises. And, as Fiona rightly pointed out, it had usually just been a way of refusing their requests.

'That's enough, you two.' For the rest of the trip home, he listened to Robbie and Fiona's friendly arguments without interrupting.

*

Once the children were in bed, Alasdair poured himself a glass of scotch – the special malt Matt had given him for Christmas – and sank into his favourite armchair – a wingback upholstered in a soft beige leather. It had belonged to his father and was beginning to show its age. He picked up the book he was reading – Michael Connolly's latest offering – planning to lose himself in the exploits of Bosch, one of his favourite detectives. But he had trouble concentrating and, after reading the same page over and over several times, he let the book drop to his lap.

Isla! If he closed his eyes, he could picture her, feel her soft skin, her lips on his. It had felt so right, as if they were meant to be together. He could almost hear Elspeth's voice telling him she approved, that she didn't want him to spend the rest of his life alone, that the children needed a mother, that Isla was the woman she'd have chosen for him.

Then he saw her with Daniel Henderson. How had she looked? He strove to remember. Had they been holding hands? Had his arm been around her? He drained his glass and, his book falling to the floor, rose to pour another. He had just unscrewed the top to the bottle when the phone rang. Damn! Who could it be at this time? He checked his watch. It was nine o'clock on a Sunday evening. It could only be bad news. He saw his sister-in-law's number.

'Kirsty! What's wrong? Is it Dad? Bel? Duncan? Not wee Jamie?'

He heard a chuckle.

'Keep your hair on, Alasdair. Why are you expecting bad news? Everyone's fine, as far as I know. Unless you know something I don't. But Dad and Bel were fine when we left, not long after you did. Jamie's fast asleep in bed, and Duncan is dozing in front of the television. A typical Sunday night in this house. That's not why I'm calling.'

Alasdair was conscious of breathing a sigh of relief. 'Why, then?'

'Now, you're probably going to tell me to mind my own business.'

That'll be a first, he thought.

'But it's been two years now...' she paused then rushed on, '...you know I loved Elspeth too, but... don't you think it's time? I mean, Robbie and Fi... they need a woman around. I know you have Anaïs, and there'll be another like her in a year's time, but it's not the same as... And you're a man too... with needs.'

Hell, she certainly didn't beat about the bush. Even from Kirsty this was going too far.

'Are you still there?'

'I'm listening,' he said tersely, wishing he'd already poured that second scotch, tempted to slam down the phone, and hoping she'd come to the point. Which of her many friends did she have in mind for her widower of a brother-in-law?

'I know I'm interfering, and have no right to make this suggestion but...'

You'll do it anyway.

'I was thinking...'

I just bet you were.

'I recently – well back before Christmas – met up with an old school friend. You know her... Isla Cameron. Oh, you probably only know her as Ms Cameron, headmistress at Fiona's school – at Glenferrie Academy.'

'And?'

'And I thought… maybe… I could invite you both to dinner,' she finished in a rush.

Alasdair almost laughed. Here he was trying to work out whether Isla was involved with his old schoolmate, while his interfering sister-in-law was trying to set her up with him.

When he didn't reply immediately, she continued, 'I know you may think it's too soon, and I know how you must miss Elspeth, but I think Isla's lonely, too…'

Lonely? If she only knew.

'Anyway – think about it.' Her voice had lost its earlier enthusiasm, no doubt at his lack of response.

'Good night, Kirsty.'

Alasdair finished pouring the dram he'd started before Kirsty's call. He took it back to his chair, picked up his book and laid it on the side table. He leant forward, elbows on his knees, glass cradled in both hands, and stared into the flickering coals.

Thirty-nine

Isla

The week passed slowly. Each day, Isla expected a text or call from Alasdair to cancel the dinner arranged for Saturday, but none came. Daniel, on the other hand, was nothing if not persistent. Despite her thanking him, but saying she didn't think it fair to see him again, his constant calls and texts had forced her to keep her phone on silent and to instruct Jean that she wasn't available to take any calls from him.

As one day followed another with no form of communication, Isla began to believe Alasdair still wanted to see her. But what if he assumed she was no longer interested in seeing him again?

Finally, on Friday, she decided to take matters into her own hands. There was no sense in her wondering what he was thinking, in trying to out-guess him. It was mid-morning. He'd be at work. With a bit of luck, he'd be in a meeting and she could leave a message. She put the phone down again, ran a jerky hand through her hair and cleared her throat. Maybe she should send a text instead?

No. Taking a deep breath, Isla pressed the numbers she already knew by heart.

'MacLeod.'

Isla's throat constricted at the sound of his voice. Prepared to leave a message, for a moment she was lost for words. 'It's Isla,' she said, hearing voices in the background. So, he wasn't alone. 'Tomorrow? Are we… do you still…?'

Instead of a reply, she heard him speak to someone else, telling them he'd only be a moment, then he spoke into the phone again, 'Sorry, I can't talk now. Tomorrow. Yes. I think we said seven.' He hung up.

Isla sat staring at the phone, a sudden coldness in her gut. Alasdair's voice had been devoid of emotion. Now she wished she hadn't called. But it established he was still expecting her to dinner. And he'd clearly had people with him, she reasoned. But she was worried nonetheless, sure she'd have some explaining to do if they were to regain their former closeness; a closeness she'd been hesitant to allow and had valued.

Damn men! She knew she'd been better off without them. She'd just let her guard down a fraction and look where it had led her – into a mire of suspicion and guilt. She was sure from Alasdair's tone that he held suspicions about her and Daniel. But it was insignificant when she considered the guilt she experienced every time she pictured the scene at the cinema – Alasdair's stunned face, and Daniel's smug expression.

*

Saturday proved to be a clear day, though the temperature was still cool enough to warrant a warm jacket, as she prepared to meet Shona in town for afternoon tea. She hadn't seen her friend since the movie with Daniel and had some questions for her about him. His persistence was verging on annoying, and she thought she'd seen his car loitering outside the school grounds on more than one occasion. She felt she was being stalked, and it was most uncomfortable, if not downright scary.

Walking up Buchanan Street to the Willow Tea Rooms, Isla rehearsed exactly what she was going to tell Shona. She loved these Tea Rooms inspired by the works of the famous Glasgow architect, designer and artist, Charles Rennie Mackintosh, and modelled on the Kate Cranston Tea Rooms from the early 1900's. A visit here was like stepping back in time.

So far, she'd kept her friendship with Alasdair MacLeod secret, but maybe now was the time to come clean. She'd got herself into a pickle and desperately needed some advice – even if it came from Shona who wasn't the world's best source of good advice when it came to men.

'You made it.' Shona rose from a seat at a corner table and gave Isla a hug. Then she held her at arm's length. 'What's up? You look rough. I think a Hendricks G&Tea for two is called for.'

Isla sat down. 'I don't think…' she began, then thought better of it. She'd barely eaten all day and the tea room's ribbon sandwiches with a glass of gin sounded exactly the sort of pick-me-up that would see her right till dinner with Alasdair. She'd always wondered what sort of women partook in the much-advertised mid-afternoon tipple. Now she knew.

Once they'd placed their orders and taken their first sip of gin, Shona leant forward and fixed Isla with a steady gaze. 'Now, what's up? You can tell your Auntie Shona.'

Isla decided to get straight to the point. 'Oh, Shona. I've got myself into such a mess. I'm not like you. I'm not used to dealing with the vagaries of the male of the species.'

Shona's eyebrows raised. Her eyes widened. 'Do tell!'

'First of all, how well do you know Daniel Henderson?'

'Daniel? Is he the cause of your angst? Not well, really. He's a pal of Hugh's. I think I told you that. Not too sure how well he knows him either, to be honest. He brought him along to the charity do and invited him to Arran but he didn't turn up. Oh, you know that too.' She winked.

Isla cringed.

'What's he done that's so bad?'

'Nothing really. It's just…' Isla took a deep breath and described the encounter in the cinema, the subsequent calls and texts and her suspected sightings of him.

But it was the mention of Alasdair MacLeod that caught Shona's attention.

'Well, you're a dark horse, Isla Cameron! What happened to the *I prefer to stay single, I don't need a man in my life?*'

'Someone told me I need to get out more.'

'Hmm. So, tell me about this Alasdair MacLeod.'

But Isla felt she'd said enough. She was now regretting confiding in her friend. 'I just wanted your advice,' she said, 'but I can see I was wrong.'

'No! Steady on. Let's backtrack. Do you really think Daniel is stalking you? That's weird.'

Isla thought it was weird too. That's why she was asking Shona about it. 'I'm not sure,' she said slowly. 'I just wanted to know if you – or Hugh – had heard anything; if he'd done anything like that before. Or if I was imagining things,' she said, giving a wry laugh.

Shona thought for a moment. 'I do seem to recall Hugh saying something about it being a good job he'd come back up here as he'd been getting a bit obsessed with a woman he knew in Oxford. I didn't think anything of it at the time. Do you think...?'

Isla shivered.

'Do you want me to say something to Hugh?'

'No!' Isla had the impression that would make matters worse. 'I guess I'll just need to be careful.'

'Does he know where you live?'

'I don't know, but it wouldn't be hard for him to find out.' She shuddered at the idea he might lie in wait for her near her home.

'Well, take care. And if there's anything I can do...'

'Thanks.'

'And you're seeing this Alasdair guy again when?'

'Tonight.' Isla checked her watch. 'And I really should be going.'

As they stood to leave, Shona touched Isla on the shoulder. 'I'm sorry I got you into this. If I'd known...'

Isla shrugged off the sympathetic touch. 'Not your fault. I could easily have met him in Orkney anyway.' But a tiny part of her questioned if the meeting there *had* been by chance, or if Shona or Hugh had inadvertently let slip that Isla would be there alone. She recalled the strange feeling she'd had when they met supposedly by chance in the park too, and shivered again. What if this was all a weird game he was playing with her? Isla shook her head to dismiss the wild fancies. She was letting her imagination run away from her. Maybe he was following her now, but the rest couldn't be true – could it?

*

Isla was still worrying about Daniel as she prepared to go to dinner with Alasdair. Wearing a new suede jacket over navy slacks and a grey cowl-necked jumper, she glanced carefully around before stepping into her car. Giving a sigh of relief when the only car in sight belonged to a close neighbour, she turned on the engine and drove away.

By the time she reached Alasdair's home, *he* was the one filling her thoughts, as she speculated about his reaction to seeing her and Daniel together. At least he hadn't cancelled dinner.

As she'd expected, the house was a large two-story, double-fronted affair, its oriel windows facing a well-maintained front yard and a long driveway – almost an exact replica of Kirsty's, and a far cry from her own tiny flat or even the house she'd shared with Morag. This evening, there was no peck on the cheek as Alasdair helped Isla off with her jacket and led her into a comfortable living room, where two leather armchairs and a sofa flanked a wide fireplace where a fire threw out a warm glow.

'This is lovely,' she said, hesitating in the doorway. Her eyes took in the wall of bookcases, a sideboard covered with family photographs, and a television in the corner. She was tempted to walk over, to pick up one or more of the photographs, to see what Alasdair's wife looked like.

'A drink?'

'What? Yes, thanks.'

'Take a seat.'

So it was back to stilted conversation?

Isla sat on the edge of a deep beige leather sofa, her fingers stroking the soft smooth surface, while Alasdair poured them both a scotch.

Her first sip hit the back of her throat, almost making her choke.

'Too strong for you?'

'No, just unexpected.'

'It was a Christmas gift from Elspeth's dad. I keep it for special occasions.'

So, he considered this a special occasion? What about Daniel? Isla decided not to mention him till Alasdair did.

He joined her, sitting in one of the armchairs, and cradled the glass made of Edinburgh crystal that held his drink.

We're like an old married couple, Isla thought. *We have nothing to say to each other, yet his company is strangely comforting – or maybe it's the whisky?*

'Have you heard from Kirsty?' Alasdair asked, breaking the silence.

Isla was astonished. Kirsty? What did she have to do with them?

'Not since I was at her book club a couple of weeks back. I met your mother-in-law there too. Nice lady. We discussed *Bloody Scotland*.' Isla knew she was babbling – anything to delay the inevitable, the questions about her and Daniel Henderson. 'Why do you ask?'

'She hasn't asked you to dinner to meet me?'

'To meet you? What do you mean?'

'She rang me the other day. Seems she has this half-baked notion we'd make a good couple, that I need a woman in my life, and you're the one she's earmarked for my attention.'

Isla didn't know whether to laugh or cry. A week ago – when they'd dined in her flat – she'd have laughed. They'd both have laughed. But now it was difficult to judge Alasdair's mood. 'Well, I haven't heard. Maybe she's thought better of it.'

'That wouldn't be like my sister-in-law. She doesn't give up easily.'

'No.' Isla remembered Kirsty's projects of old. She was like a dog with a bone once she got an idea in her head. 'You think I should be expecting a call?'

'You can count on it.'

'And should I accept?'

'Up to you.' Alasdair swilled the liquid in his glass and downed it in one. 'Another?'

'No thanks.' She held up her still half-full glass, then, taking a deep breath decided it was up to her to broach the elephant in the room. 'Last Sunday,' she said, her fingers circling the edge of her glass, 'I know it looked as if... But it was a one-off. I'm not... Daniel Henderson and I aren't...'

Isla saw Alasdair's face darken. Hell, was she making it worse?

'I didn't realise you two had met again – after the charity dinner.'

Isla dropped her eyes to gaze into her drink. 'We bumped into each other in Orkney, then again here in Glasgow, apparently by chance.' She felt dizzy and her eyes moistened as all her doubts returned. 'Look, Alasdair, I don't even like the man. I don't know why I agreed to go to see *Grease* with him. Oh, he laid on the charm, but...'

'I don't know why you're telling me all this,' Alasdair said stiffly, rising to pour himself another drink. 'Who you see or don't see is none of my business.' He sat down again, nursing his glass.

Why did she come? She should just leave now.

Isla blinked away the tears

Then Alasdair leant back, and drew a hand through his hair. 'Oh, Isla. I didn't mean that the way it sounded. I'm sorry. What I mean is that I have no claim on you. You can see whoever you like. But I *would* like to be able to have a say in it. I would like…'

His eyes met hers with a pleading look.

Did he mean?

'I'm glad Henderson means nothing to you. I hope…'

'I think he's stalking me.' The words were out before Isla could stop them.

Forty

Alasdair

Alasdair put down his glass and, moving towards Isla, took the glass from her hand and placed it carefully on a side table. He then sat next to her on the sofa, took her in his arms, and buried his mouth in her hair.

It was a long time since he'd held a woman like this. It felt right. Despite the fact he knew she was a strong, independent woman, here in his arms, Isla seemed fragile – like a little bird, as if it wouldn't take much for her to break into small pieces. He inhaled her scent – the sharp, spicy one he remembered. He wanted to crush her to him, to smother her with kisses, to...

Isla moaned softly and moved in his arms.

Alasdair loosened his grip. He tucked a stray strand of hair behind her ear. 'Better now?' he murmured, the tips of two fingers on the soft skin of her cheek.

She sat up. 'I think so. I'm sorry to give way like that. I don't know what came over me.'

'It was that bastard, Henderson.'

'Yes.'

Still holding her lightly, Alasdair asked, 'Is he really stalking you?'

Isla moved out of his grasp and picked up her drink again, taking a long swallow. 'I'm not really sure; it's a feeling I have. A creepy feeling.'

'Go with your gut, I always say. What can I do to help?'

'You're doing enough. Being here with you makes me feel safe.'

At her words, Alasdair felt his confidence grow. Did he really have a chance with this woman? At this moment he knew he wanted her, but there was a part of him – a tiny part – that felt he was being disloyal to Elspeth's memory.

But would Elspeth really want him to be alone for the rest of his life? What would he have wanted for her if he'd been the one to go first?

As if guessing what he was thinking, Isla said, 'I'm sorry. I know you're still grieving for your wife. Did I hear dinner mentioned?'

Glad of the change of subject, Alasdair pulled himself together and slid across the sofa to leave a gap between them. 'Dinner. Yes. I hope you like roast beef. It's about the only thing I can cook,' he said ruefully. 'It should be ready about now.'

'My favourite,' she said with a smile, but giving him the impression she'd have said that whatever was on the menu.

As they made their way to the dining room Alasdair tried to work out how to deal with the feelings he was beginning to have for Isla Cameron. At first, he'd been merely consumed with curiosity, surprised at the way she piqued his interest. But now, there was a stronger attraction, much stronger. And it wasn't merely physical, although his emotions while she was in his arms had a strong carnal aspect. She was unlike any other woman he'd ever met – Elspeth included, though he suspected his late wife would have liked her; would have admired her strength and independence. The two could have been friends.

'Alasdair?'

The woman who was the focus of his thoughts was looking at him strangely.

'Sorry. I was lost in thought. Take a seat. I'll fetch our meal.'

'Can I help?'

'No, not at all. You're my guest, I won't be long.'

Alasdair strode purposefully into the kitchen, but once there he stood in the middle of the room trying to work out what to do first. Perhaps they should have eaten here, where the family always took their meals. It would have been more comfortable than the formal dining room. But the table was still strewn with many of the implements he'd used to cook their meal, the sink piled with dirty dishes, and the smell of… He rushed to open the oven just in time. The meat was starting to char around the edges. He exhaled loudly. While he'd been reflecting on the appropriateness of his feelings for Isla, their dinner had almost burnt.

Alasdair piled the serving dishes and plates on the tea-trolley that, since Elspeth's death, had been gathering dust beside the back door, a repository for old magazines and newspapers. Taking one last look around the room to ensure he hadn't forgotten anything, Alasdair proudly wheeled it into the dining room.

Instead of sitting at the table where he'd left her, Isla was standing by the sideboard holding a photo in a silver frame. At the sound of Alasdair's arrival, she turned. 'She was pretty,' she said.

Parking the trolley beside the table, Alasdair joined her to examine the photo. It was an old one, taken by a local photographer on a holiday in Ayr when the children were little – before the accident. Elspeth was wearing a flowery summer dress which was blowing in the wind. He could remember the day as if it was yesterday – the stiff breeze coming off the water, the ice creams they'd eaten afterwards, even the shabby boarding house where they'd laughed at the peculiarities of the other residents.

'Yes, she was.' He sighed, taking it from her and replacing it on the cabinet, before setting two plates on the table and placing the platters of roast meat and vegetables in the middle. 'You'll have wine?' He held up a bottle of prosecco. 'It may not be the most appropriate to accompany the roast, but I thought it would go down well.'

'Thanks.'

Isla joined him at the table and began to help herself to food. 'This looks and smells delicious.'

'I just caught it in time,' he admitted with a grin, his earlier reservations forgotten in the everyday business of pouring wine and filling his plate. 'Just as well we…' He cleared his throat.

He saw Isla's porcelain complexion redden slightly. So, she wasn't unmoved by what had occurred on the sofa. He looked over at the photo she'd been studying, of the younger Elspeth, before her guilt, before her illness, and it was as if she was sending him a message – telling him it was all right to want another woman in his life; that she approved of his choice.

Over dinner, Alasdair and Isla discovered a common love for

Glasgow's history and spent the meal discussing the old architecture and the legacy of the tobacco lords which had formed much of the city. After their meal, which ended with a dish of Nardini's famous ice cream topped with frozen berries and meringue, and which Isla declared to be delicious, they retreated to the lounge room with coffee, where they seemed to talk about everything and anything. She made him laugh with tales about school life. He made her laugh with his own memories of his schooldays and the antics of Fiona and Robbie.

The evening raced on and it was late when Isla rose to leave. At the door she paused, and it seemed natural for Alasdair to take her in his arms again. This time he didn't hesitate, but pressed his lips to hers, overcome by the sense that this was what both of them had been waiting for. And when she kissed him back, one hand in his hair, he found himself almost asking her to stay.

'When can I see you again,' he whispered, breathing in her now familiar fragrance.

Forty-one

Isla

'Dinner? How lovely!' Isla tried to hide the amusement in her voice as Kirsty chatted on, apologising that she hadn't been in touch sooner, saying how glad she was Isla had joined the book club, and telling her how much she wanted to introduce her to 'some of my special people'.

The past two weeks had been a whirlwind, taking Isla's breath away. Since dinner with Alasdair, she'd been on cloud nine – the kiss at his door had undone all her good intentions and forced her to accept that this man meant something to her, that, with him, she wanted more than just friendship.

It was an odd feeling – to reverse everything she'd believed about herself for so long and to acknowledge that maybe she'd be willing to allow a man – this man – into her life.

They'd already met again several times – twice for lunch, once for drinks and once for another dinner at her flat. But, so far, kissing was as far as they'd ventured. They'd decided to take things slowly. They weren't teenagers. He'd been married – had been widowed only two years earlier – and had two children to consider, and Isla... She had to completely reorganise her thinking. She was so accustomed to being single, to making every decision for herself, it came as a shock to find Alasdair already issuing suggestions – or at least strong recommendations – as to her behaviour.

This business with Kirsty was an example. He'd warned her it was on the cards and suggested they keep their relationship – if that's what it was – secret for the moment. She had no problem with that. Where she did differ was his proposal she accept Kirsty's invitation and see where it led.

Since he'd already told his sister-in-law what he thought of her match-making, Isla didn't see how this could work. But she agreed to go along with it, despite feeling guilty at deceiving her old friend.

As a result she found herself now agreeing to turn up at Kirsty's on the following Friday at seven.

*

'And I think you know Alasdair,' Kirsty said.

Isla was standing by the fireplace talking with Will and Simone Jackson who were close neighbours of Kirsty and Duncan. She took a sip of the Aperol Spritzer she'd been handed on arriving and nodded as Alasdair entered the room with a smile of recognition in her direction. He appeared to know the other couple, who welcomed him into the group.

Simone, who had been engaged in a friendly debate on the benefits of single-sex schools with Isla, pointed her glass in his direction.

'*Your* daughter goes to Glenferrie, Alasdair. Why did you eschew your local school for an all-girls college?'

Alasdair appeared taken aback. 'I don't know that I did. I think it was Kirsty's idea. She thought Fi would get more individualised attention, that it would suit her better. And I'm pleased to say it has. She loves it there and is off on a trip to France with the school in a month or so. I can't see that happening with the local high school. Not that they wouldn't organise the trip – I have every respect for our public schools – but they haven't the resources to cater for special needs in the same way as a school like Glenferrie Academy. Ms Cameron – Isla – has been wonderful in making sure Fi feels included in all the school activities.'

'Yes, but...' Simone began, only to be interrupted by Kirsty calling them to the dinner table.

Finding herself seated next to Alasdair, Isla felt his knee nudge hers under the table and wished she hadn't agreed to this subterfuge. She felt like a teenager again, pretending to the grown-ups the boy she was dating was just someone she'd met a couple of times.

She looked up to the end of the table where Kirsty had a smug look on her face. Her project was about to come to fruition. It would have been unkind to disabuse her of that pleasure, but Isla felt guilty. She met Alasdair's eyes. They were twinkling. He was enjoying this, whereas she just felt uncomfortable.

'So, are you a stalwart of the parent body?' Will asked Alasdair, when they'd finished the dish of delicious poached salmon and were waiting for dessert to be served. 'Must be better dealing with a headmistress like Isla, here, than old Craigie at our kids' school.'

Isla blushed and hoped no one noticed the wink Alasdair gave her before replying, 'Don't have the time, Will. With work, and two kids to bring up…' He left out the *single dad* bit for Will to remember, and the other man winced.

'But you have help?' he asked.

'An *au pair.*'

This led to a discussion on the difficulty of finding good help, and the moment was forgotten by everyone except Isla who found herself reverting to the sensation of being the odd one out in a conversation to which she couldn't contribute. She remembered why she avoided evenings such as this. They were designed for married couples, people with children, people who had things in common, things that brought home how much she'd lost when Morag died.

After dinner, they all moved back into the lounge room for coffee and liqueurs. Although Isla made sure she sat well away from Alasdair, she felt his eyes on her with an amused expression, making it difficult for her to carry on a conversation. It was no surprise to her when Kirsty drew her aside. 'What do you think of my brother-in-law?' she asked in a quiet voice. She needn't have bothered lowering her voice as the chatter from the other side of the room was so loud, there was no chance of her being overheard.

'He seems very nice,' Isla replied, playing the role she'd been given.

'I know you two have met before – at the school – but I wanted you to see each other in a more social situation. It's different. I wanted him to see you as a woman, not just Fi's headmistress.'

Without thinking, Isla automatically gave her standard response. 'I'm not looking for a man, Kirsty. I'm perfectly happy being single,' adding, with a glare across in the direction of Alasdair, who appeared to be watching this encounter with interest, 'and I'm sure your brother-in-law is, too.'

To what Isla was sure was Kirsty's delight, Alasdair helped Isla into her coat and, in the ensuing hubbub of goodbyes and promises to get together again soon, he hustled her out the door into the chill of the evening before she could resist.

'Now look what you've done,' she said, in mock reproach. 'Kirsty is no doubt right now congratulating herself on the success of her ploy to get us together.'

'Well, it won't do any harm to let her take the blame,' he said, throwing an arm around Isla's shoulders. 'Where are you parked?'

'What do you mean?' She twisted her neck to look up at him, trying to judge from his expression if he was joking. She still had so much to learn about him, but had already discovered a wicked sense of humour beneath the formal and somewhat forbidding persona he showed the world. 'I'm here.' She indicated her car parked by the kerb.

'Yes, the red one. I knew when I saw that car, there was more to Isla Cameron than first appeared,' he said, his words eerily echoing *her* thoughts about *him*. 'And Kirsty – she loves to make things happen. She'd be devastated to think we'd managed to get together all by ourselves.'

'But blame?'

Alasdair pulled on one ear. 'I don't think every member of the family will be as eager as my dear sister-in-law to see me in a new relationship.' He hesitated for a moment. 'Can I follow you home? We can't let the evening end here. Kirsty would never forgive us.'

Isla laughed, slid into her car and set off, noting his BMW sitting a few cars behind her almost all the way.

When she drew into the kerb at Kelvin Drive, the road was almost deserted apart from one car – a car she didn't recognise. Alasdair's car hadn't arrived, and she was at the top of the steps, key in hand, when she sensed someone behind her. Turning quickly, expecting it to be him, her words of welcome died on her lips as she saw, not Alasdair, but Daniel Henderson staring down at her.

'You're a hard one to pin down,' he said. 'It looks as if you're trying to avoid me. You're not, are you?' His eyes glazed over, and Isla felt the hair on the nape of her neck lift.

'What are you doing here, Daniel?' she managed to say, her voice shaking.

'I just wanted to see you, Isla,' he said, his voice reverting to the smooth tone she remembered. 'You didn't answer my calls or texts. I want to know why.' He moved closer. Isla gasped, the key slipping from her fingers.

He bent to pick it up. 'Now, if you just invite me in, we can pick up where we...' He broke off as a hand appeared on his shoulder pulling him away from Isla.

'What do you think you're doing, Henderson? I think the lady has already told you she didn't want to see you again. There's a name for what you're doing and it's not a nice one. You're breaking the law, pal. Are you going to go quietly, or am I going to give you the hiding you deserve before I call the police?'

Isla gasped again – this time in relief. Alasdair had arrived just in time.

'You go inside. I'll deal with this maggot,' he said, forcing Daniel Henderson down the steps to the pavement.

For once, Isla was glad to do as she was told. She went into her flat and stood trembling in the hall till she heard footsteps. She peered through the peephole, relieved to see Alasdair standing there.

She opened the door and he took her in his arms. She was still shaking.

'It's okay now. He won't bother you again. Seems you were right about his stalking you. I'm glad I invited myself along.'

'I'm glad too,' she said, 'but what kept you? I thought you were closer.'

'That last traffic light. When I think what might have happened if I hadn't arrived...'

'Oh, I'm sure I'd have been fine,' Isla said confidently. But she knew it wasn't true. She'd been afraid. She was still trembling. Alasdair pulled her close, kissed her hair. The reality was he'd arrived in the nick of time, like a knight on a white horse charging in to save his damsel in distress. 'Thank you,' she said.

Forty-two

Bel

'Don't you see a difference in Alasdair?' Kirsty whispered as the two were clearing up after Sunday lunch.

'A difference?' Bel thought for a moment, the image of Alasdair smiling across at Robbie's antics during dinner in her mind's eye. 'Maybe. At least he seems to have sloughed off the depression that's been dogging him. I told Matt it wouldn't last. Maybe he did take his advice to see someone. I know Matt suggested he go to his GP and he gave him the name of a therapist.'

'I don't think it's a therapist who's made the difference.' Kirsty sounded smug.

'What have you been up to?'

'Remember I said what he needed was...'

'You didn't?'

'I just helped him along,' Kirsty said, grinning. 'He and Isla had already met each other. But you know Alasdair – Mr Straight and Narrow. He'd never have thought of getting to know her outside school on his own. In his mind she'd always be Fi's headmistress.'

'What did you do?' Bel folded her arms and leant back against the sink.

'We had a dinner party and invited both of them – along with some other people. And they left together.'

Bel sighed with relief. It didn't sound too bad. 'That doesn't mean anything,' she said.

'Oh, but I think it does.'

'She would be good for him, I suppose,' Bel said. 'But I think it's too soon. Not for him, maybe, but for Matt.'

'It's not Matt who has two motherless children to bring up, who goes home every night to an empty bed.'

'Kirsty!'

'I'm just saying. And I wouldn't be a good friend to him – or Elspeth...' she added with a tear in her eye, '...if I didn't try to do something about it.'

'I'm sorry I never got to know Elspeth.'

'Yes.' Kirsty stopped wiping a crystal glass and stared into space for a moment. 'She was coming around to accepting you when she died. It was a rotten shame!' She dashed away the tear. 'But life goes on and...'

'I know – Isla Cameron is on your radar.'

'And yours, I think.' Kirsty gave Bel a sly glance.

'But not Matt's. And if he ever finds out that you've been plotting this...' Bel drew a finger across her throat.

Kirsty only laughed.

'Are we done here?' she asked.

'I think so.' Bel looked around the now immaculate kitchen. 'We should join the others, they'll be wondering what we're doing taking so long.'

'Och, they'll just assume we've been gossiping.'

'Well, not a word,' Bel cautioned, worried at the gleeful look on Kirsty's face.

'Spoilsport.'

Bel had to be content with that, but wasn't entirely satisfied as they joined the rest of the family in the courtyard, which was catching the last of the sun.

'We're just talking about taking a walk,' Matt said, when the two women strolled through the French window. 'Are you up for a hike across the muir?'

'I think I'd like a breather,' Bel said, 'but don't let that stop the rest of you.'

'I'm up for it,' Kirsty announced. 'Kids?'

'Yes please,' Fiona and Jamie said together, Robbie adding, 'Not me. But, just wait. I'll be rid of these things by next week, then I'll give you a run for your money, Jamie.'

Jamie just grinned.

'Alasdair?' It was Kirsty again.

'I think I'm with Bel today. If you don't mind watching out for Fi.'

Bel smiled inwardly at the disappointment on Kirsty's face. So, she *had* intended to say something? So much for keeping her mouth shut.

Once the others had gone, after much kerfuffle with coats, and the dogs getting under everyone's feet, Robbie disappeared into the study to use Matt's computer, and Bel and Alasdair settled down with the Sunday papers.

But it wasn't long before Alasdair closed his paper and folded it. 'Bel, I'd like some advice,' he said.

'Yes?' Bel dropped her own paper into her lap and removed her glasses, unsure what advice she could offer.

'It's difficult... I... I'm seeing someone.'

Could Kirsty be right, or was he referring to a therapist?

'Someone as in a woman?'

'I'm worried it's too soon, that people might think... I've not forgotten Elspeth. I'll never do that.'

'I'm sure no one would think you have,' Bel said, aware he needed reassurance, then she found herself repeating Kirsty's words, 'but life must go on. You have two children who need a mother, and I'm sure you'd benefit from a companion,' she said, unwilling and unable to put it in exactly Kirsty's terms.

But she wasn't sure Alasdair even heard her.

'I wasn't looking for anyone. It just happened. You've met her. It's Isla Cameron – Fi's headmistress.'

'She's a lovely lady.'

'Yes, she is.'

Then Bel remembered he wanted her advice. 'What do you want me to tell you?'

Alasdair ran a hand through his hair. 'I wanted to ask you... You've been there – you and Matt. How did...? Oh, hell, I don't know if it's the right thing.'

The poor man!

'For you – or the children?'

'For all of us – and for Isla. She's had her troubles, too.'

Bel recalled what Kirsty had told her about Isla and nodded.

Alasdair went on, 'Kirsty's involved too. She tried to set us up at a dinner party.' He gave a wry grin. 'If only she knew – she was too late. We were already seeing each other.'

Bel almost laughed out loud. So, Kirsty had been outmanoeuvred. She wouldn't like that. But Bel was glad the pair had found each other without any outside interference.

Then an awful thought struck her. 'You're not expecting me to tell Matt, are you?' she asked with a heavy heart.

Alasdair looked anxious.

That was exactly what he was hoping for!

'I'll see what I can do,' she said cautiously, 'but don't get your hopes up. I don't think he's going to welcome her with open arms.' *And that's putting it mildly.*

When the others returned, laughing and out of breath, the dogs running in and jumping up on Bel, she and Alasdair were again engrossed in the papers.

'Have you and Nana Bel been reading all this time, Dad?' Fiona asked, wheeling herself alongside her father and pulling away his paper. 'Where's Robbie? He missed seeing an eagle. I bet he's playing computer games.' Without waiting for a reply, she disappeared in the direction of Matt's study.

'She knows her brother too well,' Alasdair said, folding his paper again and laying it down on the coffee table. 'We should be heading off. Thanks again Dad and Bel. These Sunday dinners are great – they're the highlight of the kids' week.'

'Not yours?' Kirsty asked with a raised eyebrow.

Bel glared at her, and Kirsty lowered her eyes.

'We should be going too, Duncan,' she said to her husband. 'Have you got everything you brought with you, Jamie?' she asked her son, as if to cover up her ill-advised remark.

*

Matt threw an arm around Bel's shoulders, and the two cars drove off. 'It's lovely to see them each week, but I'm glad to be on our own again,' he said, hugging her to him.

'Me too,' Bel replied. When she'd travelled back to Scotland to be with Matt, she'd known she would be inheriting an entire family, but the reality of it was more than she'd anticipated. She loved her new collection of step-relatives, especially the younger ones, but was happiest when she and Matt were alone.

'Coffee?' she asked, when the door was closed behind them, and the dogs, realising the family had gone, had settled down by the fire for a nap.

'Sounds good. I'll just check what Robbie's been up to on the computer and I'll be with you.' He disappeared into the study, only reappearing at Bel's announcement that coffee was ready.

'Now,' Matt said, when they were settled with coffee and the last of the stem ginger biscuits which were favourites with the grandchildren, and the dogs had moved from their warm spots to lie at their feet, 'What did Alasdair want to speak with you about?'

Bel gasped. *How did he know?*

'What do you mean?' she asked, playing for time.

'It's not like him to forego a walk, not on a lovely day like this. He had to be up to something. So, was he?'

Bel hesitated. She was afraid what Matt's reaction would be. But she couldn't keep it hidden from him. 'He wanted to ask my advice – to tell me he's met someone.'

Matt laid down his cup and exhaled loudly. 'A woman. I might have guessed it would be that. Well, he can't expect my blessing. How can he forget Elspeth in such a short time?'

'I'm sure he'll never do that. In fact, he said...'

'I don't care what he said. The man's an ass!'

Bel thought he was going to storm off, but he only picked up his cup and drained it, then sat gazing into space. As if sensing his master's mood, Hamish put one paw on his leg. Matt ruffled the dog's head, but said, 'Not now, Hamish.' The dog dropped back down to the floor.

'And I suppose you encouraged him?'

'No. I don't think I did.' Bel surreptitiously crossed her fingers. 'He thought I'd understand, since you and I...' She didn't finish the sentence as she saw Matt's pinched expression.

'That was different.'

Although aware she was in danger of treading on dangerous ground, Bel replied, 'Not so different. You'd been widowed for five years when we met. Alasdair has been alone for two. He's younger than you were and has two teenagers to bring up.'

Matt was silent.

What was he thinking?

Bel tried again. 'Elspeth was against our relationship. Remember how you felt? Do you want Alasdair to go through that, too?'

Still no response. *Had she gone too far by mentioning Elspeth?*

Matt rose. 'I'll be in the study.'

Bel bit her lip as she watched him go. She loved Matt dearly, but sometimes she just wanted to shake him. Alasdair had suffered greatly when Elspeth died. Matt knew that. Was it too much to expect him to accept his son-in-law wanted to move on with his life – that what had worked for him might also be a blessing for Alasdair? Sadly, Bel gathered their empty cups and carried them into the kitchen, before filling the dogs' bowls and walking outside in an effort to remind herself why she was here.

*

'I'm sorry.'

Bel turned over in the bed to face Matt, his eyes full of contrition. They hadn't talked much the previous evening. He'd retired to his study again immediately after dinner, and she'd fallen asleep before he came to bed.

'I overreacted. You were right.' He took Bel in his arms and she burrowed into his familiar body. 'It was a shock. I suppose I knew the day would come when he wouldn't want to be alone forever. But... not yet. I hope he doesn't expect us to meet her.'

Bel wavered, but knew he'd soon find out. Now that Kirsty was on the case, Isla's identity wouldn't be secret for long. 'You already have... It's Isla Cameron.'

'Isla...? You mean the headmistress at Glenferrie Academy? Fi's headmistress?'

'The same.'

'But that's…' He was silent as he digested this piece of news.

'She's a nice lady. She'll be good for him – and for the grandchildren.'

'Do they know?'

'I don't think so.'

'How do you know her?'

'I met her when you did, and…' Bel paused, but knew it would come out sometime, '…she was at the last meeting of our book club.'

'Kirsty's book club? I knew that interfering woman had a hand in it.'

'I don't believe she had.' *Though not without trying.*

'Hmm.'

Bel could tell he didn't believe her. Then she remembered – the next book club meeting was to be held here the following week. She could tell from Matt's expression the same thought crossed his mind – it was weird how in sync they were.

'Well, I'm glad I won't be here next Saturday,' he said, before pulling her towards him and banishing all thoughts of their son-in-law's news.

Forty-three

Isla

Isla was already regretting her decision to join Kirsty's book club. While she had loved the book they were going to discuss – the final one in Anne Cleeves' Shetland series, she was not looking forward to meeting Bel Reid again.

Over dinner the previous evening, Alasdair had revealed the substance of his conversation with his mother-in-law the previous Sunday, and it had filled Isla with horror. To think he'd seen fit to share what amounted to doubts about the future of their relationship with her was one thing. It was quite another for Isla to then turn up as a guest in her house.

Yet, here she was, book in her bag, driving out to Loch Lomond.

Isla tried to forget her reservations and just enjoy the drive. It had been a long time since she'd driven this way, and it brought back lots of memories – memories of hiking up this road as a teenager, staying in youth hostels on the way, of driving up to catch the ferry to Skye with little Morag in a child car seat in the back, of the little girl's squeals of enjoyment. She brushed back a tear.

This must be it.

Isla checked her directions again, drew in, and parked behind a line of cars. Stepping out of the car she gazed across the shining waters of the loch to Ben Lomond looming up beyond them, and took a deep breath of clean air. How wonderful to live here in the shadow of this magnificent peak. She made her way through the gate up to the house. It wasn't the cute country cottage she'd expected. Bel's home was a modern edifice of wood and glass rising up and appearing to be part of the landscape. Set back from the road, the only traditional thing about it was the dry-stone dyke dividing the garden from the road.

The door stood open and, sidestepping two exuberant small white dogs in the front garden, Isla walked in. Hearing voices in the distance she followed the sounds to find the group already seated. Bel and Kirsty were passing round cups of tea.

'Oh dear! Am I last?' Isla said as she stood at the doorway feeling awkward.

'Last but not least,' Bel said, patting her arm and giving her a meaningful look.

How much had Alasdair told her?

'I'll just close the front door. The dogs should be right out there for a bit,' Bel said.

Isla found a seat, let the chatter flow over her, and examined the room. It was large, high-ceilinged, and sparsely furnished. The floor was of slate with a couple of loose rugs seemingly carelessly thrown down. But somehow, despite the high ceiling and tall glass windows, it had a feeling of warmth, of comfort and welcome. It was a happy place.

'Bel and Matt take the rugs up when Fi visits,' Kirsty said, seeing her gaze and coming to sit beside her. 'So, how are you and Alasdair getting on?' she whispered.

Isla blushed and was saved from having to reply by Bel's return.

'Shall we start now we're all here?' she asked, and the discussion began.

The afternoon passed as quickly as the previous meeting had, and Isla thoroughly enjoyed it. Their critique wasn't restricted to *Wild Fire* but ranged over the entire Shetland series and the television version of the books, including some debate about the appropriateness of the actor playing Jimmie Perez. By the time the wine and cheese was served, the women had divided into two camps: those who loved him and those who felt the producers should have chosen someone else. Isla became so engrossed in the differing views she almost forgot this was Alasdair's in-laws' home. Almost, but not quite.

As the afternoon was coming to an end, Isla found herself sitting by Bel again, aware the older woman had deliberately moved around to make this happen.

'You know,' Isla said. There was no sense in beating around the bush. 'Alasdair told me.'

'He said.'

'It's okay.' Bel put a hand on her arm. 'He knew I would understand. Matt was widowed when *we* met. Had been for over five years. He wanted my opinion – to know if I felt it was too soon.'

Isla felt lightheaded. She'd already heard about the conversation from Alasdair, but to hear Bel's side of it embarrassed her. Alasdair was a grown man and he'd asked this woman's permission to continue their relationship? How could he? Surely he knew his own mind?

'And what did you tell him?' she asked, becoming tense.

'That it's between you and him,' Bel replied in a gentle voice. She looked away – towards the window. 'I think what he really wanted was for me to tell Matt.' She sounded tired.

It suddenly struck Isla that whereas she might have an ally in Bel, Alasdair's father-in-law was a different matter. 'He doesn't approve?' she asked.

'Give him time. He lost his daughter. You'd understand that.'

Isla gave her an incredulous stare. 'How do you know?' Then she looked across the room to where Kirsty was holding forth to two of the other women. 'Kirsty! I should have kept my mouth shut.'

'Is it such a secret? It must be hard not to talk about her.'

Isla's eyes filled. She'd tried so hard to keep her memories sealed up, only to be taken out when she was alone. It was the only way she'd been able to get through the past ten years. Then, recently, the box seemed to have sprung open – first Kirsty, then Alasdair, now Bel. It was as if her memories were spilling over into every part of the new life she'd forged for herself.

'Yes.' Suddenly Isla wanted to talk, to tell Bel about her little girl, about Morag, but the words stuck in her throat. 'I... I'd like to tell you about her, but not now.'

'I understand. I never had children myself, so I can only imagine. But I'd love to hear more when you're ready.' She patted Isla's arm again then rose.

People were beginning to leave and Bel, the gracious hostess, was farewelling them at the door. Determined not to be the last to leave, Isla found herself walking through the gate with Kirsty.

'What did Bel want?' Kirsty asked.

She didn't miss a trick.

'Nothing much. She's a nice lady and has a beautiful home.'

'Yes.' Kirsty glanced back at the house. 'Matt had it built after Ailsa – his wife – died. He was mouldering away in the old family home till Elspeth took him in hand. It was her insistence he needed to put the past behind him that gave him the motivation to make the move. The building project gave him an interest too – stopped him brooding.'

Isla could see the parallels between what had been Matt's situation, and Alasdair's. But Alasdair had no intention of leaving the house he'd shared with Elspeth. Why should he? It was his children's home. But, for Isla – and most likely for Alasdair too – it would always hold Elspeth's ghost. Maybe she was foolish to dream of a future with Alasdair.

But all thoughts of Alasdair disappeared as Isla drove home. It was Bel's final words that stayed with her. Had she been wrong to hide away her memories of Morag, to try to consign her to the past? What had at first been a case of self-preservation had become a habit. As she reached the outskirts of the city Isla made a decision. As soon as she got home, she'd unpack the photos she kept in a box on the top shelf of the wardrobe and set them on display where she could look at Morag's lively little face every day.

Forty-four

Alasdair

While Alasdair was heartened by Bel's support, he worried about Matt's reaction. It was three weeks since they'd spoken about Isla, and nothing in Matt's demeanour since then had given any indication how he was feeling. Each Sunday there had been the regular family lunch. Matt had been as friendly as ever when they were all together, but Alasdair thought he'd detected a slight cooling in his manner when the two had ended up walking side-by-side or been left alone.

He sighed. Bel had said to give him time – but how much time? Now that he and Isla were meeting regularly and talking almost every day, he wanted to bring their relationship into the open. But not at the expense of a family feud. He remembered only too well how Elspeth had railed against her father's friendship with Bel. This was no different.

The rift back then had torn Matt and his daughter apart. They hadn't spoken to each other for weeks. It had been Matt who had made the peace then, enlisting Alasdair's help. Though – Alasdair scratched his head – he hadn't been behaving too well then either. Matt didn't have that excuse. He and Bel were happy. Surely the old man could see Alasdair was ready to move on with his life. Damn, he'd been handing out advice to him to do exactly that.

Though, Alasdair conceded, Matt's advice hadn't been to find a new wife.

Wife? Is that what he wanted Isla to be? The word had popped into his head from nowhere. But he supposed they were moving in that direction, even though neither had mentioned a future together. There were the children to think of and, while Alasdair knew Fiona loved Isla as her headmistress, to have her take the place of her mother was something else. Then there was Robbie. It was difficult to know what his son was thinking most of the time. When Elspeth died, he'd gone into his shell, only emerging when the football season took off after the Christmas from hell – that first Christmas without her.

Alasdair sighed. He wondered what Elspeth would say. If only he could ask her advice, ridiculous as it sounded. He turned back to the documents he'd brought home from the office when he decided to work from home for a few days, only to be disturbed by the front door opening and the sound of Robbie's feet running up the stairs. He was glad the boy was back to normal. The young were so resilient. His leg had made a full recovery, and Alasdair had noted Robbie was more understanding of his sister's disability, so maybe his accident had been a blessing in disguise.

A car stopped and after a pause during which Alasdair pictured Anaïs helping Fiona out of the vehicle, there was the swish of tyres from his daughter's wheelchair, then his study door flew open.

'Dad!'

Alasdair looked up, a benign smile on his face. 'Fi?'

'Is it true? What they're saying about you and Ms Cameron?'

'Woah!' *Where had this come from?*

'Well, is it?' Fiona's normally cheerful face held a petulant expression.

Alasdair swung his chair around. 'Suppose you tell me what they're saying?'

Before she could reply, Anaïs poked her head around the door. 'Sorry, Mr MacLeod, I told her not to disturb you while you're working,' the *au pair* said.

'That's okay, Anaïs.' When would she learn to call him Alasdair? But that wasn't the focus of his attention right now.

Fiona took a breath, then, 'It's Deirdre Gibson. She said her mother had seen the two of you in some restaurant last weekend. Is it true? Why didn't you tell me? Deirdre's mother said you looked very cosy together, but that can't be right, can it? Were you talking about me? Have I done something wrong?'

Hell, he should have known someone would see them. They'd tried to be careful, but Glasgow wasn't such a big place when it came down to it. He thought for a few seconds before replying.

'We weren't talking about you, Fi. Or if we were it was all good. Ms Cameron and I have become friends. We met at Aunt Kirsty's. Remember that dinner party I went to? We've met a few times since. She's a nice lady – you've always told me how much you like her. We've found we enjoy each other's company. We have a lot in common. Is that so bad?' He held his breath.

'You mean… like girlfriend and boyfriend? But you're both so old!'

Alasdair hid a smile. 'I guess it is a bit like that. How do you feel about your old dad seeing your headmistress?'

Fiona stared at him for a moment, then turned her chair towards the window, her back to him. 'Does this mean… do you…?' She turned back quickly. 'Are you going to marry her?'

Alasdair's breath caught in his throat. 'It's a bit early to be thinking about marriage. Your mum…' He cleared his throat. 'But if, in the future… how would you feel?'

Fiona appeared to give the question serious thought before replying, 'It would probably be okay. Would it mean I'd get special treatment at school? The others mightn't like that, I could get teased. But,' she brightened, 'I guess I could handle it. Do Grandpa Matt and Nana Bel know?'

'Yes.'

'What do they think?' Then without waiting for a reply, she asked, 'Is that why Grandpa has been a bit off lately?'

Alasdair sighed again. His daughter was so perceptive. He nodded, not trusting himself to speak.

'I suppose he doesn't want you to marry again. Mum was his daughter, and I guess he doesn't want anyone in her place,' she said in a matter-of-fact tone. 'But I think it would be good for you to have someone of your own age to talk to. Anaïs is a bit young.'

And with that, she wheeled herself out of the room, leaving Alasdair staring after her, his mouth open in surprise.

Dying to share this conversation with Isla, but deciding to wait till after dinner, Alasdair tried to continue with his work, but Isla's face kept intruding on his thoughts, till he gave up and went through to pour himself a glass of scotch.

Dinner progressed smoothly, with only the usual skirmishes between Fiona and Robbie as they vied over who should have the last piece of apple pie and who had received the largest serving of ice cream.

'That's enough, you two,' Alasdair said almost automatically, as he saw Robbie try to elbow his sister when he thought his dad wasn't looking.

'Guess what, Robbie?' Fiona said, clearly determined to gain some sort of supremacy over her brother.

'What?' he muttered.

'Dad has a girlfriend.'

'Dads don't have girlfriends.'

'Yes, they do! And guess who it is?'

Robbie looked up, his eyes going from his sister to Alasdair and back again.

'Ms Cameron!' she announced, and sat back waiting for his reaction.

'Gross,' Robbie said, pushing back his chair and disappearing, his feet pounding on the steps as he ran upstairs.

'Now you've done it,' Alasdair said, wishing he'd been the one to break the news to his children.

'Sorry, Dad.' Fiona looked penitent. 'Was it a secret? I didn't know Robbie would…'

'No, Fi. It's not your fault.' Alasdair drew a hand through his hair. 'I should have told you both before now. I didn't know how. Robbie'll be fine when he's had time to think about it,' he said, hoping it was true. He didn't need another member of the family opposing him and Isla.

Once Fiona had gone to bed, Alasdair knocked gently on Robbie's door and pushed it open, almost deafened by the loud music, to see his son was sitting on the bed with his back to him. He walked over to turn down the music.

Robbie whirled around. 'I was listening to that.'

'Can't you use your earpods instead of keeping the whole house awake?'

Not a good start, Alasdair reminded himself, but the boy had to learn to think of others. He thought he and Elspeth had taught him that, at least. But when Robbie turned round, Alasdair saw he'd been crying.

'What's up, son?' he asked, sitting down beside him on the bed.

'Is it true, Dad? What Fi said? Mum...'

'Would it be so bad if it was, Robbie? I loved Mum, too. I miss her all the time, but... sometimes I need company.'

'You have us.'

'And I'm so grateful for you both. But I mean adult company – to talk about the things Mum and I talked about.'

'You've got Grandpa Matt and Nana Bel and Uncle Duncan and Aunt Kirsty and...' Robbie seemed to run out of other adults, and Alasdair realised how few of their friends – mostly Elspeth's friends – he'd remained in touch with.

How could he explain it to his son?

'That's true,' he said, pushing back a lock of Robbie's hair, and appreciating how upset his son was when he didn't flinch or draw away. 'But us grown-ups are strange creatures. Sometimes we need someone special to share things with.'

'And this Ms Cameron of Fi's, she's someone special?'

'I think so. I'm sorry I didn't tell you and Fi about her myself. I was waiting till...' He wasn't sure himself what he'd been waiting for. For Matt's acceptance? That might never happen, though he hoped it would. 'But I'm glad you know now.'

'But...' Robbie seemed to be trying to come to grips with the situation. 'She's not going to come here and take Mum's place?'

'No one could do that.'

'Okay, Dad.' Robbie shied away, clearly eager to get back to his music.

'Right, son.' He patted Robbie on the shoulder and stood up, hesitated for a moment, then walked out, closing the door behind him. He stood in the hall and took a deep breath before heading back downstairs to call Isla.

'Isla!'

'Alasdair?'

It was such a relief to hear her voice – a glimmer of sanity after the tussle with Robbie.

'What's the matter?'

How could she tell? Had his voice held all the emotions of the past few hours?

'Fi and Robbie – they know. Fi found out at school. Some girl called Deirdre? Her mother saw us.'

Forty-five

Isla

Alasdair was leaning up on one elbow and gazing at her. Isla felt a quiver of pleasure in the pit of her stomach. She smiled lazily. She'd known what would happen as soon as he'd asked to come over. They'd both known. It had been hovering over them the last few times they'd met – waiting. But they'd resisted, hadn't talked about it. She'd been afraid – afraid she was out of practice, afraid he'd be disgusted by her forty-four-year-old body which wasn't as supple and toned as it used to be. She wasn't sure why *he'd* hesitated. Maybe he was still grieving, maybe he didn't want her that way – there could be a thousand reasons.

'You're beautiful,' he said, pulling her towards him.

Isla glowed with pleasure at his words – and at her feeling of wellbeing, despite the fact they'd just made love on the floor in front of the fire, and her skin was itching from the carpet fibres. How attractive he looked, the glow of the fire and the shaded lamp casting shadows across his handsome features.

He kissed her again, then drew away with a sigh. 'It must be after midnight. I should go.'

Isla was disappointed. She wanted to hold him, to keep him with her all night, to take him to her bed and wake up with him in the morning. But she understood. He had two children. He had to go home to them, to be with them at breakfast. And she had school to go to in the morning. She slid away and, rising, moved around to pick up the clothes that lay scattered across the floor where they'd been discarded before…

Alasdair dressed quickly then took her in his arms again. 'Thanks. I… I'm glad I…'

Isla put a finger on his lips to silence him and he took it in his mouth, making her want him all over again. 'You'd better go now, or…'

His teeth nibbled on her finger reigniting a spiral of desire.

'Go!' she put both hands on his chest and pushed him gently.

'Tomorrow?'

'Tomorrow.'

*

Isla awoke with a start. A weak sun was peeping through the blinds, and Sooty was curled up in the hollow of her knees. He must have snuck up there during the night. She had a flash of memory. Had Alasdair really been here? Had they made love, or had it been a dream? She stretched her legs aware of the ache in parts of her body unaccustomed to exercise and smiled. It wasn't a dream. She'd made love with Alasdair MacLeod. She sighed with pleasure, then leapt up. She had a full day ahead, and now everyone knew about their liaison.

Why should she worry? They were both free agents. But that counted for nothing where the Glasgow gossip mill was concerned. As headmistress at the prestigious Glenferrie Academy, she was expected to be beyond reproach – and, in some quarters, that meant having no personal life at all. And for years – ten years – it hadn't bothered her. She'd been content to live in a bubble.

Shona had encouraged her to get out more – to have a life. But getting out didn't include sleeping with the father of one of her students. She'd managed to do that all by herself. Isla was well aware how sanctimonious many of the mothers were, not to speak of the Board of Governors. The image of Rachel Callaghan loomed up behind her eyes – the woman who was searching for a titbit exactly like this to destroy her.

In the ensuite, Isla examined her face in the mirror, seeing a glow which hadn't been there the day before, and the slight rash on her cheek from whisker burn. She touched it, remembering, then gave herself a shake. A shower and make up was what she needed. Then she could face whatever the day might bring.

*

'You're looking chipper today,' Maree greeted her, arms full of folders which she dropped on Isla's desk. 'Here are the itineraries for the Colmar trip – one for each student with details of all the visits, host parents, and contact details. You said you wanted to check them over before we handed them out.'

Isla didn't respond.

'Is everything all right?' Maree's brow furrowed.

'Sorry. Thanks. Yes, fine. Have you heard anything?'

Her deputy looked puzzled. 'Heard anything? About what?'

'Nothing. The meeting's this afternoon, isn't it?'

'Three o'clock in the French room. We decided the girls only this time as they might have questions they don't want the parents to hear. Okay?' Maree still appeared perplexed.

'Of course. I'll look through them now. See you at three.'

'If you have any questions before that you know where to find me.' Maree swept out, her perfume lingering, as she closed the door behind her. French, of course.

Putting all thought of Alasdair from her mind, Isla picked up the master folder to check the list of hosts and the revised itinerary for the trip. After making the initial contacts, she'd left the planning to Maree who, as her deputy and French Mistress, was nominally in charge of the excursion. She scanned the first sheet – a list of the students alongside details of the host families. All looked in order. Maree had handled it well. It was no mean feat to arrange accommodation for twelve teenage girls in a foreign country. She was pleased to note most of the host families had children of much the same age as her students, which could make for ongoing communication between the two schools.

Isla made herself a cup of tea before continuing then, cup in one hand, itinerary in the other, she continued to scan what Maree had arranged. Everything followed her suggestions exactly till she came to the visit to a vineyard. She'd hesitated over that one, wary of the memories it might evoke, but eventually had named one on the other side of the valley from the one where she'd met Ollie.

Vignoble Carlier, Isla read. She blinked. It couldn't be. She'd expressly identified *Vignoble Beauchêne* as the location of their visit. *Vignoble Carlier* was owned by Ollie's uncle – or had been. It was where...

She picked up the phone. 'Jean,' she said when her secretary answered, 'Can you check if Maree is in class, I need to see her.'

'Will do. She was here a minute ago. I think she's still free.'

Barely a minute later, Maree breezed in again. 'Something wrong?' she asked, seeing the open folder on Isla's desk. 'Did I screw up?'

'This vineyard.' Isla tapped the page. 'It isn't the one we discussed.'

'No.' Maree seemed relieved. 'The local travel agent I was dealing with said the other one was pretty much run down and put me on to that one. Evidently, it's had a recent makeover – new equipment, state-of-the-art processes. She was keen for us to see what she regarded as a local icon. I didn't think it would matter. Was there something special about the other one?'

'No, no. I just wondered at the change.'

'It was a minor one; I didn't think I needed to bother you with it. Is that all?'

'Yes. Of course. You were quite right.'

Maree gave Isla a strange look before leaving again.

This would have to happen today.

Isla closed her eyes, seeing the *Vignoble Carlier* she remembered.

It was a sunny day and Ollie was stripped to the waist. Isla had cycled over from the tiny gite where she was staying. It was the last day of her holiday; she had to catch the 2.23 train to Paris if she was to make her flight. She'd come to say goodbye.

For a few moments she watched the body of the young man she'd spent so many pleasurable hours with as he moved between the vines. Then he noticed Isla and ran towards her.

'You came!'

'I wanted to see you one more time.'

When he'd left her bed in the early hours, they'd said their farewells. He'd begged to see her today, and she'd refused, knowing it would only delay their inevitable parting. But this morning, she knew she had to see him one more time before they parted forever.

Ollie picked her up in his arms and whirled her around heedless of the whistles and catcalls of the other workers. 'Come with me,' he said as he put her down and, taking her hand, led her to a shed in a shaded corner of the vineyard – one she'd never noticed before.

'One more time,' he repeated as he laid her down on the ground covered by a thick layer of straw, and, removing her thin dress, covered her body with his.

That final lovemaking had been like a special gift. Isla couldn't be sure, but she strongly suspected that's when Morag had been conceived – right there, on the straw, in the middle of the vineyard. And now she was going back.

But, she reasoned, the name meant nothing. Many of those vineyards kept the name generations after the owner of the name had moved on or died. What were the chances the Phillipe Carlier who'd known her and Ollie was still there?

She crossed her fingers.

Forty-six

Isla

Isla was a bag of nerves.

A few days ago, when Alasdair suggested it was time she met the children properly, she'd readily agreed, but now the time had come, she wasn't so sure. Fiona would be okay. Alasdair had said as much, and she'd caught a gleam of amusement in the girl's eyes when they passed in the corridor that afternoon. But Robbie was an unknown quantity. It was years since she'd had anything to do with teenage boys – not since she'd taught in Maryhill. And, from what Alasdair told her, Robbie had been upset on hearing about his dad's relationship with her.

She checked herself once more in the mirror and took a few deep breaths. What would Robbie see? Isla didn't look anything like his mother – Elspeth had been fair, pretty, more… motherly. Isla gave a derisive grin at the image of the slim, elegant career woman which met her gaze. She would have been a mother too, if… But she wasn't going to go there. Not tonight.

'Okay, Sooty,' she said to her cat who was watching her from his perch on the back of the sofa. 'Wish me luck.'

As she slid into her car, Isla reminded herself that it was two children she was going to meet. They weren't monsters. But, despite her attempts to reassure herself, she almost turned back.

She was being daft. They wouldn't eat her. Alasdair had said Fiona was even excited that she was going to get to meet her headmistress outside school. Isla was reminded of a colleague she'd had in Maryhill – a man whose wife had taught in the local primary school very close to where they lived. One day he'd told them how her pupils would knock on the door on weekends then stand there staring at her – as if they couldn't believe she led a life outside of the classroom.

She turned on the radio in the hope it would take her mind off the evening ahead, then turned it off again remembering she was going empty-handed. That wouldn't do. She should at least take a bottle of wine with her for dinner. But what about Fiona and Robbie? What might appeal to them? What could she find at this time of night? Or would it be stupid to try to appease them as if they were small children? They – especially Robbie, she suspected – would see through her right away.

The wine was easy. A quick detour via Byers Road and that was sorted, with a bottle of Rioja carefully tucked away in the back seat. She was just about to turn into Great Western Road when she remembered. Loop & Scoop. The women on staff had been talking about it and it seemed to be popular with the students. Making an instant decision, instead of turning left into Great Western Road, Isla drove straight on then doubled back at the roundabout and, after a short wait in the busy ice cream bar, had added a selection of churro cups – cup-shaped churros dipped in cinnamon sugar and filled with gelato – to the wine.

*

All too soon, it seemed, Isla drew into the driveway of the Anniesland house. Lights were streaming from the tall windows and the globe above the porch sent out a welcoming glow. Isla turned off the engine and sat there, her heart in her mouth. But now she was here, she knew she had to go in. Taking three deep breaths, she picked up her offerings from the back seat, and started towards the front door.

It opened as she reached it, and Alasdair's welcoming hug did a lot to allay her concerns.

'Come on in. dinner's almost ready. Fi and Anaïs have been helping. I'm not a great cook, as you know.'

By this time, Isla was inside the house, and Alasdair's hand on her elbow led her, not into the dining room where they'd eaten before, but into the more friendly kitchen, where the table was set for four with a gaily coloured tablecloth and napkins.

'This is Anaïs,' Alasdair said, drawing forward a slight young woman with shoulder-length dark hair. 'Anaïs, this is Ms Cameron. She'll be going to France with you and Fi.'

'*Madame.*'

'It's lovely to meet you. I'm so glad you agreed to help on the trip.'

'*Je t'en prie.*"

'Anaïs is going out for the evening,' Alasdair explained as the girl surreptitiously looked at her watch. 'You should get going now, Anaïs. You've been a big help.'

'*Merci.*'

She left with a smile, and Isla heard a familiar swish of wheels as Fiona appeared in the doorway. 'Ms Cameron!' She grinned. 'It's funny to see you away from school. What are those?' she asked, seeing the packages in Isla's hands.

'Oh, these need to go in the fridge,' she said. 'I stopped off at Scoop & Loop and thought maybe you and Robbie would like them for dessert.' She looked apologetically at Alasdair. 'I hope that was all right?'

'Loop & Scoop,' Fiona corrected her. 'Great! Robbie'll enjoy that, too. I'll take them.'

'Sure.' Alasdair said. 'And I assume the wine's for us? Thank you.' He took the bottle and set it down on the table. 'Fi, where's Robbie?'

'Where he usually is.' Fiona rolled her eyes. 'He lives on his iPad,' she said to Isla, sounding oddly grown-up.

Alasdair stepped into the hallway, and Isla heard him call up the stairs, 'Robbie! We have a visitor. Can you stop what you're doing and come down here? Now!'

She was standing in the middle of the room feeling awkward, while Fiona bustled around the table checking everything was in place.

Alasdair returned, followed by a tall, lanky boy who was his double, or would be when he filled out. He had the same thick blond hair, the same blue eyes, but, whereas Alasdair was smiling, Robbie's face held a stubborn expression.

'This is Ms Cameron, Robbie.' Alasdair gestured towards Isla.

'Robbie. It's good to meet you at last. Your dad's told me so much about you. I was sorry to hear about your accident, it must have been hard to miss the rest of the season.' She held out her hand.

'Yeah,' he said, and to her relief, accepted the handshake. 'So, you're the headmistress Fi goes on about? You don't look like I expected.'

'Robbie!' Alasdair admonished, but Isla put up a hand to silence him.

'It's okay, Alasdair.' She turned to Robbie. 'What did you expect?' she asked with a chuckle.

'I dunno. Someone… older… and sort of dried up.' He blushed.

'Don't be daft, Robbie,' Fiona said. 'Ms Cameron's nothing like that. She wouldn't be Dad's friend if she was.'

'I guess not.'

'Dinner anyone?' Alasdair asked, as if determined to break up this conversation.

All three took their places at the table, and Alasdair set dishes of chicken, potatoes and vegetables in the centre. 'Help yourselves,' he said, opening the wine. 'Isla?'

'Yes, please.' She gave him a grateful glance as he filled her glass.

The meal passed without any awkward moments. Isla had boned up on the current music scene and football, and they spent several minutes sharing their impressions of *Grease*.

The children were enjoying their churros when Alasdair said, 'You'll never guess where Ms Cameron lives.'

Robbie and Fiona looked at him in surprise.

'She lives in Kelvin Drive.'

'Oh!' said Fiona. 'Do you live near *Isobel's Place*? My Nana Bel established that – and she's bought the house next door too, and…'

'They're only a couple of old houses,' Robbie said.

'They're not! They're a special respite care home for people like me. Do you live near them?'

Amused by the exchange, Isla took a moment to reply. 'Along the road,' she said. 'I noticed some work going on.' She remembered how she'd had to skirt a group of workmen when out walking the previous weekend. 'Your nana must be a very special person to do that.'

'She is!' Fiona said, beaming. 'You met her at the Art Show, didn't you?'

'I did. And I belong to a book club with her – and your Aunt Kirsty.'

'You know Aunt Kirsty too?' Robbie asked, his curiosity clearly getting the better of him.

'We were at school together.'

'Is that how you met Dad?'

Isla looked at Alasdair who gave a slight nod.

'We met at a party she gave on Christmas Eve. But it wasn't till a lot later – after we'd met again at Glenferrie – that we became friends.'

'Mmm.'

'And now you're really good friends,' Fiona said.

'We are,' Alasdair said. 'How do you guys feel about that?'

Isla felt her heart rise to her mouth. She sat like a statue waiting for their reply.

'I like it!' Fiona said immediately.

'Robbie?' Alasdair raised an eyebrow in his son's direction.

'I suppose. Does that mean...' He put down his spoon and traced a pattern on the tablecloth with his finger, before raising his eyes to meet his dad's, '...you two will be getting married?'

'Steady on, son.' Alasdair threw a glace towards Isla who was trying, unsuccessfully, to look blasé – she could feel herself redden. 'We're friends – good friends. For now, that's all. What might happen in the future...' he spread his hands '...it's too early to say. What's important to me at this point is that you get to know Isla and like her.'

That seemed to satisfy Robbie.

'Okay,' he said, before going back to his ice cream.

After the meal, Fiona and Robbie disappeared, leaving Isla and Alasdair to take their coffee into the living room.

'Well,' Alasdair said, once they were both seated on the sofa, 'that seemed to go well. Don't you think?'

'Mmm.' While Isla was relieved at Robbie and Fiona's responses, she still had her own doubts to deal with. And, now she'd met the two of them, she understood even more fully what her future might hold if she and Alasdair...

'Come here!' Alasdair took her into his arms and nuzzled her hair.

Isla inhaled his masculine scent and allowed herself to be seduced by his nearness. She let herself enjoy his attention for a few minutes then, conscious of his children only a few doors away, drew apart. 'I should go.'

'Already?'

'I feel… your children… this house…'

'Okay.' He withdrew his arm and stood up. 'Let's get your coat then.'

At the door, Alasdair took her in his arms again. 'Tomorrow?' he murmured, his lips on her eyelids.

'Tomorrow,' she agreed.

But on the drive home, Isla felt confused. She was falling in love with this man, but still wasn't sure it was right for her. When she was with him, she was filled with an excitement she'd never thought to feel again. He was able to dispel her doubts and lead her to believe he was all she wanted. But in the clear light of day – or night as it was now – these doubts persisted.

Forty-seven

Isla

Speech night had arrived.

It seemed only yesterday they were meeting for the beginning of the summer term, and now it was ending, and the Colmar trip was less than a week away.

Isla changed into the blue linen dress that had been hanging on the back of her office door all day, shrugged into her academic gown, and freshened her make-up. The sandwich she'd bought at lunchtime lay uneaten on the desk. There had been so many things to finish off before tonight. She'd got through what she could, but knew she'd be back for a few days next week to clear her desk.

But tonight was about the students, the girls who were her reason to get up each day, who were the only family she had. She enjoyed the ceremony of the occasion. It was one of the few opportunities she had to get dressed up in the black silk gown and matching hood lined and edged with purple, and bordered on the outer edge with scarlet cord, which was the signature of Glasgow University's Bachelor of Arts degree. The girls loved it, and the parents felt it added a sense of grandeur to the evening. She drew the line at adding the cap, instead merely drawing her fingers through her short hair and giving it a pat.

She grinned at the thought of Alasdair seeing her like this. Of course, he'd probably seen her in her full regalia in previous years but then they weren't lovers, then he wasn't going to join her in her bed later that evening with a glass of the prosecco which was cooling in her refrigerator.

Sitting on the dais listening to the guest speaker, Isla knew she'd chosen well. Hannah Grayson was a former pupil who was now an internationally renowned author of the paranormal books so many of the girls enjoyed reading. Her speech was humorous and inspiring and was followed by an enthusiastic round of applause.

Rising to announce the prize-winners, Isla was careful to avoid seeking out Alasdair's eyes. She'd seen him sitting in the audience, flanked by other members of his family, and knew they'd be proud of Fiona's achievements. When Fiona was helped onto the stage to accept her awards of distinction in English and French and the Art Award for most promising Junior School Student, the whole room broke into spontaneous applause. At that moment, Isla did sneak a glance towards where Alasdair sat to see his beaming expression.

Afterwards everyone filed out into the school grounds where tables of food and drink were set up. It was a tradition which Isla had been delighted to continue. It gave her the opportunity to mingle with parents and students, to congratulate them on a productive year and to accept their congratulations in turn. It also served as an excellent public relations exercise.

She was in the process of grabbing a well-earned cup of tea, when Alasdair and Fiona appeared at her side, followed by Bel and her husband.

'This is Ms Cameron!' Fiona announced proudly.

'Isla,' Alasdair said with a twinkle in his eye, 'Quite a performance. And this one didn't do too badly this year.' He smiled fondly at his daughter and pulled on her ponytail. She shook off his hand.

'Hello, Isla. I have to agree with Alasdair. You have done well. Kirsty was right to suggest sending Fi here. Don't you agree Matt?'

Isla turned her gaze to the tall man standing beside Bel, whose intent stare made her feel uncomfortable. Did she have a spot on her nose, crumbs on her lips? She felt as if she wanted to check.

'So you're the famous Isla Cameron?'

'Not so famous.' Isla tried to laugh. 'Infamous, perhaps? At least that's what some of my students would say.'

'Matt!' Bel whispered so low, Isla barely caught it.

'And you're off to France soon?' Bel asked, in an obvious attempt to reduce the tension emanating from her husband.

'Yes. Next Friday,' Isla said. 'We're all looking forward to it. I'm so glad Fiona is able to join us.'

'Mind you take care of her. She's precious to us,' Matt said, and Isla saw Bel give him a nudge, before he added, 'It's been good to meet you properly.'

'You must have Alasdair bring you along to lunch one Sunday after you get back,' Bel said, with a glare at her husband, who seemed to be about to say something before thinking better of it. 'Alasdair?'

'Yes,' Alasdair said, but now *he* looked uncomfortable.

'Come and meet Ms Smythe, Nana and Grandpa. You didn't get to talk with her at the Art Show.' Fiona wheeled herself away, Bel and Matt following and leaving Alasdair and Isla together.

Alasdair drew a hand through his hair. 'I'm sorry about that. Matt's still not comfortable with me seeing you. I'm not sure what to do about it. Bel said to give him time, but…'

'There's no rush.' Isla was conscious of referring to her own feelings as well as those of Matt Reid's. She was loving her time with Alasdair, the way they had fallen into a close relationship, but it had all happened fast – too fast? She wasn't sure about that. And she wasn't sure where it was leading, where she wanted it to lead. They hadn't talked of the future. Did they have a future together? Did Isla want what a future would entail? It would mean giving up her single status, the independence she enjoyed as a single woman. She'd be inheriting two teenagers who still missed their mother, a home which belonged to another woman, a family who was grieving. It was too much to think about.

'I should join them,' Alasdair said, his eyes following the rest of his family. 'Tonight?' he whispered, his lips so close to her ear she shivered.

Isla nodded, unable to trust herself to speak, mystified how his nearness could send her emotions into a spin so easily. She was glad she was off to France next week. Despite having twelve students to look after, it would be good to have a break from her routine, to be away from Glasgow for a bit, away from Alasdair. It might give her time to think; to work out how she really felt, without his presence to distract her.

*

Lying in bed in the after-glow of making love, the empty prosecco glasses beside them, their legs entwined, Alasdair dreamily said, 'I really care for you, Isla. I want you to be part of my future – *our* future. The kids like you. They'd accept you.' He traced her lips with one finger, then tipped up her chin. 'What do you say?'

Isla's stomach churned with an emotion she couldn't identify. *Was it excitement or fear?*

'As I said, there's no rush. Let's wait till we get back from France.' Maybe by then she'd have a clearer understanding of her feelings, have put a few ghosts to rest, and be ready to think about the future. 'In fact…' she pulled back from his embrace and met his eyes, '…I have a lot to do before we leave so…' she took a deep breath, 'I think we should leave it all till I get back.'

'All? You mean…?'

'We shouldn't meet again till we return.'

Seeing the disappointment in Alasdair's face, Isla almost changed her mind. But it was something she'd decided driving home from school. She was consumed with a set of contradictions. She needed to clear her thoughts. Now he'd mentioned the future, it was even more vital. She loved being with him, had never felt this way before, but was it enough? Enough to give up what she had, enough to withstand the opposition of his father-in-law, enough to change her entire way of life?

Conflicting emotions flashed across Alasdair's face. The disappointment was followed by something akin to understanding, combined with a sense of loss. 'I'll miss you,' he said softly, pulling her into a tight hug before releasing her. 'I'd better go.'

Isla watched him dress. It was a strange relationship. They met frequently, made love often. But always in *her* flat, in *her* bed. And they never spent the entire night together as he needed to be home for the family breakfast. In one way, it added to the excitement, but she knew it couldn't continue like this. A relationship had to move forward, or it would die. What she had to decide was if she wanted to move forward at all.

*

Whereas it had seemed wisest to tell Alasdair she wouldn't meet with him again till after France, next morning in the cold light of day, she began to regret her decision. The school term was over. She had six days before she had to leave. They seemed to stretch before her like a long empty tunnel.

She rose from bed, dislodging Sooty who had curled up in his usual spot, and stepped into the shower letting a stream of cool water flow over her, as she itemised all the things she needed to do before the following Friday.

Today, she was meeting Shona, who'd be eager for the latest on her relationship with Alasdair. Isla wished she hadn't told her friend about him, but it was too late now. Shona was keen to meet the man who'd snared her attention; who'd managed to do what Shona hadn't, despite years of trying.

The sun was shining with a hint of the summer to come when Isla set out to walk down to Byres Road where she'd arranged to meet her friend. She arrived first, took a seat by the window, and ordered coffee while she waited for Shona to arrive.

'What's up?' was Shona's greeting when she finally joined her. 'Sorry I'm late. Men!' She rolled her eyes, but had a smug look on her face. 'I couldn't get Hugh to leave. How's Alasdair?'

Isla's expression must have communicated her inner conflict. 'Don't tell me he's finished it.'

'No, nothing like that.' Isla almost envied Shona's uncomplicated love life. Her relationships were either full-on or finished, and if on, her men stayed with her overnight. 'I told him I didn't want to see him till I got back.'

'Back? Black coffee, please,' she said to the hovering waitress. 'Oh, that's right. You have this school thing – this *trip down memory lane*. Are you sure it's a good idea?'

'No,' Isla sighed. She wasn't sure at all, especially now they were to visit the *Vignoble Carlier*. But it might be all for the best. 'But we leave on Friday for ten days.' She fiddled with her teaspoon. 'Alasdair's talking about the future. I met his children.'

'Well that's all good, isn't it? You *are* keen on him?'

'Yes, but it's a big step. Their mother's only been gone for two years. I know his daughter quite well – Fiona's a delightful girl – but being her headmistress is a bit different from being her father's…'

'Mistress? Sorry, I couldn't help it.' Shona chuckled, then sobered, 'So it's serious with you two, then?'

'Maybe.' Isla drew patterns on the table with her finger. 'But I don't know. I've been on my own for so long. What if…?'

'If you want to know what I think, I think you're making too much of this. How many men are you going to meet who want to introduce you to their family? Wish Hugh did.' She gazed into space, apparently lost in thought. 'I say you should go with the flow. What's the worst that can happen? You like him. Sounds as if you like his daughter, too. Who else is there? A son?'

'A son – Robbie – and his in-laws – I've met them too. Kirsty's an old school friend, and…'

So what are you worrying about?'

Isla could see her friend didn't understand. And maybe she *was* making too much of what she saw as a problem. But she knew it would continue to worry her until she worked out what she wanted.

The rest of their conversation focussed on Shona and her plans to spend her holidays travelling up the west coast of the States. Isla listened while she radiated enthusiasm about visiting LA, Yosemite and Yellowstone and driving through the Redwoods, but couldn't manage to evince any interest in the trip. After an hour, she rose to leave.

'Sorry, Shona. I really need to go. I have a pile of work on my desk.'

'But you're on holiday,' Shona objected. 'Can't you forget about that school for once?'

Isla smiled at Shona's lack of understanding. Her job wasn't one she could walk away from when term ended.

But, as she drove towards the well-loved building, Isla wondered if Shona had a point. She'd made the school the focus of her life for so long, it had *become* her life. Was it time to draw back, to devote at least some of her energies to making a life for herself outside of work?

Forty-eight

Isla

It was the day Isla had been dreading. After a week of sightseeing, visiting the older parts of the city, churches, museums and a side trip to Strasbourg, today they were to visit the vineyard. No matter how often Isla told herself the old man she remembered would be long gone, she was reluctant to risk reliving the past.

'*Nous sommes ici,*' Maree announced, following their stated goals to speak French with the girls wherever possible. They all tumbled off the bus and unloaded Fiona's chair. Although the students had been warned that there would be no wine tasting permitted, they were all interested to see how the wine was made, eager to report back to their parents.

Isla followed the others towards the building she remembered. It was freshly painted and appeared in better shape than on her previous visit, and she hung back from the group, memories of that other time filling her mind.

She was shocked out of her dreaming by a voice in her ear.

'*Madame? C'est vous?*' Then he reverted to English. 'It has been a long time.'

She turned to see a wizened old man she recognised as Ollie's uncle.

'Monsieur Carlier. Yes, it's me. But still Mademoiselle. And with my school party, as you see.'

'*Ah oui.*'

'I should catch them up.' But she hesitated. She had to know. 'Ollie – your nephew, who I met last time I was here. He is well?'

She was surprised to see his face cloud over. 'You do not know? It was after you left.'

Isla felt something twist in her stomach. *What had happened?*

'It was bad – the accident, *vous savons.*'

'Accident?' *Ollie had been injured?*

'*C'était déroutant.*' He shook his head. 'He fell, you see, into the *trémie.*'

'The hopper?' Isla asked beginning to tremble. 'Did he…? Was he…?'

The man shook his head again and repeated, '*C'était déroutant.* The machinery. My brother's only *fils.*'

Isla thought she was going to faint. Her legs began to give way. She felt dizzy. The next thing she knew she was being helped into a chair and a glass of water was being put into her hand. She sipped gratefully.

Ollie! Dead! And she hadn't known! All those years when she'd imagined him happily married, running his own vineyard with a clutch of children, he'd been dead.

'Are you all right? I did not mean to shock you.' The man was hovering at her shoulder.

'Fine, I'll be fine,' she said, wondering if she was, if her legs would hold her.

'Ms Cameron?'

It was Anaïs. Alasdair's *au pair* had come to find her.

'Everything's okay, Anaïs. I just had some bad news.' She struggled to her feet. '*Merci. Mes condoléances,*' she said to the old man, then managed to join Anaïs and walk towards the rest of the group.

The remainder of the visit passed in a blur for Isla as she tried to come to grips with the news. It was almost impossible to believe that the vital young man she'd known was no more – hadn't been for years. He hadn't been alive when his daughter had been born, or when she'd died, hadn't returned to his family in California, to his fiancée. It was such a waste!

Back in the hotel where they'd arranged for the adults in the party to stay, Isla finally broke down. Amidst her tears, she railed at the injustice, at the quirk of fate that had taken the life of Ollie, the young man who'd seemed invincible, who'd laughed at the world, who'd given her so much pleasure, who'd fathered her daughter. He'd been gone for over ten years but, for Isla, it was as if he'd died that day. It brought home to her how fleeting life could be and made her think of Alasdair.

Alasdair, who'd lost one wife, but was willing to take a second chance, to risk loving again. Because that was what he'd meant when he'd talked of the future. He hadn't needed to put it into words. It was too soon – for both of them. And *she'd* balked at the thought of losing her independence!

Next day was their final one in France, and this evening the host school had organised a special dinner and entertainment for the Scottish group. Isla dried her tears, rinsed her face with cold water and redid her make-up, before going downstairs to join the others.

Next morning, the girls gathered outside the school in a noisy group, excited to be going home, but sorry to be leaving their new friends. Scottish accents mingled with French as the students made their final farewells.

'Can we make one more visit to the market?' one of the older girls asked. 'Jeanne,' she gestured to one of the French students, 'has been telling us about the stalls we missed last time. Please!'

'As if you need more mementoes,' Isla laughed. 'Well, if you're careful and Jeanne is in charge.' Jeanne was the head girl at the French school which was hosting them and had proven to be extremely reliable.

'Can I go, too?' Fiona asked with a wide smile.

Isla hesitated, then nodded. 'As long as Anaïs is with you.'

Fiona grinned and headed off to join the others. Isla saw Anaïs hurrying to keep up.

'All set?' Maree appeared in the doorway as Isla was watching the group moving away. 'They got round you, did they? I said it was your call.'

'We'll be home this time tomorrow. It seemed like a small thing for them to ask.'

'Well, it gives us a few minutes to ourselves. Coffee?'

'Good idea.'

The two settled at a small round table outside a café adjoining the hotel and ordered the *café crème* they'd become addicted to during their stay.

'Glad it's over?' Maree asked. 'You haven't been yourself the past couple of days. Did something happen?'

'I had some bad news,' Isla said, unwilling to explain further. 'And yes, I'll be glad to get home. You?'

'I guess. Though I don't have much waiting for me. I may take a trip down south.'

Another one, Isla thought. Like her, her deputy was wedded to the job. It was sad that two women in the prime of their lives had so little going for them. This was a novel thought for Isla who'd never before considered what a narrow life she led.

They were enjoying their second cup of coffee when two of the girls arrived in a flurry. 'Miss, you have to come!' one said, breathless from running. 'There's a big argument…'

Isla rose, and Maree joined her. Led by the two girls they raced towards the market where a group of the girls were engaged in some sort of a dispute with one of the stallholders and Jeanne was obviously trying to pacify him.

'Leave it to me,' Maree said, moving into the group and sending the girls back to stand with Isla who immediately instructed them to make their way back to the hotel, deciding she'd investigate later. Then she realised one of the group was missing.

'Where's Fiona MacLeod?' she asked, peering around. A few girls shook their heads.

'Anaïs?'

'She went after her,' a tall bespectacled girl offered, 'when Fiona went off on her own.'

Damn! Of all the girls to get lost, it would have to be Fiona! Her determination to be independent sometimes led to her being headstrong, but so far on this trip she'd been a model of correctness.

Throwing a glance at Maree and Jeanne who appeared to be making progress with the aggrieved stallholder, Isla set out in the direction the girls indicated. This led her further into the market then down a side street where she saw Anaïs trying to reason with Fiona. As she got closer, she could hear the *au pair* saying, 'We must go back, Fi. We are not supposed to leave the group. Ms Cameron will be angry. She will blame me.'

'Fiona!' Isla called. The two girls turned around, and Fiona wheeled herself toward her.

'Ms Cameron. I was just trying to find a wee shop we saw the other day. There was a purple scarf in the window that I know my Nana Bel would love.'

'I tell her, Miss, *mais*...' Anais threw her hands up in the air.

'Well, let's get back now. You need to pack. We're leaving tomorrow. I'm sure you can give your grandmother something else.'

'There it is!' Ignoring Isla and Anaïs' warning cries, Fiona propelled herself across the road, just as a car came careering around the corner.

Anaïs stood horror-struck, but Isla didn't hesitate. She ran towards the wheelchair and gave it a hefty push, falling onto the road in the process. She felt a blast of air as the car grazed her leg, then everything went black.

Forty-nine

Bel

Bel opened her computer, a cup of tea beside her, and smiled to see an email from Fiona. 'We have another one!' she yelled to Matt who was filling the dogs' bowls.

'Be there in a minute,' he called back.

By the time he joined her, Bel had already opened the YouTube app. Matt stood behind her and leant over her shoulder as she clicked *play*. Fiona appeared on the screen waving both hands, a wide grin on her face, before moving on to some street scenes of medieval buildings and video of a vineyard, while music played in the background.

'Looks like she's having fun,' Bel said, leaning back into Matt. 'She's so talented – to be able to put all this together.' This was the most recent of the six videos their granddaughter had posted since she arrived in France, and the first in which she'd appeared herself.

'A chip off the old block,' Matt said proudly, when they'd watched the video for a second time. 'Nothing from Andrew today?'

'I haven't checked the other emails yet. I opened Fi's first. Let me see.' Bel scrolled through the list of emails that seemed to grow longer each day, deleting many advertising sales or announcing breaking news items. 'Oh, here it is.' She opened the email they'd been waiting for and read aloud,

'The work is finished at last. Contact me to set a time for your final inspection. We should be ready for an August opening. Regards, Andrew.

'At last,' Bel breathed. 'I thought it'd never get done.'

'It did take longer than we expected. But it was worth redoing the trusses like we had to do in your Aunt Isobel's house. Better safe than sorry.' He squeezed Bel's shoulder. 'Shall we go today? I can call Andrew and set it up.'

'Yes, please.' Bel turned her head slightly to drop a kiss on the hand which was still on her shoulder. How had she managed on her own all those years? It was so good to have Matt in her life, to have him to rely on. Everyone needed someone. Her thoughts went to Alasdair and to Isla Cameron. By all accounts the headmistress was a strong independent woman, just as she, Bel, had been. She'd make a good helpmeet for Alasdair – and a good mother to his children. If only Matt wasn't so obdurate.

An hour later, they were on their way. The beautiful morning had encouraged Matt to take the little sports car rather than the larger sedan which was their usual mode of transport into town, and Bel relished the wind in her hair as they sped south along the side of the loch. The fine day had brought out several water-skiing enthusiasts who vied for space with the small fishing boats and kicked up a deafening racket.

'This is lovely,' she said. 'It reminds me…' Matt turned his head and grinned, both of them remembering the first time they'd travelled together in this car. They'd barely met when Bel had been persuaded by her aunt to drive up with Matt to his home on the lochside. The rest, as they say, was history.

When they arrived at the house on Kelvin Drive, Andrew was waiting for them.

'I think you'll be pleased,' he said, handing Bel a key. 'I expect you'd like to do the honours.'

With a glance at the two men, Bel accepted and, walking up the steps, fitted the key into the lock. But, before turning it, she closed her eyes for a moment to remember the man who'd made this possible, the man she'd been married to, the man who'd appeared back in her life when he was dying, the man who'd almost destroyed her relationship with Matt.

'Everything all right?' Matt came up behind her and put a hand on her elbow.

'Sure. I was just thinking how this is all thanks to Pete. I wonder what he'd have said if he'd known what I'd do with his money.'

'Something sarcastic, no doubt.'

The two men hadn't seen eye-to-eye when they met in Bel's Sydney house. In fact, at one point, she thought they might come to blows.

'Ready?'

Bel gave him a grateful glance and turned the key in the lock.

Immediately her nostrils were assailed with the smell of new paint and carpets. She coughed.

'It's been shut up since the workmen left,' Andrew explained. 'The smell will soon dissipate. What do you think?' He waved an arm to encompass the freshly painted walls, the tiled hallway and the light shining in through the large windows. 'Upstairs is the same configuration as next door, but here…' He led them through the hall to where one large room had been equipped as a games room and another set up for exercise and rehabilitation. 'Just as you stipulated.'

Bel gazed around in delight. 'It's perfect,' she said. 'And the connecting doors?' She peered at what appeared to be a solid wall.

'Here.' Andrew touched a pad on the wall and it slid back to reveal the hallway of the next-door house from which came the sound of happy voices and music.

'It's yourself.' A smiling Annie Baird walked through the opening to greet Bel with a hug. 'We've been waiting for you.' Behind her was a group of children who now spilled into the empty rooms, filling them with their chatter.

'We can open it up to more residents now, Annie,' Bel said. 'I'm afraid it's taken longer than we anticipated. Can you handle that?'

'Bless you. We have a list as long as your arm waiting for places. It's summer holidays and that's always a busier time. I'll get Wendy onto it right away and… furnishings?'

'Can I leave that with you, too? You know what's needed. Just have them send all the bills to me. You're doing a great job here. You'll be looking for a physio and occupational therapist too?'

'Steph and Pippa can manage for a bit,' she said naming the two young women she already employed at *Isobel's Place*, 'but we may need to take on some part-time help.'

'Right. Just let me know. We should have a grand opening, but…'

she turned to Matt, '... I'd like to get Fi involved. Let's wait till she gets back before we organise it.'

'Fine with me. Do you want to check out upstairs before we leave?'

They made their way upstairs, Bel sliding her hand over the newly sanded and stained bannister as they went and peering into one room after another before heading back down again.

'Thanks, Andrew,' she said to the young man who was waiting for them in the hall. 'You've made sure it was all done perfectly. I'm delighted with the result. It's even better than I imagined. When I think of what it was like...' She shook her head in disbelief.

*

It was late afternoon when Bel and Matt arrived home, the dogs rushing to greet them as soon as the car stopped.

'Did you miss us?' Bel asked, stooping to pat the two little white balls of fur as she and Matt tried to make their way into the house, with Hamish and Toby running between their feet.

'I'll feed and water them if you put the kettle on,' Matt said. 'Or is it too early for a glass of something?'

He didn't wait for a reply, and Bel was filling the kettle when the phone rang. With the kettle in one hand she picked up the phone to hear Alasdair's voice.

'Bel,' he said, his voice breaking, 'I've had a call from one of the Glenferrie Academy governors. There's been an accident.'

Fifty

Alasdair

Alasdair gripped the phone tightly, the sweat on his hands making it slippery. He heard Bel gasp and call for Matt. He could imagine the two of them supporting each other.

'Is it Fi?' Bel said. He could hear the fear in her voice – the same fear he'd heard in his own when he took the call from Bernie Houston and heard his measured tone giving him the news.

He heard Matt take the phone. 'What's happened to Fi, Alasdair?'

'There's been an accident,' Alasdair repeated. 'In France. I don't have all the details, but it seems...' his voice broke, '...Fi and Isla were caught up in it. Fi's in shock and Isla... They're both in hospital. I'm going there as soon as I can get a flight.'

He heard Matt exhale loudly and Bel's voice in the background asking something.

'Is there anything we can do, son?'

'No. I just wanted to let you know. Kirsty's going to have Robbie while I'm away.'

'Right. Call us when you have more news.'

'I will. Now I need to go and arrange a flight.'

Alasdair hung up, then dialled the travel agent he always used. He tapped his fingers on the desk impatiently while the agent told him how busy the flights were as it was the holiday season, but finally she

247

found him a seat on one leaving at 7.55 which would reach Colmar at around eleven next morning.

Alasdair's next call was to the hospital where a very formal ward sister told him, 'Fiona has been sedated and is recovering from the shock.'

'And Isla – Mademoiselle Cameron?' he asked.

'Are you a relative?'

'No, but... she was with Fi. She's...' He dragged a hand through his hair in frustration. How could he explain to this woman in far-off France what Isla meant to him when he didn't really know himself? 'Never mind. I'll be there in the morning.'

He slammed the phone down, only to have it ring again.

'Yes?' he said, irritably. He didn't have time for conversation.

'Mr MacLeod? It's Maree Stoddart here. I'm...'

'I know who you are.'

'I expect you've already heard about the accident. Mr Houston said he'd let you know. But I wanted to tell you that Fiona wasn't badly hurt. Isla – Ms Cameron – managed to push her out of harm's way when the car... but her chair tipped over and I'm afraid she fell onto the road. She was shocked, of course, but only seems to have sustained a few grazes and bruises. They've kept her in hospital for observation.'

'And Ms Cameron?'

'She's more seriously injured, I'm afraid. The car missed her by a hair's breadth, but she's suffering from concussion. I don't have a next-of-kin for her, so I'm at a loss...'

'Yes, yes. I'll be there myself in the morning.'

She hesitated. 'We were all due to leave tomorrow, and I can't delay the departure of the rest of the group, but Anaïs? She's in a dreadful state, saying it was all her fault. She and Fiona went off from the group, you see, and Isla followed them...' Her voice tailed off.

'Tell her I don't blame her. And I think she should return with the others. There's nothing she can do there.'

Alasdair put the phone down and went out of the study, closing the door firmly behind him. He didn't intend to take any more calls. Throwing a few essentials into an overnight bag, he locked up the house and hopped into his car for the drive to the airport.

*

Alasdair gave a wry grin at Colmar airport when he picked up the hire car the travel agent had arranged for him. The red Peugeot was a twin of the one Isla drove in Glasgow, the one he'd mentally derided. Isla! He was desperate to find out the severity of her injuries. She had to recover. He couldn't bear to lose anyone else. He couldn't bear to lose *her*.

Throwing his bag into the back seat, he took out the map and was soon on his way to the Hospital Louis Pasteur.

Fifteen minutes later, he found his way to the hospital reception, then to the ward where Fiona was now sitting, propped up by a bank of pillows.

'Dad!' She reached out her arms to be enfolded in his hug. Alasdair buried his face in her hair to hide his emotion. His little girl was safe.

'How is Ms Cameron?' Fiona said, when he finally released her. 'They won't tell me anything. She saved my life.'

Shocked, Alasdair hugged Fiona again. 'Tell me exactly what happened.'

'First, can you find out about Ms Cameron? They'll tell you – you're a grown-up.'

Alasdair wasn't so sure, but released his daughter and went to the nurses' station to enquire.

The nurse on duty was more obliging than the one he'd spoken to on the phone. She directed him to the appropriate ward and, with a quick word to Fiona, he headed for the lift.

He stood at the door of the single room which held the woman he now knew he wanted to spend the rest of his life with, stunned to see her lying surrounded by medical equipment. There was no sign of life and a multitude of cords and tubes protruded from her body, all aimed at keeping her alive.

His breath caught in his throat. She looked so tiny lying there, so fragile, not the strong, elegant woman he knew.

'*Vous* êtes *sa famille?*'

He turned to see a young doctor standing behind him.

'Not a relative, no. She was with my daughter; she saved her life. Fi wanted me to find out how she was.'

'Mademoiselle Cameron, she is concussed, her shoulder it has the fracture, and the leg it is badly gashed.'

'She'll live?' Alasdair felt his legs go weak.

'*Mais oui, je pense que…*'

'*Merci.*' Alasdair turned away, his eyes misting, and made his way back to Fiona.

'Well?' Her eager face met his.

'She's still unconscious, but the doctor says she should recover.' He crossed his fingers as he spoke, hoping the doctor was right.

'I want to see her.'

'Maybe later. Now, what happened?'

Fiona explained how she'd left the others in the market to find a scarf and how Isla had pushed her out of the way. 'I don't know what happened to my chariot,' she said. 'It landed against some parked cars. It's probably damaged. I'm sorry, Dad.'

'Don't worry about the chair. We can get another one. The important thing is that you're okay.'

'*Monsieur?*'

Alasdair looked up to see the nurse he'd spoken to earlier.

'It is the time for *le déjeuner pour la petite.*'

'And you want me to leave?' Alasdair sighed. 'I'll go find a hotel, Fi. Then I'll be back.' He dropped a kiss on her forehead and left.

Alasdair knew the name of the hotel in which Isla had been staying and was able to find a room. Once he explained to the concierge who he was, he was allocated the room Isla had vacated. It still contained all of her belongings which the concierge apologised he had not yet removed. It appeared that Maree Stoddart had requested they be packed up ready for Isla when she was released from hospital. Alasdair wished he could be as optimistic.

He dropped his bag on the bed and sat down. The room still smelt of Isla, her spicy perfume filling it with her aroma. Alone, Alasdair gave way to tears – tears of relief that Fiona was okay, and tears of despair that Isla might not be. Then he sluiced his face with cold water and headed out to find something for lunch. He'd be no good to either Fiona or Isla if he keeled over from lack of food.

After a quick lunch of *un café américain* and a *croque monsieur*, Alasdair returned to the hospital to spend the afternoon and early evening with his daughter. Fiona was in good spirits despite continuing to blame herself for the accident and again demanding to see Isla.

Before leaving, he managed to obtain an assurance that, all being well, Fiona could be discharged next day and that they'd enquire about the possibility of her visiting Isla's room. Alasdair then detoured to the *soins intensifs* to see Isla again.

There was no change. She still lay there as if dead. He stood silently at the door mouthing her name, then turned away.

*

Next morning everything looked brighter as Alasdair awoke to the loud noise of traffic and the cheerful rattle of a trolley full of dishes making its way along the corridor. A cool shower helped him awake and, after another *café américain* and a buttery croissant, he was ready for the day.

His first task was to get information about Fiona's wheelchair and, as she'd anticipated, it was only good for the tip. That meant he'd have to find some way of hiring one until they got home.

That done, and the chair folded into the car boot, he returned to the hospital where Fiona was awaiting him with a wide grin.

'They say I can go home,' she said, 'but I want to see Ms Cameron first.'

Alasdair frowned. He knew what Fiona was like when she got an idea in her head, but how would she feel seeing Isla lying there unconscious? 'If the doctors permit it,' he said at last. 'But she looks… she's still unconscious.'

'It doesn't matter. I want to tell her… to thank her. She may be able to hear me.'

The discharge process seemed to take forever, but they were finally free to leave. Helping Fiona into the hired chair, Alasdair pushed her to the *soins intensifs*, worried about Fiona's reaction to seeing her comatose headmistress.

They stopped at the door, a nurse gesturing to indicate they were permitted to enter. Alasdair held back, but Fiona turned her head up to face him. 'Please, Dad?'

'I'll be at *le poste des infirmières*,' the nurse said and left them to go into the room which was silent apart from the hiss and beep of the medical equipment.

Alasdair heard Fiona's intake of breath, much like his on the previous day. 'You don't need to...' he said.

'I do, Dad,' Fiona replied, wheeling herself up to the bed, leaving him to follow.

Alasdair held Fiona's hand tightly in his as they sat together at Isla's bedside. He could see the tears begin to slide down Fiona's cheeks and wasn't far off weeping himself. He blinked. Then he felt Fiona squeeze his hand and heard a soft whisper, 'Dad.'

He opened his eyes. Fiona nodded toward the motionless figure in the bed. Was he imagining it, or was there a slight fluttering of her eyelids? He pressed the button for the nurse.

Fifty-one

Isla

Isla felt herself coming back from a long way away. All she could see through her eyelashes was white – a white ceiling, white walls. She'd been dreaming. She'd heard Fiona MacLeod's voice – and her father's. Where was she? Was she still in France? What was Alasdair doing here?

The effort of opening her eyes fully was too great and she descended again into oblivion. But this time, she was disturbed by voices, by someone holding her hand, by her name being called in a French accent. Wearily she attempted to open her eyes again. She blinked at the strange face leaning over her.

'*Vous* êtes *de retour avec nous, Mademoiselle Cameron?*'

Isla tried to smile and move, only to be gently restrained. '*Pas encore. Plus tard.*' The doctor, if that's what he was, turned to someone else and issued orders in rapid French which Isla couldn't comprehend, then there was silence.

'*Vos amis,*' the nurse said, gesturing to the door.

Isla tried to move her head, but it ached. She heard a swish of wheels, then Fiona's bright face, filled with concern, gazed at her. Behind Fiona was Alasdair.

What were they doing here? What had happened? Isla tried to remember. But everything was a blur.

'I'm sorry I caused so much trouble,' Fiona was saying. 'Thank you so much. You saved my life.'

Isla felt herself drifting off again, just as Alasdair said, 'We should go now, Fi,' in a choking voice.

*

Had she really been here for two weeks? Isla looked around the tiny hotel room which had been her home for the past fourteen days. It had taken her several weeks to recover. Then, after being subjected to a CT scan and various other tests, she'd been permitted to leave the hospital, but the doctors had insisted she remain close by and have plenty of rest until they were sure she was fit to travel. Since her arm was also in a sling for the fractured shoulder, staying here alone was no hardship. She'd loaded her kindle up with the books she never took time to read back home, and settled in, only venturing out for meals and the odd cup of coffee.

Now she felt more relaxed than she had in years. It was fortunate this had happened during the school holidays when there were no more urgent demands on her time. She'd called Shona to tell her the news, and Alasdair called and emailed almost every day.

Alasdair! She savoured his name on her tongue. He and Fiona had stayed in town for four weeks till she was discharged from hospital. Fiona was delighted at her father's relationship with her headmistress and asked if she could call her Isla 'not at school of course'.

But now, it was time to return to the real world. Her bag was packed, her flight booked, and her taxi would be arriving any minute to take her to the airport. She couldn't wait to get home to her own flat, to see Sooty again, to see Alasdair.

He'd promised to meet her at the airport, citing her inability to drive as a reason, though her shoulder was healed now, if still a little tender. Her flight was due in at 4.50 and Alasdair had assured her he could easily finish work early. On their call last night, he'd sounded eager to see her again. There was a lightness in her chest as Isla stepped into the lift and made her way down to street level.

She dozed fitfully for most of the flight, a sure sign she hadn't yet completely recovered, only coming fully awake when the announcement was made that the aircraft was preparing for landing.

A frisson of excitement began to build up as the familiar landscape took shape below her, and the aircraft finally touched down on the tarmac. She exited the plane and, after collecting her luggage, walked through the barrier to see Alasdair's tall frame, head and shoulders above the others waiting for loved ones.

'Isla!'

His arms went around her, and Isla felt she'd come home. She sank into his embrace, delighting in the feel of his lips on her hair, inhaled his familiar scent, then drew away.

'Your bags?' he asked.

'Yes.' She indicated the trolley.

Alasdair took charge of Isla's luggage and led her to his car.

'I'm free for the next few days,' he said, as they drove out of the airport. 'Anaïs is off with friends, the kids are with Matt and Bel and,' he glanced at her sideways, 'I thought we might join them for Sunday lunch. It's a family tradition – has been since Bel and Matt married.'

Isla, who had been enjoying just being with Alasdair, felt overwhelmed. 'Maybe,' she said cautiously. 'Can I decide later?'

'Of course.'

They drove in silence, Alasdair's hand on Isla's knee filling her with a sense of belonging, of certainty that this was right. She knew all the obstacles were still there, but had confidence they could – *must* – be overcome. She closed her eyes, filled with the joy of being home.

*

'How's the shoulder?'

They were sitting up in bed, drinking tea which Alasdair had made and brought in to her. The weekend papers were strewn about, and Isla felt warm and loved. After arriving home yesterday, they ordered a takeaway then retired to bed where they made up for lost time. During their weeks apart, they'd come to know each other better, sharing confidences through their calls and emails, so that, now they were together again, it was as if they'd known each other for years.

'Still tender, but okay really.' Isla flexed her shoulder as she spoke. 'Don't worry. You didn't do any damage.' She smiled at the memory of

Alasdair's gentle lovemaking. 'You treated me with kid gloves. I won't break, you know.'

'Would you like a rougher lover?' he asked, putting his mug down on the bedside table, grasping her in mock he-man style, and almost tipping her tea all over her in the process.

'Careful!' She set her own cup aside to kiss him on the forehead. 'I like you just as you are,' she murmured, her words muffled as Alasdair moved to cover her lips with his, and lower his body over hers, sending the papers to the floor.

*

'About lunch.' Alasdair paused in the midst of breakfast to give Isla a quizzical look. 'Have you decided? You've met them all before.'

'I know Kirsty, and I like Bel, but... your father-in-law... I don't think he approves.'

'Matt's okay. It's just that... Well. He's Elspeth's father, and I guess he doesn't like to see anyone take her place. But I'm not going to let him rule my life. And he'll be perfectly polite. I don't think he knows how to be rude.'

'Mmm.' Isla wasn't so sure. But, if this relationship was going to continue, she knew she'd have to do it sometime. 'Okay, if it means so much to you.'

'Thanks.' He laid a hand over hers on the table. 'It does. I want you to be part of the family, part of *my* family.'

Isla glowed at his certainty. She was still becoming used to the idea her single life might be a thing of the past. Alasdair hadn't actually asked her to marry him, but all the signs were there and, if he did, was she going to accept? Where would they live? Would he expect her to live in the house that had been Elspeth's home, that his wife had no doubt decorated with delight? Could she do that? Could she leave this flat that had been her own special place?

It was a big step, but Isla knew a future with Alasdair was what she wanted, and she'd have to be prepared to accept all it entailed.

As if reading her mind, Alasdair rose to come around to her side of the table. Standing behind her, he cradled her head in his arms and rested his chin on her hair. 'You know how I feel about you, Isla. You're my sun and stars. You've brought me out of the dark place I was in, taught me to live again, to love again when I never thought it was possible. I hadn't planned to say it this way. I intended to arrange a romantic setting – champagne and all the trimmings. I love you, Isla Cameron. I want you to be my wife. Will you marry me and make me the happiest man alive?'

Isla's heart lurched. She was lost for words. A raft of emotions vied with each other. It was too soon. It was wonderful. It was everything she wanted. It was terrifying.

She tipped her head back and looked up into the face she knew she loved more than anything, and always would, regardless of what might happen, of what it might cost.

'Yes,' she said. 'Yes I will, Alasdair.'

Fifty-two

Bel

Bel checked her messages while Matt was in the shower.

'Alasdair's bringing Isla Cameron to lunch,' she said, wandering into the ensuite to join him.

'What did you say?' He turned the water off and stepped out of the shower stall.

Bel repeated her words.

'Hmph. Why did he tell you, not me?'

'I'm the one preparing lunch, and he probably knew what your reaction would be. Don't you think it's time you opened your mind to Alasdair having a future? I know it's difficult for you, but...'

'I know what you're going to say.' Matt grabbed a towel and began to rub himself dry. 'But she was my daughter, and I can't bear to see her being replaced.'

'Is that what you think I did?' Bel asked, taking the towel and rubbing Matt's back, then placing a kiss on his naked shoulder. 'Did I take Ailsa's place?'

'No. But that was different.'

'Elspeth didn't think so,' Bel said, daringly. 'She hated the idea of anyone in her mother's place.' She paused. 'Much like your attitude to Isla. It isn't her fault Elspeth died. She wasn't even around back then. Alasdair only met her recently. She's a good woman, Matt. And she saved Fi's life.'

She paused again to let her words sink in. 'Why don't you give her a chance?'

Matt didn't reply immediately, instead pulling on his pants and taking a shirt out of the wardrobe.

Bel buttoned her lips and went to the kitchen, where she was greeted by their two dogs. 'Good morning, you precious creatures,' she said, letting them out for a run, then filling their bowls ready for their return.

'Morning, Nana Bel.' Fiona appeared in the kitchen, a worried look on her face. 'Did Dad text you, too? He says Ms Cameron – Isla,' she added shyly, 'is coming to lunch today. Will that be okay with Grandpa?'

'Yes, he did. And of course it will,' Bel said, trying to sound more certain than she felt.

Fiona pressed a button and spun around. 'Thanks again for this. It's brill!'

Bel smiled. Despite his objections that he could afford it himself, she'd prevailed on Alasdair to allow her to buy Fiona's new chair – an electric one. It made her glad some of Pete's money was being used to benefit her new family. In an odd sort of way, she thought he'd have approved. Although he and Matt had been at loggerheads, Pete had always had a soft spot for children, the children they'd never been blessed with.

'Who's coming to lunch?' Robbie, hair askew, joined them and perched in one of the high stools at the kitchen bench.

'Ms Cameron – Isla.' Fiona said proudly.

'Your headmistress?'

'She's Dad's friend, too. And she...'

'I know, I know. She saved your life. So you keep telling us. How did she manage to do that? You never said.'

'It was all my fault,' Fiona said, with a frown, 'I wanted to find this little shop where I'd seen a scarf for Nana Bel. I never did get it.' She gave Bel a sorrowful look.

'No worries. I have lots of scarves, sweetheart,' Bel said.

'Anyway, she followed Anaïs and me and, when a car almost ran me over, she pushed me out of the way.'

'Trust you, Fi,' Robbie said. 'And Dad's grateful, I suppose.'

Bel and Fiona exchanged a glance.

'Something like that,' Bel said. 'Now, who's for breakfast? I was planning to make pancakes. We can have them in the courtyard. Can you let the dogs in first, Robbie?'

'Pancakes. Yum,' Fiona said.

Robbie slid off the stool to open the sliding glass door. As the dogs came bounding in to put their noses into their bowls, Fiona picked up a bundle of placemats. 'Help me set the table, Robbie.'

With a grunt, he took a handful of cutlery from a drawer and joined her outside.

As Bel prepared the pancake mix, she thought how different her life was now from the one she'd enjoyed in Sydney, and had some inkling of how Isla must be feeling. Like the younger woman, Bel had been an independent woman, enjoying her single life, when, quite unexpectedly, Matt had arrived on the scene – a widower with a relative who didn't approve of their friendship. Although in Bel's case, it had been a daughter, not a father, the effect had been the same.

She was still remembering how isolated Elspeth had made her feel, how she'd despaired of a future with Matt, unwilling to come between him and his family, when Matt himself appeared.

He came over to where Bel was standing, took the spoon out of her hands, and hugged her. 'I'm sorry,' he said. 'You're right. There's been enough division in this family. I may not entirely agree with Alasdair on this – I still feel it's too soon – but if she's the one for him, it's not up to me to stand in his way. Kirsty likes her; you like her; Fi idolises her. I'm a mere male. What do I know?'

'You know a lot.' Bel smiled in relief. 'But I'm glad you've decided to see sense at last. I knew you would – eventually.'

'How come you're so smart?' Matt kissed her.

'I'm your wife,' she replied, 'and I know you very well. Now, why don't you join your grandchildren outside and take the dogs with you, while I fix breakfast?'

*

Kirsty, Duncan and Jamie were first to arrive, the dogs greeting them by barking wildly and running around in circles. In the general commotion, Kirsty whispered to Bel, 'Alasdair here yet?'

'Not yet,' Bel whispered back. 'And he won't be alone.'

Kirsty raised one eyebrow, a smug smile on her face. 'No prizes for guessing who? She's back from France, then?'

Bel was saved from replying by the arrival of Fiona, who had managed to scoop Hamish into her lap. 'Have you heard, Aunt Kirsty? Dad's bringing *Isla* to family lunch.'

'It's Isla now, is it?' Kirsty chuckled.

'She said I could call her that. But not in school.' She whisked herself away again.

'She seems none the worse for her adventures,' Kirsty said, gazing after Fiona. 'It's amazing how at that age, everything *is* an adventure. She could have been killed.'

'Yes. We have a lot to thank Isla Cameron for.'

'And Matt?'

'He's come around. I knew he would.'

'The match has his blessing?'

'I'm not sure he's at that stage yet,' Bel said. 'But, yes. He's come to realise Alasdair has his own life to live – and the similarities…'

Kirsty nodded, evidently pleased with herself and what she imagined was the result of her matchmaking efforts.

Just then, there was the sound of another car arriving, and Matt's voice could be heard welcoming Alasdair and his companion, followed by Isla's more dulcet tones.

'Good to see you.' Bel hugged Isla and gave her a peck on the cheek. 'You've fully recovered?'

She glanced up at Alasdair who was hovering protectively behind her. 'Pretty much. I'm glad there are still a couple of weeks of the school holidays to go, though I'll need to be back there before term begins.'

'And I'm going to make sure she doesn't do too much,' Alasdair said, moving forward to hug Bel and Kirsty.

'Dad!' Fiona appeared again. 'You're here!' She saw Isla behind him and faltered a little. 'Isla! Dad said you'd be coming.'

'How are you, Fiona?' Isla asked, as if unsure how to handle the situation. 'You're looking well. And is this a new chair?'

'Nana Bel got it for me. Isn't it cool?' She proceeded to demonstrate by speeding across the slate floor, spinning in a circle, then turning and coming back to the group.

'Steady, Fi,' Alasdair remonstrated.

'But how *are* you?' Fiona asked Isla. 'You had to stay in France for a long time.'

'I'm fine now. And your dad's been great.' She threw Alasdair a glance which Bel thought contained more than gratitude.

*

The meal was over. There was talk of a walk on the muir, and the children were about to disappear, when Alasdair stood up. Everyone stopped talking and looked at him.

'I have something to say,' he said, then took Isla's hand.

Isla looked up at him, her eyes so full of love that Bel felt tears come to her eyes. *Could it be?*

'I wanted to say this when we were all together,' he said. 'I know Fi has already guessed, and maybe the rest of you have too.' He cleared his throat. 'As you all know, these past two years have been hard for me – hard for all of us. But in recent months, I've found a way out of the darkness that seemed to shroud me like a fog that wouldn't disperse. I met this lady.' He smiled down at Isla who dropped her eyes. 'Not only has she revived this old guy, but she saved young Fi here.'

Fiona beamed.

'Well, to cut it short, I've asked her to marry me and she's said yes.' He grinned, and Bel thought she'd never seen Alasdair look so happy and content.

'Oh, congratulations!' Bel said before anyone else could speak.

'Congratulations!' Kirsty echoed.

'Well done,' said Duncan.

Matt rose, and Bel held her breath. Was he going to spoil the moment? But he went over to Alasdair, shook his hand, and said, 'My congratulations too, son. I hope you'll both be very happy.' Then he bent down to give Isla a peck on the cheek. 'Welcome to the family,' he said. 'We have a lot to be grateful to you for.'

'Can we go now?' Jamie wanted to know, clearly bored by the adult talk.

'Of course,' 'Kirsty said.' But we grown-ups shouldn't waste time on the muir. This calls for champagne.'

While Matt fetched a bottle, and Bel found glasses, Fiona wheeled her chair over to Isla. 'I'm glad for you and Dad,' she said.

'Thanks Fiona. I'll never try to take your mother's place, you know.'

'I know that. But now you're going to be part of the family, there's one thing you must do.'

Isla looked puzzled.

'You must call me Fi.'

'But not in school,' the two of them said together and laughed.

'To Isla and Alasdair!' Matt held up his glass.

'To us!' Alasdair clinked his glass with Isla's and gave her a kiss.

Isla beamed with happiness. She had found love. She had been welcomed into the family. Her days as a single woman were numbered.

THE END

If you enjoyed this book, I'd love it if you could write a review. It doesn't need to be long, just a few words, but it is the best way for me to help new readers discover my books.

Now read on for an excerpt from the first book in my
Oregon Coast Series – The Sand Dollar

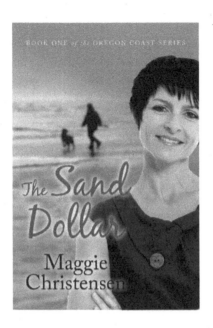

Prologue

Florence Oregon, July 1950

The red Chevy convertible roars into life, breaking the silence of the early morning and throwing the young couple back in their seats. The girl turns to her companion and laughs, her long dark hair rippling on her shoulders.

"We've done it!"

"Not yet, but we'll be in Mexico tomorrow if we drive all night. We'll be safe then."

"Dad'll never think of looking for us there." She hugs herself in glee. "We couldn't have managed without help."

The boy pushes a hand through his jet black mane and looks over with a tolerant smile. "We'd have found a way. You and me, we belong together." He reaches over and grabs her hand.

"*Together forever!*" *The girl stretches out, head back against the seat.* "*Faster, honey. I can't wait to get there.*"

The car speeds on. It's early morning and the roads are clear. All is well, till they come to a sharp corner with a rock face on one side and a steep drop on the other. The car accelerates into the bend throwing the girl hard against her companion.

"*Not that fast,*" *she laughs, then her laugh turns to a scream as the car hits the rock face and ricochets out of control.* "*What's the matter?*" *she finally manages to yell, as they sway from side to side down what is now a steep incline.*

"*The brakes…they won't…*"

The girl screams again and her hands reach down to protect her unborn child before she is engulfed in darkness, oblivious to the crash and the continuous blare of the horn which follows.

One

"I didn't get it!" Jenny's shoulders drooped as she sank into the chair beside her friend's desk, her eyes beginning to mist. She wiped them angrily with the back of her hand. She'd held the tears back this far, she could last out a bit longer.

"Hang on a tick." Rosa finished the email she was writing and pressed *Send*. "Now, let's grab a coffee and you can tell all. You can't go back to the office looking like that."

Trust Rosa to be honest with her. She must look like death warmed up if the chill in her bones was anything to go by. Jenny's friend picked up her purse and mobile and shooed her out the door. "Coffee's on me today."

"I'll just pop to the loo first."

Somehow Jenny stumbled to the nearest toilet. *What is it about women that we take our sorrows to the loo?* she thought, using a tissue to mop up the tears, which were now streaming down her face.

"What a mess," she said aloud, as she looked at her face in the mirror. *Did they consider her too old?* Jenny examined herself carefully. She might be close to sixty, but she wasn't quite over the hill yet. An open face with wide violet eyes looked back at her. A few lines around the eyes, a few more round the mouth. Too much laughing – though not today. Her hair looked tidy, the dark bob framing her face suited her sharp features; the high cheekbones and pointed chin. She stepped away from the mirror as the door opened.

Jenny gazed out of the window while Rosa bought the coffees. The palm trees trembled in the breeze and the bright red, orange and purples of the bougainvillea assaulted her eyes. The heat haze shimmered on the hard surface of the car park, reminding her summer was not yet over. She loved the ambiance here. This hospital campus had been part of her working life for as long as she could remember, but she might not be seeing it for much longer. Suddenly the familiar view blurred. It was as if she was viewing it through a haze. Jenny brushed a hand across her eyes, as tears threatened to erupt again.

"Now tell me." Rosa placed two coffees on the table and looked up expectantly.

"Well, I didn't get it. That's all. They didn't appoint anyone. They're going to re-advertise and I've been offered a redundancy and/or an executive coaching session. Just like that. I don't know why they advertised the position in the new structure if they didn't intend to appoint any of the local candidates." Jenny dropped her eyes and played with her spoon as she spoke.

"Wow. Well, I did say you were too good for them. You'd have shown them up in no time at all. Talk about the blind leading the blind…"

"It hasn't sunk in yet. How will I tell my team? How can I face them looking like this?"

"Send them an email and go home," advised Rosa. "It'll all look better after the weekend. And think of the opportunities."

Opportunities! Jenny sniffed. That wasn't the word she'd use. She thought of her ten staff members. She'd been their leader and mentor for the past ten years. They'd never considered anything like this could happen. An email would certainly be an easy way out; give her time to consider her options. *What would she do? How was she going to handle the humiliation of being tossed aside with everyone knowing?*

"Tell you what," Rosa offered. "Do it from my office then you won't have to avoid anyone on the way."

"What would I do without you? What *will* I do without you?" Jenny sighed, as the reality of the situation began to sink in. "I guess they would find me another position, but I won't become a victim. I've seen that happen too often. I'm not ready for the scrapheap yet." She sat up, stiffening her back and straightening her long, elegant neck as she considered her options.

"First things first. Get through the weekend. Use it to relax, then come back refreshed on Monday."

Refreshed? Who did Rosa think she was talking to? This was the Jenny who was the perfectionist in everything she did, the high achiever from way back. How could she relax with all of this happening and her future uncertain? She should be making plans. Plans had always been her lifesaver when times got tough, and this was a tough time – no doubt about that.

*

Thank goodness for the weekend, Jenny thought when she awoke next morning to the raucous cackle of a kookaburra, and the sunlight streaming in her bedroom window. She didn't need to face anything or anyone for two whole days. Nevertheless, the meeting with Carmel, her boss, was still going around and around in her head as she started on the routine Saturday chores. She realized that it was the apparent devaluing of all she'd achieved over the past ten years that saddened her the most. Jenny knew she needed to rise above it and move on, but it wouldn't be easy. She'd been aware of her bravado when speaking with Rosa, but today she was alone and she couldn't fool herself. It was okay to talk about moving on, but moving on to where?

Jenny's eyes began to fill. Now she was on her own, she could give way to her emotions. The tears trickled down her cheeks as she indulged in a bout of self-pity. She let them flow unchecked, washing away all the anger and unfulfilled ambitions. *Everything had been going so well. It just wasn't fair!*

Around lunchtime Jenny received the weekly phone call from her daughter. At first it was the usual catch-up call, but after Jenny had recounted what she thought was a humorous account of her work situation, something in her daughter's voice caught her by surprise.

"Is everything alright, Helen? You sound a bit stressed."

"Oh, Mum," Helen's usually self-contained voice broke, "it's the baby. He's not sleeping, and Bradley's going through a difficult stage. And Alan is working late most nights. I don't know how I can cope."

There was a pause. "You couldn't... no, I guess you're going to fight this decision in your usual stubborn way. Your career has always come first, and now, when it looks like folding, you'll still be putting yourself first."

Jenny sat down with a thump, swallowing the angry words which threatened to erupt. This, on top of everything else. Helen had been fiercely independent since she left home at eighteen. Now, ten years later, she lived on the leafy North Shore of Sydney with her architect husband and two children. This was the first inkling Jenny had that everything wasn't right in Helen's world. She took a deep breath before replying.

"Now hold on, Helen. You know I'm always here for you." They talked for another half hour by which time Helen had calmed down and was sounding more like herself.

"Thanks, Mum. You've really helped. It was good to talk to you like this. Tom is beginning to drop off so I'll put him down. Just caught me at a bad time."

As she hung up, Jenny started thinking. If she gave up work, took the redundancy, she could be there for Helen, move closer, take some of the load, offer to babysit and maybe Helen could even go back to work. She knew some of her friends had taken on this role in retirement and seemed to be enjoying it. They loved to talk about their trips to the zoo, the aquarium, the beach. It was food for thought, but was it really what she wanted to do with the rest of her life?

The call made Jenny think back too. She'd sacrificed a lot for her kids over the years and thought they'd been proud of her. She remembered Helen asking her advice regarding careers in her late teens. Jenny had been glad at that time she had something to offer, that she'd not been one of these stay-at-home mums. Not like the mothers of many of Helen's friends. Had her daughter forgotten all of that? So it seemed.

She went back to her weekend routine, more unsettled than before. Maybe Helen did resent the time she'd spent away from her and her brother. Maybe now was the time to make up for that by being there for Helen and her children and allowing her to enjoy the sort of career path Jenny herself had followed. By the time she was ready for bed she still hadn't reached a decision.

Jenny was awakened on Sunday by a call from her son, Hugh. It was as if she'd been sending out smoke signals. She should have known her news would get around. Helen and Hugh had been very close all of their lives, and the story of her impending redundancy was sure to be no secret.

"Never mind, Mum. You couldn't have stayed there forever anyway." *When had her son become so patronizing?* After voicing a few platitudes, Hugh asked, "Why don't you move to Brisbane? You could see more of your grandchildren and Karen is dying to go back to work again. It would fill in your time too."

Jenny really had to bite her tongue this time. *Were these the children she'd raised?* She came off the phone more thoughtful than ever. While it was nice of her children to be concerned about her future, she was a bit surprised they saw their mother as no more than a glorified babysitter, someone who was past it and needed something to keep her busy. She should have been amused, but was so shocked she lost her sense of humor. However, the idea of a change of some sort did have its merits. She'd allowed herself to get into a rut. She needed time to ponder her future.

After dinner, Jenny set to emptying out the bottom drawer of her bedside table, a task she'd been putting off for ages. A round object fell to the floor. She picked it up and rubbed her thumb over the surface. She looked down at the white object dotted with five holes and her fingers traced the star-like shape on its surface. It took her back to her childhood. She had been about six or seven and wandering on an Oregon beach when she'd picked it up.

"Look what I've found, Maddy!"

Her godmother had bent down to the height of the little girl and explained. "It's a sand dollar, Jenny Wren. It was once a sea creature and this bleached skeleton is all that's left." Maddy had gone on to spell out its significance, which Jenny had long forgotten. What she *did* remember was her belief as a child that this white disc held magical qualities.

Jenny sighed as she absentmindedly dropped it into her pocket. She could do with some magic right now.

*

San Francisco California,

"Are you sure about this?"

Mike Halliday looked up from the box he was filling with books. "There's nothing to keep me here now. Oregon calls," was his terse reply.

His colleague sat down on the desk, fixing him with a level gaze. "Mike, Mary died only two weeks ago. Don't you want to wait a bit longer? It's a drastic step you're taking."

Mike stood still, book in hand, and sighed. "Thanks, Bob. Appreciate your concern. But you know Mary has been gone from me for more than three years. Alzheimer's took the Mary I knew. It's just her shell I've been visiting in the nursing home. Now even that's gone, best I go too... to Oregon I mean," he quickly added, seeing Bob's shocked expression. "We have a great place up there. Always meant to retire there together." He looked into the distance. After a long pause he went on, "There's only me now, and I'm going."

"Why not finish the semester? It's not like you to leave anything half finished."

"You're right there, but I don't have a teaching load this semester. I'm really on sabbatical. I only stayed around the university to be close to Mary. I can do my research just as well in Seal Rock, better in fact."

"So you're still on about the Native American tribes in that region?"

"Yeah, the Confederated Tribes of Coos, Lower Umpqua and Siuslaw Indians. It's an interesting story..."

"Not now," Bob laughed. "I don't want to get you started on your pet hobby horse. Remember you're having dinner with Cathy and me tonight. Remind you of what you'll be missing up there in the sticks."

"The smog, the traffic, the hectic lifestyle, I know. It'll actually be good to get away from all that. I feel as if I'm starting a new life. I told you I'd put the house on the market, didn't I? It's far too big for one person."

As Bob left with a cheery wave, Mike reflected how he'd be glad to get rid of the old place. Since Mary had gone into the nursing home, it had been so depressing going back to the empty house every night. The place had been like an albatross hanging around his neck. He really spent very little time there. This office had been more of a home to him. He looked around the now denuded bookshelves and the piles of discarded papers and folders lying beside the overfull wastepaper bin. Well, it would belong to someone else soon; some bright young academic, no doubt, full of how he was going to change the world. It had been a long time since Mike had thought that way. Now he was content with the research for his book.

He hadn't been completely honest with Bob. There were some things he *would* miss. Mike ran his fingers through his thick hair and tugged on his beard, a habit he'd developed over the years. He'd miss the camaraderie of the staffroom, having like-minded individuals with whom to discuss his ideas; the delightful moment when one of his graduate students made a breakthrough in a research project. But who was he kidding? He certainly wouldn't miss the backbiting, the jockeying for promotion, the lack of respect for his own area of research. The Dean had suggested he continue with some postgrad students, but he'd decided to make a clean break. He was looking forward to leading a solitary life in a spot which held such fond memories for him.

Back home, Mike was greeted by Ben, the black labrador he and Mary had raised from a pup, and who was now his faithful companion. Once inside the house, Mike's gaze took in the boxes he'd packed for his trip north. They contained mainly books and a few clothes. The realtor had told him the house would sell better furnished, so everything else was still in place, just as it had been for years. He ran his hand over the arm of the sofa, the feel of its soft surface bringing back memories of happier times. He sat down in what had been his favorite armchair, the springs sagging under his weight with the wear of over twenty years. He rubbed his eyes, tired already at the thought of the long drive ahead and wishing he could avoid the farewell Bob had planned for him. He'd never been a social animal. Mary had understood that. His eyes fell on the letter he'd been handed by his lawyer after the funeral. It was lying on the coffee table where he'd thrown it, unable to handle what it contained. He picked it up, the words blurring as he tried to read it a second time. His darling Mary had been thinking of him, even as the darkness of her illness engulfed her. She spoke of their love and the wonderful years they'd shared, but it was the final words that had thrown him, and still did as he re-read them.

"I know you are a solitary soul, my darling, but you do occasionally need a companion to share your days and your thoughts. I know that, alongside everything else we shared, I was there for you. I hope you won't draw so deeply into your shell that you forget our closeness and the comfort it gave both of us. I want you to find that closeness with another. Should the right person appear, please think of my wish for you, and let her into your life."

Mike folded the letter carefully and slowly replaced it on the table. His fingers reached down to touch Ben's head. The dog nudged his master gently.

To read more of The Sand Dollar go to books2read.com/TheSandDollar

From the Author

Dear Reader,

First, I'd like to thank you for choosing to read *A Single Woman*. When I wrote my first Scottish tale *The Good Sister*, I had no intention of writing more. I just wanted to tell my aunt's story. Then I realised Matt and Bel's story hadn't ended so there came *Isobel's Promise*. But so many of you readers enjoyed reading about Bel and Matt again and also wanted to hear more about Fiona, that I wrote this book. Isla Cameron was a character who kept popping into my head and I wasn't exactly sure where she would fit, but as soon as I started thinking about this book, she came to life as the slightly frosty headmistress of Glenferrie Academy.

If you'd like to stay up to date with my new releases and special offers you can sign up to my reader's group.

You can sign up here
https://mailchi.mp/f5cbde96a5e6/maggiechristensensreadersgroup

I'll never share your email address, and you can unsubscribe at any time. You can also contact me via Facebook Twitter or by email. I love hearing from my readers and will always reply.

Thanks again.

MaggieC

Acknowledgements

As always, this book could not have been written without the help and advice of a number of people.

Firstly, my husband Jim for listening to my plotlines without complaint, for his patience and insights as I discuss my characters and storyline with him and for being there when I need him.

John Hudspith, editor extraordinaire for his ideas, suggestions, encouragement and attention to detail.

Jane Dixon-Smith for her patience and for working her magic on my beautiful cover and interior.

My thanks also to early readers of this book –Helen, Anne and Louise, for their helpful comments and advice. Also to Carole and Mandy for ensuring the accuracy of the details about Orkney and Glasgow, and to Annie of *Annie's books at Peregian* for her ongoing support.

And all of my readers. Your support and comments make it all worthwhile.

About the Author

After a career in education, Maggie Christensen began writing contemporary women's fiction portraying mature women facing life-changing situations. Her travels inspire her writing, be it her frequent visits to family in Oregon, USA or her home on Queensland's beautiful Sunshine Coast. Maggie writes of mature heroines coming to terms with changes in their lives and the heroes worthy of them. Her writing has been described by one reviewer as *like a nice warm cup of tea. It is warm, nourishing, comforting and embracing.*

From her native Glasgow, Scotland, Maggie was lured by the call 'Come and teach in the sun' to Australia, where she worked as a primary school teacher, university lecturer and in educational management. Now living with her husband of over thirty years on Queensland's Sunshine Coast, she loves walking on the deserted beach in the early mornings and having coffee by the river on weekends. Her days are spent surrounded by books, either reading or writing them – her idea of heaven!

She continues her love of books as a volunteer with her local library where she selects and delivers books to the housebound.

Maggie can be found on Facebook, Twitter, Goodreads, Instagram or on her website.

www.facebook.com/maggiechristensenauthor
www.twitter.com/MaggieChriste33
www.goodreads.com/author/show/8120020.Maggie_Christensen
www.instagram.com/maggiechriste33/
www.maggiechristensenauthor.com/

Printed in May 2019
by Rotomail Italia S.p.A., Vignate (MI) - Italy